BOUND

THE ELITE SERIES: BOOK ONE
CHARLEY BLACK

C.BLACK PUBLISHING

CONTENTS

Digital ISBN: 979-8-9923095-1-5

Print ISBN: 979-8-9923095-5-3

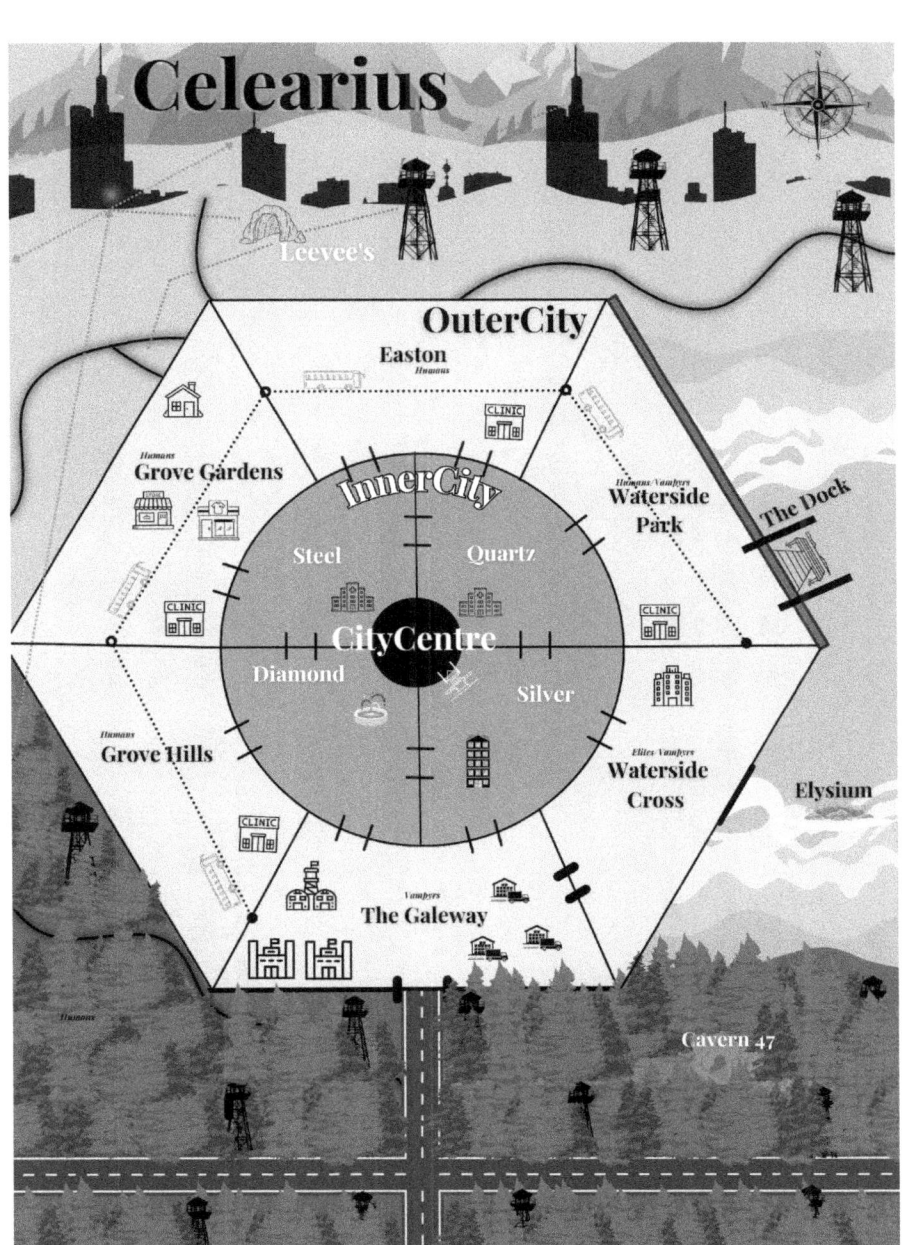

For anyone who would burn the world down to save the ones they love.

CHAPTER ONE

SERENITY

The Elite Program.

Every person, regardless of age or hatred for the vampyrs, yearned to be selected. Deep down, they craved the privileges of being an Elite: the ones who willingly offered themselves to the vampyrs.

But not her.

Serenity had no such desires; she refused to be a meal for anyone, no matter how tempting the rewards seemed. Yet her personal feelings were irrelevant now. This program was her last hope. If it didn't work, she'd have to turn to Jax, and that was a road she desperately wanted to avoid.

Sighing deeply to calm her rising nerves, Serenity surveyed the office. Four white walls enclosed a space stripped of comfort, furnished only with a simple desk, a utilitarian chair, a computer, a printer, and a cold metal filing cabinet. No pictures adorned the walls, no plants softened the corners. The message was clear: this was a place of transaction, not connection.

The subtle metallic scent in the air, barely perceptible but unmistakable, told her vampyrs frequented this place. The overhead lights were dimmed to a level that would be comfortable for their sensitive eyes, another reminder of who truly controlled this facility.

The environment's lack of warmth showed her what she was truly signing up for and how she'd be treated as soon as her application was approved.

And they would approve it. She had no doubt about that.

Serenity possessed the type of blood that vampyrs wanted... and craved. At least, that was what her father had told her. Only those with the rarest of blood types were selected as Elites.

The hierarchy was clear: A and B types automatically entered the system as donors. O positives rarely made the cut, while O negatives had better chances only when specifically requested. AB positives, the rarest tier until AB negatives entered the conversation, were treated like gold and matched with the wealthiest vampyrs, proving that despite their claims, money still talked within vampyr society.

According to the locals, AB negatives like her were a myth, believed to represent a divine gift in vampyric lore, 'ambrosia,' so treasured that only the upper echelons of vampyr society knew of their existence. She almost felt violated knowing that such an intimate part of her was seen as a commodity, a delicacy to be consumed with primal delight.

The Elite program was supposed to bring balance and peace between the two races, a part of the treaty humans and vampyrs signed after the Great War twenty years ago. Yet the vampyrs ruled their lives in practice, despite humans sitting on the city's governing Council. Every rule seemed bent toward the vampyrs' survival, not humanity's.

It was infuriating. Her father's careful protection made a new kind of sense now: he hadn't only been shielding her from vampyr attention, but from a system built to exploit the desperate.

When the office door opened, Serenity turned in her chair to see a petite woman in black scrubs walking through. The woman had caramel-colored skin and dark eyes. A laminated card clipped to her shirt read "Sheila" in bold capital letters.

"Can I have your name, please?" the nurse asked, sitting on the other side of the desk and placing a clipboard with an application next to the computer.

Such a simple question, yet for Serenity it meant surrendering to the inevitable. She made herself say it aloud. "Serenity."

The words felt like a prison sentence once they left her mouth. A cold weight settled in her stomach, her instincts urging her to bolt for the door while she still could.

But she couldn't leave.

Her mother's diabetes had progressed to the point where she needed daily in-sulin injections, and her sister's severe asthma attacks had become more frequent and dangerous, often leaving her gasping for breath in the middle of the night. They needed expensive medications neither could afford nor qualify to receive as Elites themselves.

The image of her mother last week flashed unbidden in her mind: she'd found her slumped against the kitchen wall, skin ashen and clammy, mumbling incoherently as her blood sugar plummeted dangerously low. They'd used their last emergency glucose injection that day. There would be no more unless Serenity did this.

Why did Grove Gardens have only one small clinic with outdated equipment while the Inner City boasted multiple state-of-the-art medical complexes? Mrs. Chen next door was rationing her heart medication, and the Johnsons' youngest had been coughing for weeks without proper treatment. Her family's situation wasn't unique. It was the same pattern repeated in every house on the block.

Sheila's kind smile and soothing voice washed over her but did little to quiet the storm building inside her. "What is your full name, honey? You don't have to be nervous. You may not even get approved. This is just the application stage," she assured her.

She forced the words out. "Serenity R. Wright."

Sheila punched her name into the machine, attempting to assess her medical history. Her father had been methodical in keeping her hidden: burning records, homeschooling her, developing protective scents, even insisting on the light-brown cloak she wore everywhere. Today, without these familiar protections, she felt exposed.

Had he known this day would come? Had he only been buying her time, not sparing her from it?

Serenity's fingers instinctively reached for the cloak that wasn't there, remembering how she'd draped it over her sister's thin shoulders three nights ago. The girl had been hunched over in their shared bed, her lips tinged blue as she wheezed through another attack, the empty inhaler clutched uselessly in her small hand.

As Sheila stared intently at the screen, Serenity knew she was seeing the bare minimum of information.

"The only record we have of you in the system is your birth date. Have you never had a physical?"

"My father was a doctor. He handled all my physicals and medical records," Serenity explained, her voice softening. He had trained her in basic nursing skills

before his sudden death, but that knowledge meant nothing without the medications her family couldn't get.

"He didn't update your records." Sheila glanced back at the screen. "What was
his name?"

"Dr. Richard J. Wright." She knew the screen would come up empty. He never
officially returned to practicing medicine after the Great War, working only as an
informal doctor for their neighbors and friends.

The nurse's brows scrunched in concentration. "I can't find him in the system,
and your records have not been updated. We'll need to do a physical today and
draw blood to get your blood type for your application. Let me see if we can
squeeze you in with Dr. Bradford."

Serenity had anticipated this moment, had mentally prepared for it. Yet dread
still rose, threatening to engulf her. Soon, they would know her secret, and she
would be in danger. But her family would be saved.

The Elite program wasn't a solution. It was a band-aid that required sacrificing
one family member to save the others, and it only worked if you happened to have
the 'right' blood type.

She held herself still, careful to betray nothing. When Sheila looked up expec-
tantly, Serenity squared her shoulders.

"Don't worry, honey. The physical exam is painless, and the blood draw is
quick. Over before you know it."

Sheila typed a few more notes on her computer. "Alright. I managed to fit you
in with Dr. Bradford. She is wonderful. This way."

As she stood to lead Serenity from the room, she paused, her expression turning
serious. "Are you sure you want to do this? Once we walk out the door, there is
no turning back. Your name will be filed into the system forever."

Even if she wasn't approved by some chance of fate, her name would still
be recorded in their databases, making her a potential target in a future blood
drought. It was one of the risks she took by even walking into the clinic, but it
was her only choice.

"I understand your concern, and thank you for it, but I have to do this."

Sheila nodded slightly and opened the door. Her eyes, wide with uncertainty,
met Serenity's briefly before she stepped into the hallway, closing the door behind
them.

Serenity followed close behind, heart pounding as she contemplated what lay ahead. Beneath her immediate fear for her family's survival, a larger truth was crystallizing, one her father had died trying to expose.

CHAPTER TWO

SERENITY

As Sheila led Serenity to an exam room, her hesitant steps betrayed the nerves coiling in her gut. A chill met them as they entered the sterile, unwelcoming space, one more proof of what she'd committed herself to.

This was Serenity's first time in a doctor's office. Her father's stories from before the Great War had painted a different picture: one of compassionate healing rather than clinical processing. Now reality clashed with those nostalgic tales, leaving her disillusioned. Had the war changed everything, or had her father simply been protecting her from this truth too?

The room contained standard medical equipment, but some instruments looked sleeker, more elegant, clearly designed for vampyr use. Despite her unease, she reminded herself this was for her family.

"You can have a seat right there." Sheila pointed to the chair and handed her a clipboard. "Please fill this out as best you can. All the information is optional, except for your family's medical history and your own."

"Dr. Bradford will be in soon." Sheila gave her an encouraging look before closing the door, leaving Serenity alone.

Settling into the uncomfortable chair, she focused on the medical form, hoping the task would steady her. Her name was already pre-filled at the top. She wrote her date of birth: June 4, 2020.

The day was historically significant: the date the peace treaty was signed, ending thirty years of brutal war between humans and vampyrs. Her father had told her how the vampyrs emerged during the climate crisis, claiming they could no longer watch humans destroy Earth. The war that followed devastated both sides until, at last, peace came.

What would her father think of her now? The thought ached. He'd spent his whole life keeping her hidden from them, and here she was, offering herself up. But what choice did she have?

She continued down the form. Address: Grove Gardens, one of the modest human districts far from the gleaming towers where vampyrs dwelled. For her phone number she gave her workplace. Rack n' Reynolds was the only place with a reliable phone, and Lenny wouldn't mind.

She skipped most personal questions, only answering medical ones. In the family history section, she noted her sister's severe asthma and her mother's diabetes. They were the reason she was here.

When her father died, he'd left only enough medicine to last a short while. A few months ago, they ran out. She'd been getting supplies from a bootlegger named Swindle until the Outer City Police raided him. The pharmacy wanted a prescription and $600 for her sister's inhaler alone, impossible on her meager wages from Rack n' Reynolds.

Why should life-saving medication cost more than most families in Grove Gardens made in months? The question gnawed at her as she finished the paperwork. This was their only way out.

A knock sounded, three sharp taps.

"Come in," she called, her voice less steady than she'd have liked.

The door opened to reveal a tall, striking woman with sun-kissed blonde hair and deep blue eyes that held intelligence and kindness, and beneath them an unspoken depth that seemed to see right through her. The woman stood unnaturally still, not even appearing to breathe. In that instant, Serenity knew: vampyr.

She looked so normal, yet everything her father had told her was true: the unearthly beauty, the ancient eyes, the peculiar stillness gave them away.

"Hi. I am Dr. Joy Bradford, and I will be doing your exam today." She glanced at the paperwork. "I see your father was a doctor. What kind of medical professional was he?"

Serenity hesitated, unsure whether sharing that was safe.

Dr. Bradford looked up when no answer came. "It's okay. There's no need to disclose that. I was merely curious." Her nostrils flared slightly, almost imperceptibly.

Serenity nodded. Despite her father's warnings to be wary, she couldn't help feeling at ease with Dr. Bradford's warmth.

"Do you mind if I sit near you?"

The woman glided across the room, grabbing a rolling stool. As she approached, she caught herself and drew back, giving Serenity space.

"Is this the first time you have been around one of us?"

Serenity nodded stiffly, her chest tight. She'd always been taught to avoid vampyrs, yet here she was. The guards at the gates separating Grove Gardens from the Inner City had looked distant and unapproachable, but Dr. Bradford seemed almost human.

Her father had been the one to interact with vampyrs when he ventured into the Inner City. He'd given her crucial warnings: never let blood be exposed in their presence. Scent could be disguised, but blood was nearly impossible to hide.

"There is no need to be afraid. I will not harm you. I am only here to give you a physical and take a blood sample. That is all, I promise."

Serenity held her gaze and chose to push her fears aside. "I believe you."

"Good." Dr. Bradford smiled. "I just have a few questions, okay?"

The questions were routine: menstrual cycle, sexual activity, birth control. Serenity answered honestly. Her period had ended four days ago (five days she wasn't allowed out, because they couldn't afford the specially made products that masked blood scent), she wasn't sexually active now but wasn't a virgin, and no, they couldn't afford birth control.

"I'm going to have you change into this gown," Dr. Bradford said, standing. "I'll grab the hemoptic extractor and be back shortly."

Hemoptic extractor: a fancy vampyr term for a blood-drawing device, Serenity supposed. With trembling fingers, she changed behind the curtain. The irony wasn't lost on her. Her father had taught her to be invisible to vampyrs, and now she was laying herself bare before them.

When Dr. Bradford returned, the examination proceeded smoothly. The vampyr's enhanced hearing meant no stethoscope was needed. Her hands were surprisingly warm as she worked through the standard checks.

"You smell lovely," Dr. Bradford commented while writing notes. "Lemon and vanilla. I like it."

Fear gripped Serenity before relief washed through her. The comment was about her protective fragrances, not her natural scent. Still, the way Dr. Bradford's nostrils had flared made her wonder if the vampyr caught a trace of what lay beneath the herbal mixture.

The blood pressure check and brief examinations went quickly. Then came the moment Serenity dreaded most.

"I just need to take the blood sample, and you'll be all set."

Bradford opened a kit containing an oddly shaped black device, the hemoptic extractor. It gleamed under the lights, its surface marked with vampyr symbols etched in silver. This wasn't ordinary medical equipment; it was built to handle blood safely around vampyrs.

Panic overwhelmed her. Instinct took over, and she shoved the device away.

With inhuman speed, Dr. Bradford caught it before it hit the ground. Serenity's eyes widened at the reflexes. She hadn't even seen the vampyr move.

"Sorry to startle you," Dr. Bradford said, her movements easing back to a human pace. "It's simple and won't harm you." She demonstrated on her own arm. "Quick, easy, and painless. The extractor takes the sample and instantly seals the puncture site."

"I'm sorry." Serenity reluctantly held out her arm. There was no escaping this now.

Dr. Bradford gently placed the device against her upper arm. Serenity felt the slightest pressure when the button was pressed, nothing more.

"That's it. You're all set. I'll submit your exam and bloodwork immediately."

The doctor's posture went rigid. Her head whipped toward Serenity, her whole bearing sharpening to a point that sent a cold prickle down her spine. Her sapphire eyes bored into her, glowing with an unnatural light that burned away the kind demeanor and left only the ancient predator beneath.

Serenity went cold all over. Her father had told her their eyes only glowed like that when blood was present, but the device held her sample securely.

Why was she staring? What had she done wrong?

The silence stretched between them, heavy and unspoken, that glowing stare pinning her where she sat. Her heart hammered, and she felt like prey.

CHAPTER THREE

SERENITY

Serenity's eyes widened as she glanced down at her arm. A drop of bright red blood slid along her skin, and the sight sent ice crawling up her spine.

"Oh no," she whispered. She was in trouble.

Dr. Bradford didn't move, her eyes fixed on the small drop of blood. Her inner turmoil was plain as she glanced toward the medical cabinets, then shut her eyes as if trying to leash herself.

Serenity stayed as still as possible, knowing any sudden move could push Dr. Bradford past control. The smell was already in the air; there was no hiding it now.

When Dr. Bradford finally opened her eyes, Serenity became rigid. The kind physician who had examined her moments ago was gone. In her place stood a predator: eyes transformed from soothing blue to burning crimson, radiating unholy fire. Her gentle hands curved into claws, and her professional calm twisted into a thing ancient and monstrous.

This was what her father had warned her about. The vampyrs' true nature beneath their civilized veneer.

Serenity had to move fast, or she wouldn't make it out alive. She searched for escape routes, but none would protect her. Her best chance was to scream and pray someone would come.

Before she could even reach for the stool, Bradford yanked it away.

Terror gripped her as she scrambled behind the exam table. Her breaths came in short, frantic bursts while she tried to put distance between them. This couldn't be happening, not when her family depended on her survival.

"You smell divine, like honeysuckle, jasmine, and roses. Like heaven." Bradford's haunting voice filled the room as she inhaled deeply. "I will drink you slowly."

Reality crashed down on Serenity. She'd underestimated the power of her blood. Aware of its rarity though she'd always been, she had never imagined it would lead to her death so quickly. Perhaps her family would receive compensation for a death on government property, a cold comfort.

She scanned the room with trembling hands for any way out, knowing her only option was to flee.

"You can run, but not fast enough. The chase is the best part," Dr. Bradford taunted.

Serenity's heart slammed against her ribs as she watched the doctor closely. Then she glanced at the window.

Dr. Bradford laughed. Seizing the moment of distraction, Serenity bolted toward the exit, knowing she would never make it. Fear and adrenaline drove her forward faster than she'd thought possible.

She never reached the door.

Dr. Bradford caught her by the neck. "Where do you think you are going?"

Her grip tightened around Serenity's throat, making it hard to breathe. Panic flooded her as she struggled against the hold, the doctor's breath warm on her cheek.

"God, you smell so damn good. I must taste you."

Serenity stilled as Dr. Bradford turned her head aside, baring her neck. She was going to die here. She could only hope her family would benefit from the credits her death would bring, especially on government property.

She closed her eyes, accepting her fate.

The door burst open with such force it shook on its hinges. Dr. Bradford's grip loosened but didn't release completely.

"Release her, Bradford," commanded a deep, resonant voice.

Bradford hesitated, her hold easing slightly at Serenity's throat.

"Release her," he repeated with lethal authority.

A heavy silence pressed into the room. Serenity could feel the tension against her closed eyelids, but Bradford's grip warned her to stay still.

"No, she is mine," Bradford growled, dragging Serenity closer.

"I will not ask you again." The cold voice carried a deadly undercurrent.

"Never," Bradford declared.

A blur of motion crossed Serenity's peripheral vision. A sharp crack rang out like contained thunder, and a heavy weight struck the wall. Bradford's grip vanished.

Breathing hard, Serenity opened her eyes to find Bradford crumpled on the floor, a spiderweb of cracks in the plaster marking the force of impact. She looked up, and her gaze met the most striking pair of silver-blue eyes she had ever seen.

They fixed on her with an intense, almost unnerving focus, icy depths that seemed to see right through her. Yet there was warmth there too, threaded beneath the cold.

"You are safe."

The authoritative voice held a touch of gentleness, surprisingly steadying. The man before her was imposing. Kane Draccus stood like a force of nature, over six feet of coiled power. His midnight-black hair framed sharp angles and strong planes, but it was those mesmerizing eyes that captured her: ancient, penetrating, somehow seeing beyond her surface.

She found herself lost in his gaze as his strong hands reached toward her. Carefully, he lifted her onto the exam table and inspected her neck.

"You will be sore for a few days, but there should be no lasting damage," he reassured her. Her pulse leapt. This was Kane Draccus, head of the Human Vampyr Council.

Kane crossed to the sink for gauze. Serenity held still, but her eyes were drawn to Dr. Bradford on the floor.

"She won't harm you anymore," Kane said, pressing gauze to her arm and gently wiping away the blood.

As he cleaned the wound, Serenity tensed when his eyes kindled to bright silver. But unlike Bradford's feral transformation, the change in Kane held reverence woven through restraint. Where Bradford had been chaos and hunger, Kane was control and purpose. His nostrils flared at the crimson stain, yet his movements stayed precise and gentle.

"Your apprehension is understandable but unnecessary," he said, his voice a deep balm. His eyes met hers, holding centuries of wisdom and a quieter thing she couldn't name.

When he finished bandaging her arm, he stepped back. His expression was unreadable, but the muscle ticking in his jaw hinted at emotion held in check. The stern set of his lips eased when their gazes met again.

Why wasn't her blood affecting him the way it had the others?

"Breaking protocol is a severe offense," Kane murmured, sealing the bloodied gauze in a hazard bag before returning to her. "Do you require anything else?"

She blinked up at him and managed to shake her head. "No," she stuttered, barely above a whisper, as it struck her: Kane Draccus was truly standing before her. His image had been on posters throughout the district, glimpsed on screens in the library, but she'd never imagined meeting him.

"We are sorry this happened," he said with surprising sincerity. "If you wish, I can have your application pulled and your name removed from the system."

Serenity found her voice, stronger than she felt. "How?" she gasped.

"Excuse me?"

"How are you able to control yourself?" she asked tentatively.

The unspoken question hung heavy. She watched emotions cross Kane's face before he steeled his features.

"It's not easy," he admitted after a long moment. "The thirst is always there, a constant, relentless companion."

Drawing a slow breath, Kane glanced away before meeting her eyes again with quiet determination. "It requires decades of discipline. Years of learning restraint under unyielding hunger. And not inhaling also helps."

"Thank you for your honesty," Serenity said with newfound respect. Despite her fear, she felt drawn toward him. His scent tugged at her senses, an intriguing blend of sweet aroma and warm leather.

"Would you like me to remove your name from the system?"

"You would let me walk away so easily?"

Kane studied her, then nodded.

An option. The word landed oddly in her chest. She hadn't thought she'd be given one.

She closed her eyes and could almost picture walking out as if none of this had happened. But then she remembered her mother's labored breathing, her sister's terrifying wheeze. She thought of half-empty insulin bottles and a sputtering inhaler.

"If I become an Elite," she asked, her voice steadier now, "will my family receive medicine right away?"

Respect flickered across Kane's expression. "Yes. Medical care begins immediately for Elite families. It's part of the compensation."

"Then no." She drew a breath. "Please submit my application."

Kane's brows lifted, the only hint of surprise in his stoic demeanor. She caught something flicker in his gaze. Concern? She couldn't read this man, and that realization both terrified and thrilled her.

"As you wish. Your application will be submitted," he murmured as another figure stepped into the room.

This new vampyr was tall and imposing, his lean frame radiating quiet strength. Short, dark hair framed sharp features, lending him an otherworldly beauty that unsettled her.

As he inhaled, his eyes flared wide and locked on her. Kane moved in a blur to plant himself in front of him.

"I need you to focus on me, Rhy, and stop inhaling," Kane commanded, his body tense and coiled.

Rhyzan nodded, his piercing gaze snapping to Kane. "I am trying. She smells fucking delicious," he murmured with a charming accent. His attention drifted back to Serenity, scrutinizing her.

"Calm yourself," Kane urged, pressing a firm hand to Rhyzan's chest. "You are scaring her."

"Easy for you to say," Rhyzan retorted. "It's not easy when she smells like heaven."

Kane whispered something, and Rhyzan visibly settled. "I'm in control."

Kane nodded and stepped back, jerking his head toward Dr. Bradford's motionless body. Rhyzan examined the doctor, hissed with displeasure, then lifted her.

"I will take care of her," he declared coldly before glancing at Serenity. The glint of warmth in his eyes told her he wouldn't harm her. He was in full control, unlike Dr. Bradford.

"What will happen to her?" Serenity couldn't stop herself from asking.

Kane's expression hardened. "She broke the law by attempting to feed on an unconsented human. The Council will determine her punishment." The grim set of his jaw suggested severe consequences.

Kane gathered her paperwork and the sample box Dr. Bradford had abandoned. As he read through the documents swiftly, his gaze flicked toward her with curiosity.

"Again, I apologize for what happened today, Miss Wright."

"Thank you," she said, unable to hide the tremor in her voice despite both vampyrs' show of control.

His gaze lingered before moving toward the door. "We will be in touch."

"I understand," she replied.

Kane nodded, his stoic façade softening briefly before settling back into place. Then he left, closing the door behind him.

She took several slow breaths, trying to soothe the adrenaline still coursing through her. Once steadier, she got dressed, unable to believe what had happened. It all seemed surreal.

Kane Draccus had saved her.

She opened the door cautiously and stepped into the empty hallway. Following the signs to the exit, she passed closed examination rooms, each eerily normal despite her unsettling encounter.

After navigating the labyrinthine corridors, she reached the front desk, where a tired-looking receptionist barely acknowledged her before returning to her computer.

Hurrying through the front doors, Serenity nearly sagged with relief at the fresh air. She moved quickly to the transit stop as the bus approached.

Had she just signed away her freedom for her family? But what choice did she have? Without medicine, her mother's body would slowly poison itself, and her sister's lungs would close until she could no longer breathe. At least this way, they would live.

She climbed onto the bus and took the seat farthest back, feeling exposed. The mundane reality of public transportation jarred against her brush with death. How could the world go on as normal when everything had changed for her?

Staring out the window, she watched them pass Easton's identical ranch-style houses, where the prestigious humans lived, those who worked directly for the military or the vampyrs. One more marker of the hierarchy that governed their world.

As they approached Grove Gardens' gates, she knew there was no turning back. Yet strangely, through the fear, she found herself replaying how Kane had looked at her: not as prey, but as something valuable, someone worthy.

The guard ran his quick check before waving them through. She'd always prayed they would never notice her.

At last she breathed easier as they passed Rack n' Reynolds, housed in an old grey factory. They drove on through her neighborhood, similar to Easton but pocked with abandoned, burned, or collapsing houses. The contrast spoke volumes about how resources were shared in their supposedly equal society.

Serenity pulled the bell at her street and stepped off, looking back toward Easton. Even with distance between them, she knew the consequences of her actions would follow. And somewhere in the Inner City's gleaming towers, Kane Draccus would be reading her file, learning everything about Serenity R. Wright, the girl with ambrosia blood.

CHAPTER FOUR

KANE

The glass in Kane's hand shattered as his fingers involuntarily clenched, sending shards and synthetic blood spraying across his pristine office. He stared dispassionately at his bloody palm, watching the cuts seal within seconds. This was the third time this week his control had slipped, a warning sign he couldn't ignore.

With a low growl, he wiped his hand clean and moved to his desk, where the computer screen had dimmed to black. He couldn't concentrate; his thoughts kept circling back to Rhy's words about the human woman.

Serenity. Even her name was a cruel irony. There was nothing serene about the turmoil she had unleashed within him.

Her scent haunted him, that otherworldly fragrance of jasmine, honeysuckle, and roses with the unmistakable undertone of ambrosia. In his centuries of existence, he had encountered that particular aroma only once before, at a lavish ball in his younger years. That night had ended in bloodshed when his father and uncle transformed into savage creatures upon catching the scent. The screams still echoed after all these years.

Now that same scent had returned to tempt and torment him, so potent he could almost taste the coppery tang of her blood in the air.

As head of the Council, his dealings with humans had been mostly limited and professional. He may have initiated the Elite program, but Rhyzan and Evelyn ran it smoothly, with only minor incidents like today's.

A sharp knock at his door jolted him from his reverie.

"Enter," he commanded, his voice fully controlled, none of the tumult evident.

His assistant, a young vampyr named Kaelen, stepped inside with reports. "The security briefings you requested, sir. And Councilmembers Artin and Elise are asking for your position on human district funding before tomorrow's preliminary vote."

Kane's expression stayed impassive as he accepted the files, though his fingers gripped the edges too tightly. Artin and Elise, vampyrs who believed humans should be kept as livestock rather than equals, had been thorns in his side since Celearius's founding.

"Tell them my position remains unchanged. The human districts require adequate funding to prevent further unrest."

"Yes, sir." Kaelen hesitated, his nostrils flaring slightly. Kane realized he hadn't cleaned all the synthetic blood from his desk.

"That will be all, Kaelen."

When the door closed, Kane allowed himself a moment of weakness. The mask of control he wore grew heavier by the day. Her scent had filled his senses and left an indelible mark on his memory; beneath the fragrances of lemon and vanilla, he could still detect jasmine and roses kissed by honeysuckle. Ambrosia.

Kane had fought countless wars and faced unspeakable horrors, but nothing compared to the war he waged within himself when near her. The primal urge to sink his fangs into her tender flesh was almost unbearable.

Yet there was a pull beyond mere physical desire. Despite himself, Kane was intrigued by her spirit. Her resilience reminded him of humanity's stubborn determination to survive, a spark that somehow managed to shine amid ruin and despair.

Her scent had inadvertently become her salvation. Kane hadn't planned to visit the clinic that day; he and Rhy had stopped by to collect files when warmth invaded his senses. Lemon and vanilla drifted through the air, but beneath those artificial fragrances lurked a far more intoxicating note. He'd tried to ignore it, to focus on the task, but found himself following the trail until her screams pierced the air and he came upon Bradford holding her by the throat.

He could have taken her then and there, sated the hunger that flared. But he was not that vampyr anymore. He was not his father or uncle.

He'd been surprised by the human's calm in the face of imminent death. Despite her racing heart and obvious fear, she didn't weep, scream, or beg as most humans would. Perhaps choosing to become an Elite had steeled her for danger. He couldn't forget the hesitation when he'd offered her freedom.

Shaking his head, Kane tried to clear his mind. He had work to do. Reading the paragraph for the fifth time, his brain finally registered General McGraff's words.

His request for more human police in Waterside Park and credits for the human military wasn't surprising. They would discuss it in Wednesday's Council meeting and promptly deny it.

As General of Celearius's human army, McGraff's only concern was protecting Waterside Park, not the other three human districts: Grove Gardens, Grove Hills, and Easton.

Why should one district receive all the military protection while others struggled for basic security? The inequality grated at Kane, but his role was to maintain balance, not interfere in human governance.

None of the humans holding Council seats advocated for their districts, only for themselves, except Councilwoman Caroline, who tried to keep Easton decent and protected. Councilman Peter occasionally requested building repairs for Grove Hills's appearance, but Councilman Gary was the worst of all, never lifting a finger for Grove Gardens.

Perhaps that was why places like Grove Gardens bred desperation. When your own representatives abandoned you, what choice did families like Serenity's have?

His job wasn't to interfere in human affairs but to ensure humans and vampyrs didn't slaughter one another. One duty was overseeing the vampyr academy; every vampyr entering human society required his approval. Vampyr incidents were down twenty-five percent over fifteen years.

Except for incidents like today's. The doctor had held back from biting Serenity, but a young vampyr would never control himself around that scent, no matter the training.

He needed to know her blood type before she entered the larger selection pool. Her blood could ignite trouble he didn't need, especially with a human uprising on his hands and a general who thought it was myth.

Six vampyr murders had occurred in six months, carried out by humans calling themselves the Human Liberation. They always left a skull and crossbones with "H.L." at the crime scenes. At the last murder, they'd left a note detailing how they'd keep killing vampyrs until they were eradicated.

Rising from his desk, Kane crossed to the window and gazed out at Celearius, the city he'd built over twenty years. Unlike other vampyr territories, Celearius embodied his vision of coexistence, however imperfect its execution.

To the north lay Bosa, where Nicolai ruled with an iron fist, granting humans no authority. Southwest sprawled Clowell, where Isis treated humans as livestock. Only Kregan to the northwest shared any likeness; Deyja and Xavier had divided their city into separate human and vampyr districts.

Here in Celearius, Kane had established the Human Vampyr Council, a radical experiment that gave humans actual seats at the table. The delicate balance he'd held for decades now threatened to collapse entirely.

His phone vibrated. Evelyn's name appeared on the caller ID.

"Yes?"

"Another Elite has gone missing," Evelyn informed him.

His stomach dropped. The fourth Elite missing this month, and the timing couldn't be worse. The Human Liberation grew bolder, their attacks more frequent. He didn't doubt they were behind the disappearances.

"When?" he asked gruffly.

"Kalhoun called. Ricky didn't return last night after visiting his sisters."

"Have we interrogated the sisters?"

"They reported it and are with Kalhoun now."

A vein ticked in Kane's neck. "Send Nox to pick them up and inform Rhy. I want them questioned."

"Rhy knows. He'll pick them up since he's closer."

Kane exhaled heavily. If the Human Liberation kept gaining support, it could lead to all-out war.

"Good." Kane was ready to end the call, but Evelyn cut in.

"Wait. I want to discuss getting you an Elite. We have strong candidates this round."

"Evie, I don't have time for this. I'm fine." Kane's voice was strained.

"But I don't think you are."

He sighed, rubbing his temples. "It's been a long day, Evie."

"I'm worried about you, Kane. Rhy told me about the young woman from the clinic."

"Did he?" Kane replied, instantly alert. "And what did he have to say?"

Evelyn paused. "That her scent affected you in a way we haven't seen before."

Kane's gaze hardened. "And did he mention his own loss of control?"

A silence stretched across the line. Kane could all but feel Evie glaring at Rhy.

"I'll deal with him later, but Rhy is concerned, and so am I," Evelyn replied firmly. "When was the last time you fed?"

"I don't need an Elite, Evie," he responded, his voice harsher than he intended. The image of Serenity flashed in his mind, honey-brown eyes wide with fear yet defiant. There was a quality to her scent that sent his senses spiraling. But trusting an Elite with his desires would invite ruin into his private world.

"Kane Draccus, you are Head of the Human Vampyr Council. You need to take care of yourself."

"I am fine."

"Don't shut me out, Kane," Evelyn pleaded. "You can't bear the burden alone. Let us help."

"I know, but I don't need an Elite."

"Kane—"

"This conversation is over. Keep me updated." Kane ended the call.

He turned back to the cityscape. Through his window, flickering lights spread across Celearius's distinct sections, vivid testimony to harmony and discord living side by side.

His hands pressed against the glass as he sought control over the power coursing through him. His own illuminated silver eyes glared back at him. The city lights stung his oversensitive eyes, another sign his hunger grew too strong.

His hunger was a beast straining to break free, clawing its way to the surface. He could feel it swell in his veins, demanding release.

"No. I am in control," he gritted through his teeth.

Kane went to his mini refrigerator and grabbed bottles of Syn and vodka. He poured a glass and downed it before forcing the synthetic blood down his throat. The metallic taste was satisfying. His hunger subsided for the moment, his mind clearing.

Leaning against his desk, his thoughts wandered back to Serenity and her sweet smell. She would taste like the real thing, rich and full of life. Even the thought had his fangs elongating. But he pushed the image away.

"Control," he reminded himself, commanding his fangs to retreat.

He needed to choose another Elite. Syn could only hold his hunger at bay for so long, and eight months was too long without real human blood.

Until six months ago, he'd gotten sustenance from the Cataract Club on Waterside Cross's edge, until Styxx, the owner, became one of the first killed by human rebels. The club burned down, the one place he'd trusted.

Once more his mind drifted to Serenity Wright, who had willingly chosen to become an Elite despite being attacked. Her choice compelled him, a desperate act for credits, yet made with surprising clarity and resolve.

The strategic calculation was clear: if her blood proved what he suspected, claiming her himself would be safest. Her death would be swift and painless, her family generously compensated. One decisive act to satisfy his growing hunger before it became uncontrollable bloodlust.

Yet another thought surfaced. What if he could resist? What if he could make her his Elite, taste her blood without taking it all? The challenge tempted him almost as much as her scent did, the chance to prove he was not his father, not his uncle, not a slave to his nature.

Kane shook his head. Such thoughts were dangerous indulgences. Better to end it quickly than risk losing control. And yet Serenity Wright had awakened something in him beyond mere hunger, something he hadn't felt in centuries.

CHAPTER FIVE

RHYZAN

Rhyzan paused outside Kane's office door, taking a moment to compose himself. The human woman's scent, Serenity's, still lingered in his nostrils, a haunting echo that refused to fade. His centuries of disciplined control had nearly crumbled in that examination room. If he, as head of the vampyr academy, had struggled this much, Kane's reaction was all the more perplexing.

He'd expected Kane to show possessiveness, territorial rage, or fierce hunger. Instead he'd witnessed something else entirely: a restraint born not merely of duty but of a deeper thing, one he hadn't seen in Kane for over a century.

Drawing a slow breath, Rhyzan squared his shoulders and entered without knocking.

Kane's office reflected the man himself, impeccably organized yet touched with antiquity that hinted at a much longer history. An extensive bookshelf dominated one wall, while floor-to-ceiling windows offered a commanding view of the city's skyline.

Kane was a study in barely leashed tension. Seated behind his desk, his jaw worked steadily as he examined the report. His silver-blue eyes sharpened with each line, veins standing prominent on his hands as his fists curled and uncurled without thought.

"Bad news," Kane finally muttered, his voice carrying a restrained unease though his gaze stayed fixed on the papers.

Rhyzan stepped forward. He knew the contents. Elite disappearances spelled danger for them all, especially for Kane, who carried the city's weight on his shoulders.

"The disappearances are worrisome," Rhyzan agreed. "But I believe we have another matter requiring immediate attention."

Kane's penetrating gaze rose to meet his. "What could possibly demand more attention than this?"

"The woman from the clinic. Her blood is unlike anything I've encountered in centuries."

Kane's eyes darkened, a muscle twitching in his jaw. "What of it?"

"Kane, your refusal to address this doesn't exempt you from its reality." Rhyzan spoke with measured authority. "We both felt it. I barely held control in that room, while you..." He left the observation hanging.

The silence stretched as Kane stared toward the city beyond his window. "I am aware," he finally admitted, though the words sounded hollow.

"Aware but unwilling to act," Rhyzan pressed. "Your control over hunger is unrivaled among our kind, but after what I observed..." He leaned forward, genuine concern cracking his usual stoicism. "The Council must be informed about a human with blood potent enough to bring even you to the edge."

"You already informed Evie," Kane seethed. "She will know what to do once she gets the blood results. Now, how is Dr. Bradford?"

Rhyzan held his ground, returning the look Kane leveled at him. They both knew Evie wasn't a Council member.

"She is slowly on the mend," Rhyzan replied calmly. "But we'll keep her away from the blood clinics for now."

He'd smelled many kinds of human blood before, but this woman's carried a unique velvety quality, like deep red wine. Sweet and fragrant, it stirred something primal in him. She wasn't just blood walking around in human form; there had been steel in those honey-brown eyes, a fierce dignity beneath the fear. The way she'd refused to run, even facing certain death. That wasn't mere stubbornness; it was rare courage.

"Her blood sample will be processed with the others."

From Kane's pensive look, Rhyzan suspected he'd guessed the type as well. "As soon as they have results, have her application brought to me."

"Of course." If the results came back as they thought, Kane would be the only one who could protect her. "So we're going to ignore both our reactions, because mine was definitely different from yours. I wanted to sink my teeth into her. You wanted to—"

"Enough, Rhy," Kane interrupted, a raw edge to his voice. "Whatever you're thinking, it's irrelevant."

"It's not 'enough' or 'irrelevant,'" Rhyzan insisted, crossing his arms. "I've been your friend for centuries, Kane, and what happened today was unprecedented."

"Unprecedented how?" Kane's amusement was thin, a transparent deflection.

Rhyzan held his gaze with unwavering resolve. "You protected her. Not just from Bradford, but from me as well. Not as Head of the Council preserving order, but as something else entirely."

Kane's eyes hardened, yet beneath the steely exterior lurked a thing Rhyzan hadn't glimpsed in decades: uncertainty. Kane looked away for a moment, the first crack in his formidable composure.

"This isn't merely about our control," Rhyzan continued, his voice softening. "This is about the balance we've fought so hard to maintain. You've gone without an Elite for far too long, especially when the city needs you strongest. The tremors in your hands, the red veins in your eyes. We both know where this path leads."

Kane shot him a sharp look, silver-blue eyes reflecting storms beneath the surface. His jaw set as if he were grappling with some inner contradiction.

"I will deal with this after we've handled the Elite disappearances," Kane decreed, though the words came from a desperate need for control rather than conviction.

Rhyzan exhaled heavily, knowing this conversation would ultimately fail. Kane was notorious for holding to his decisions, regardless of what anyone said.

He turned to leave, but Kane's next words made him pause.

"Rhy," he called out, and Rhyzan reluctantly glanced back.

"I understand your concern. I will consider it if the woman becomes an Elite and if her blood is as unique as we suspect," Kane finally conceded.

Rhyzan nodded and left, relief washing over him. He and Evelyn had been pushing Kane to take another Elite for months; his last one had tried to kill him.

As he slipped into his classic Chevy El Camino, he couldn't help but smile despite his worries. After months of pushing, Kane had finally asked for an Elite's application. Serenity Wright's, specifically.

Kane's fervor when speaking of her echoed the dangerous passion he'd shown centuries ago with Becca. That parallel was both promising and terrifying. If Kane claimed Serenity as his Elite, it might save him from the encroaching bloodlust. Or, if his control shattered, it could plunge Celearius into ruin.

The selection process wasn't designed for connections like this. Most pairings were clinical arrangements; the highest-ranking vampyrs got first choice of the rarest blood types. But an AB negative... there hadn't been one in the system for decades. The last one had nearly caused a blood war.

He drove through the quiet Silver District streets, noting the increased patrols, until he reached the Waterside Cross gates. Two heavily armed guards stepped forward; security protocols had tightened considerably.

"Identification," the first guard demanded, though they knew who he was.

Rhyzan held his wrist to the scanner. "Blood signature verification, Rhyzan, Academy Director, security clearance Alpha."

After verification, he drove to Evelyn's office in the distinctive dark gray and red brick building that stood out among the area's bright, pastel-colored bungalows.

He took the elevator to the fifth floor and stepped into Evelyn's office after getting past Maeve, her gatekeeper.

Evelyn sat at her antique glass-topped oak desk, attention fixed on her computer screen. Her auburn hair was pulled back into a neat bun, and her piercing emerald eyes stayed trained on her work.

"Knocking would be polite," Evelyn said without moving her head.

"And when have you known me to be polite?" He smiled faintly, remembering their first meeting in Paris, 1789, during the Revolution. She'd been just as composed then, calmly stitching his wound while lecturing him on combat technique.

"True. I'm assuming you came with good news." Evelyn kept typing.

"Better than I expected, actually. It seems our stubborn friend might be coming around."

"Oh?" Evelyn's fingers paused, her interest clearly piqued.

"Kane wants the application on his desk as soon as it's processed. He wants to know her blood type." Rhyzan settled on the only clear part of the couch, a slight smile still on his face.

"And how exactly did you manage that?" Evelyn turned to look at him, plainly skeptical.

He shrugged. "I believe he was already considering it. Having her walking around Celearius with her blood type is too dangerous. I'm surprised she lasted this long."

"Indeed," Evelyn said, her green gaze turning thoughtful. "A woman with AB negative blood walking around unclaimed can start a blood war. We have to act fast."

She grabbed a Syn bottle from the mini fridge. "And he asked for her application specifically?"

Rhyzan nodded. "You think we can convince him to take her as his Elite?"

She chugged the contents while Rhyzan watched, his stomach turning. It had been years since he'd touched the vampyr-made nutrient; its vile taste, like ashes and iron, staved off hunger for only hours. Being academy leader had its perks, including access to blood donations.

"I think she may be able to convince him."

Evelyn furrowed her brow.

"Her blood will convince him. If I barely held control from a single drop, convincing him won't be the problem. But Evie, he was different with her. Gentle, if I had to put a word to it."

"Gentle? Kane?" Evelyn raised an eyebrow, emerald eyes glinting with doubt. "Kane being gentle is like a hurricane causing no destruction. Even his kindness has a temper."

"Believe it or not, Evie, Kane had this... gentleness when he was with her. Something in the way he looked at her. I haven't seen that look since..." Rhyzan let the words trail off; their shared memory didn't need revisiting.

Evelyn's smile faded at the unspoken name. The echo of tragedy they'd long tried to bury drew her shoulders tight. She knew exactly who he meant.

"Interesting. That could prove useful." She leaned back, crossed her arms, and regarded him thoughtfully. "We need to come up with a plan, and fast."

"What's the woman's name? Let me see what's in the system." Evelyn spun around in her chair.

Rhyzan reached into his pocket and read from his paper. "Serenity R. Wright."

Evelyn's fingers danced across the keyboard. After a moment, results appeared.

"If she wasn't interesting before," Evelyn remarked, intrigued, "she certainly is now."

"Why? What did you find?" Rhyzan came to stand beside her.

"Not much. Her father was a military doctor who served under General Harris. He died a year ago. Never registered as a doctor after the war. Says he had a wife and two daughters. Neither was registered for school. That's all."

"How is that possible? For a military doctor to leave so little behind..." If Kane looked into her background, he'd grow suspicious.

They needed more. Real, substantial detail to put in the system.

"I'll send Sebastian to dig up more on the girl and her family. We don't want Kane suspicious if he looks into her."

"What's the plan for getting them in the same room again?" Rhyzan sat on the couch. Evelyn understood Kane better than anyone; she'd known him longest, and he trusted her more than anyone else.

"Why do I have to come up with the plan?" Evelyn frowned.

"You know him better than I do," Rhyzan said simply.

"But he listens to you more."

"He'll find it suspicious if I broach the topic, but if it comes from you, it'll be believable."

Her brow creased as she examined her schedule. "I've got it. Kane has a meeting with me Friday at 3 p.m. You need to make sure she's here."

"I can do that," he said, pulling out his cellular device. "But your plan is?"

"I'll let you know as soon as I confirm her application and test results."

Rhyzan stood, trusting her judgment. As he turned to leave, a troubling thought surfaced.

"Evie," he said, pausing at the door, "if this doesn't work, if Kane refuses her, or worse, if he loses control, we both know what's at stake."

"We both remember what happened after Becca," Evelyn said softly. "The bloodshed, the vengeance."

"If history repeats, the Human Liberation would have exactly the ammunition they need. War would be inevitable."

"Then we make sure it works," Evelyn said, her voice hardening with resolve. "We've come too far to let Celearius fall now."

Rhyzan nodded grimly. Everything depended on a human woman with AB negative blood and the ancient vampyr who would either save her or destroy them all.

CHAPTER SIX

SERENITY

The acrid smell of burning trash mingled with the metallic tang of approaching rain as Serenity pushed open the worn metal door of Rack n' Reynolds General Store. The harsh fluorescent lights inside had given her a headache, and the early evening air felt like freedom after being cooped up all day.

Jax, her best friend of eleven years, sat perched on a milk crate in his faded uniform shirt. He ran his hands through his dark curls, his hazel eyes fixed on the laundromat across the street. They always coordinated their breaks, a small distraction from the monotony of working in Grove Gardens, a district that hardly lived up to its name since there were no gardens except the one she tended with her sister in their backyard.

"Did you hear about what happened to Michelle last week?" Jax passed her a cool can of water from his lunch bag.

"Yeah. She went to the Blood Clinic and got the call to become an Elite three days ago." Opening the can, she drank it down.

Jax made a face. "I can't believe she's going to be an Elite. I could never."

Serenity's muscles tensed at the unmistakable disdain in his voice. If only he knew where she'd been today. She remembered how last winter, when her mother had taken a turn for the worse, Jax had spent three nights at their house, keeping the fire going while she slept. He'd given them his extra blankets and half his food rations without being asked. How could she betray that kind of loyalty?

Kane's sharp silver-blue eyes flashed through her mind. She couldn't shake the pull toward him, how alive she'd felt in his presence. The way his hands had been so careful when cleaning her wound, how his deep voice had commanded the room. Despite knowing the danger he posed, she couldn't bring herself to fear him.

What would Jax think if he knew where her mind kept drifting?

He'd always harbored a deep hatred for vampyrs. They'd taken his family, including his baby sister, a year before the war ended. His only surviving relative, his sixteen-year-old cousin, had taken him in but joined the Elites five years ago, leaving only a note seeking forgiveness. Jax had severed all ties with him.

"She has nothing left," Serenity said, watching Jax's hardened expression. "Her mother passed away six months ago, and she hasn't been able to find a job."

His jaw clenched. "She should have come to me. I would have helped her."

"Yeah, but only for so long. You help enough people as it is."

"She made her choice," he snapped. Silence engulfed them. Then he asked, "How's your mom and sister doing? I've been meaning to stop by, but I've been helping Mrs. Ives with her house."

He would offer his support if he knew how much they needed, but she couldn't let him take on more.

"We've been doing fine. Parts of the garden are still growing, so we'll be alright when winter hits," she lied.

His watch beeped, fifteen minutes up.

"I have to get back. I'll see you tonight at Levees?"

It would probably be her last time at the old makeshift bar.

"Yeah, I'm bringing Clyde and Victoria."

"Stay safe," he said, walking toward the overpass.

Sadness spread through Serenity as she realized it might be the last time she saw all her friends.

She remembered clearly the first announcement of the Elite program. She'd been eight, huddled beneath her threadbare blanket, feigning sleep while her parents whispered urgently in the kitchen. The next morning, broadcast screens throughout the district flashed with promises of luxury and security. Her father had shut off their screen at once, his face a mask of dread.

That same day, he'd begun putting in place the precautions that would define her childhood: no school, no doctors, no ventures into the Inner City. When she turned twelve and got her period, she finally learned the truth. She was AB negative. The myth. Her father told her vampyrs called her blood ambrosia. Every month, she'd have to hide in the sealed basement room for five lonely days.

Walking back into Rack n' Reynolds, Serenity's mind buzzed with the Elite program and Jax's hatred for vampyrs. She took her place behind the old wooden counter, the cash register a silent reminder of how few customers they had.

The door jingled, echoing like a warning. The man who entered seemed to carry a different atmosphere, something sleek and polished that didn't belong in Grove Gardens.

He had silvery hair that set off bright blue eyes, and sun-kissed skin that had clearly never known outdoor labor. He moved with fluid grace, each step calculated yet effortless. His clothes were simple but cut from materials she'd only seen in Inner City broadcasts.

"Hello," he greeted casually. "You must be Serenity."

"Do I know you?" she asked, puzzled.

"No, you don't," he replied. "The nurse at the blood clinic told me you worked here."

Panic rose within her. She didn't want her family to find out before she could tell them.

"I'm just here to follow up on the incident today," he continued with a smile that did little to comfort her.

"I'm fine. There's nothing else to say." Serenity stood, busying herself to avoid his eyes.

"My name is Sebastian. I want to know more about you, and why there's no information about you in the system."

She should have known they'd be curious about that.

"My father was old-fashioned. He'd seen enough war and didn't want us too deep in the system, in case things turned bad and we needed to run."

"In case you needed to disappear with little trace. Let me guess, you were born in the caves." His accuracy unsettled her.

"How did you know?"

"I lived in those caves too. I was six when they signed the treaty, eighteen when I became an Elite. I've been through two vampyrs already. I'm on my third now." He took off his jacket and hopped onto the counter. "My parents died before the war ended. My aunt and uncle died when I was sixteen."

Why was he sharing such personal details? Was he trying to manipulate her?

"Why are you telling me all this?" she asked cautiously.

"So you know I can be trusted." He lay back on the counter. "I was Derek's blood slave for almost a year before the HVC discovered his little blood brothel. They cleaned me up and stuck me with Hilda, a proper vampyr lady."

As he spoke about being a blood slave, his casual demeanor slipped. His hand drifted to his neck, tracing what looked like a faded scar. His eyes clouded over briefly before he resumed his carefree posture.

"I despised her, but without her, I'd never have been found by Evelyn, who rescued me. Do you have anything to drink?"

Serenity grabbed a can of water. "Your life has been crazy, but why do I need to know you can be trusted?"

Sebastian drank deeply. "Evelyn finds you curious. She wants to know why your father kept you out of the system."

"So they don't know yet." Her blood type results weren't back.

"She'll find out soon enough. Your blood is rare. How rare?"

She bristled. "Rare enough."

"So why choose to become an Elite? What happened?"

Serenity hadn't been able to tell anyone about this. "My mom and sister are sick. I can't afford their medicine. My dad had a supply, but we're down to our last few doses. The only job that would give me enough credits—"

"Is becoming an Elite," Sebastian supplied, his voice carrying an unexpected understanding.

"My best friend will hate me, and I'll hardly see my family, but I'll make sure they get the medicine they need."

"I understand." Sebastian's eyes softened. "You know, it's not all blood and luxury. You'll have your own room, private space that's yours. Three days a week are feeding days, but the rest is yours. Some Elites study, others take up hobbies." He paused meaningfully. "The very rare smart ones use their position to help their communities."

A weight sat under his tone, hinting at more than the words said.

"But choose your battles carefully," he continued, straightening up. "The wrong vampyr can make your life hell, while the right one..." He smiled, and this time it reached his eyes. "Not all vampyrs are like the stories."

Sebastian put on his jacket. "I'll make sure Evelyn places you with a good one. You've been selected. Report here Friday at 3 p.m." He set a card on the counter. "Oh, and Serenity? Sometimes the best way to help your family, and others like them, is from the inside. Think about that."

Before she could ask what he meant, he was gone.

Damn. She hadn't gotten to ask what being an Elite was really like.

A pit opened in her stomach as it sank in that she'd been chosen. Fear and excitement chased each other through her. In three days, she'd meet her patron.

Would it be Kane? The thought set her pulse racing. She remembered how his silver-blue eyes had shifted when he looked at her, his gentle touch despite the power beneath his controlled exterior. But why would they choose her for the Head of the HVC?

Then doubt overwhelmed her. What if she wasn't ready?

She didn't have a choice. This was what they needed. She would meet it head-on.

With trembling fingers, she picked up Sebastian's card. The heavy cardstock felt foreign, its surface embossed with a simple symbol, a rose intertwined with a vine. She turned it over: "Friday, 3 PM."

Sebastian's words echoed in her mind. *Sometimes the best way to help your family, and others like them, is from the inside.*

She slipped the card into her pocket. There was no turning back now. Yet perhaps there were ways to help beyond her own family's survival. Ways that her father, with his hidden journals and careful documentation, might have approved of.

Think about that, Sebastian had said. And despite everything, she found herself doing exactly that.

CHAPTER SEVEN

SERENITY

Glancing at the wall clock, Serenity grabbed her bag, zipped up her jacket, then locked the shop's front door. Sebastian's card weighed heavily in her pocket, the Friday appointment looming. Three days until everything changed.

The blue-line bus took forever, but eventually she was let off at Del and Surge St. amid the deadened atmosphere of a once-bustling neighborhood. Now all that remained were crumbling buildings and boarded-up windows, ghosts of what life had been before the Inner City's wall went up.

The resources hadn't drained away by accident, she thought, starting the three-mile walk home. They'd been redirected. When had the decision been made to let the Outer City decay while the Inner City gleamed?

Her father used to tell her stories about life before they came here, when this place wasn't so desolate. People had roamed the neighborhood to see him, drawn by his reputation as a skilled doctor. Although he'd had little medicine left from his war days, medical care was expensive and hard to come by, even in this tight-knit community.

Their humble home hugged the wall of the narrow alleyway. She climbed the rickety porch stairs, the third step creaking dangerously. One more thing they couldn't afford to fix. Since her father's passing, the house had slid into disrepair, one more sign of how fast things fell apart without resources.

She reached for the screen door handle, and the front door flew open. Her twelve-year-old sister stood there, tears streaming from panicked hazel eyes.

"Oh! Serenity, thank God! It's Mom," she cried, running her hands frantically through her short, curly brown hair.

Serenity rushed past Beth into the house. She found her mother in her blue night robe on the living room floor, pale and unmoving. Her eyes were closed, but the shallow breathing and faint bluish tint to her lips told Serenity exactly what was happening.

Classic signs of insulin shock. Her father's training kicked in. She knelt beside her mother, checking her pulse, slow and thready, but there. Her skin felt cool and clammy.

Look for perspiration and monitor respiratory depression, her father's voice echoed in her memory, as though he'd somehow known she would need this.

She gently eased her mother into the recovery position, then looked up at Beth in the doorway, tears running down her face.

"Beth," she said, forcing a reassuring smile, "I need you to go to Father's shed and grab one of the red needle cases. Quick."

"The one with the g-glucose?" Beth stuttered, picking at her frayed sleeve, a nervous habit she'd developed after their father died.

"Yes, that one. And be careful crossing the yard."

As Beth sprinted out the back door, Serenity looked down at her mother, fury and helplessness warring inside her. Her mother had been rationing insulin out of fear they'd run out, and now she was paying for it.

How many other families in Grove Gardens were going through this exact crisis right now? The question landed with a hard, sudden clarity. How many mothers were rationing medication while the Inner City overflowed with it?

Soon, she thought, soon she would have enough credits to buy all the medicine they needed. After Friday, her family wouldn't have to ration anything. But what about Mrs. Chen next door? What about the Johnsons? What about all the other families Sebastian had implied she might be able to help "from the inside"?

Beth burst through the door, gasping and clutching a red metal case.

"I need you to take a deep breath. Can you do that for me?" Serenity said gently. "Give me the case, then use your inhaler."

"But Mom said I shouldn't use it unnecessarily," Beth wheezed.

"Beth, please. I promise I'll get you more if you run out."

Finally Beth moved toward her room. Serenity opened the case and drew out the syringe, remembering her father's steady hands guiding hers. *The angle matters, Serenity. Too steep and you hit muscle. Too shallow and the medication won't absorb properly.*

She inserted the needle into her mother's thigh at a forty-five-degree angle, holding her breath. The glucose solution would raise her blood sugar quickly, but they needed to wait fifteen minutes.

The Inner City hospitals wouldn't send ambulances this far into the Outer City, and even if they did, the cost was prohibitive. One more barrier that seemed built on purpose to keep them isolated.

When Beth returned, her breathing steadier, they lifted their mother onto the couch. Serenity draped the soft, faded crochet blanket over her, once vibrant with color, now muted like everything else in their lives.

It felt like an eternity. Her mother had come around instantly the first two times, but this time was different. Serenity knew why her mother's health was slipping. She wasn't taking the insulin correctly, stretching it to make it last.

To distract herself, Serenity went to make tea. The kitchen wore the marks of their poverty: chipped countertops, an old stove with only two working burners. It would be different in the Inner City, where everything gleamed with wealth and privilege. After Friday, would she live in a place like that?

"Serenity! She's awake!" Beth's voice broke the silence.

Serenity rushed back to find her mother's eyes fluttering open. Relief poured through her as she knelt beside the couch.

"I'm okay, baby," her mother said weakly. "I'm sorry. I'll be alright."

They wouldn't talk about the incident. Her mother refused to see the situation for what it was. But Serenity was beginning to see it with hard, unsparing clarity, not just her family's crisis, but the pattern behind it.

As they sat together watching Golden Girls, the only clear channel besides news, Serenity felt her mother's chest rise and fall. Laughter filled the room, but her mind was far away.

Sebastian was right. This wasn't only about her family. This was about a system that forced desperate choices on families like theirs while abundance sat idle just miles away.

Later, she went to the backyard and gathered ripe tomatoes before heading to the small shed. She marked off the needle she'd used on her inventory list.

Just as she'd suspected, only two more needles left. Her sister had three inhalers, but nothing beyond them if she had another attack. Two more chances before they had nothing at all.

The truth settled hard in her chest. This was why she'd gone to the blood clinic, why she'd applied to be an Elite. In three days, she would walk away from everything she knew and offer her blood to a vampyr. There was no other choice.

But Sebastian's words lingered: helping "from the inside." What had he meant by that, exactly?

As she prepared dinner, dicing tomatoes and adding herbs, Beth appeared in the doorway with a grim expression.

"Is Mom going to die like Daddy?"

Serenity came over to rub her back. "No, Mom is going to be fine. She needs more medicine, and I'm working on that. I'm going to get you both more."

And maybe, she thought, remembering Sebastian's words, maybe there were ways to get medicine to more families than just her own.

"You are?" Beth asked, twisting her fingers nervously.

"Yes, I am. So don't worry, okay? I promise everything is going to be alright."

Beth wiped her tears and hugged her. "Can I help you make the pasta?"

"Of course." Serenity lived to see that smile. "The pot is over there. You remember how much water?"

"Yes! Three cups!" Beth grabbed the pot, excited.

After Friday, Serenity would have to find a way to tell her family what she'd decided. It hurt to leave them, but it was the only way to keep them safe. She trusted that Jax would look after them, even if he despised her choice.

As she watched her sister carefully measuring water, remembered her mother's close call with death, and felt the weight of Sebastian's card in her pocket, she knew she'd made the right choice.

Not just for her family's survival, but maybe for something larger. Sebastian had planted a seed, the notion that she might help beyond her own front door. The access Elite status could grant, the position it might offer...

She didn't know precisely what he'd meant, but his words had lodged in her, and they wouldn't let go.

For now, she would focus on Friday. On meeting her patron. On taking the first step into a world that might give her the chance to make a difference.

For them. And perhaps, somehow, for others too.

CHAPTER EIGHT

EVELYN

The blood results stared back at her from the open manila folder. Evelyn's breath caught as her eyes locked on the two words that would change everything: AB negative.

"Ambrosia. Fuck yes." The words escaped her in a reverent whisper.

Evelyn set down the empty Syn bottle, its metallic tang still lingering on her tongue. In the vampyr world, finding a human with this blood type was like stumbling onto a mythical creature. The legendary ambrosia blood, carrying its distinctive scent of jasmine, roses, and honeysuckle, was believed to hold properties beyond mere sustenance.

For centuries, vampyr scholars had theorized that AB negative blood held transformative power: the potential to rejuvenate aging vampyrs, sharpen existing abilities, even trigger genetic mutations. Unproven though they were, these theories had driven vampyrs to war over such rare humans.

Kane wouldn't be able to resist her, nor could he afford to let her remain unclaimed. A human with this blood walking freely would inevitably trigger a feeding frenzy among lesser vampyrs, perhaps even draw challenges from Council members. Only Kane, with his unmatched authority, could put down any challenge for her.

Evelyn's gaze drifted to the portrait on her wall, a hand-painted image of the Elder Council from 1716. Kane stood at the center, looking much as he did now, though without the weight of centuries in his eyes. She'd been at his side through revolutions and wars, through the rise and fall of nations. She couldn't lose him now to bloodlust.

No one could know about this yet, not until she made certain Kane would claim Serenity. Evelyn moved to her computer with purpose, pulling up the woman's file and methodically altering the results to read AB positive. Then she grabbed the matches, striking one to set the original results ablaze.

She carried the burning paper to the open window, waiting until the flames nearly touched her fingertips before releasing the evidence into the night breeze. The lab records would need altering too, but Martin, her devoted assistant who owed her his family's lives from the Great War, would handle that without question.

As she watched the last glowing ember vanish into the dark, Evelyn mapped her next moves with a chess master's precision. Kane's condition was deteriorating faster than he admitted. The red veins in his eyes, the increasingly violent outbursts, the tremor in his hands all pointed toward bloodlust. She'd witnessed this progression before, most memorably in London, 1888, when a vampyr called Jack had descended into madness and bred a terror that humans still whispered about.

Kane had been the one to end Jack then. Who would end Kane if he fell now?

She was about to reach for the phone when Sebastian strolled into her office and dropped onto the antique leather couch.

"The Outer City sucks." He ran a hand through his blond hair. "It's nice being back in the Inner City. Cleaner air." He smirked.

"You know that's not true. Now, spill. What did you find out about the woman?" Evelyn went to her fridge, took out water, and handed it to him before joining him on the couch.

"She's interesting, with an interesting story. You already know her blood is rare, right?"

"Yes. So she knows her blood type?" She had to know what it meant.

"Yes. She said her father was old-fashioned and didn't trust the system."

Sounded like bullshit. "Why did she apply to be an Elite?"

"Desperation." He shrugged, but for a brief beat, something flashed across his face, a genuine concern that broke through his carefully built indifference.

Evelyn raised her brow, waiting for more, but Sebastian wasn't forthcoming. "Care to explain?"

"The usual. Wanting out of the Outer City, hoping to help her family." Sebastian turned toward her, draping his arm around her neck. "So, what do I get for this favor, mistress?"

She should have guessed he'd want something. He was never one for doing anything free, but she never minded paying his price.

"What would you like?" she drawled.

His hand slipped under her lab coat, then dipped into her shirt to cup her breast. His thumb dragged over her nipple, drawing it taut.

"I think it's lunchtime." He smiled before freeing her breast and dipping his head to claim the peak. Sebastian sucked deeply, sending jolts of pleasure straight to her core.

Fuck, she loved his mouth on her. A shockwave rolled through her as his tongue flicked over the tip before he gave it a small nip.

"Sebastian," she sighed as her fangs lengthened. "You know we can't do this here."

"I know, but it's my duty to feed you when you're hungry." Lifting his head, he stared deep into her eyes. "And I know you're just as hungry as I am."

He wasn't wrong. She could see her own hunger reflected back at her.

Sinking to the floor between her legs, he pulled up her shirt, baring her other breast. Returning his lips to her warm flesh, he suckled and tweaked the bud with his fingers.

His long strokes drove Evelyn wild as he worked back and forth from one peak to the next, scattering hot sparks low in her belly.

A soft sigh slipped out as he slid his hands up her thighs, stopping just short of her center. Her hips bucked forward in anticipation.

Tugging at her skirt's waistband, she lifted herself so he could draw it off. Once it was gone, she lay back, fully exposed to his ravenous gaze.

His deft fingers slid the silken fabric aside, baring her glistening sex. A single finger ran along her folds, pulling a moan from her as she arched against him.

"See? You're so ready to feed me." His tongue slid up her slick heat and circled the swollen crown of her clit. She gasped, lost in sensation.

"Fuck, Sebastian," she breathed. Her hands twisted into his hair, clutching at him as need tingled through her.

"My sweet little Eve." He drew her tender bud into his mouth and swirled his tongue around it. Pulling back, he murmured, "You want to make sure your Elite is nice and satiated?"

She tried to swallow the moan and failed. His tongue plunged into her wetness like a blade, his lips hot around the swollen peak.

"Now, you don't want us to get caught, do you? You know how your kind has excellent hearing. Be quiet, or I'll be forced to stop."

Evelyn bit her lip, knowing he was right. She nodded, and his mouth was back on her, rubbing, licking, sucking. The pressure built inside her like a gathering storm, and she squirmed even as she ground herself harder against his tongue, chasing release.

His tongue flattened against her as his fingers thrust against her G-spot, and the shockwave tore through her. Her core detonated, sensation ripping outward as he sucked, riding her orgasm until she was shaking and breathless.

Before she could think, she had him flat on his back, guiding his cock into her as she straddled him, taking him in until there was no space left between them.

He stared up at her, devastating blue eyes blown wide, pupils dilated. He smirked, his hands rising to grip her breasts, squeezing gently as she sank her fangs into his neck. She savored the sweetness of his blood filling her mouth while he thrust into her until he reached his climax.

When she'd finished, Evelyn licked his neck, making sure the punctures had sealed before sliding off him.

"Sebastian, spill. I know there's more you didn't tell me." She grabbed her skirt and pulled it back on as he sat up, tugging his pants into place.

Still on the floor, he leaned back against her desk. He studied her for a moment, then said, "Her mother and sister are sick."

For an instant, his carefully maintained facade cracked. His voice dropped, raw with feeling. "Her mother has diabetes, her sister severe asthma. They're down to their last doses of medication. She can't afford the medicine, so this is her only option." The emotion in his voice was unmistakable, his own past surfacing in Serenity's desperation.

Sebastian swallowed hard, visibly gathering himself. "She's giving up everything to save them. And she doesn't even know what she's walking into."

"She's forced into the system to save her family." Evelyn moved behind her desk and noted the crucial detail in Serenity's file. This could be the emotional leverage to deepen whatever connection formed between Kane and his new Elite.

Desperation made people do unexpected things. It made them willing to take risks they'd never consider otherwise.

Sebastian stood, watching her with those radiant blue eyes. "You're not going to use this against her, are you?"

Beneath his casual demeanor, she glimpsed the same protective fierceness that had surprised her years ago, when she'd first found him bloodied and broken in Hilda's private chambers. She'd meant only to rehabilitate and release him. But seeing the intelligence behind his fear, hearing the resolve in his voice once he'd begun to trust her, she'd found herself keeping him longer than any Elite before.

"No," she answered truthfully. "I just want to place her where she can stay close to her family."

There was a quality to Sebastian's interest in this particular human that felt unlike his usual detached reports. More... invested.

Sebastian's lips curved into a real smile as he came around the desk. He tilted her chin up gently and drew her into a kiss that spoke of their peculiar but profound bond.

"I'll see you at home later?"

She nodded. "Yes."

He would be waiting naked for her when she got home, a thought that made her bite her lip in anticipation.

After he left, Evelyn's mind returned to the pressing crisis. Kane's condition posed a terrible dilemma. If this Elite, this Serenity with her ambrosia blood, didn't stabilize him, Evelyn would face the unthinkable duty of destroying her oldest friend to protect Celearius.

The signs of his decline were unmistakable and accelerating. His refusal to take an Elite for eight months had driven him dangerously close to the edge. Without Styxx's Cataract Club, burned by rebels six months ago, Kane had lost his last discreet source of human blood.

The timing of that attack had been... convenient. Almost as if someone had known exactly how to pressure Kane into accepting an Elite.

Evelyn picked up her phone and dialed Rhyzan's number. "It's confirmed," she said when he answered. "Friday at 3 p.m. We need to make sure Kane is there." She paused, listening. "Yes, I'll handle the paperwork. Just make sure he attends the meeting."

After hanging up, she pulled out the special file folder marked with the HVC's seal, the formal Elite assignment documents. Normally these would go through a committee, but as Chief Medical Officer, she had the authority to make emergency placements.

With calculated precision, she began filling out the forms that would bind Serenity Wright to Kane Draccus, potentially saving him from bloodlust while planting a desperate young woman in the heart of vampyr power.

Strange, how cleanly the pieces were falling into place.

CHAPTER NINE

SERENITY

Serenity made sure her mom and sister were safely tucked into bed before finally leaving to join Jax at Levees. Sebastian's card weighed heavily in her pocket. Two more nights of freedom before everything changed. This would likely be her last visit to the makeshift bar, her last chance to be just Serenity from Grove Gardens before she became someone's Elite.

She slipped through the dark gray plank hidden in the thick wall, one street from her house, a secret passage created years ago when Ol' Irving's furnace explosion had accidentally breached the barrier. The city had merely patched it with planks, inadvertently leaving a shortcut that spared residents the long walk through the official tunnels.

How many other "accidents" had opened convenient passages between districts? she wondered.

The barren wasteland between the ruins and the wall was treacherous, rumored to be prowled by rogue vampyrs. After meeting Kane, she wondered whether the true predators weren't these mythical wanderers but the ones who operated within the system's sanctioned spaces.

Following the faded blue arrows painted on the wall, she reached the dead tree marking her turn, then continued until she found the cave entrance. The ceiling glowed with luminous mushrooms, casting an ethereal light onto the black door.

"Password?" Kurt's voice called from the other side, tenser than usual.

"I am no bird, and no net ensnares me: I am a free human with an independent will." The Jane Eyre quote, Kurt's small rebellion against the system, rolled off her tongue after so many years.

The door opened to reveal Kurt's burly frame, his piercing blue eyes scanning the darkness behind her before he ushered her in with unusual haste. "Everything alright?" she whispered.

"Fine," he muttered, not meeting her eyes. "Just heard rumors of increased patrols tonight."

Increased patrols. A cold prickle crawled up her spine as she moved on through the dark cavern.

Levees unfolded in all its makeshift glory, a sanctuary cobbled together from necessity and determination. Sweet, yeasty beer mingled with musty earth, layered over pine-scented candles that barely masked years of spilled drinks and sweat.

Tonight the crowd seemed thinner than usual. Old Sam's chess table sat empty, and Fred was nowhere behind the bar, replaced by an unfamiliar face. Small signs that something wasn't right.

She found Jax in a back booth with Clyde and Victoria, who were nestled together opposite him. Jax's smile took her back to when they were twelve, hiding in her father's shed after "borrowing" his medical textbooks. She'd miss that smile more than anything.

"Hey, I almost thought you weren't coming. We waited for you at the stop." Jax scooted over to give her room.

"Sorry. My mom had an incident earlier, and I wanted to make sure she was sleeping before I slipped out."

Worry etched Victoria's face. "Is she alright?"

"Yes, she's fine. She just forgot to take her medicine this morning."

Another lie. Her mother hadn't forgotten; they were rationing what little remained.

"You haven't been able to find your father's supplier?" Jax asked, filling a glass from their pitcher.

"No, it's too risky to ask around. I wish he'd left some kind of clue."

"Don't be cruel to yourself," Jax cut in. "We'll figure it out. We always do."

We'll figure it out. If only he knew what she'd already done, the choice that would take her away from all of them. She remembered how he'd stayed with her family for two weeks after her father died, rebuilding their steps and fixing the roof without being asked. He would go to the ends of the earth for her, but she couldn't let him keep sacrificing himself.

When Clyde offered moonshine shots, for once she didn't decline.

"Woah! Serenity's taking a shot tonight! It's about to get rowdy!" Clyde yelled.

"Are you sure?" Jax asked, concern in his voice.

The taste would carry her back to that night after her father's funeral, when grief had blurred into need. She'd regretted using him for comfort ever since.

"Yes. I've had a rough couple of days. Just one."

The moonshine burned like fire, crude corn and sugar and whatever else was cheap and on hand. Grove Gardens had no bars or liquor stores; only homemade brews were to be had. Easton had one bar, but its prices were impossibly high.

Only certain humans, those with credits, could afford to drink there. Councilman Gary Hensen, who represented their district, spent most of his time in Waterside Park and surfaced only during election season.

Serenity was never sure why he always got re-elected.

Clyde lifted his glass. "OC Bitches for Life!" Victoria slapped his head. "Ow. I meant OC Friends for Life!"

They laughed, clinked glasses, and downed their shots. The moonshine scorched Serenity's throat as it worked its way to her stomach.

"How are you feeling?" Jax asked, always trying to take care of her.

She smiled. "I'm fine, but Tori looks like she's itching to dance."

Serenity pressed her hand to Victoria's and drew them toward the makeshift dance floor. The moonshine moved warm through her veins, loosening the tension. She closed her eyes and let the music take her, forgetting her responsibilities, forgetting that she'd soon have to tell her best friend she was leaving to keep her family alive.

It would be so hard, but just like her father, she knew what had to be done.

A deafening crash from the entrance shattered the harmony like lightning splitting the night sky.

Serenity's instincts seized as panic broke out around her. She grabbed Victoria's hand, eyes hunting for Jax. She found him steering Clyde toward the back, his gaze meeting hers in understanding.

The tunnels. They needed to reach the tunnels. Fast.

Her heart slammed against her ribs as she pulled Victoria through the press of bodies toward the tunnel entrance. Adrenaline sharpened every sense. The air hung thick with fear.

Through the crush, she caught a glimpse of the intruders, the distinctive black uniforms and silver badges of the Outer City Police. But something was off. Mingled among them were figures moving too fast to be human, their eyes gleaming with unnatural light.

Vampyrs. The OCP had brought vampyrs.

This wasn't a routine patrol. This was coordinated. Planned.

Time was running out. If the OCP found her here, she'd never make it to Friday's appointment. And if the vampyrs caught her scent, her real scent, everything would be lost.

CHAPTER TEN

SERENITY

The deafening crash from the OCP raid still rang in Serenity's ears as they scrambled through the bar, dodging panicked patrons. The four of them quickly found the hidden exit deep within the walls, ducking inside just as flashlight beams swept across the space they'd vacated.

From the outside, the exit seemed to lead nowhere, but inside lay a tunnel running underground. Jax went first, followed by Serenity, Victoria, and Clyde, who helped Theodora, an elderly woman whose arthritis made the steep descent difficult.

"Hurry," Jax whispered urgently. "I think I heard someone at the entrance."

A distant shout confirmed his fears, driving them deeper into the dark. Faintly glowing mushrooms lit only a few feet ahead at a time, throwing a pale blue cast on their frightened faces. They followed the path until it split three ways.

"Theodora, you should take the middle path with the others," Clyde said gently. "It'll lead you straight back to Grove Gardens."

The old woman nodded, her weathered face tight with fear. "You kids be careful." With a final worried glance, she joined the group heading down the middle tunnel.

They took the tunnel farthest left while the others chose the remaining paths back to the Outer City. Their tunnel ran deeper into the barren lands, a forbidden place that had never once stopped them.

As they pressed on, the dirt walls turned from rough to smooth, and the mushroom glow began to fade. Jax grabbed an old, rusty lamp resting at a cave juncture. With a flick, dim light pierced the dark, throwing long shadows as they continued.

"Think anyone followed us?" Victoria whispered, glancing nervously over her shoulder.

"The OCP never ventures this far into the tunnels," Jax answered, but his tone lacked conviction. "Too afraid of what might be living down here."

Or maybe they had other reasons for staying away, Serenity thought. Maybe some places were meant to stay hidden.

Their footsteps echoed through the cavern as they followed the twists and turns of the old sewer system. The air turned musty and damp, a sharp contrast to the lively atmosphere they'd left behind. Water dripped somewhere in the blackness, each drop counting off the seconds spent underground. At last they reached the makeshift ladder of old planks and rusty nails.

Clyde held the lamp while Jax climbed, each rung creaking under his weight. At the top, Jax lifted the metal lid and peeked out carefully, going still for one held breath before continuing. He climbed out, easing the lid shut behind him.

They waited in silence for Jax's signal: one bang for danger, two for caution, three for all-clear. Seconds stretched into what felt like hours as Serenity held still. A moment later, three clear bangs rang through the air. The collective sigh of relief was audible.

As they climbed out of the opening, dust coated the floor, swirling up into the air. The moon shone brightly through the dirty, cracked windows of the abandoned warehouse loft, casting long shadows across the concrete. In the distance, the gleaming towers of the Inner City pierced the night sky, their lights twinkling like stars, so close yet impossibly far. In two days, Serenity would be there among those lights, living a life these friends couldn't imagine.

Amid the debris on the floor, they'd gathered furniture from nearby buildings and thrown blankets over it for comfort. A tattered Cougars banner, the city's pre-war baseball team, hung crookedly on one wall, alongside faded posters of bands none of them had ever heard play. They kept water cans and beer in Clyde's old cooler to make it a decent hangout. Nobody ever bothered them here.

"Home sweet home," Jax sighed, collapsing onto a faded armchair that released a small cloud of dust. "Another clean getaway from Celearius's finest."

Another escape. Victoria and Clyde had stumbled onto this place years ago after a wrong turn while evading the OCP. But Serenity and Jax used it for more than hiding; they'd often vanish here for days, sometimes venturing further into the barren lands than anyone was supposed to go.

"Think the raid was random?" Serenity asked, settling onto a threadbare couch.

"Nothing's random anymore," Jax replied grimly. "Word is the OCP's been cracking down on anything that smells like a human gathering place. They've shut down three underground bars in the last month."

Three bars in a month. The pattern was coming into focus. Someone was systematically targeting the places where humans gathered freely, where they might organize or share information.

Clyde went to the cooler and looked inside. "Sweet, they're ice-cold. Catch!" He tossed a beer toward Jax, who caught it and popped it open.

A few weeks ago, the two had turned up a case of what might have been twenty-year-old beer while exploring. Serenity had told them to throw it out, but clearly her warning went unheard.

"I guess Victoria and I will just start digging holes now, since we can't afford credits for funerals," Serenity said, wrapping a blanket around herself.

Victoria plopped onto the couch, dust flying. "You think we can say they wandered off into the barren lands and got eaten by radioactive wolves, so we don't have to dig holes?"

Serenity laughed, loving the idea. For a moment, the raid, her looming departure, all of it dissolved in the easy comfort of their friendship.

"Laugh it up all you want. You two are missing out on some great beer," Clyde remarked, walking over to Victoria.

"Go away, Clyde." Her voice went flat as she lifted her arm to cover her face, pretending to sleep.

"Just a sip, baby," he taunted, tipping the bottle until amber liquid splashed against her cheek.

"Bastard!" she screamed, jumping up and chasing him up the jagged stone steps into a room with a pallet of blankets.

Serenity sighed heavily, throwing them a disdainful look before turning away. Grabbing Jax's hand, she led him outside the building, away from the room with no door. She refused to listen to their moans of passion.

Taking refuge in the only patch of grass around, Serenity spread a blanket so they could lie back and watch the stars. The full moon's silver light washed over their faces as crickets began to chirp. From this hillside, the Inner City's gleaming spires stood in stark contrast to the crumbling ruins of the Outer City districts, a visible map of the divide that would soon cut her off from everything she knew.

"I wish they'd be less obvious about what they're going to do," Jax said, taking a sip from his beer.

She chuckled. "Why? There's no less obvious way to sneak upstairs to have sex, especially when there are only four of us. It only bothers you because you have no one to sleep with."

He glanced at her. "We could—"

"Don't even think about it. Once was enough. We've talked about this, several times. I don't want to ruin our friendship. Besides, there are plenty of girls who want you." The weight of her secret pressed on her like a stone. How could she explain that in two days she'd be gone, claimed by some vampyr she'd never met?

He turned toward her, looking straight into her eyes. "But I don't want them."

"Jax." She hated the guilt he stirred in her when he got like this. It was worse now, knowing she'd vanish from his life without warning.

"I know. I know." He leaned over her. "Can I kiss you? Just one kiss, that's all."

Serenity held his stare and read the clarity in his eyes. She opened her mouth to refuse, then stopped. What if this was her last chance? After Friday, she'd belong to a vampyr, her blood and body no longer hers to give. This might be the last time she'd ever feel truly human, truly free.

The moonlight caught in his dark curls, lighting the face she'd known for so many years. The same face that had been there after her father died, that had laughed with her through their best moments.

She let her eyes drop, reluctant, before finally relenting. "Okay."

Surprise lit his face, and he leaned in close as if waiting for confirmation. After a few tense seconds, she nodded.

When his lips touched hers, a familiar current rushed through her, and her chest warmed. His tongue brushed against hers, gentle yet purposeful. His fingers traced her thigh, kindling a low heat in her belly.

The scent of him, bleach from the laundry, the herbal soap her mother made, and something uniquely Jax, wrapped around her and brought the memories flooding back. The crescent scar above his eyebrow from when they'd climbed the water tower at fourteen. The calluses on his hands from years of manual labor. All the small details that made him home.

Every instinct screamed at her to stop, but the thought of never seeing him again carried her on, until his hands moved from her thigh to skim the sides of her breasts.

She gasped and caught his hand, reluctantly breaking away. "Jax."

"I know. I'm sorry. I can't help it when I finally have you in my arms." He leaned in, lips parting slightly, eyes half-lidded.

She felt it coming and turned her head at the last second. He exhaled heavily and sank back against the blanket.

She regretted agreeing in the first place, but guilt had gotten the better of her. How could she tell him the truth? That in less than forty-eight hours she'd be gone from Grove Gardens, living in the Inner City, her blood sustaining some vampyr she'd never met?

"We should probably start heading back." Serenity stood. When he didn't look at her, she knew he needed a minute. "I'll get the two lovebirds."

She went back inside and found Clyde and Victoria coming down the stairs, smiling. Serenity couldn't help a twinge of envy. They were so damn cute. She still remembered when they'd hated each other; now they couldn't live without each other. Would she ever find that kind of bond, or would becoming an Elite strip her of even that?

Victoria saw her first. "We're ready to head back."

"Same." Jax spoke from behind her. He threw the blanket over one of the chairs, and they made their way back through the tunnels.

They took the one farthest right this time, which let them out near a junkyard in Grove Gardens. They went their separate ways from there. Jax, of course, walked her home.

Halfway to her house, he took her hand, and they walked in silence. The streets were empty, the only sound an occasional distant bark of a dog or the hum of electricity from the walls surrounding the district. The familiar route, with its cracked sidewalks and abandoned storefronts, had never felt so precious. She tried to memorize every detail: the crooked lamppost at the corner, the faded mural of the pre-war city on the old grocery store, the maple tree her father had planted the year she was born, now towering over their street.

When they reached the front of her home, he finally spoke. "Serenity, I'm sorry about earlier. I didn't mean to—"

"Shh." She pressed her fingers to his lips. "I'm not mad. Let's take it for what it was... just a kiss."

The flicker of sadness in his eyes made her chest ache, but she refused to give in, showing him instead a smile that hid the emotions churning beneath.

"I understand. Friends?" His lips formed a weak, barely there smile as he looked away.

"Always." Serenity's heart broke as she pulled him into a tight embrace, breathing in his scent one last time, trying to fix it in her memory.

She clasped her hands tightly at his back, hoping he would forgive her as a tear slipped down her cheek. She wiped it away before pulling back.

They said their goodbyes, and he walked away. She watched until he rounded the corner and was gone from sight.

Serenity drew a slow breath and whispered a silent prayer, hoping she'd made the right decision as she looked up at the night sky. The porch light flickered behind her, lighting the worn welcome mat her mother had made years ago, the swing where her father used to rock her sister to sleep, the garden where they'd grown vegetables every summer. All the pieces of a life she was about to leave behind.

Tomorrow she would write the letter explaining everything. Tonight, she would hold on to these last precious moments of being simply Serenity Wright from Grove Gardens.

CHAPTER ELEVEN

KANE

The scent of her lingered in his memory: jasmine, honeysuckle, and a note uniquely hers that called to the darkest part of him. Kane stared at the half-empty bottle of Syn on his desk. His fangs throbbed painfully against his gums as her image flashed through his mind: honey-brown eyes, the pulse visible beneath the delicate skin of her throat, that single drop of blood that had nearly shattered his legendary control.

This had to stop. He was the Head of the Human Vampyr Council, not some fledgling unable to master his urges.

A rap on his office door pulled him from the dangerous thoughts. Rhy and Evie stood in the doorway, their faces drawn tight with worry. His stomach seized in dread.

Something had happened.

"Another murder?" he asked quietly as they settled into the chairs facing him. The Human Liberation had grown bolder in recent weeks, with more vampyr killings than ever before.

After a tense pause, Rhy spoke, his voice solemn. "No. We have the results on the woman."

Relief washed through Kane. He went on putting his notes away. "And?"

"Kane, her blood type is AB negative," Evie revealed.

If her blood were ever exposed to the public, the city would descend into mayhem. Wars had been fought over her blood type. If any vampyrs found her before they did, she'd be either dead or locked away and used until there was nothing left of her.

Celearius already teetered on the edge of collapse, and he didn't need this woman adding to the unrest.

"I know." Kane stood and began to pace. His fangs extended fully, the sharp points pressing against his lower lip. He tasted his own blood as they pierced the skin, the metallic flavor a bitter reminder of his waning control.

How had she survived in society this long without being caught? Unless she'd stayed hidden in the Outer City.

"Take her as your Elite," Rhy said, utterly serious.

Kane stopped and turned, silver-blue eyes locking onto Rhyzan's. The suggestion hung in the air like lead, heavy and impossibly daunting.

The silence stretched until Kane finally broke it, his voice barely louder than a whisper. "That is not an option."

Rhyzan held his gaze without faltering. "Why not? You're one of the few who could actually keep her safe."

Kane's gut churned at the proposal. Taking her as his Elite would mean committing on a level he hadn't since he lost his wife. Becca's face rose in his mind: her gentle smile as she tended their garden in the moonlight, the way she'd cup his face in her small hands, the lavender scent that always surrounded her. For three centuries, he'd kept that wound closed, refusing to let anyone near enough to reopen it.

But taking Serenity would also mean direct protection, a loophole to shield her from prying eyes and opportunistic vampyrs.

He was silent for an eternity before he finally answered, "I don't think she would agree to it once she learns what it means."

Evelyn fixed him with a look of exasperation that somehow still held sympathy. "You don't know that until you ask her, Kane. And right now, we don't have many options."

"As your Elite, she'd be under our protection. Her identity and blood type can stay secret," Rhy explained.

"And stand a higher chance of being discovered," Evelyn added, drawing their attention.

"Evie is right," Kane agreed, heat in his voice, his eyes flashing. "The vampyrs are always sniffing around my Elites."

"But you are Kane Draccus," Rhyzan countered calmly. "Both vampyrs and humans respect you. Fear you. You have a control none of us do."

Kane ran a hand through his hair and exhaled heavily, looking out at the cityscape beyond his office. Celearius lay sprawled beneath them like an intricate board game, each district beating with its own rhythm. The gleaming towers of the Inner City stood in stark contrast to the dim lights of the Outer City, a visible map of the divide between abundance and scarcity.

He thought of the woman's face, those innocent eyes blind to the depth of her appeal to their kind. Even in this fractured world, there was a magnetic purity about her that drew him in.

Was he considering this because he craved her blood? Or truly to protect her? Or perhaps for a reason that ran deeper, one he couldn't quite name?

Each possibility coiled tight in his chest. He had vowed long ago to keep his emotions locked away after losing his wife. But now she was beginning to unravel everything he'd sworn to bury.

He thought of the fear that would surely etch across those delicate features once she learned her fate. The image stirred a primal instinct in him, an old code of protection that had long lain dormant.

As his thoughts churned, his mind strayed to the Human Liberation, whose operations were seeping through Celearius like a spreading disease. He was certain they were behind the missing Elites, but he still had no proof.

The recent raid on underground gathering places showed their growing boldness. How long before they escalated from targeting individual vampyrs to something far larger? The systematic nature of their attacks suggested a coordination he hadn't fully appreciated before.

Would they see her as a symbol of salvation or another pawn in their deadly game? Their recent actions held nothing but ruthlessness, and he feared they'd stop at nothing to seize power.

"Honestly, Kane... she needs you." Evelyn's voice cut through his brooding.

The words struck a deep chord. When was the last time anyone had truly needed him? Not his authority, not his power, but him?

Kane's gaze drifted to the city below, to the endless rows of lights stretching into the distance. In all his years as leader, he had built walls, enforced boundaries, kept order. But had he ever truly protected those under his care? Had he ever made a difference in a single life, not merely in the abstract idea of society?

He turned back to Rhyzan and Evelyn, his resolve hardening. His fist clenched at his side as he met their gazes with a new conviction.

"I'll do it," he said firmly, the words rising from a place he hadn't reached in centuries. "I will take her as my Elite."

Kane allowed himself one long breath before leaning back into his chair. Despite their heated debate, their faces held nothing but understanding and worry.

"But only if she consents. I will not force this upon her," he said, stubbornly resolute.

Rhy and Evie nodded, their shoulders easing as they saw his expression soften.

Evie pulled out her cellular device and tapped a few buttons. "I have a meeting with her tomorrow at 3 p.m. at the Easton Blood Clinic. You can meet her then."

Kane nodded, feeling the heavy weight of his decision settle on his shoulders. He wanted to take it back, but in his heart he knew this had to happen. Evie and Rhy rose to leave.

Evie touched his shoulder, smiling softly. "Thank you."

In silence, they left his office.

As the door closed behind them, Kane pulled open a drawer in his massive mahogany desk and lifted out an old drawing of his wife. The parchment was yellowed with age, the charcoal lines faded but still holding Becca's gentle expression. What would she think of him now, preparing to take another under his protection after all these years?

He traced her face once more before carefully returning the drawing to its place. Becca would have sided with Evie and Rhy; she had always seen the best in him, even when he couldn't see it himself.

Kane poured another glass of vodka and drank it down in one motion. The alcohol burned down his throat, a pale imitation of the heat that real blood would bring, and useless against the warring desires inside him. Taking Serenity as his Elite would force him to risk what he hadn't risked in lifetimes. It would mean facing his hunger every day, testing his control against the most powerful temptation he had ever known.

The strategic calculation was plain: claiming her himself was the safest course for her and for Celearius. But the personal cost was beyond measure. His fangs lengthened of their own accord at the mere thought of her blood, rich and sweet, unlike anything he had ever tasted.

And there was the other concern. If the Human Liberation truly was growing more organized, more methodical, then leaving someone with AB-negative blood unprotected would be like handing them a weapon. They could turn her into a symbol, a rallying cry, or worse, a bargaining chip against vampyr leadership.

No. Better to keep her close, where he could safeguard her and watch for any risk she might pose.

With a heavy breath, Kane gathered his things and left the office. As he walked out into the night, the lights of the city spread below him, he caught sight of a lone figure crossing one of the distant Outer City districts. Too far to identify, but the slight frame tugged at him, reminding him of her. Serenity.

Tomorrow, everything would change. For both of them.

CHAPTER TWELVE

SERENITY

Serenity was caught in a whirlwind of emotion as the two days flew by. She fought to keep herself composed while carrying out her duties.

She made sure the medicine logs were up to date. Each entry was a knot pulling tighter in her chest, knowing the supply was running out. Leaving instructions for Beth and her mom on how to make remedies and ration the last of the medicine was its own quiet torment.

Writing the note to Jax was the hardest task of all. As her best friend, he'd been her rock, and the thought of breaking the news to him was heart-wrenching.

Jax, I know you'll hate me for this. You'll say I didn't trust you enough, that I acted alone when we could have found another way. But I need you to understand. I couldn't risk waiting. I couldn't risk losing them... or you.

You've always been my rock, the one person I could count on when the world felt like it was falling apart. And I hope—no, I pray—that you'll still look out for them, even if you can't forgive me for this. I won't blame you if you walk away, but Jax, please know that you'll always be my best friend. Always.

Her tears blurred the ink as she signed her name, sealing words she could never say aloud. She drew a slow breath and tucked the note away, knowing it would be one of the last things she left behind.

The morning of her appointment dawned beneath a leaden sky. She spent the early hours memorizing her mother's face, the way her sister's hair curled at the temples, small details she feared forgetting. With trembling hands, she packed a small bag with her few possessions.

Now Serenity stood in front of the Easton Blood Clinic, remembering how she'd nearly died the first time she came here. Gathering her courage, she walked through the automatic doors, the sharp smell of disinfectant filling her nose.

She stopped at the desk, where a stern-looking woman in a white coat sat behind a computer screen.

"Name and ID, please," the woman said without looking up.

"Serenity. I have a meeting here at 3 p.m. I'm not sure—"

The nurse stood. "Right this way."

She didn't have time to take out her ID. For some reason, she'd thought she would be treated differently now that she was an Elite. The woman didn't even wait to see whether she'd follow.

Serenity hurried after the nurse through stainless-steel doors and down a long hallway. The fluorescent lights flickered overhead, throwing a harsh glow across the stark white walls.

The woman led her to a small room with a cozy feel, nothing like the cold, sterile space she'd been in before. Soft cream walls created a welcoming ambiance. A plush tan loveseat beckoned, a matching armchair nearby. Fresh flowers sat on a low coffee table.

It was a space built for comfort and conversation. Serenity realized this was where they put Elites to tell them who their patron would be.

"You can have a seat. They will be with you in a minute."

The nurse closed the door, leaving her alone with her thoughts. Every part of her wanted to flee, if only she could.

Serenity stood when she heard shuffling footsteps and hushed voices down the hallway. The conversation grew louder, as though an argument was about to break out.

The steps paused outside the door, and a voice barked, "Enough."

The handle twisted, and the door opened. She recognized the vampyr from before, Rhyzan. His presence still carried an edge of danger, but the glint of warmth in his eyes settled her nerves.

Then a beautiful woman with long auburn hair and deep green eyes entered. She wore a lab coat, marking her as a doctor.

Serenity's breath caught. The white coat triggered an instant cascade of images: cold metal tables, harsh fluorescent lights, antiseptic threaded through fear-sweat. Her heart hammered as phantom sensations crawled over her skin, rough hands holding her down, the bite of restraints, voices discussing her like a specimen.

She pressed back into the chair, muscles coiling for flight. Logic reminded her this wasn't the same doctor, but her body only remembered the helplessness, the violation of being examined like livestock.

"She won't hurt you," Rhyzan told her, his voice gentler than she expected. The reassurance loosened some of the knots in her.

"Hi, Serenity. I am Evelyn, and you've met Rhyzan." She gestured toward the vampyr.

Serenity extended her hand toward him. "Hi. We never introduced ourselves. It's nice to meet you. Also, thank you."

Rhyzan glanced down at her hand, then at Evelyn, before reaching out and gently clasping it. "Pleasure to meet you. Thank you for what?"

"Not killing me." She could have sworn she saw the ghost of a smile before his face went stoic.

"We can sit," Evelyn said, motioning Serenity toward the loveseat. She took the armchair across from her. Rhyzan stayed standing, his eyes never leaving Serenity's face.

"We're here to discuss your potential patron," Evelyn began. "First, I want you to know we take our responsibility very seriously here. We're sorry for what happened in our clinic, but we're glad you decided to continue with the application."

Serenity nodded, her pulse still unsteady.

"Your test results have come back, and we have good news. You've been matched with a patron."

Evelyn's expression turned serious. "Your patron is a very powerful vampyr, one of the most respected and feared in the community. He is known for his generosity and his commitment to his Elites."

Powerful and feared. Unease prickled along her arms as she recalled the stories she'd heard about such figures.

"But before we reveal his name, we want to make sure you understand what becoming an Elite means, especially his. Once you sign the contract, you'll have twenty-four hours to pack before being escorted to your new residence. Your patron will go over the feeding schedule."

The feeding schedule. Her chest tightened at the words. The air felt thin as she fought to keep her composure.

"Are you ready for this?" Rhyzan asked, his voice low and deep.

Ready? No, but she was here, and there was no turning back. She had to meet her choice head-on. This was for her family.

Serenity drew a breath and nodded, steeling herself.

Evelyn smiled, sensing her resolve. "Good, because for you there is a bit more."

"More?"

"Yes," Rhyzan explained. "Because of your blood type. We had to place you with someone who can protect you."

"Your blood type is rare, which makes it dangerous," Evelyn elaborated. "AB negative is less than one percent of the human population. The last recorded case in our city was over eighty years ago, and it nearly started a civil war among the vampyr houses. They call it 'ambrosia' for a reason."

Evelyn leaned forward, her voice dropping. "The patron we have selected can shield you from any harm. He is an elder vampyr."

"He is one of the most powerful beings in our world," Rhyzan added with deep respect. "Kane Draccus, the Head of the Human Vampyr Council."

Serenity's mouth fell open. Her eyes went wide, her hands trembling.

"I know this must be a lot to take in," Evelyn said softly, "but your safety is our top priority."

Kane Draccus would be her patron. Despite everything, she couldn't get past the news that it would be him. She remembered his striking silver-blue eyes and the strange warmth in them.

"Serenity," Rhyzan said gently, "I understand your apprehension. But you have to see this for what it is, an opportunity."

"An opportunity?" she echoed, bewildered.

"Yes," Evelyn chimed in. "He has the resources to protect you and your family. He'll make sure they get everything they need."

Protect her from what? The other vampyrs. They would want her blood, the way Dr. Bradford had.

She drew a shuddering breath. "I understand."

A sharp rap on the door jolted her from her trance.

"He's here," Evelyn said, a thread of hesitation in her voice.

Serenity swallowed, her pulse leaping. "I am ready," she said shakily.

Evelyn gave Rhyzan a subtle nod. They rose, and Serenity followed as Rhyzan opened the door with a soft creak.

Rhyzan bowed his head and stepped aside to let the man enter.

Serenity's eyes landed on him, and her breath caught in her throat.

Kane Draccus.

He stood before her exactly as she remembered. Taller than Rhyzan, his commanding presence seemed to draw all the air from the room. His tailored black suit clung to his muscular frame with precision, and his harsh silver-blue eyes fixed on hers the moment he crossed the threshold.

For a fraction of a second, those eyes widened with something close to recognition, perhaps even pleasure, before his expression settled back into careful neutrality. But she had seen it, that brief flash of vulnerability.

The room seemed to shrink until all she could sense was him, the sharp, intoxicating scent of cedar and leather. It was the sheer force of him, like gravity pulling her closer until she had to lock her knees to stay standing.

Kane crossed the room with slow, measured steps, his eyes never leaving hers. When he stopped before her, he loomed close enough that the faintest shift would close the gap between them.

"I realize," he began, his voice smooth, low, and dangerously intimate, "we never properly introduced ourselves."

The tension between them was almost a physical thing, a magnetic pull drawing them together. "Serenity Wright," she breathed, her voice steady despite the storm inside her.

Kane extended his hand, the movement slow and deliberate. She hesitated before finally grasping it. The instant his cool, firm grip enveloped hers, the world tilted. A current surged through her veins, kindling heat low in her belly.

"Kane Draccus," he replied, his name wrapping around her like velvet over steel. His thumb grazed the back of her hand before he let go, but the ghost of his touch lingered.

"Have they thoroughly explained," he continued, his tone darkening as his gaze cut to Rhyzan and Evelyn, "the situation to you?"

"Yes," she managed. "They made it clear I would be safer with you... because of my blood."

"Is that so?" He scowled and turned sharply toward Rhyzan and Evelyn, the air around him charged with authority. "Get out," he ordered, the command slicing through the room.

Serenity's pulse stuttered. Fear and curiosity rose together inside her.

Evelyn hesitated. "It's not usually customary—"

"Out," he repeated, his tone brooking no argument.

Rhyzan gave her a brief, unreadable glance before nodding and steering Evelyn out. The heavy door clicked shut, leaving Serenity alone with him.

The silence stretched until she felt it might smother her. The room seemed to answer their isolation, the air thickening, the scent of fresh flowers swelling and mingling with Kane's cedar and leather.

She cautiously raised her eyes to him. Their gazes connected, and he pinned her with a fiery stare that made her feel transparent, as if he could see through every defense she'd built.

His expression shifted by a fraction as he noticed her struggling, and in one swift motion he was beside her, a hand steadying her elbow. "Sit," he commanded, his voice gentler than she expected.

She sank onto the loveseat, grateful for the support as her legs threatened to give. Kane stayed standing, towering over her, his presence filling every corner of the room.

"Look at me," he demanded. Reluctantly, Serenity lifted her head to meet his icy blue gaze. He held her there as if he could read the secrets in the depths of her eyes.

A flicker crossed his expression then, too fleeting to name. His nostrils flared, his jaw tightening as his gaze dropped briefly to the curve of her neck. She caught it, the way his hand flexed at his side, his fingers curling into a fist.

What was that, she wondered.

The moment passed too quickly, and when his gaze returned to hers, it was sharp and unyielding.

"Why are you here?" he asked at last, his voice deceptively calm but edged with something sharper. "Why have you chosen to be an Elite? Don't lie to me. I will know."

"For the credits," she said finally, barely above a whisper. "Medicine."

"I know you are not sick. I have read your file. So, for whom?"

Serenity exhaled, her gaze dropping to the floor. "My mother and sister need it. They both suffer from illnesses that require medicine."

The silence that followed felt like judgment. Then Kane surprised her by asking, "When was the last time they saw a doctor?"

"When my father was alive, over a year ago."

He didn't answer right away. Then, slowly, he reached out, his fingers brushing a loose curl and tucking it behind her ear. The touch was achingly gentle, yet it sent a current straight through her.

"Being my Elite will not be easy. You may be targeted by others who disapprove of our decision," Kane warned. "You will have to be prepared."

Targeted by others. The phrase sent a cold ripple through her. What others? Other vampyrs who wanted her blood? Or were there threats she didn't yet understand?

"I don't have a choice," she said, her voice small but steady.

His lips tilted into the barest suggestion of a smile. "You always have a choice," he said, his voice drifting over her like smoke. "But remember this: once you are mine, there's no turning back."

Once you are mine. The possessiveness in his voice should have frightened her, but instead it sent heat spiraling through her chest.

His eyes narrowed for a moment, then closed. When he opened them again, she read what looked like resignation. "I accept you as my Elite. I will expect you tomorrow."

Before she could respond, he was moving toward the door, his long strides carrying him away as abruptly as everything else about their meeting.

"Wait—" she began, but it was too late.

The door closed behind him with a soft click, leaving her alone with a storm of emotion. Relief that her family would be cared for mingled with fear of an unknown future and, strangest of all, a peculiar disappointment that he had gone so quickly.

Tomorrow, she would step into a new world, one bound by blood and obligation, with a man whose very presence made her feel more alive than she ever had.

But his warning echoed in her mind. *You may be targeted by others.* What had he meant? What dangers awaited her that even Kane Draccus, Head of the Human Vampyr Council, felt the need to warn her about?

And why did the thought of being *his* feel less like captivity and more like... protection?

Serenity sank deeper into the loveseat as the enormity of it all washed over her. Tomorrow, everything would change.

CHAPTER THIRTEEN

SERENITY

The moment Serenity stepped through the doorway of her home, dread sank into her bones like a cold, suffocating weight. The paperwork had been signed, the seal of the Vampyr Council pressed into the document. A car would arrive within twenty-four hours to take her away from everything she had ever known.

But she hadn't told anyone.

The thought of breaking the news to her family filled her with paralyzing fear. The air felt heavier than usual as she stepped into the living room, a sharp chill racing down her spine. She froze mid-step.

Jax stood in the center of the room, his broad shoulders stiff with rage, his jaw set tight. His hazel eyes blazed with fury, darker than she had ever seen them.

Her gaze shifted to her mother and sister, sitting on the worn couch, their faces streaked with tears. Her mother's cheeks were pale and hollow, her chest heaving with muffled sobs. Her sister's small frame trembled as she clung to their mother.

"What happened?" she cried out, panic flooding her voice. "Did someone die?"

And then her gaze met Jax's. His eyes were ice, piercing and unforgiving, filled with an anger that wasn't merely rage. It was betrayal.

He knew.

"How did you find out?" she whispered.

Jax's nostrils flared, his lips curling into a sneer. "Clyde's sister, Rainn, works at the Easton clinic. She saw your name on the Elite Match list this morning."

Serenity cursed herself under her breath. Of course. She'd been a fool to think she could keep it secret.

"You told them." Her voice rose, raw with accusation. "You had no right!"

Jax stepped forward, his voice thundering through the room. "I had every right to tell them! Your family deserves to know the truth. They deserve to know how foolish you're being, throwing your life away for some vampyr bastard to drain you dry!"

"Don't!" Serenity snapped. "Don't act like you did this for them. You did this because you couldn't stand it. Because you hate them."

"Of course I hate them!" he roared. "They're monsters, Serenity! Blood-sucking demons who see us as nothing but cattle. And now you're just handing yourself over to them!"

Her mother's wail cut through their shouting, the sound so broken and despairing it silenced them both.

Serenity's anger crumbled as her mother rose unsteadily from the couch. Her tear-streaked face turned to Serenity, her expression caught between grief and disbelief. "Baby," she choked out. "Why? Why would you do this?"

Serenity knelt before her mother, her trembling hands clutching the woman's frail ones. "Because I have to. So you and Beth can get the treatment and medicine you need. So you can get better."

Her mother's hand cupped her cheek. "But not at the cost of losing you," she sobbed.

"You won't lose me," Serenity said, though the words tasted bitter.

Her mother shook her head. "You can't promise that."

Jax's voice sliced through the air. "She's right. You can't promise her that."

"Just go, Jax," Serenity whispered.

His eyes widened in shock, but when she repeated it, his expression hardened.

"The paperwork is signed," she continued, cold and resigned. "My patron has been selected. I leave tomorrow."

His lips twisted into a snarl. "You're making the biggest mistake of your life. And when they kill you, don't expect me to mourn you."

The words cut deeper than she'd thought possible, but she didn't flinch.

"Get. Out," she said, barely above a whisper.

Jax stood frozen before storming out, slamming the door hard enough to shake the walls.

Serenity's heart shattered at the sound. She turned back to her mother and sister, her arms wrapping around them both as they clung to one another, their sobs mingling in the silence.

The first rays of morning sunlight peeked through the lace curtains. Serenity's sister lay beside her, still lost in peaceful slumber, but their mother was nowhere to be found.

The rich aroma of herbal tea drifted through the living room, woven through with the subtle scent of cinnamon, her mother's special blend for difficult days.

Serenity found her mom in the kitchen, staring out the window into the yard, a steaming cup of tea in her hand. She walked up behind her and hugged her tightly.

"You know I would never have done it if we'd had any other option," she said, her hands shaking. "I'll be able to pay for a doctor, maybe even a nurse. And I'll be able to get the medicine you both need. I can't bear to watch you both suffer and die."

Tears glistened in her mother's eyes as she stayed silent.

She finally let out a heavy breath. "Will we ever see you again? Will they take care of you?"

"I don't know, but I will try," Serenity said. "Every vampyr is different and has different rules for their Elite. Some allow visits home once a month. Others never..." She swallowed hard. "I'm having most of my pay put into your account, so you and Beth can keep buying food, clothes, and whatever else you need."

Her mother gripped Serenity's shoulders. "I understand why you did it, but I wish you'd talked to me first. We could have found another way."

Her mother pulled her into a tight embrace. She buried her face in her mother's shoulder, guilty and grateful all at once for the love wrapped around her.

Her mother drew back, wiping the tears from her eyes. "Come. I need to give you something."

She led her to her parents' bedroom, moved the nightstand aside, and lifted a wood panel from the floor. She reached in and pulled out a worn wooden box.

Serenity's eyes widened as her mother brought out a tiny silver pocket pistol.

"Do you know what this is?"

Serenity nodded slowly. "Yes. It's a gun."

"Yes. A pocket pistol. It has six small silver bullets."

If anyone knew she had this, it would mean instant death for her and her family. "Mother, where did you get this? You shouldn't have this."

"I know. It was a gift from your father, to protect us if anything happened to him." She sighed, her eyes taking on a distant look. "Do you remember how he used to take you into the woods when you were small? Teaching you which herbs could heal and which could harm?"

Serenity nodded. "He said knowledge was the greatest weapon."

"And he was right. But sometimes..." Her mother's eyes hardened. "Sometimes you need more than knowledge." She pressed the pistol into Serenity's palm. "Now I want you to have it. You must keep it hidden, but if you are ever in danger, you use it, do you understand me? Then you run. Fast. It will only slow them down, but it will be enough for you to get away."

"I understand."

"Do you know who your patron is?"

"Yes." Serenity was almost reluctant to tell her. "It is Kane Draccus."

Her mother sucked in a sharp breath, her face twisting into an agonized expression. "Kane Draccus," she echoed.

"The same Kane Draccus that presides over the Council?"

"Yes. It's him," Serenity managed.

Her mother sank onto the edge of the bed. A long silence followed before she seized Serenity's wrist in a vice-like grip.

"Serenity." Her voice quivered as she held her daughter's gaze, fierce and unwavering. "You need to be extremely careful around him. He is more dangerous than any other vampyr, especially with your blood type. They say he can smell a specific blood type from miles away, and that he's killed Elites who displeased him with nothing but a look."

Serenity's mouth went dry. She was well aware of his dangerous nature, yet she'd never once felt in danger with him. If anything, she felt the opposite, safe and secure.

"I'll be careful, Mother," she reassured her softly.

"Vampyrs are clever creatures, child. They know how to charm, to manipulate, to deceive. And Draccus is the oldest and most cunning of them all. They whisper that he's lived for a thousand years, feeding on the blood of those who trusted him. Do not mistake his behavior for genuine care or decency."

But there was something else in her mother's voice, not just fear. Something deeper. Almost like... recognition.

"I understand that I must stay cautious, and I will."

"Good girl," she murmured. "Just remember, you are stronger than you think. You have your father's strength and determination."

Her father's strength. The words carried weight beyond their surface, and Serenity found herself wondering what else her father might have passed down to her, what other legacies beyond medical knowledge and a protective instinct.

Her mother returned the gun to the box and handed it over. "Please be safe, baby. I understand and trust your decision. Just please come home to me if you can."

"I will. I promise."

The car arrived promptly at noon, and Serenity found herself standing outside her house with a single suitcase. The sleek black car looked out of place in her small neighborhood, a symbol of the world she was about to enter.

The driver, a tall, imposing figure in an all-black suit, opened the door and waited patiently as she said her tearful goodbyes. Her heart ached as she handed her mom the letter for Jax, knowing he would come to check on them despite his anger.

Reluctantly, she let go of her family and stepped into the car. The door closed with a definitive click, sealing her decision.

The car glided silently through her familiar district, passing places she knew so well: her job, the laundromat where Jax worked. She hadn't even gotten the chance to say goodbye to him.

As they drove past the different neighborhoods, Serenity felt a pang of regret. She had always watched her neighbors from a distance, knowing her father had treated their ailments. But she'd never taken the time to truly know them. Now she wondered what stories they might have shared, what struggles they'd faced that mirrored her own.

The systematic raids on gathering places, the difficulty getting medical care, the way families like hers were forced into impossible choices. Maybe her neighbors carried their own tales of hardship she'd never heard.

As they approached the imposing gates to the Inner City, Serenity's heart thudded with a mix of fear and fascination. This was the closest she had ever been, a place she'd only heard about in stories.

Her father had always warned her to stay away from the police, especially the vampyr police, fearing they might discover her unique blood and try to take her away.

But looking at the gates now, she understood they weren't only about protection. They were about control. Keeping humans separated, preventing them from seeing how resources were divided, making sure they couldn't organize or measure their lot against anyone else's.

The barriers weren't just physical walls; they were built to isolate people and choke off information.

Celearius was divided into three distinct cities: Outer City, Inner City, and CityCentre. The Inner City was open only to those with a work badge, an Elite ID, or a visitor's pass granted by a Council member.

Serenity supposed it was meant to limit contact between humans and vampyrs, though she suspected the truer purpose was the same one those gates served. Humans mostly inhabited Easton, Grove Hills, and Grove Gardens, while the more fortunate ones lived in Waterside Park. They could smell the salty ocean air near the docks, but a high wall blocked their view, keeping them from ever seeing the sea.

They were confined to their own world, cut off from the rest of Celearius by boundaries no less potent for being invisible.

The driver slowed only enough for the gates to open. She didn't see him flash anything; they simply let him through.

The ease of passage struck her as telling. No questions, no delay, as if the car itself were recognized and expected. It made her wonder about the networks and systems running behind these walls, the careful coordination it took to keep such control in place.

The car glided through the Diamond District, and Serenity couldn't help but marvel at the opulence around her. The district was a vibrant canvas of shops and storefronts, each more extravagant than the last. The air here carried exotic scents, spices and flowers she couldn't name.

Yet for all her old dreams, Serenity had never believed the Diamond District was worth the risk of becoming an Elite. The lure of fine things could never outweigh the danger of such a choice.

They continued until they reached the Silver District. Unlike the Steel District, it lay quiet. No one walked the streets. The hush was profound, almost eerie, as if the whole district were holding its breath.

They drove on until they reached what looked like the tallest building in the district. The driver pulled into the garage beneath it, finally stopping to use an ID card to open the gate.

He walked to the elevator, which scanned his ID before sliding open.

"Please step in. He is waiting for you upstairs. I will bring your things to your room," the driver told her.

Good to know she would have a room. Hopefully it would have a bed and not a cage, she thought as she stepped into the elevator. The driver pressed the top button, then stepped back as the doors closed.

This was it. Her choices had carried her to this exact moment, her life now hanging in the balance at the mercy of Kane Draccus. As the elevator began to climb, Serenity's blood rushed in her ears, her heart slamming against her ribs.

But beneath the fear lay something else, a strange sense of purpose she was only beginning to understand. Her father's lessons about knowledge being the greatest weapon, her mother's fierce protectiveness, the hidden gun now tucked among her belongings, and the dawning awareness that she wasn't merely a victim of circumstance but, perhaps, something more.

Whatever fate awaited her at the hands of the most powerful vampyr in Celearius, she would meet it with the same determination that had brought her this far.

CHAPTER FOURTEEN

KANE

Kane stood in the opulent foyer, his eyes fixed on the sleek elevator doors. The cool marble beneath his boots reflected the golden glow of the overhead lights, its chill a stark contrast to the heat building inside him. The entire building was a testament to control, from the contemporary art meticulously placed on the walls to the air itself, precisely scented with sandalwood and citrus.

But his thoughts weren't on the grandeur around him. They were on her.

He clenched his jaw, exhaling a slow breath that frosted faintly, a subtle sign of his agitation. This place would undoubtedly overwhelm her. The comforts of her simple human life would pale against the calculated extravagance he used to ensnare his Elites. For most, such grandeur worked like an opiate, dulling the reality of their servitude.

But she wasn't like the others. He had seen the defiance blazing behind her fear.

This wouldn't distract her.

Yet Kane found himself wanting to see to her comfort, to make sure she wanted for nothing. Not just as her patron, but because...

Because why?

He frowned, adjusting the high collar of his black shirt. The nervous gesture was foreign to him, centuries of practiced composure crumbling at the mere thought of her arrival.

He hated this. Hated how one human woman had managed to dismantle the composure he'd spent lifetimes mastering.

A flash of memory struck him: her scent at the clinic. The hunger that had twisted inside him like a living thing, clawing to break free. Her blood. Rare. Forbidden. The kind that shouldn't exist.

The kind that could destabilize everything if it fell into the wrong hands.

When he first caught her scent, the primal part of him had surged forward so violently he'd nearly staggered. For a moment his vision had sharpened unnaturally, the world bleeding into stark relief, her pulse visible beneath the skin of her throat, thundering in his ears like a siren's call.

Kane felt the memory in his body, his gums aching as his fangs threatened to descend. He swallowed hard, tasting copper.

It wasn't only her blood's rarity that made it irresistible. It was her.

Her wide eyes had brimmed with fear, but there had been a fire in her gaze that refused to be put out. The vulnerability of her trembling form sat against the quiet strength she carried, a paradox that had drawn him in despite himself.

He had wanted her. Not just for her blood. Not just for the hunger that writhed within him. No, he had wanted her in ways he hadn't allowed himself to want anyone in centuries.

And that terrified him.

The Elder Council would execute him without hesitation if they discovered his weakness. Vampyrs of his station were forbidden from forming attachments to their Elites, a rule established when such bonds had begun to tear their society apart.

But there were other dangers now. The Human Liberation's systematic targeting of Elite gathering places, their coordinated attacks on vampyr assets. If they discovered her blood type, she wouldn't merely be a target. She'd be a weapon they could turn against the entire vampyr hierarchy.

The soft chime of the elevator broke through his thoughts, snapping him back to the present. He straightened, his mask of calm sliding into place. The doors slid open.

And there she was.

She lifted her head to meet his eyes, cascading black curls bouncing with the movement. The honey-brown eyes that had haunted his thoughts stared back at him.

Serenity stepped out hesitantly, her movements wary. She was smaller than he remembered, yet her presence filled the space. Her gaze lingered on the lavish details, wide with disbelief, before landing on him.

The room felt too small. The air between them hummed with electric current.

Her eyes held his, and something passed between them, an unspoken recognition she didn't seem to understand. But he did.

She could sense the predator beneath his skin.

Kane forced himself to focus, burying the thought deep where it couldn't hurt either of them. His senses sharpened against his will; all at once he could hear the blood rushing through her veins, count each beat of her heart, catch the faint trace of soap beneath the intoxicating scent of her blood.

Once again he tried to slip past her mental barriers, his mind brushing against hers like smoke against glass. Nothing. Only silence met his probe.

The anomaly both fascinated and unsettled him. No human had ever blocked him before.

"This way to my office. We have matters to discuss before you settle in."

She hesitated, studying him. Her lips parted as if to speak, but no words came. Instead she nodded and followed.

Kane walked ahead, forcing himself to fix on the rhythmic click of her shoes rather than the steady thrum beneath her skin. With each step, small bursts of her scent reached him, jasmine and honeysuckle, tinged with a note that was entirely her own.

Though he had vowed to keep his distance, he knew this would be a battle he fought every moment of every day. Not just for him. Not just for her. But for the beast that lived within him.

Kane opened the door to his office and stepped aside. "After you," he said, his voice steady despite the roaring in his ears.

She hesitated, then walked in, her steps soft but sure. The instant she passed, her nearness shattered what remained of his composure.

First came vanilla and lemon, the human scents of soap and shampoo. Then it struck him. Her true essence. Jasmine and rose with honeysuckle undertones. Divine.

His pupils dilated until only a thin ring of color remained. A primal hunger surged through him as every cell in his body recognized what stood before him, the rarest blood type among humans.

His jaw locked, his fangs extending partway behind closed lips. He swallowed hard, forcing his feet to move as he stepped into the office and shut the door behind them.

He gestured to the chair opposite his desk. "Please, sit."

She approached with careful, measured steps. Kane caught the rapid flutter at her throat, the way her eyes cataloged every possible exit. She sat down, her back straight, hands folded, a picture of calm belied by the fine tremor in her fingers.

Kane moved behind his desk, each step a battle against the thing clawing inside him. He settled into his chair, gripping the armrests until the wood creaked. He pulled out a brown folder, desperate to focus on anything but the way her blood called to him.

Control. You've mastered this for centuries. You are not the hunger. You are not the beast.

He glanced up briefly, his irises now rimmed with crimson. She looked past him, her attention drawn to the bookshelves and paintings. Her lips parted slightly, but she stayed silent.

Her calm exterior was practiced, a shield he recognized too well. He could hear the quickened rhythm of her heart, smell the adrenaline coursing through her. She was afraid, yet determined not to show it.

Clearing his throat, Kane leaned forward. "First," he said, his voice carefully measured, "I work all day and won't return until evening. Today is an exception." He paused, watching her reaction. "You'll have unrestricted access to the apartment, except for this office and my bedroom, unless invited."

Her lips tightened for an instant, a flicker of defiance crossing her features before she masked it. Her gaze drifted to the window and its view of the Diamond District and, beyond it, Grove Hills and Gardens. Her former home.

"It's a significant adjustment," he said, his voice softening against his will. "Leaving your family, coming here. If you need anything at all, tell me."

She looked at him then, her expression unreadable. The silence stretched until she finally said, "I'll learn to adjust."

The words were polite but hollow, weighted with the cost of her sacrifice. For a moment her carefully built mask slipped, baring a sadness so deep it made his chest constrict.

Then the moment passed, her walls rebuilt.

He nodded, returning to the folder. "Cameras are positioned throughout the apartment, excluding bathrooms and bedrooms. The elevator will be your primary access."

Her brow furrowed. "What if there's a fire?"

The practical question caught him off guard. "The emergency system will direct you to the nearest exit."

She nodded thoughtfully, glancing back toward the window. Kane watched her, noting the way her eyes filed away details, the view, the exits, the layout. Even in her nervousness, she was observant.

"I have some personal questions," he said, his tone clinical despite the heat building beneath his skin.

She stiffened, her eyes widening before dropping to her lap. A soft blush spread across her skin.

"When was your last menstruation?" The question was standard protocol, yet it felt uncomfortably intimate.

"Last week," she answered quickly. "I'll need special pads to mask the scent."

The mention of blood sent a wave of heat through him. His vision sharpened, the world taking on a reddish tinge. With tremendous effort, he dragged himself back from the edge.

"You'll find some in your room," he managed. "If you need more, tell Evelyn during her visits."

"When was the last time you were sexually active?"

Her blush deepened, eyes downcast. "Over a year ago."

"Did you leave someone behind?"

"No," she replied firmly, a challenge in her tone.

Relief washed through him, an emotion he had no right to feel.

"You may pursue relationships," he said coolly, "but if you become pregnant, you must resign."

The thought of her with someone else sent a territorial surge through him. The hunger inside him snarled, the sound nearly escaping his lips. The lights flickered overhead.

"I understand," she said quietly.

He nodded, dropping his gaze back to the papers. Vampyrs were forbidden from touching pregnant women or children, the most sacred law in their society.

But her relationships could become security concerns. Anyone she grew close to could be leveraged against her, or against him. The Human Liberation had shown increasing sophistication in its intelligence gathering.

Her scent intensified as her discomfort grew, and Kane's control frayed further. Unbidden, an image formed: rising from his chair, circling the desk to stand before her. She would look up, those innocent eyes widening as he leaned down, his mouth brushing hers before his fangs pierced the vein beating beneath her skin.

The fantasy dissolved as he caught her expression. Fear. Pure, unmistakable fear. She was staring at his eyes, which he knew now glowed with crimson light.

He bit back a curse.

He closed his eyes, inhaling deeply as he forced the beast down. The temperature in the room slowly normalized. When he looked at her again, his eyes had returned to their natural state.

Guilt stabbed through him. He was hiding his struggle from her, letting her believe she was safer than she truly was.

He closed the folder and reached into his desk drawer, retrieving a small box containing her Elite ID, keycard, and cell phone.

"These are yours," he said, placing the box before her.

She examined the contents with cautious curiosity.

"This is your Elite ID," he explained, lifting the black bracelet with its silver identification panel bearing his surname. "Let me secure it to your wrist."

She extended her arm slowly. As he clasped the wristband, his fingertips brushed her pulse point. The sensation, her warm skin, the rhythmic throb of life beneath it, sent electric currents through his body.

With tremendous effort, he withdrew his hand. "It remains on at all times. You'll use it for any purchases."

He lifted the silver keycard next. "This grants you access to the apartment. Guard it carefully."

Finally he presented the cell phone. "For emergencies only. Evelyn will use it to schedule your check-ins."

She picked it up with obvious uncertainty. "I've never used one before."

The admission underscored the divide between their worlds. "Nox will show you how it works."

She nodded, gathering her new possessions. "Is there anything else I should know?"

His expression hardened as he leaned forward. "No one enters this apartment without my explicit permission. Evelyn, Rhyzan, and Nox have clearance. Anyone else will face consequences."

The security protocols weren't only about his privacy. They were about protecting her. If the Human Liberation discovered her location, her blood type, what she represented...

The atmosphere chilled as she trembled faintly. "Understood. I won't let anyone inside."

"Good." Kane rose and moved to the door. "Let me show you to your quarters."

He led her down the corridor, past paintings of landscapes from before the Great War. They climbed the metal staircase, their footsteps forming a rhythmic duet.

"Your keycard grants access to your room. Only you, Evelyn, and Nox in emergencies are permitted entry."

She swiped her card against the black panel. The doors unlocked with a soft click.

Kane pushed them open and stepped aside. He had never before troubled himself with an Elite's comfort beyond basic necessities, yet he'd deliberately chosen the pastel furnishings and plush carpeting for her.

"You may change anything to suit your preferences," he offered as she surveyed her new home.

The distant chime of the elevator announced Nox's arrival with her belongings.

"Nox will bring your things shortly," Kane said, "and return in an hour to collect you for a tour."

He turned to leave when her touch stopped him, the lightest brush against his arm. "Wait. Please."

He froze, his body answering even that fleeting contact with a surge of heat. "Yes?"

Her honey-brown eyes met his, wide with uncertainty. "You never mentioned your feeding schedule."

A heavy breath escaped him. He had hoped to avoid this conversation.

"I don't feed often," he admitted, though lately his abstinence had stretched dangerously long. The hunger coiled inside him now, restless and alive. "I'll inform you when necessary."

Confusion crossed her features; she'd clearly expected something more structured. Something safer.

"I'll leave you to settle in," he said abruptly, retreating as Nox arrived with her luggage.

Kane strode down the corridor, putting distance between himself and the temptation she presented. He had brought her here to protect her from others, only to realize the greatest threat might be himself.

But there were other threats to weigh. The systematic nature of the recent attacks, the coordinated raids on human gathering places. If the Human Liberation discovered what she was, where she was...

He would have to be more than careful. He would have to be strategic.

Kane entered his private chambers, locking the door behind him. The cold truth settled in his bones: he would have to stay away from her as much as he could, or risk losing himself to the hunger.

And he would have to make certain no one else discovered what she truly represented, not the Council, not the Liberation, not anyone who might use her as a weapon in the growing conflict.

Because if that happened, she wouldn't survive.

CHAPTER FIFTEEN

SERENITY

I'll inform you when necessary. What exactly did that mean? Did he not feed regularly? And if he didn't, why was she even here? Questions tumbled through Serenity's mind as she pressed her fingertips to her throat, feeling her pulse quicken beneath the skin. The thought that her blood, the very thing that had marked her as different her whole life, would soon flow into him sent a shiver down her spine that wasn't entirely fear.

"Do you need anything else?" the man named Nox asked.

She stared at him, lost in thought until his words registered. "Umm..." She glanced around the spacious room, brighter than any she had ever seen. Soft pastels of yellow, pink, blue, and white covered the walls and furniture, an atmosphere that contrasted sharply with the dark, masculine tones of Kane's apartment.

Nox stood tall, his broad shoulders lending him an air of authority. His close-cropped beard framed his face, sharpening his stern expression. His dark eyes studied her with an edge that made Serenity uneasy, and she noticed he didn't seem to blink. Not once since entering the room.

She realized he was waiting on her answer.

"Do you need anything else?" he repeated, his tone professional and measured. The words came out too precisely enunciated, as if each syllable had been practiced countless times.

"No. I'm fine." She studied him in turn, her father's voice surfacing in her memory. *Pay attention to details, Serenity. A good nurse notices what others miss.* She found herself cataloging the unnatural stillness, the too-careful speech, the absence of human mannerisms, the kind of assessment she'd done at her father's side for years without ever questioning why he'd drilled it into her.

His features were flawless, unnaturally so. He wore an impassive expression, standing so still that she couldn't detect the rise and fall of breath. Curiosity bubbled up in her, too insistent to ignore.

"Are you... human?" she ventured.

One eyebrow arched at the question, the movement too smooth to be natural. His composure held. "No," he replied simply, offering nothing more. "If there is nothing else, I will leave you to get settled."

"Thank you," she said, watching him turn and go. His movements were fluid yet somehow mechanical, like water flowing through a carefully cut channel. The door clicked softly behind him, leaving her alone with her thoughts, and with the growing awareness that everything in this place would be watching, analyzing, reporting.

She had never realized those observational skills might be useful for anything beyond a sickroom.

Looking around, Serenity found herself running the systematic assessment her father had drilled into her: room layout, potential hazards, available resources. The lavender and pale-pink hues cast a calming glow through the space, but she noticed the things that mattered, the lack of personal touches, the strategic placement of what looked like small sensors, and, most telling, the frosted windows that let in sunlight while denying any view of the outside world. Beautiful barriers that both protected and imprisoned.

One corner held a queen-sized bed dressed in silk sheets that felt like liquid under her fingertips when she brushed them, a stark contrast to the scratchy blankets and worn mattress she'd shared with Beth in the Outer City. The memory of her sister's small form pressed to her back at night, her quiet breathing a reassurance in the dark, hardened her resolve.

"I'm doing this for you," she whispered to the empty room. "Both of you." She touched the silver bracelet at her wrist. His name engraved on it. His ownership marked on her body.

The room held a delicate vanity with a silver-framed mirror, a plush armchair angled to watch both the door and the window, and a sleek desk near the glass. Fresh flowers in a crystal vase gave off a gentle fragrance. She caught herself noting the chair's line of sight, the desk's placement, before she could even name why.

These trappings of luxury felt less like a home than a beautifully decorated patient room, comfortable but, in the end, institutional.

She sat at the vanity and met her own eyes in the mirror. The girl looking back seemed tired, overwhelmed, but resolute. Three days ago, she'd believed her future held nothing harder than caring for her family and perhaps helping her father with his patients. Now she was an Elite, bound to a vampyr whose very presence seemed to unravel her composure.

The thought sent her hand drifting to her throat, where her pulse beat hard beneath the skin.

She just had to focus on surviving this and earning enough to help them.

Opening the drawers beneath the vanity, she found cosmetics she'd never seen: deep red lipsticks in shades that reminded her of blood, vibrant blush palettes, volumizing mascara. She also found a small, unremarkable compact mirror. Her father had carried one like it, claiming it was useful for examining patients' throats and catching unconscious signs of distress. She pocketed it without thinking.

Her attention shifted to the bathroom door. The beautifully appointed en suite revealed gleaming fixtures, an inviting bathtub, and marble floor tiles. Fluffy towels lined the shelves, and she found herself noting the ventilation almost automatically, the way her father had taught her, though here she couldn't say why it should matter.

She was beginning to understand why some women volunteered for Elite positions beyond the money. The luxuries made the arrangement feel less clinical, more like being a pampered patient than livestock. But comfort, her father had always warned, could mask serious underlying conditions. *Never trust first impressions, Serenity. The most dangerous symptoms hide behind healthy appearances.*

Standing amid luxuries she'd only seen in old magazines, her mind drifted back to the office and the charged tension that had filled the air. Kane. She had felt his gaze on her, sharp and unrelenting, as if he were dissecting her with every glance, peeling back the layers she'd fought to keep intact. The pull of that stare left her both unnerved and inexplicably drawn to him.

She trailed her fingers along the sink's edge, slow and contemplative. She replayed how his voice had deepened over those personal questions, questions that should have embarrassed her but instead left her feeling strangely exposed. When their eyes had locked, something unspoken had passed between them, not just tension but a quiet battle, an unyielding push and pull she didn't understand yet felt in her bones.

And then the moment his eyes had changed, that supernatural glow breaking through his careful facade. The flare had been brief but enough to remind her what he was, the danger he carried, even while seated behind a polished desk speaking with calm authority. Yet despite that flash of fear, despite knowing what he was capable of, she hadn't been able to pull away.

She should have been terrified, trembling at the thought of being alone with him. Instead she'd been hyperaware of the distance between them, of how his voice wrapped around her like a tether, holding her in place. She had caught herself wondering what it would feel like, his fangs against her skin, drawing her blood into him. The thought sent heat rushing to her face.

She needed to focus. This was about survival, and about understanding what her father had really been doing.

She reached for the thin silver bracelet, running her thumb over the embossed letters of Kane's name. There was something about him that called up her father's stranger lessons, the way he'd taught her to read people's faces, to notice when someone was lying or hiding something. Skills that had seemed excessive for nursing and now felt oddly precise.

"This is just a transaction," she whispered to herself. "Nothing more."

Yet as she prepared to return to the bedroom, she wondered whether Kane had noticed something different about her, the way she mapped rooms and tracked details on instinct. Did he suspect she was more observant than the average district girl?

She went back to her bedroom and opened her suitcase carefully, suddenly conscious that she might be watched. She set the family photograph by her bedside, a true reminder of why she was here. She arranged a few favorite books on the shelf near the door, including the medical text her father had given her last Christmas. Maybe someday she'd understand why he'd insisted she memorize passages that seemed far beyond basic nursing.

She turned to the shopping bags Nox had brought. The clothes were her exact size, information that could only have come from close observation, or from her medical records. The thought unsettled her, but she tried to focus on the practical side rather than the privacy of it.

Don't borrow trouble, as her father used to say. *Deal with what's in front of you.*

Deciding to test the room's privacy, she locked the bathroom door and swept it carefully, using the techniques her father had taught her for checking patient rooms for hazards. Finding no obvious surveillance, she filled the bathtub and added jasmine bath gel. The familiar scent carried her back to her father's medical garden, where he'd grown herbs while teaching her to identify each plant's properties.

As she sank into the warm water, she let herself take in the strangeness of it all. In three days her entire world had shifted. She'd gone from a district girl desperate to save her family to an Elite bound to one of the most powerful vampyrs in the city. And somehow the skills her father had given her, skills she'd believed were only for nursing, felt more relevant than ever.

Father, what were you really preparing me for?

She ran her hand over the surface of the water, watching the ripples spread outward. Like her decision to become an Elite, every action would carry consequences reaching far beyond herself. But unlike that first desperate gamble, this path might lead her to her father's legacy, whatever it truly turned out to be.

When the water cooled, she reluctantly climbed out and wrapped herself in the impossibly soft towel. Back in the bedroom, she chose her comfortable sweater and jeans, holding on to some thread of who she'd been before everything changed.

She tried one of the new bras, noting how it shaped her figure, wondering whether appearance would matter in her role as an Elite. Her father had always said presentation could be as important as competence in earning trust.

Nox would be back in twenty minutes.

She let herself rest on the luxurious bed, though her mind kept working. The mattress felt excessively soft, built for comfort rather than the practical firmness her family's had. She thought of Beth, who would sleep alone tonight for the first time since their father's death.

Tonight there would be no one. Just her and her thoughts in this beautiful prison.

But her family would be safe and well. That was what mattered. She only hoped the medicine would arrive sooner rather than later. She needed to set boundaries with Kane, to make sure her family got everything she'd promised them. His apparent agreeableness was encouraging, but Serenity knew better than to trust first impressions, especially with a vampyr.

She remained particularly curious about his lack of a feeding schedule. Sebastian had said most Elites had structured arrangements with their patrons, at least three times a week. Kane's vague answer unsettled her. Would she get any warning? Would it hurt?

The question made her stomach flutter with a feeling that wasn't entirely dread.

Whatever came next with Kane, whenever he decided to feed, she would face it with the same determination that had carried her this far. She would survive this. She had to.

CHAPTER SIXTEEN

KANE

Ten minutes after three, Kane hung up with Councilwoman Ruess while Nox stood at his office door, waiting. The overhead lights flickered briefly, answering Kane's agitation after the tense conversation about rising rebel activity in the outer districts.

He raised a brow at Nox, curious about his presence. "Aren't you supposed to be giving the Elite a tour?"

Nox's face lifted into a sheepish grin, though a thread of tension ran beneath his usual ease. "Yes, I am, but unfortunately, they need me in Cavern 47. So it looks like you're on tour duty."

Kane's enhanced senses caught the subtle shift in Nox's heartbeat, barely perceptible, but there. Something more urgent than routine maintenance was happening at their security facility. "And why do they need you there?" Kane pinched the bridge of his nose, the veins at his temples darkening beneath the skin.

Nox shrugged, the motion too fluid to be human. "I need to rewire a panel so they can set up the cameras outside Easton and Grove Gardens." A pause. "Rhyzan picked up some unusual electromagnetic signatures near the district borders. Could be nothing, but..."

"Rhy still thinks he'll catch something out of the abandoned districts." Rhyzan had been trying to get cameras installed beyond those walls for ages, but the Council had kept ruling it unnecessary, until the vampyr deaths began to climb.

Kane's vote had finally tipped the scales in Rhyzan's favor. "Though if he's reading unusual activity, perhaps his paranoia is warranted."

The systematic nature of the recent attacks pointed to coordination far beyond random human violence. Someone was organizing the rebels, feeding them intelligence about vampyr movements and weaknesses. The thought that they might have reached into the outer districts set his jaw.

"You know Rhyzan. Once he fixates, his mind won't budge." Nox came further into the office and dropped into a seat, though his usual relaxed posture seemed a touch forced. "Remember when he became obsessed with finding Bianca and nearly burned Paris to the ground? He was convinced she was working with Gabriel, but they'd just been lovers, long ago."

Kane rolled his eyes, a memory flaring through his mind: Paris, 1797, the sky crimson with fire, the air thick with ash and screams. But Rhyzan had been right about the larger conspiracy that time, even if he'd misread the personal part. "Yes, I remember the mess I had to clean up. And don't worry, Rhy knows to keep his obsession in check. Why don't you give the Elite her tour before you go?"

"No, I can't. I don't have time." Nox's voice carried an urgency Kane rarely heard from his unflappable friend. "Rhyzan wants the surveillance expansion live by tonight. With everything that's been happening..." He let the sentence hang, but Kane understood. Three vampyr deaths in two months. Coordinated attacks on Elite gathering places. Someone was escalating the campaign.

Kane felt the protective instinct surge, not just for his people, but for the woman sleeping upstairs. If rebels were operating closer to the city center, if their intelligence networks were sophisticated enough to track Elite movements...

"Besides," Nox continued, "you'll do fine. Just remember what we discussed about keeping your distance." His dark eyes studied Kane with rare gravity. "I know what she is to you. What her blood must smell like. But I also know you, Kane. Better than anyone except perhaps Evie. You've resisted greater temptations."

Kane wasn't so sure. The scent of the Elite, of Serenity, was unlike anything he'd encountered in his long existence. It woke something primal in him, a thing he'd thought he buried centuries ago. And if Rhyzan's suspicions about rebel infiltration held, she could be walking into danger he hadn't anticipated.

Nox stood and smirked, though it didn't quite reach his eyes. "I think she may be exactly what you need. But right now, she needs you to keep her safe."

"What does that mean?" Kane growled, the glass on his desk trembling.

"It means you've been alone too long," Nox said simply, then added, more seriously, "And it means the security briefing Rhyzan gave me this morning suggests we may have underestimated how close the rebels have gotten to our operations. Not all Elites are like Hannah and Ava, but some have been... compromised."

The implication hit Kane like a physical blow. Elite women vanishing, only to surface weeks later as rebel sympathizers, or worse, as suicide bombers targeting their former patrons. The psychological warfare was every bit as devastating as the physical attacks.

Kane grumbled under his breath as Nox headed for the door, knowing he had no choice but to give the Elite her tour. But that tour now carried an added weight. He would have to gauge not just her comfort, but her vulnerability to outside influence.

He rose from his desk, the chair sliding back with unnecessary force. As he reached for the door handle, unease settled in the pit of his stomach and spread through his veins like ice. The conversation with Nox had reshaped the afternoon ahead. This wasn't only about managing his hunger around Serenity. It was about protecting her from threats she couldn't even see coming.

And making certain she isn't already compromised, a darker voice whispered in his mind.

He pushed the thought away. Rhyzan's paranoia was infectious, but Kane refused to let it poison his judgment of every human who entered their world. Still, as he climbed the stairs toward her room with preternatural grace, he found himself cataloging security weaknesses with fresh urgency.

The air grew warmer the closer he got to her quarters, as if her very presence shifted the atmosphere around her. He stopped outside her door and leaned in close, his enhanced hearing reaching for any movement inside. Silence. A complete stillness that could mean peaceful sleep or careful concealment.

He glanced at the keypad and saw the light glowing green. She hadn't locked the door, a sign of either trust or naivety that troubled him more than it should have. Without thinking, he opened it.

The instant he stepped into her room, the air changed, turning sweeter, thicker, charged with her presence. His eyes adapted at once to the dimmer light, scanning the space methodically now, hunting for signs of disturbance or contact with outsiders. Instead they found her, asleep on top of the bedding, vulnerable and unaware.

Guilt hit him like a tidal wave. He had told her he wouldn't enter without permission. But beneath the guilt lay something more tangled: relief that she was here, safe, seemingly untouched by the unrest beyond these walls.

He crossed to the bed and sat on the edge, the mattress barely dipping beneath his weight. Her peaceful expression stirred the warring pull of protector and predator, but now it sharpened his tactical mind as well. How easily could someone reach her here? What if the rebels already knew about her blood type?

Kane brushed a strand of hair from her face, his fingertips lingering a fraction of a second too long. Her hair felt impossibly soft, like silk slipping through his fingers. The faint scent of vanilla and lemon reached him first, artificial human scents, the products she'd used to wash. Ordinary. Manageable.

As she exhaled, her true essence escaped, jasmine, rose, and honeysuckle, deepening with each breath. The hunger rose in him as expected, but now it came twined with a fierce possessiveness that startled him. *Mine to protect. Mine to feed from. Mine to keep safe from those who would use her.*

His senses sharpened further; all at once he could hear not just the blood moving through her veins, but the sounds beyond the apartment, footsteps in the building's corridor, the distant hum of vehicles on the street below, the electronic whisper of his security systems keeping their watch.

A glint of light caught his eye from the nightstand: the family photograph she'd placed there, her smiling face staring back alongside the people who depended on her survival. The image struck him harder than he expected, a reminder that she wasn't only his Elite, but someone with loved ones who would suffer if anything happened to her.

They could use her family against her. The realization landed with cold clarity. If the rebels knew about her blood type, they'd know about her reasons.

The thought sent a chill through him that had nothing to do with his nature. The rebels had grown only more sophisticated in their psychological warfare; they wouldn't simply target Serenity directly. They would threaten the people she loved most.

Kane stood abruptly, his protective instinct fully roused. This tour wouldn't be about showing her his home. It would be about making sure she understood the dangers and the measures in place to keep her safe. And perhaps, if Nox's concerns held weight, about quietly assessing whether she showed any sign of outside contact or coercion.

He would have to do more than guard his own control. He would have to watch for any trace that the growing rebellion had already found its way into his home.

Because if it had, both their lives, and the lives of her family, would be in immediate danger.

CHAPTER SEVENTEEN

SERENITY

Beep-beep. Beep-beep.

Serenity rolled over and fumbled for the alarm clock, her hand searching until it found the snooze button. She pressed it, but the beeping went on. Confusion swirled through her as she finally opened her eyes, disoriented for a moment by the unfamiliar ceiling above her. The beeping stopped.

Reality crashed over her as she took in the luxurious room. This wasn't her cramped bedroom at home with Beth's sleeping form beside her. The silk sheets felt foreign against her skin. She sat up and rubbed her hands over her face, the weight of her new status settling on her shoulders. She was an Elite now. Kane Draccus's Elite.

Glancing at the digital clock by her bedside, she gasped. 6:32 PM.

Her twenty-minute nap had turned into hours. Would he be angry?

Her heart fluttered. She wasn't sure what protocol demanded. Should she stay and wait for him to come to her? What if he'd already tried? But he couldn't enter without the keycard, right? Her gaze darted around the room until she spotted it on the nightstand where she'd left it, beside the compact mirror she'd found in the vanity drawer.

Beep-beep. Beep-beep.

The sound wasn't coming from the clock. She moved the pillow and found the cell device Kane had given her vibrating against the sheets. The screen lit with the name "Evelyn."

Anxiety gripped her chest. She didn't even know how to answer it. The device kept beeping, more insistent with each repetition. She pressed the green button on the screen, hoping it would work.

"Serenity," a feminine voice said as the small screen glowed blue, displaying "Evelyn" with a four-digit number beneath it.

"Yes?" Her own voice sounded small, uncertain in this new world of technology and secrets.

"Are you okay?" The woman's tone carried genuine concern, unexpected in a place where she'd anticipated only coldness and formality.

"Yes. I'm fine," Serenity replied, turning the sleek device over in her hand, noting the number beneath Evelyn's name and the way it seemed to track calls, technology far beyond anything in the districts.

"Kane was a little concerned when you didn't leave your room."

A fresh wave of anxiety washed over her, followed by an odd flicker of opportunity. If Kane was concerned about her whereabouts, then he was keeping track of her movements. Useful, if her instincts about this place were right.

"I'm sorry," she said, guilt threading through the words. "I took a nap, and it lasted longer than I meant." The admission felt childish, but she filed away how Evelyn responded to it.

"Oh, no worries." Evelyn's voice softened. "Kane is waiting outside your door. He wants to give you the tour. We need to make sure you eat. I believe your dinner should have arrived by now. I'm sorry I can't be there, but I'll definitely come by tomorrow."

Serenity blinked in surprise. An apology? From a vampyr? Unexpected kindness could reveal as much as hostility. Perhaps it was genuine, perhaps calculated to lower her guard. Either way, worth noting.

She glanced toward her door, picturing Kane standing just on the other side, waiting. Her pulse quickened, but beneath the nervous attraction lay something else, a growing sense that this tour might reveal more than the layout of his home.

"Okay, thank you. I'm sorry again."

"It's not a problem. Now, go get something to eat, and I'll see you tomorrow."

She nodded, then realized Evelyn couldn't see her. "Sounds good."

The screen went dark, and Serenity stared at it a moment. Two buttons remained visible, one shaped like a phone, another like the outline of a head. If her father had been teaching her to observe for reasons beyond nursing, then understanding how these systems worked might one day matter.

She rose from the bed, steeling herself for Kane's possible displeasure, and for whatever the tour might show her. Every environment told a story if you knew how to read it. Tonight she would start learning to read Kane's.

She smoothed her clothes and tucked a strand of hair behind her ear, then paused. Appearance could be a tool; people often gave away more when they felt at ease. Grabbing her keycard and slipping the compact mirror into her pocket, Serenity drew a breath and opened the door, finding Kane leaning against the wall nearby. His posture was casual, but nothing about him was truly relaxed. His body held a coiled energy, a predator at rest yet ever alert.

To her surprise, his face softened at the sight of her. Where she'd expected irritation, she found only gentle concern in his silver-blue eyes. The reaction struck her as real.

"I'm sorry she woke you, but she insisted you needed to eat," he said, his deep voice sending a tremor through her that she tried to examine objectively. Physical attraction, yes, but also something close to recognition, as if part of her was answering something familiar in him.

"No, it's okay. I overslept by a lot." Serenity stepped out and lowered her eyes, playing the intimidated district girl while quietly mapping the hallway. "I didn't mean to. I'm sorry."

When he didn't immediately respond, she cautiously lifted her gaze to his. Unlike the harsh rumors of the Outer City, which warned she'd be reprimanded severely for such a lapse, Kane seemed unbothered.

He offered a small smile and ran a hand through his slightly disheveled hair, a surprisingly human gesture that made her wonder what other human traits he kept, what vulnerabilities lay hidden beneath his vampyric nature.

"No need to apologize. Your dinner arrived, so I'll show you the kitchen first, and you can eat."

The simple kindness caught her off guard, though she made herself weigh it. Genuine care, or careful manipulation? Her father had taught her both were possible, sometimes at once.

As they headed down the stairs, she noted Nox's absence with interest. Where was Kane's security detail? What did that say about his confidence, or about this place's defenses?

Their path led toward the elevator, then veered left through an open doorway into the kitchen. The space was expansive and pristine, gleaming black marble countertops reflecting everything like dark mirrors. A large refrigerator and freezer stood side by side, while three ovens lined the adjacent wall, more cooking equipment than her entire neighborhood had owned. At the center island, a covered plate waited.

"I believe that is for you," Kane said, gesturing toward it. "You can cook your own food if you prefer, but a catering service is available. We always arrange catering on the first night, since the transition can be overwhelming."

We. The phrasing suggested she wasn't his first Elite, that there was a system in place. How many others had there been? What had happened to them?

He pulled out one of the stools and gestured for her to sit. The courtesy was so at odds with his imposing presence that Serenity felt momentarily off balance, but she filed the observation away as she settled onto the stool.

"Thank you," she said, lifting the metal cover to reveal steaming penne in rich tomato sauce, strips of grilled chicken scattered through it. The aroma was intoxicating after years of bland ration meals.

Her hands trembled faintly as she unrolled the napkin around the silverware, and she couldn't tell whether it was hunger, nerves, or the growing awareness that all of this was more tangled than she'd first understood.

The first bite nearly brought tears to her eyes, not only from the flavor, but from the realization that this luxury came at a price she was only beginning to grasp. As she ate, she studied Kane from the corner of her eye, noting how he watched her, how he placed himself in the room, how his attention seemed to shift between protective and predatory.

When she finally set her fork down on the nearly empty plate, she leaned back with a contented sigh, forgetting for a moment that she sat on a stool. She felt herself tipping backward, panic flaring—

A warm, firm hand pressed against her back, steadying her. The touch sent a jolt of electricity through her, and she turned quickly, her breath catching as she found herself mere inches from Kane's face.

He was closer than she'd realized, his tall frame looming over her. His lips curved into a faint, almost teasing smile, but his eyes told another story, stormy and dark, swirling with an emotion that quickened her pulse and set her mind racing.

"Careful," he murmured, his voice low and rough, wrapping around her like dark velvet.

"I... I forgot I was on a stool," she managed, barely above a whisper. She tried to straighten but went still when she realized his hand stayed on her shoulder, not heavy, but grounding, warm, unexpectedly intimate.

"I think I'm all right now," she added, testing whether he would release her or hold on.

His gaze captured hers, silver-blue depths that seemed to hold centuries of secrets. For a moment she felt herself pulled into them, her analytical mind going quiet as pure instinct took over.

Time seemed to slow, each second stretching long. Kane's hand twitched, and she couldn't tell whether he meant to pull away or draw her closer. The moment hung between them, charged with possibility.

Kane's jaw tightened, conflict flickering across his features. With visible reluctance, he withdrew his hand and stepped back, opening space between them. The absence of his touch left her skin tingling, her mind spinning with what that reaction meant, both for her safety and for whatever larger purpose her father had been preparing her for.

"I hope the meal was satisfactory," he said, his voice quieter but still edged in a way that made her pulse jump.

"Yes... yes, it was delicious," she replied, barely audible. Her cheeks burned, and she stood quickly, smoothing her jeans while trying to make sense of what had just happened. Was this normal between a patron and Elite? Or had something else passed between them?

She carried her plate to the sink, grateful for the moment to gather herself, and noted the view from the kitchen window. She could see street level from here, useful if she ever needed to signal someone or find a way out.

"Just leave it by the sink. Nox will take care of it," Kane said.

As they left the kitchen, Kane began the tour. He showed her the living room with its circle of plush couches and a mahogany coffee table, pointing out the lighting controls and the fireplace, while she mapped sight lines and took in the expensive artwork that hinted at the resources behind his operation.

The bathroom was more luxurious than anything she'd seen, the heated floors likely to mask footsteps, the large windows both an asset and a vulnerability depending on the moment.

The workout room's floor-to-ceiling windows offered a breathtaking view of the city below, and more than that, they showed her exactly where they stood in relation to the district boundaries and the major transit routes.

When they reached the library, Serenity's breath caught, not only at its beauty, but at what it represented. This much knowledge, these resources, marked Kane as far more than a powerful vampyr. He was someone with access to information, someone whose reach extended well beyond what she'd first understood.

She moved toward the nearest shelf, her fingers hovering over the spines with reverence, cataloging titles that might prove useful. History books, technical manuals, political treatises, the collection of someone who needed to understand the world more deeply than most.

Kane stepped closer behind her, his breath warm against her neck, and she felt that same electric awareness as before. But now it carried weight. When she turned to find herself nearly pressed against him, the moment felt different, charged not just with attraction, but with the growing sense that they were both hiding something.

"Would you like to choose a book?" His voice resonated in the space between them, and she wondered if this was part of some test, some read on her interests.

"I... I wouldn't even know where to begin," she admitted, though her eyes were already cataloging titles that might help her understand her situation.

Kane reached around her, his arm briefly caging her against the bookshelf as he plucked out the volume she'd been examining. "How about this one, then? It's a favorite among many."

He placed it in her hands, a book on political theory and social movements. Coincidence, or did he know something about what she might find useful?

"Thank you," she whispered, looking up to find him studying her closely enough to make her forget to breathe. He wasn't simply looking at her. He was assessing her, trying to work something out.

What did he suspect? What was he trying to figure out?

The moment stretched between them, heavy with unasked questions. Then she saw it, a shift in his eyes, the silver flaring from within, glowing with otherworldly light. Her breath caught, uncertainty replacing the tentative comfort she'd felt.

Was this it? Was he finally going to feed from her? Or was this something else, a response to suspicions about her true purpose here?

Her foot caught the edge of a low table, and she lost her balance. A gasp escaped her as she began to fall, but Kane moved with inhuman speed, catching her before she hit the floor.

His arms around her were like iron, his touch electric where their skin met. As she tried to steady herself, his grip tightened, his eyes blazing with that strange light.

Time suspended as they stared at each other. Despite everything, despite the growing complexity of her situation, Serenity felt no immediate fear. If he chose to end this now, there was nothing she could do to stop him. Yet the realization came with a strange calm rather than panic.

She closed her eyes and tilted her head, baring the curve of her neck, the ultimate submission, and perhaps the ultimate test of whatever game they were both playing.

A moment passed, then another. Instead of fangs, she felt his grip loosen. She opened her eyes to find his face contorted with what looked like pain, as if he were fighting something inside himself.

"I'm sorry," he whispered tightly. "I shouldn't have—I shouldn't have gotten so close. I'm sorry."

Confusion washed over her. Was this restraint real, or was he testing her reactions, her expectations? Her father had taught her that meaning often lived in what people chose not to do as much as in what they did.

Before she could form a question, a throat cleared from the doorway. Kane released her completely and turned to face the newcomer.

Rhyzan stood watching them, his posture rigid, his features sharper and colder than Kane's, his eyes bright with a calculating intelligence that snapped her own to attention. This was someone who missed nothing, who weighed everything. If she was going to navigate whatever she'd walked into, she would need to be especially careful around him.

"I hope I am not interrupting," he said, his words clipped and deliberate, his gaze flicking between them with knowing assessment.

"No," Kane replied. "I was just showing her around. That concluded the tour."

Rhyzan's gaze shifted to Serenity, one eyebrow arching. "Has he gone over his feeding—"

"Yes," Kane interjected quickly.

"No," Serenity answered at the same instant, then immediately wondered if she'd just made a crucial mistake. The contradiction seemed to expose something about the dynamic between Kane and the people around him.

Rhyzan's lips thinned as he glowered at Kane, disapproval in every line of his face. "I am sure he will go over it soon. For now, we must go. Another murder has occurred."

A cold weight dropped through Serenity at the casual mention of death. Murder. The way Rhyzan said "another" marked it as part of a pattern. The urgency in his voice said it was serious enough to cut Kane's evening short.

Who had been killed? Human or vampyr? And what did it mean for her?

Kane's features had hardened, grief and fury warring in his eyes. For the first time, she glimpsed the shape of responsibilities that reached far beyond managing a single Elite.

"If you need anything, please ask Nox," Kane said, his voice strained as he visibly fought to hold his composure.

Before she could respond, both vampyrs were gone, moving with that supernatural speed that reminded her exactly what they were. The air where they'd stood seemed to shimmer a moment before settling into stillness.

Serenity stood alone in the library, the fallen book at her feet, her thoughts racing with new understanding. The mention of murder had shattered any illusion that her role here was simple or contained. Kane wasn't only a vampyr who needed her blood; he was caught up in matters of life and death, politics and power, something far larger and more dangerous than she'd realized.

She bent to retrieve the book, her fingers trembling faintly. As she traced the golden lettering on the cover, Serenity wondered what she had truly walked into, and whether she would survive long enough to keep her promise to her family.

CHAPTER EIGHTEEN

KANE

Rhy drew a sharp breath as the elevator doors slid closed. He glanced at Kane, who stood motionless beside him, tension radiating from his shoulders after those charged moments with Serenity. The memory of her pulse beneath his fingertips lingered, an echo of temptation that set his jaw.

"Evie's not going to be happy you haven't set up a feeding schedule with her yet," Rhy said quietly, his usual sarcasm replaced by genuine concern.

Kane's eyes flashed silver, a momentary slip. He looked away, afraid his oldest friend would see too much. "Then keep it to yourself," he grumbled, the weight of expectation bearing down on him.

Rhy shook his head. "It's not me. She's going to ask about it tomorrow. She'll know." His voice dropped. "You can't starve yourself forever, Kane."

The truth of it landed harder than Kane wanted to admit. It would be the first thing Evie asked Serenity tomorrow. The feeding issue couldn't be put off much longer, not when he was already pressing the edges of his hunger.

The elevator dinged, and the doors opened onto the underground garage. Rhy's bright red Chevy El Camino gleamed under the fluorescents like fresh blood.

They slid into the car, the leather seats cool against Kane's overheated skin. The engine rumbled to life, something mechanical and predictable, unlike the tangled realm of politics he navigated daily.

Kane forced thoughts of Serenity aside, feeling the burden of leadership settle back over him. "What happened? Who died?"

"Nat. Car exploded on his way into the Quartz District from Waterside Park." Rhy's knuckles whitened on the steering wheel. "He'd been with us since before the Treaty."

The name hit Kane like a physical blow. Nat had been steady, reliable, one of the ones who remembered what the war had truly cost. "Fourth incident this month," he said, jaw twitching. "Was the symbol there?"

"Yes."

The mocking skull with H.L. written on the forehead, crossbones beneath, and that cryptic message no one could decipher. A calling card left by killers growing bolder by the week.

Kane had warned the Council for months, laying out evidence and patterns. They'd waved off his concerns as paranoia, a leftover of post-Treaty tension. Even some vampyrs thought it imagination, as if he would manufacture terror for political advantage.

"Is Sullivan at the scene?" Kane asked, his voice dropping to that dangerous register that made most beings instinctively step back.

"Always the first one," Rhy replied, steering through empty streets. "He believes you. Has from the beginning."

Small comfort, but Kane would take what allies he could get. "Hopefully they were sloppier this time. We need something concrete."

The attacks were growing more sophisticated, more targeted. Kane feared they would soon escalate beyond isolated murders into mass violence, the kind that had marked the darkest days of the Great War. He remembered too clearly: burning flesh, screams that lasted years, hunger driving vampyrs to extremes.

The Treaty had been hard-won through painful compromise. The Elite program was his answer to the blood shortage that had driven the original war, willing donors, fairly compensated, protected by regulations. It wasn't perfect, but it had held the peace for nearly a century.

Until now.

When they arrived, the crime scene blazed with artificial daylight. Human officers held the perimeter while vampyr investigators moved through the debris. Kane's enhanced senses picked up acrid explosives, burnt metal, and beneath it all, the distinctive copper tang of vampyr blood, sharper than human blood, with ancient undertones.

Sullivan stood examining twisted metal, his weathered face marked by count-less battles. The scar running from eyebrow to jawline caught the harsh light as he turned toward Kane's approach.

Then Kane spotted it, a small metal box near the driver's side door, lid open, fine silvery powder blowing across the pavement.

The sight hit him harder than he expected. Silver. Refined, processed silver, the kind that could burn through vampyric flesh in seconds, stop a vampyr heart for good. During the war, humans had discovered silver dust was more effective than bullets; it could be inhaled, enter the bloodstream through the smallest cut, blind and disable before the killing blow.

After the Treaty, all silver had been carefully regulated, most of it melted down for controlled industrial use, stored under heavy guard in jointly monitored facilities.

Kane's stomach twisted as old memories surfaced: sizzling flesh, burning skin, the screams of friends as silver dust filled their lungs. He'd nearly died of silver poisoning during the siege of Old Chicago, saved only by a transfusion that took three donors.

"What do we have?" Kane asked, keeping his voice steady despite the primal fear.

Sullivan turned, recognition and respect flickering across his features. "Same signature as the others. Symbol, precise explosive placement, and now this." He gestured toward the silver. "This is an escalation. They're moving beyond targeted kills."

"How is this possible?" Kane muttered, his enhanced vision catching particles drifting in the night air. He felt a faint burn wherever they touched exposed skin, tiny cauterizations that would be agony for lesser vampyrs. "Silver's been outlawed for decades. Our repositories are under Council control."

Sullivan shook his head. "High-grade, too. Not crude extraction. Someone knew what they were doing."

Kane crouched beside the car, preternatural senses taking in details human investigators would miss. Military-grade explosives, precise device placement, refined silver of a purity that demanded specialized equipment.

A cold, ancient fury built in him, calculated violence aimed at destabilizing the fragile peace he'd spent decades nurturing.

The scene blurred for a moment, replaced by a memory from 1943: a similar car, a similar explosive signature, silver dust in the air. That time, human leaders had been targeted by vampyr extremists who felt the newly signed Treaty favored humans. Kane had tracked down the culprits himself.

He still remembered their surprise when he'd executed them, vampyrs stunned that one of their own would enforce justice against them for killing humans. A necessary message at a crucial time.

Kane stood, knees cracking, a reminder that even immortality had its limits. "We need to find how they accessed this silver. Start looking into repository security protocols. Be discreet," he ordered. "If Council members are involved..."

The implication hung heavy. Rhy nodded grimly, already pulling out his phone.

Kane moved toward the box, extending his senses. This silver carried a particular resonance, oddly familiar, tugging at memories he couldn't quite place. The particles were uniform, suggesting mechanical processing. The box itself was expensive, polished mahogany with brass fittings, the kind used for Council commendations.

This wasn't just a weapon. It was a message.

Sullivan approached quietly. "We need to handle this carefully. If word gets out about the silver..."

"I know." Kane felt the weight of his position settle over him. The balance between human and vampyr interests had never felt more precarious. "But we need to move quickly. Whoever's doing this wants war."

"I'm sending this for analysis immediately. Special containment protocols."

"Hourly updates," Kane ordered, then swept his gaze across the scene. Four murders in a month, each more brazen, and now silver, a direct challenge to vampyr authority.

Time for an emergency Council meeting. Force them to face what they'd been denying.

As he walked back to Rhy's car, an image of Serenity flashed unbidden through his mind, her honeyed scent, her pulse jumping beneath his fingers, the way she'd offered her neck without fear. The memory was an unwelcome distraction, yet some part of him held on to it, a reminder of what was at stake if this fragile peace failed.

He pulled out his device and called Kaelen, his assistant of thirty years.

"Yes, sir?"

"Emergency Council meeting. Now," Kane said without preamble. "Vampyr attacks using silver. I suspect our kind is involved. Everyone there within the hour."

Silence, then: "I'll send the call immediately. The chamber will be prepared."

Kane ended the call and leaned back, closing his eyes for a moment. The pressure built behind them, the tension headaches that had grown more common over the last decade.

"You look like hell," Rhy observed, sliding into the driver's seat.

"Feel it too," Kane admitted, a rare vulnerability with one of the few he truly trusted. "We're running out of time."

Rhy squeezed his shoulder, a gesture worn smooth across countless battlefields and council chambers. "We'll figure it out. We always do."

Kane gave him a thin smile that didn't reach his eyes. For the first time in lifetimes, he wasn't certain. The situation was unraveling faster than he could contain it.

The drive passed in silence. Kane stared out at his city, the one he'd helped rebuild from the Great War's devastation. He'd personally designed many of the integration systems that let humans and vampyrs coexist.

The Silver District gleamed with unnatural brightness, its towering structures housing the wealthiest vampyrs and their Elites. Beyond it, the modest human districts stood in shadow. From this distance, they looked peaceful. But Kane knew better; beneath the surface, tensions simmered, old hatreds festered, and now someone was deliberately stoking the flames.

The Council building dominated the central district, sleek steel and glass purposely designed to blend human and vampyr aesthetics. Another of Kane's initiatives, a physical embodiment of cooperation and compromise.

The private elevator whisked them to the top floor, where paired guards, one human, one vampyr, stood at attention. Everything about the Council was carefully balanced, every detail weighed for political implication.

The circular chamber's high ceiling displayed scenes from both histories. The central table was crafted from ancient oak, a gift from the last human president before the war. Twelve chairs surrounded it, though only nine were regularly occupied, a reminder of the lives lost crafting their fragile peace.

Elise and Artin were already seated, dark heads bent in quiet conversation. They fell silent as Kane entered, golden eyes tracking his movement. As transport overseers between cities, they wielded considerable power.

Elise's lips curved into a smile that didn't reach her eyes. "Kane. This is unexpected."

"Necessary," he replied curtly, taking his seat at the head of the table. He could smell their anxiety beneath the composed exteriors.

The remaining Council members filed in: Marcus with his military bearing; Sian, white-blonde hair gleaming; General McGraff, his human heartbeat steady despite being surrounded by predators; Gary Hensen, nervous as always; Caroline Ruess, politically savvy; and Peter Fulton, whose family had helped draft the original Treaty.

Once the privacy protocols engaged, all eyes turned to Kane.

"As you know, we've been investigating vampyr deaths in the city. Tonight, I'm formally declaring them what they are: targeted assassinations." He let the word hang, watching the reactions. "And I have evidence suggesting a coordinated effort between human rebels and vampyr collaborators."

Artin leaned forward, skepticism plain. "What evidence? We've heard these theories before."

Kane met his gaze steadily. "Silver shavings at the latest murder scene. Council-grade refined silver, not black market scrap."

Shock rippled through the room. Vampyrs stiffened; humans exchanged worried glances. Silver was the nuclear option, internationally regulated, production monitored, stockpiles under multilayer security. Its presence at a murder scene was unprecedented in the post-Treaty era.

Elise broke the stunned silence, her golden eyes wide. "Silver shavings? But have we ruled out that it was planted to incriminate vampyrs?" Her fingers tapped a nervous rhythm, unusual for her typically composed manner.

"We're running comprehensive analyses," Kane replied, noting her agitation. "But preliminary examination suggests it's consistent with silver stored in Council repositories, specifically the Diamond and Steel District facilities. This isn't scrap. This is weapons-grade."

Sian's features hardened. "Are you suggesting we can't control our own repositories? That someone in my district is involved?"

Kane held up a placating hand. "I'm stating facts. Council-grade silver was used in a vampyr assassination. That silver came from somewhere, and the most logical source is our repositories. Whether obtained through corruption, coercion, or theft remains to be determined."

General McGraff cleared his throat. "You're right, Kane. We need to find who's behind these murders, human or vampyr, before this escalates."

Caroline nodded. "We can't let fear and hate consume us again. We must work together to protect both communities."

Kane noted the careful rhetoric. Humans were quick to speak about justice, yet none had volunteered concrete help locating rebel cells in their districts. They insisted it was just "rogue elements," a convenient fiction that let them ignore the growing anti-vampyr sentiment.

Peter Fulton stroked his beard thoughtfully. "What about the rebels' ultimate goal? Simple destruction, or something strategic?"

Kane exhaled heavily. "Based on the attack patterns and the increasing sophistication, I believe their goal is destabilizing the Treaty itself. Create enough fear and suspicion that vampyrs and humans turn on each other. Reignite the war." He met Peter's gaze. "If vampyrs are involved, their motives are similar, those who believe the Treaty favors humans too strongly."

Elise's eyes widened in apparent shock. "That's monstrous! To deliberately push us back into war after everything we've sacrificed?"

"That hatred has always lurked beneath the surface," Sian said bitterly, an unusual alliance forming with Elise. "But we won't let them succeed. We'll find those responsible."

Kane noted the shift, a tentative unity forming against an external threat. Whether it would translate to actual cooperation remained to be seen.

Artin leaned forward, surprisingly pragmatic. "We'll audit the silver repositories. Every gram accounted for. And we need better intelligence on the rebel cells."

Kane turned to Caroline, whose informant network was reputed the most extensive among the human representatives. "You have contacts who might have useful information?"

She nodded, though Kane caught the hesitation. "Yes. I'll activate my networks and report back directly."

"Daily updates from all of you," Kane said, his tone making clear it wasn't a request. "Full security audits of your districts, increased border patrols, every silver repository checked by morning. We reconvene in three days with preliminary findings."

As the meeting broke up, Elise lingered, approaching with uncharacteristic hesitancy. "Kane, I know we've had our differences," she began, her voice softer than usual. "But I want you to know I'll do everything I can to help with this investigation. This affects all of us."

The sudden conciliatory attitude from someone who'd so often opposed his policies set off warning bells. Elise had been among the most vocal critics of the Elite program, arguing for less regulation and more vampyr autonomy. This felt calculated.

"I appreciate that, Elise," he replied carefully. "I hope we can all work together."

She gave him a small smile before departing, the scent of anxiety lingering after her. Kane watched her go, mentally flagging the exchange. Her heart had raced when he mentioned the silver repositories, a physiological response difficult even for vampyrs to control.

Lifetimes of politics had taught him one truth: when an adversary suddenly becomes an ally, it's rarely genuine.

As the chamber emptied, Kane remained seated, the weight of leadership heavy on him. Something about Elise's demeanor troubled him, a nervousness unlike her usual confidence, a forced quality to her concern.

As he finally rose to leave, his thoughts turned once more to Serenity, waiting in his apartment. If war came again, if the fragile peace crumbled, what would happen to her and the other Elites? Would they become targets, caught between the species they served and the families they'd come from?

The thought sent an unexpected surge through him, fierce and possessive. He'd brought her into his home to shield her from those who would exploit her rare blood. Now he might need to protect her from something far worse, a war that could tear apart everything they'd built since the Treaty.

With renewed resolve, Kane strode from the chamber. He would find who was behind these murders, who was trying to destroy the peace he'd sacrificed so much to create. And he would not let himself be constrained this time by Council politics or procedural niceties.

Whatever it took, he would hold the line for what mattered: the Treaty, the city, and the woman with honey-brown eyes who had begun to matter more than he could afford.

CHAPTER NINETEEN

SERENITY

As she stepped out of the steamy shower, her heart leapt at a voice behind her. She quickly grabbed a towel and turned to see Evelyn in her bedroom doorway, wearing faded jeans and a plain tee, her hair loose around her shoulders instead of tucked into its usual bun. Without the lab coat, she was almost unrecognizable, more approachable, yet no less dangerous.

Serenity clutched her towel tightly, the sudden exposure leaving her painfully vulnerable. The luxury of unlimited hot water and a locked door had lulled her into a false sense of security.

Evelyn stepped back, hands raised innocently. "I apologize. I didn't mean to alarm you. I did knock, but you didn't answer." Her voice was gentler than at the clinic, almost sympathetic. "I wanted to make sure you were doing okay. Some Elites have trouble with their first night."

Her mesmerizing eyes held what looked like real concern, but Serenity stayed wary. In her experience, kindness from those in power often came with expectations, or with information gathering.

"I'm fine, Evelyn," she said at last, brushing a stray curl from her eyes, struggling to keep her dignity while standing nearly naked before a vampyr.

"Please, call me Evie," Evelyn replied, a soft smile spreading across her face. The familiarity felt like an offered hand, one Serenity wasn't sure she should take.

"Why don't you get dressed? We can talk afterward."

Serenity quickly grabbed her clothes and ducked into the bathroom. Her heart hammered as she pulled on worn jeans, conscious of how her father had always taught her to stay observant around those in authority.

When she emerged, Evelyn offered an encouraging smile from her perch on the edge of the bed.

"All better now?" She tucked a loose strand behind Serenity's ear, a gesture both intimate and presumptuous. "Have you had breakfast yet?"

Serenity shook her head. "Not yet."

Her stomach had been growling for hours, but she'd been hesitant to venture from her room. Back home, breakfast was her mother's homemade oat bars and herbal tea, though she hadn't had any in months, making sure Beth got at least two meals a day.

"We can grab something at the market. They have delicious coffee."

Coffee. Her father had brought it back once from the Inner City, a rare treat that had cost him half a day's wages. The memory of his smile, so rare in those final months, made her chest ache.

"Okay," she agreed, pushing the grief aside.

Serenity slipped her feet into worn-out shoes, the soles nearly separating from the uppers. She caught Evelyn's raised eyebrow, the first hint of judgment in her otherwise welcoming manner.

"Those are the only ones you have?"

Shame burned along her skin. These shoes had been re-soled twice, the laces replaced with twine. "Yes," she said quietly.

"We'll add clothes shopping to our errands. Did the clothes in the bag fit?"

Serenity nodded before looking away. The "bag" had held more clothes than her entire family owned put together.

"There's no need for that," Evie said, her tone softening. "I won't bite." A small smile played at her lips. "But speaking of... has he fed from you yet?"

The question sent a flutter through Serenity. Her hand moved on its own to her neck, fingers brushing the pulse point where Kane's gaze had lingered.

When Serenity stayed silent, Evelyn's face eased into a knowing smile.

"I'm taking that as no. Come, let's find him." Evelyn took her hand and led her downstairs.

The apartment's vastness still disoriented her after Grove Gardens' cramped quarters. Here, you could get lost between rooms.

They found Kane in his office, deeply absorbed in reports. When Evelyn burst in without knocking, he didn't look up.

"Oh, there you are. I'm taking her shopping, and I need your card," Evie announced, walking over and holding out her hand with casual entitlement.

His office was breathtaking. Floor-to-ceiling windows revealed clouds drifting around the building, as if it were suspended in the sky itself. In the Outer City, windows were small, practical things, sources of light, not views.

Serenity wanted to approach the glass but stayed in the doorway, noting that the bookshelves had parted to reveal televisions, some showing news channels, others displaying security feeds of the apartment. Beauty and surveillance side by side.

Without a word, Kane set down his paper and pulled out his wallet, handing Evelyn a black and silver card. The casual way he surrendered what represented more wealth than her family might see in a lifetime made her stomach clench. He picked his report back up, reading without acknowledging her.

His dismissal stung more than it should have. She was only a blood source, a contractual obligation, nothing more.

"Thank you." Evelyn smiled, walking toward the door.

"Before I go." Serenity saw Kane visibly cringe as Evelyn turned back toward him. "A little birdie told me you haven't set up a feeding schedule with this wonderful Elite yet?"

Kane sat silent, seemingly engrossed in the paper. The tension thickened until Serenity found it hard to breathe. Evelyn stepped closer, leaning in to whisper something in his ear, too low for human hearing, but whatever she said drew a visible stiffness across his shoulders.

Kane slowly raised his head, his eyes boring into Serenity's with such force she had to look away. Even across the room, his attention felt like standing too close to flame.

"Evelyn, when I am ready to make a feeding schedule, I will speak with the Elite," he said, each word clipped and deliberate.

The woman tutted. "She has a name, by the way. It's Serenity."

The fine hairs along her nape rose as she felt his unblinking stare. She kept her eyes averted as he offered a soft "I know," two words that somehow carried more weight than they should.

"Good. You should make a schedule soon. I'll give you until tomorrow." With that ultimatum hanging in the air, Evelyn left, pulling Serenity along behind her.

As the elevator descended, Serenity couldn't shake the feeling that something unspoken had passed between the vampyrs, some tension or understanding that left her outside it. The politics between them seemed as tangled as the treaty relationships her father had tried to explain, though his simplified version, vampyrs protecting humans in exchange for willing blood donation, now seemed naively incomplete.

The Diamond District was another world entirely. Where Grove Gardens had dirt paths lined with salvaged brick, here smooth stone gleamed in the sunlight. Where home had communal water pumps and weekly ration lines, here fountains flowed freely and food vendors offered delicacies without restriction cards.

Evelyn guided her through bustling streets, past displays of wealth that made her dizzy. Each store window showcased items worth more than her family's entire dwelling. The scents were different too, subtle perfumes and polished wood, not the earthier smells of her district's communal gardens.

They approached Glamour Couture, a high-end boutique with mannequins displaying clothes that looked untouched by life or labor. Serenity hesitated at the entrance, suddenly aware of how out of place she must look.

"Don't worry," Evie said, noticing her hesitation. "You belong here now."

But did she? The words "Elite" and "Kane Draccus's Elite" might open these doors, but they didn't change who she was inside, a woman from Grove Gardens who'd learned to stretch beans for three days and patch clothes until the patches needed patching.

Inside, luxury saturated the air. Clothing racks stood in perfect order, each garment evenly spaced. The carpet beneath her worn shoes was thicker than her mattress at home, and mirrors surrounded them, multiplying her discomfort.

Eventually she selected two pairs of jeans and two simple shirts, practical choices that wouldn't mark her as different when she returned home. Because she would return home, wouldn't she? She needed to read that contract again.

Evelyn rounded a corner with an armful of dresses in jewel tones, their fabric catching the light like cut stones. She scanned Serenity's modest selections with barely concealed disapproval.

"Oh no," she began, her tone making Serenity shrink inwardly. "You're an Elite now. You can't go around in plain jeans and T-shirts. Besides," she added with a dismissive wave, "it's on Kane's dime."

The words stung with their casual indifference to what such spending meant. In her district, people went hungry to save for new shoes. Here, Evelyn spoke of dresses costing hundreds of credits as if they were nothing.

After trying on the clothes Evie selected, Serenity felt a strange disorientation at her own reflection. The tailored blouses and designer jeans fit her body in ways her hand-me-downs never had. No gaps, no stretched seams, no places where fabric had been reinforced with mismatched thread.

Each garment represented a different version of herself, one she hadn't known could exist. Her stomach churned with a mix of guilt and excitement. Who was she becoming?

The true revelation came when she tried on a burgundy silk dress that slid over her skin like water, cool and sensuous. It clung to her body, accentuating curves usually hidden beneath shapeless clothing. The deep color made her skin glow, and the perfect fit left her feeling both elegant and strangely powerful.

Evelyn knocked before entering, her eyes widening at the transformation. "You look absolutely stunning," she breathed. "I can't wait for Kane to see you in it."

The mention of his name sent heat rushing to her cheeks. Despite his cool demeanor that morning, the memory of his stare lingered, the way he'd looked at her in the library, the strange inner light in his eyes.

Standing there, transformed by silk and expert tailoring, it was hard not to imagine his reaction if he saw her like this. The thought was presumptuous, dangerous even. She was an Elite, a contracted blood donor, not a potential romantic interest for one of the most powerful vampyrs in Celearius.

Being practical, she settled on three outfits Evie had chosen, including the burgundy dress, and basics that wouldn't draw attention in her home district when she visited.

Shopping with Evelyn was like being caught in a whirlwind. In four hours, she'd tried on more clothes than she'd owned in her entire life.

Her stomach eventually growled loudly enough to interrupt Evelyn's enthusiastic discourse on proper foundational garments.

"Shit," Evelyn muttered, looking genuinely contrite. "I forgot to feed you."

The phrasing, so close to how one might speak of a pet, struck Serenity, but she pushed the discomfort aside. "It's okay."

"We'll stop by one more store. Then we can get you something to eat," Evelyn promised.

Evelyn led her to Secret Illusion, an exclusive lingerie boutique that seemed to glow from within. Unlike the utilitarian undergarments back in Grove Gardens, these pieces were works of art.

As she studied herself in the fitting room mirror, these lovely, impractical things seemed to embody all that separated her old life from this new one. Part of her felt like an impostor, playing dress-up in clothes she hadn't earned. Yet another part thrilled at the transformation, at the possibility of being someone different.

With three new bras selected, she was ready to leave. But as she went to find Evelyn, a shimmer of gold caught her eye.

On a central mannequin stood a golden dress unlike anything she'd ever seen. The metallic fabric seemed alive, catching and throwing back the light with each small stir of air. Its halter neckline and body-hugging silhouette radiated a confidence and sensuality she'd never associated with herself.

She was drawn to it despite herself, transfixed by its raw elegance. It was extravagant, impractical, outrageous, everything she wasn't supposed to want. Yet she couldn't look away.

Unbidden, an image formed: Kane seeing her in this dress, his cool composure faltering as those silver-blue eyes lit with appreciation. The fantasy was foolish. She barely knew him, and what she did know suggested he saw her as nothing more than a necessity.

A gentle touch on her arm made her jump. She looked up into Evelyn's knowing green eyes.

"You want it, don't you?" Evie asked softly, her voice neither mocking nor judging.

Heat rushed to her cheeks. "It's beautiful," she admitted.

"Then take it." Evie's directness startled her. "A beautiful dress for a beautiful woman. You deserve to have something that makes you feel beautiful."

Deserve. The word snagged in her. What did she deserve? In Grove Gardens, survival wasn't about deserving; it was about necessity. Beauty, pleasure, desire, these were luxuries no one could afford.

"Why are you doing this for me?" she asked, the question rising from genuine confusion.

Evelyn sighed, her ageless face revealing a flicker of weariness. "Because you are more than just an Elite here to serve Kane. You are also a woman deserving of things that bring her joy."

The simplicity struck her deeply. All her life she'd defined herself by usefulness, by responsibility, daughter, sister, caretaker. The idea that she might deserve joy for its own sake was revolutionary.

Taking the dress felt like a small rebellion, not against Kane or the system, but against the limits she'd placed on herself. She could fulfill her duties to her family and still find moments of joy. The two weren't mutually exclusive.

The true highlight came when they passed Sound Haven, a music store glittering with devices she'd only heard about. When Evelyn led her inside and bought a Zunie, a sleek device preloaded with thousands of songs, Serenity felt a childlike excitement overtake her.

The thought of having private music whenever she wanted seemed almost as magical as the golden dress. In a world where so much was uncertain, where her body was no longer fully her own, having this small thing of beauty felt profound.

"Let's get you something to eat, then head to the salon," Evelyn suggested.

Serenity ordered a black bean burger with sweet potato fries, noting the absence of the greasy food stalls that dotted Grove Gardens. Here, even "casual" food seemed designed for optimal nutrition.

"How was your first night?" Evie asked as Serenity ate in Gwen's Spa's waiting area. "Do you always visit Elites like this?"

Evelyn hesitated, her usual confidence faltering. "Yes... and no."

Before she could elaborate, a spa attendant approached.

They were guided through glass doors into a space that defied understanding. Sunlight streamed through a massive skylight, scattering patterns across marble floors. Greek statues stood in silent judgment while a crystal fountain sent rainbow reflections dancing over the walls.

"She needs the full works, nails, hair, and wax," Evelyn instructed the beautician. Then, her voice dropping to a dangerous register, she added, "She is human. If one drop of her blood is spilled, it will be your death."

The threat, delivered so casually, reminded Serenity of what lay beneath Evelyn's friendly surface. The predator was always there, ancient and deadly, just out of sight.

Hours later, as they massaged her feet with oil that smelled of lavender and mint, Serenity felt herself drifting into a relaxed contentment. She could almost forget why she was here, what awaited her when she returned to Kane's apartment.

In the Relaxation Room, plush couches and ambient lighting created a sense of calm. Evelyn joined her on a small couch in the corner.

"He's my friend," Evelyn said suddenly, breaking the peaceful silence. "I don't do this for Elites. A Health Inspector checks on them every two weeks, but I want this to work. I need this to work."

The abrupt confession caught Serenity off guard.

"Why do you need this to work?" she asked.

Silence filled the room before Evelyn spoke, her voice uncharacteristically vulnerable.

"For several reasons. One is that he needs to take better care of himself." She turned to face Serenity. "Another is that Kane is lonely. It has been years since he's had a true companion. He needs someone like you, Serenity."

The implication stunned her. Someone like her? A woman from Grove Gardens with no special skills, whose only value was rare blood?

"Me?" she stammered. "Why would he need someone like me?"

Evelyn studied her for a long moment. "For eons, we've existed on a precipice. Eternal beings trying to carve out happy endings in fleeting moments. Kane... he carries this world in ways even I cannot fully understand."

The words painted a picture of Kane that clashed with his cold demeanor, not just the intimidating head of the Human Vampyr Council, but someone shouldering burdens she could scarcely imagine.

"What if I can't adjust to this life?" The question rose from her deepest fear.

"There is more at stake here than you realize, Serenity," Evelyn replied. "Not just for Kane, but for all of us. As an Elite, you have the chance to offer him companionship and understanding he hasn't known in centuries. This alliance will also strengthen your position here, give you a voice and protection among vampyrs, especially now, when tensions are rising and loyalties are being tested."

Serenity filed away that last part, remembering the murder that had called Kane away so urgently. There were larger forces at work here, ones she didn't understand but could feel gathering around them.

"The Elites are more than caretakers," Evelyn continued, her gaze unwavering. "They're a link between vampyrs and humans, a symbol of a fragile peace. And you and Kane, given current circumstances, could lay the groundwork for stability when we need it most."

Stability. The word carried a weight Serenity couldn't fully grasp, though she sensed its importance.

"I understand," she said softly, though she wasn't sure she fully did. "What happens if he doesn't want to feed from me? Would I still get paid?"

Evelyn's expression shifted, a flicker of something, concern, or fear, crossing her face. "I know I shouldn't ask this, and you have no reason to be truthful with me, but I need you to tell me if he doesn't feed. Please."

The request grew more desperate until Evelyn, to Serenity's shock, dropped to her knees before her, eyes pleading.

Serenity stared, weighing her options. Agreeing to report back on Kane's feeding felt like a betrayal, though of whom, she wasn't sure. Yet there was something in Evelyn's desperation that resonated.

"Okay," she finally agreed, reluctant.

Evelyn exhaled sharply in relief. "Thank you, Serenity. Truly."

"If he doesn't feed, will I still be paid?" Serenity repeated.

"Yes," Evie answered, looking away. "You will still be paid."

The confirmation loosened the knot in her chest. With newfound courage, she decided to ask for what she truly wanted. "Do you think I could see my family? Or at least get a cellular device to them so we can talk?"

"You'll have to speak with Kane about that," Evelyn replied evenly. "We usually have Elites wait two weeks before contacting family, so they adjust to the transition, but it's at his discretion."

Two weeks without hearing her mother's voice felt like an eternity. But she would ask Kane somehow, gather the courage to approach the imposing vampyr with her request.

After their final treatment, Serenity stared at her reflection in disbelief. The person looking back seemed like a stranger, tight spirals turned into light, bouncy curls, eyebrows arched with precision. Even her skin seemed to glow.

"How about you wear that green sundress we found?" Evelyn suggested.

Their final stop was a market unlike anything in Grove Gardens. Where Rack n' Reynolds offered mostly canned goods and limited produce, this place was a cornucopia of fresh food.

As she walked the aisles, she instinctively reached for things her family would appreciate, rice, beans, root vegetables. But halfway through, reality hit. These weren't for her family. They were for her, in Kane's apartment.

Reluctantly, she put many of the items back, unsure what to choose for herself alone.

"Is that all you're going to buy?" Evelyn asked, peering into the nearly empty basket.

"Honestly, I'm not sure what to buy," Serenity admitted.

"It's okay. I'll show you how to order food online for delivery. You can try new things and figure out what you like."

Walking to Evelyn's car, a sleek black vehicle that hummed rather than rattled, Serenity noticed how the late afternoon sun brought out the auburn highlights in Evelyn's hair. Despite her earlier wariness, she found herself growing comfortable in the vampyr's presence.

"Can I ask you something?" she ventured.

"Of course," Evelyn replied warmly.

"It's about Kane. I know you're his friend, but I wanted to know if he's always so... intense?"

Evelyn's expression softened with understanding. "Yes, Kane can be intense. He's passionate about his responsibilities and carries the weight of our community." Her voice dropped lower. "But beneath that exterior is a good man. He cares deeply about Celearius, about all its people, human and vampyr alike. He'll do anything to protect them. Especially now."

Serenity caught that last word again, the same quiet pressure that seemed to weigh on everyone around her.

"I didn't mean to offend him earlier about the feeding schedule," she confessed. "I want to fulfill my part of the agreement."

"I understand," Evelyn assured her, placing a comforting hand on her shoulder. "And I don't think Kane was offended. He's... complicated. Takes getting used to." A shadow crossed her face. "And the recent security concerns have made him more cautious than usual."

The pieces of a larger puzzle were beginning to surface, though Serenity couldn't yet see the whole picture.

As they drove back toward the Silver District, the scenery shifted dramatically. The colorful bustle of the Diamond District gave way to sleek, minimalist architecture, glass and steel reaching toward the sky like the ambitions of those who lived there.

When they pulled into the underground garage, Nox stood waiting by the elevator. As Evelyn stopped the car, the trunk opened on its own, and he moved to collect the shopping bags with efficient grace.

Evelyn turned to Serenity with a warm smile. "I'll call you tomorrow to check how things went with Kane. I have to run, but call me if you need anything." She squeezed Serenity's hand.

"Thank you," Serenity said, meaning it despite her lingering questions about Evelyn's true motives. "For everything today."

They rode the elevator up in neutral silence. Serenity followed Nox upstairs, watching as he waited for her to unlock the door before setting the bags inside.

"Will you be needing anything else?" he asked politely.

"Actually, yes," she replied, suddenly aware of how little she knew about the modern kitchen. "Maybe later you could show me how to work the stove."

In Grove Gardens, they'd cooked on gas. Everything here was electric, gleaming appliances that might as well have been spacecraft controls.

"Just let me know when you're ready. I'll be in the library if you need me," Nox replied with professional courtesy.

Alone again, Serenity surveyed the bags holding her new possessions. She should unpack them, hang the beautiful clothes, arrange the new toiletries. But suddenly the day's events crashed over her, the overwhelming newness, the constant calculations about what to say and how to behave, the uncertainty of what awaited her when Kane returned.

Exhaustion pulled at her limbs. The bed beckoned, promising comfort she'd never known before yesterday.

Just a quick rest, she told herself, lying down fully clothed. She would unpack later, before Kane returned. She would prepare herself for whatever the evening might bring.

As sleep began to claim her, Serenity's last conscious thought was of the golden dress, carefully folded in one of the bags. Not a reminder of what she lacked, but a symbol of possibility, that perhaps in this new world she could find beauty alongside purpose.

She would wear it someday, she decided as consciousness slipped away. Not to impress Kane or anyone else, but because it made her feel like more than a blood source. Like a woman with choices, with desires, with a future that might hold more than mere survival.

Outside, the city continued its endless rhythm, unaware of the quiet revolutions taking place within one young woman from Grove Gardens, now an Elite in the Silver District, caught between two worlds, belonging fully to neither, yet perhaps finding a place for herself in both.

CHAPTER TWENTY

KANE

When Kane stepped off the elevator, the last thing he expected to hear was Nox laughing, a sound that had grown rare since tensions between humans and vampyrs began escalating months ago. The baritone echo bounced off the walls, jarring in its unexpected joy.

The first thing to hit him was her scent, no longer just the clean, natural essence he'd caught earlier, but now laced with the rich aromas of herbs and spices. His gums tingled faintly, an unconscious response his body had developed over centuries. Not hunger exactly, not yet, but awareness, like a predator catching the first hint of prey on the wind.

Walking into the kitchen, he found Nox holding open a cookbook for Serenity as she stirred a pot on the stove. The domesticity of the scene struck him as bizarre, his security officer and his Elite, carrying on like old friends in his kitchen. A long-dormant ache twisted in his chest at the sight.

Kane let himself breathe fully for the first time in weeks, drawing the aroma deep into his lungs. Human food hadn't appealed to him in hundreds of years, but whatever was in that pot stirred something forgotten. His mouth watered, a reflex he'd thought had died with his humanity.

"This stove cooks faster and at a higher temperature, so you'll have to adjust the recipe for the fourth time, stubborn human," Nox scolded, his normally impassive face animated with amusement.

"I know. I am adjusting," Serenity replied, determination in the set of her shoulders.

"Not too much seasoning." She glared at Nox without breaking her stir. He laughed again, the sound still a surprise. "It will not get done any faster, no matter how much you glare at me."

"I'm supposed to put two teaspoons. It says it right here." Serenity pointed to a line in the book. Their shoulders touched as they leaned over it together.

Something shifted inside Kane. Jealousy. It surged through his veins like poison, darkening the edges of his vision. His muscles coiled, ready to move, to separate them, to—

He caught himself, horrified at the possessive rage burning through him. He had no claim on her beyond their contract. She was not his wife. She wasn't even truly his Elite yet; he hadn't fed from her. She was free to interact with whomever she chose.

The rational thoughts did nothing to quell the territorial fury that had his fangs pressing against his gums.

Nox turned, his preternatural senses catching Kane's presence and the dangerous shift in his energy. Recognition of that possessive rage flickered across his face. "Sir," he said sternly, a reminder rather than a greeting.

Kane forced his features into neutrality, though he could feel the telltale heat behind his eyes that meant they'd begun to glow. "I apologize for interrupting, but it smells delicious in here," he managed, his voice steadier than he felt.

Serenity turned slowly, her movements carrying a grace he hadn't noticed before. Her lips curved into a smile that transformed her entire face, lighting her eyes and sending an unexpected warmth through his chest. For a moment he forgot his jealousy, forgot the constant hunger, forgot everything but the strange flutter in his stomach at the realization that his presence had brought that expression to her face.

Then her smile vanished, replaced by widened eyes and parted lips as she held her breath. Fear leaped into her expression, a reminder of what he was, and what he was not.

Nox stepped between them, his back to Serenity. "Sir. Your eyes," he whispered, too low for human hearing.

Fuck.

Kane closed his eyes, drawing on centuries of discipline to rein in the hunger and the jealousy. He focused on his breathing, on the cool marble beneath his feet, on anything but the temptation standing a few feet away. When he opened them again, Nox nodded once, confirmation that the vampyric glow had faded.

"Nox tells me vampyrs don't normally eat food, but they can," Serenity said softly, nervousness threading beneath the casual words. She glanced at him before looking back at the pot. "Would you like to join us?"

He hesitated. Eating with her meant prolonged exposure to her scent, to the sound of her pulse, to all the little human mannerisms that proved so distractingly appealing. His mind screamed at him to refuse, to retreat to the safety of his office.

"Yes," he heard himself say instead, the word escaping before he could stop it. "I would love to."

Surprise flashed across Nox's face before he schooled it. Kane rarely ate, and never with Elites. The deviation was as telling as his glowing eyes had been.

"Awesome. It should be done in ten—"

"Fifteen," Nox corrected, resuming his place at her side.

She gave him a sidelong glance that carried more personality than Kane had seen in all their previous interactions. "Fifteen minutes. I can come get you when it's ready," she said, her voice brightening.

Kane found himself smiling back, a real response rather than a calculated one. "I look forward to it."

As Nox turned to stir the pot, Kane's eyes drifted back to Serenity. The green sundress she wore, new, he noted, left her neck and upper back bare. He could see the delicate knobs of her spine, the elegant curve where neck met shoulder, the faint blue tracery of veins beneath the skin.

This wasn't the usual hunger, the manageable craving he'd disciplined himself to endure for weeks between feedings. This was more demanding, more urgent, the kind of hunger he hadn't felt since his early centuries, when control was still something he struggled to hold.

Before he could take off his coat and settle in his office, his phone buzzed. He snatched it up, grateful for the distraction. Rhy's voice greeted him, tense with suppressed excitement.

"We caught one. He was installing a bomb on one of the Elite doctors' cars."

Kane's body went still, the predator in him fixing instantly on this new prey. "Is he human?" he asked, though he already knew the answer.

"Yes."

At last, proof that couldn't be dismissed by the Council as coincidence. They'd managed to capture a human rebel, evidence of the coordinated effort Kane had been warning about for months. All that remained was keeping the prisoner alive and making him talk. Kane needed to uncover the rebellion's leadership and locate their headquarters.

With that, he could finally show the Council the true danger and secure the resources he needed to crush the rebellion before it gained further momentum.

"Rhy, bring him to Cavern 47. Make sure he gets there alive. No one is to know."

"Received." The line went dead.

Rhyzan would carry out the order flawlessly; he always did. But Kane couldn't shake a sense of unease. After months of evading capture, why had this rebel been caught so easily? It felt deliberate, like bait in a trap.

Suspicion clouded his thoughts as he turned over the possibilities. Humans were unpredictable, their short lifespans lending them a recklessness that often confounded vampyric strategy. But to let one of their own be captured seemed uncharacteristically sacrificial.

The rebels had a message to deliver; that much seemed certain. The question was whether it was genuine or a carefully crafted deception.

Kane sighed heavily, sinking into his chair. When he'd been asked twenty-five years ago to lead the Council, he'd accepted reluctantly, knowing he was the only one he trusted to wield such power responsibly. But the burden had grown heavier with each passing year. Vampyric politics were exhausting enough; adding human rebellion threatened to wear through even his considerable patience.

Sometimes he found himself longing for the quiet solitude of his castle in the Irish hills, far from the constant machinations and tensions of Celearius. But duty had always been his guiding principle, even when desire pulled him elsewhere.

Almost without thinking, his hand moved to the gold locket he kept close to his heart. He opened it with practiced ease, revealing the miniature portrait inside, his wife's amber eyes staring back across three centuries of grief and memory.

Even now, three hundred years after her death, Becca remained a daily presence in his thoughts. She had been so vibrantly alive, so determinedly human in her passions and principles. So unlike the cool calculations of vampyr society.

Rage still simmered beneath his grief when he thought of how she'd died, trapped in the schoolhouse fire set by a jealous husband who believed his wife was having an affair with another teacher. The flames had spread too fast for even Kane's supernatural speed to save her. She'd died trying to rescue the children in her care, her final act one of selfless courage.

The locket snapped shut with a soft click, bringing Kane back to the present. He tucked it safely away and pulled several folders from his briefcase, determined to focus on work until dinner.

The top report detailed another missing Elite, the third this month. The pattern was becoming hard to ignore. If the disappearances continued, the media would eventually take notice, handing the human rebellion exactly the kind of publicity it sought.

He was reviewing the case details when a soft knock sounded at his door. At once his senses sharpened; he could smell her unique scent through the solid wood, could hear the slightly elevated rhythm of her heart. His own pulse answered, a sympathetic reaction he hadn't felt in decades.

He pressed the button beneath his desk, and the door clicked open. Serenity stepped through, and Kane was momentarily startled by the change in her appearance. Her hair, tightly curled when she'd arrived, now fell in loose waves around her shoulders, framing her face differently, drawing out the delicate structure of her cheekbones and the fullness of her lips.

"Dinner is ready," she said softly, tucking a strand behind her ear in a gesture that struck him as endearingly self-conscious.

"You changed your hair," he said, the observation slipping out before he could weigh its appropriateness.

She touched it again, a nervous habit he was beginning to recognize. "Yes, Evelyn had the salon do it. I've never had my hair done before." Uncertainty flickered across her face. "Should I change it?"

The question caught him off guard. She was asking his opinion, as if his preferences mattered to her. As if she wanted to please him. The thought sent a complicated surge through him, pleasure tangled with guilt, desire knotted with responsibility.

"No," he said, the word firmer than he intended. Her answering smile made his chest tighten, a sensation so long forgotten he barely recognized it. "I'll be out in a minute."

"Okay," she replied, closing the door with a quiet grace at odds with the nervous energy she usually showed in his presence.

Alone again, Kane faced an uncomfortable truth: Serenity was becoming more than an Elite to him, more than a source of the rare blood his body craved. She was becoming a person in his eyes, a dangerous development given how fundamentally unbalanced their relationship was.

His mind drifted to his previous Elites, a stark reminder of why such entanglements were perilous. Ava had seemed perfect at first, quiet, resilient, with a defiance that assured him she'd never seek to become a vampyr. He'd thought they understood each other, believed they'd built a mutually beneficial arrangement.

He'd been wrong. Her hatred of vampyrs had run deeper than he realized, ending in an attempt on his life that left him wounded and her imprisoned. The betrayal hadn't been personal; Ava would have tried to kill any vampyr. But it reinforced his decision to stay solitary.

Before her had been Hannah, whose desire to be turned had manifested in increasingly disturbing ways. She'd nearly drained herself, slicing open her own veins in a desperate bid to force his hand, believing he would turn her rather than let her die.

He'd sworn then that he would never take another Elite. The risks were too great, the potential for tragedy too high. Yet here he was, drawn once more into the dangerous dance of Elite and patron.

But it wasn't only her blood that captivated him, and that was the truly disturbing part. Unlike his previous Elites, she carried a genuine gentleness that seemed at odds with the harsh realities of their world. Not weakness; he'd glimpsed the steel beneath her soft exterior, but a quiet grace. She didn't hate him for what he was, didn't seem to fear him beyond natural caution. She didn't crave transformation, didn't view him as a means to power or immortality.

She simply was who she was: a young woman trying to save her family through the only means available to her. The purity of that motivation touched a place in him he'd thought long dead.

Pushing the troubling thoughts aside, Kane left his office and made his way to the kitchen. He expected to find Nox still there, a buffer between them, but was surprised to find Serenity alone at the island table.

"Where's Nox?" he asked, keeping his tone casual despite the sudden quickening of his pulse.

"He said something about a last-minute errand," she replied, uncertainty in her voice, as if she suspected his departure wasn't entirely coincidental.

"Did he now?" Kane murmured, making a mental note to have words with his security officer about such transparent manipulations.

He sat beside her, acutely aware of her nearness, the soft sound of her breathing, the subtle shifts in the air as she moved, the warmth radiating from her skin. His enhanced senses registered details no human could perceive: the slight rise in her body temperature, the faint tremor in her hands, the way her pupils dilated a fraction when she looked at him.

His gaze fell to the plate before him, steam rising from pasta coated in rich red sauce. Despite the centuries separating him from any physical need for human food, the scent woke memories of his mortal life, of meals shared with family, of simple pleasures most vampyrs surrendered in exchange for immortality.

He took a bite, surprised by the burst of flavor on his tongue. His sensory perception, heightened by the change, had always made eating somewhat over-whelming in the rare instances he indulged. But this was different, complex yet balanced, the acid of the tomatoes softened by herbs and a hint of sweetness.

"How was your day with Evelyn?" he asked, slowing to savor the unexpected pleasure of the meal she'd made.

Serenity finished her bite, setting her fork down carefully before answering. "It was good," she said, tucking a strand behind her ear. "She took me shopping, then to the salon for my hair. She's very kind to me."

Her smile as she spoke of Evie seemed genuine, easing a worry Kane hadn't realized he'd been carrying, that she might feel intimidated by his oldest friend.

As Serenity spoke, Kane found his attention drawn helplessly to her neck. His hunger, briefly forgotten during the first bites of food, came roaring back.

Despite the artificial lemon-vanilla scent she'd applied, he could detect the sweet undertone of her blood just beneath the surface. It called to him with a potency he hadn't known in centuries, making his fangs ache and his vision sharpen unnaturally.

"I'm glad," he managed, forcing his gaze back to his plate. But his mind stayed fixed on the pulse point at the base of her throat, on the imagined taste of her blood.

"Kane?"

Her voice broke through the dangerous reverie. "Would you like more?" she asked, apparently mistaking his stare for interest in the food rather than in her.

"Yes," he answered, his voice rough with the effort of restraint. But it wasn't pasta he hungered for now.

She rose, carrying his plate to the stove for a second serving. He used her brief absence to draw a deep breath, fighting to center himself. His hands gripped the edge of the counter, leaving faint indentations in the marble where his fingers pressed too hard.

When she returned, he reached across the table to take the plate. Their fingers brushed, sending an electric current through his entire body. It wasn't just hunger this time; it was something more complicated, more human. The skin-to-skin contact, brief as it was, affected him more powerfully than he would have believed possible after centuries of isolation.

From the widening of her eyes and the sudden catch in her breath, he knew she'd felt it too, whatever it was.

Kane withdrew quickly, fixing his attention on the marble countertop as if studying its patterns might save him from his own impulses. "I hope you're settling in nicely," he said, desperate for neutral conversation to break the charged atmosphere between them. "I know being here will take some getting used to. If you have any questions, don't hesitate to ask Nox... or me."

"I..." Her voice trailed off, and he glanced up to find her gaze fixed on her hands, fingers fidgeting with the silverware, another of those endearingly human gestures that made her seem so alive next to the calculated movements of most vampyrs.

"Yes?" he prompted, curiosity briefly outweighing hunger.

She looked up, meeting his eyes with a determination that surprised him. "I was just wondering," she began, her voice gaining strength with each word, "about your feeding schedule."

The directness caught him off guard. Most Elites approached the subject obliquely, either too frightened or too eager to address it plainly. But Serenity looked at him steadily, only the slight quickening of her pulse betraying her nerves.

A peculiar tension filled the space between them, not just the predator-prey dynamic that usually marked such discussions, but something more nuanced. In her question he sensed not duty or fear, but a real wish to understand what would be expected of her. To define the shape of their unusual arrangement.

And for the first time since she'd entered his home, Kane found himself truly considering the answer he would give, not just to her question about feeding, but to the unspoken one beneath it: what, exactly, would she be to him?

The captured rebel pressed at the edges of his thoughts, a reminder that the conflict was tightening around them. Whatever was forming between him and Serenity would have to survive not only their personal complications, but the danger closing in from every side.

CHAPTER TWENTY-ONE

SERENITY

The moment the words "feeding schedule" left Serenity's lips, the air in the kitchen seemed to crystallize around them. Kane's shoulders tensed, and the temperature in the room dropped perceptibly, as if his vampyric nature had briefly overtaken the space. A flicker crossed his face, fear, or frustration, she couldn't tell, and she immediately regretted raising the topic.

Her hands turned cold despite the warm kitchen, while heat rose to her cheeks and she wished she could take the question back.

He sighed heavily, a sound that carried the weight of centuries. "She said she would contact you tonight to make sure I set it up?"

Serenity nodded silently, not daring to meet his eyes. Her pulse fluttered fast while her fingers twisted beneath the counter, a nervous habit her mother had always tried to break her of.

"Come to my office when you're finished, and we'll take care of it." Without another word or glance, he was gone, leaving nothing but a slight disturbance in the air where he'd stood.

So much for a pleasant dinner. She looked down at her plate. The food that had tasted so good moments ago seemed flavorless now as she tried to muster an appetite. The weight of his displeasure pressed on her shoulders.

This wasn't her fault, a defiant voice rose in her. Why should she feel guilty for doing what Evelyn had asked? The contrition gave way to a spark of irritation.

She was tired of walking on eggshells around vampyrs, first at the clinic, now here. This was a business arrangement, not a social visit; they both had obligations to fulfill.

She gathered their plates and stacked them neatly, the mundane task soothing her jangled nerves. After searching for a container for the leftovers, she loaded the dishwasher as Nox had shown her earlier. The array of buttons and settings remained bewildering, so she left it for later, afraid of making yet another mistake in this unfamiliar territory.

Drawing a breath, she recalled Nox's advice as he'd helped her prepare dinner. *Don't let him intimidate you. His bark is worse than his bite.*

She'd laughed then at the ironic choice of words, but now found herself clinging to them. Kane was a vampyr, not just any vampyr, but the Head of the Human Vampyr Council that governed the entire city. There was no avoiding being intimidated by him, but she would try. For her family's sake, if nothing else.

That reminder straightened her spine as she made her way to his office. She needed to get this over with. Soon she would receive her first payment, which would help her mother and sister get the medicine and treatment they desperately needed. That was all that mattered, not Kane's mood, not his imposing presence, not the strange jolt she felt whenever his eyes met hers.

Still, her feet dragged and her hand trembled as she stood before his office door. Before she could knock, his voice came from inside.

"Come in."

The door clicked open on its own, another reminder of the technological gulf between her world and his. She stood apprehensively at the threshold before stepping in. He sat at his desk, eyes fixed on his screen, the blue light casting sharp shadows across the planes of his face.

She moved closer, unsure of her place in this space that was so clearly his domain. A chair rose from the floor beside her, another bit of luxury and innovation she'd never known in Grove Gardens, where furniture was patched and repaired until it literally fell apart.

"You can have a seat," he said, not looking up.

She obeyed, perching on the edge rather than settling in. Her back stayed straight, a physical sign of her determination not to be cowed. Kane worked at his computer a few more minutes, whether finishing something important or deliberately making her wait, she couldn't tell.

When he finally turned toward her, his silver-blue eyes seemed to see straight through to her core. She squirmed under the weight of his stare, her fingers digging into her palms as she fought to keep her expression neutral.

"Do you understand how feeding is done? Did they explain it to you?" he asked, his voice softer than she expected.

"Yes... sort of." He waited patiently for her to elaborate, his stillness absolute in a way no human could achieve. "You would be... taking blood from one of my arteries. Either my wrist or neck. Every few days, or at least once a week."

The clinical words felt strange in her mouth, at odds with the intimacy they described. In the Outer City, the relationship between Elites and their patrons was the subject of constant speculation and whispered rumor. Some said the feeding was agonizing, others claimed it was euphoric. There were stories of Elites who emerged from their contracts changed, some harder, colder, as if something essential had been drained from them along with their blood. Others supposedly gained a strange glow, a secret knowledge that set them apart from ordinary humans. But these were only rumors, stories passed down through the districts, impossible to verify since no Elite from Grove Gardens had ever returned to tell the truth.

Which would she be?

Kane turned away, clicking a few buttons on his computer, then walked around the desk to stand before her. The space around them seemed to shrink, the air growing heavy with his nearness. He leaned back against the desk, his tall frame looming over her without seeming to intend it.

"My teeth will penetrate your skin, and I will drain one pint of blood," he explained, his tone clinical yet somehow intimate. "It is usually the wrist or neck, but according to the contract, I can take blood from any viable artery of my choosing, as long as it doesn't kill you, and I only take what I need."

Any viable artery? The implication sent unexpected warmth spiraling through her lower abdomen. Unbidden, an image flashed in her mind, Kane's head between her thighs, his lips against the sensitive skin there, tracing the line of her femoral artery. The thought both horrified and thrilled her, sending a shiver racing along her nerves.

She rubbed her thighs together without thinking, trying to banish the inappropriate fantasy. His eyes tracked the movement at once, and she froze. The heat in his gaze shifted from clinical to something darker, more primal, making her breath catch. The familiar signs of vampyric interest flickered across his face, the slight dilation of his pupils, the almost imperceptible parting of his lips, before he mastered himself and went on.

"I'll only need to feed from you once or twice a week, more likely just once."

He pushed off the desk and walked to the window, putting distance between them. Was it for her comfort or his?

"To give us privacy, it will be conducted in your bedroom, where you'll be most comfortable. Unless you would prefer mine?"

The question hung in the air between them, laden with unspoken implication.

She swallowed hard, her throat suddenly parched as she weighed it. The thought of him entering her bedroom, her one sanctuary in this strange place, felt invasive yet oddly intimate, like sharing a secret. But the alternative, being in his private space, surrounded by his scent, his possessions, perhaps even his bed, seemed even more dangerous.

The silence stretched until he spoke again, still gazing out the window. "Let's see how things go. We can start tomorrow at 8 p.m. Make sure you eat and drink beforehand," he instructed, his tone leaving no room for negotiation.

Serenity nodded, then realized he wasn't looking at her. Without thinking, she stood and crossed to him, drawn by some impulse she couldn't name. If they were going to commit such an intimate act together, perhaps they should know each other a little first. The thought of him feeding from her while they remained near strangers felt wrong somehow.

He turned as she approached, a flicker of surprise registering before it smoothed into careful neutrality. His silver-blue eyes raised the hair on her neck, but she held her ground, refusing to look away. She realized with strange certainty that she wasn't afraid of him. Wary, yes; intimidated, certainly; but not afraid. Not in the way she should be.

"Would it be alright if we had dinner together before you..." she trailed off, unsure of the right term. "Feeding" seemed too clinical, "biting" too crude for what would happen between them.

"Before I feed from you," he supplied, the words rolling off his tongue with an ease that reminded her of the vast gulf between their experiences. For him, this was routine; for her, it would be transformative.

Serenity swallowed, feeling the movement of her throat, muscles he would soon be intimately acquainted with. "Yes, before you feed from me."

He didn't speak, only studied her with a focus that made her skin prickle with awareness. Was he trying to read her mind, to discern her motives? Did vampyrs have that ability, or was that just another Outer City myth?

She looked away first, unable to hold the connection without revealing too much of herself. A strange tension hummed in the space between them, neither comfort nor fear.

"If your other dishes are anything like the one you prepared tonight, I'll gladly join you," he finally said, a warmth in his voice she hadn't heard before. "This way, I can also make sure you eat and drink beforehand."

"I can't promise they'll all be as good, but I'll try my best." Looking at him again, she found him still studying her, as if working through a puzzle. She shifted under the scrutiny, feeling transparent and exposed, as if he could see past her carefully built barriers to the confused, frightened girl beneath.

To her surprise, he lifted a hand to her cheek, his touch gentle yet somehow possessive. His skin was cooler than a human's, but not cold, more like the pleasant coolness of a pillow's underside on a warm night. She found herself leaning into the contact, seeking a comfort she hadn't expected to find in his touch.

Her heart skipped as their eyes locked. She couldn't help being drawn to him despite their situation, despite the voice in her head screaming that this was dangerous, foolish, reckless. He was a vampyr, powerful, ancient, lethal, and soon he would feed on her blood. She should be holding him at an emotional distance, not craving his touch. But something about him made her feel paradoxically safe, as if the very danger he embodied somehow guaranteed her protection from every other threat.

"Great, then it's settled," he said, his smile transforming his severe features.

Serenity nodded, unable to find her voice. She felt caught in a web of her own making, unable to escape the spell that seemed to form whenever they were close. He was so near that she could catch the subtle scent of him, cedar and night air, ancient and masculine. She could easily reach up and press her lips to his, closing the small distance between them.

But she didn't.

Remember why you're here. Remember who's depending on you.

She took a step back, breaking the contact. She couldn't afford to grow attached to Kane, couldn't risk the complications it would bring. He was using her for her blood; she was using him for the credits that would save her family. It was a transaction, nothing more.

Whatever she felt wasn't real, she told herself firmly. It was the strange circumstances, the stress, the isolation from everything familiar.

"Okay," she said softly, looking at the ground, unable to meet his eyes without revealing the war raging within her.

She was about to turn away when his hand shot out, catching hers in a grip that was firm yet gentle. Before she could process what was happening, he pulled her toward him, the movement so swift human eyes could barely track it.

Serenity gasped as she stumbled forward, finding herself pressed against his hard, muscular frame. The sudden nearness sent a shock through her, part alarm, part exhilaration. He gazed down at her with a heat that blazed through her defenses, igniting a response she couldn't control. The hunger in his eyes went straight to her core, dissolving every rational thought in a wave of pure sensation.

His lips descended on hers in a searing kiss that obliterated every boundary she'd tried to build between them. The touch lit a fire in her unlike anything she'd known before, not the tentative fumbling with Jax, not the occasional intimate dreams that left her flushed and confused on waking. This was consuming, overwhelming, devouring.

She was lost in him, in the feel of his mouth on hers, the press of his body against her own. It was as if he were claiming her, marking her as his in a way more fundamental than any contract could establish. Her body answered instinctively, molding to his, seeking more of the intoxicating contact.

A moan escaped her as his hand traced down her back, pulling her closer until there was no space left between them. The world beyond them ceased to exist, no Council, no Outer City, no sick mother or hungry sister. There was only this moment, this connection, this dizzying surrender.

This is wrong, a distant part of her mind protested. You're here for your family, not for this. He's a vampyr. You're human. This can only end badly.

But the voice was drowned out by the roar of blood in her ears, the desperate pounding of her heart. Her hands clutched at his shirt, fingers tangling in the smooth fabric as she pulled him closer, deepening the kiss. She felt rather than saw the world tilt around them, as if reality itself were bending to accommodate the impossible thing happening between them.

His sharp fangs grazed her lower lip, not breaking the skin, but a promise, a reminder of what he was and what tomorrow would bring. The contact sent electric tingles racing down her spine, drawing another soft sound from her throat. The sensation was so unexpectedly erotic that her knees nearly buckled.

She surrendered to his embrace, letting him take complete control. In one swift motion he lifted her, and she instinctively wrapped her legs around his waist. Their hungry kisses only deepened, growing more desperate, more primal. She could feel the evidence of his desire pressed against her, and answering heat pooled low in her belly, shocking in its force.

But as suddenly as it began, it ended. He pulled away and gently let her legs slide back to the floor, steadying her as she swayed. She was left gasping, disoriented by the abrupt shift from passion to separation.

"I'm sorry," he whispered, his eyes still blazing with barely leashed desire. "I shouldn't have done that."

The words fell like ice water on her heated skin. As the spell broke and reality reasserted itself, Serenity became acutely aware of where they were, what they'd done, what lines they'd crossed. She stumbled back, confusion and embarrassment flooding her.

Her heart kept up its frantic rhythm, and the longing that had been briefly satisfied now burned anew, stronger for having been acknowledged. She wanted to reach for him, to ask what this meant, for her, for him, for their arrangement. But words failed her, trapped behind the lump forming in her throat.

"Kane," she started, her voice barely audible, "we shouldn't—"

"I know," he cut in, his voice rough with restrained emotion. His silver-blue eyes, still luminous with vampyric arousal, held regret and something deeper, more complex, an emotion she couldn't decipher. He stepped back further, running a hand through his dark hair, now mussed from her fingers.

The space between them felt both too vast and not vast enough. She wrapped her arms around herself, suddenly cold in the absence of his heat. Vulnerability washed over her as her mind whirled, guilt at betraying her purpose here, desire still throbbing insistently through her veins, confusion about what had just happened.

Her family's faces flashed in her mind, her mother's lined face drawn with pain, her sister's too-thin frame, both of them depending on her to fulfill this contract and send home the credits that would save their lives. She wasn't here to indulge in forbidden romance; she was here to ensure their survival. The realization sent a wave of shame through her.

Kane's expression softened as he watched the struggle play out across her features. "It's okay," she said softly, finding her voice at last. "We were both caught up in the moment."

"Please forget it happened," he said gently, his tone almost apologetic.

"Okay," she murmured, avoiding his gaze, knowing it for a lie even as she spoke. How could she forget the way her body had ignited at his touch? The way something in her had recognized something in him, like two halves finding their match? These weren't sensations she could easily dismiss or forget.

He stepped further away, widening the physical distance between them as if that could somehow erase what had occurred.

Serenity nodded, her heart still hammering, her lips still tingling from his kiss. Pretending it never happened was probably best for both of them, but she couldn't suppress the sadness that settled in her chest at the thought.

He cleared his throat, drawing her attention back to the present. Kane turned away, his broad shoulders rigid beneath his expensive shirt. When he faced her again, his eyes had regained their usual icy detachment, every trace of the passionate man who'd held her moments ago carefully concealed behind a professional mask.

"Any other questions?" he asked, his voice formal and distant.

"Not at the moment," Serenity replied, matching his tone though it cost her real effort to seem so unaffected.

"Then you may go. Now you can happily report to Evelyn that we've made a schedule." He returned to his desk, sitting with precise movements. "I have work to do." With that dismissal, he began typing, effectively ending their conversation.

She walked toward the door on unsteady legs, as if moving through water. As she opened it, she paused, some impulse making her turn back. "Thank you for joining me for dinner tonight," she said, the simple courtesy a poor substitute for everything she couldn't say.

Then she was through the door before he could reply, unwilling to see whether her words had any effect on his carefully rebuilt composure.

The corridor seemed longer than she remembered, the walk to her room an exercise in keeping her dignity when all she wanted was to collapse against the wall and process what had happened. Her keycard shook in her hand as she unlocked the door, a testament to her unsettled state.

Once inside, she leaned back against the closed door and brought a trembling hand to her lips. They still tingled from his kiss, the sensation a physical proof that she hadn't imagined what had passed between them.

Serenity squeezed her eyes shut, giving herself a moment. Her heart kept its erratic rhythm, her body still humming with unfulfilled desire. The memory of

Kane's hands on her, his mouth against hers, the feel of his body pressed to her own, it all swirled through her mind in a dizzying loop.

It was foolish. It was dangerous. They came from different worlds, different species even. Their relationship was contractual: she provided blood, he provided credits. Anything beyond that would only complicate an already precarious situation.

Yet she couldn't deny the pull she felt toward him, a magnetic draw that seemed to override her common sense. Even now, part of her wanted to return to his office, to finish what they'd started, consequences be damned.

In Grove Gardens, those who formed relationships with vampyrs were viewed with suspicion at best, revulsion at worst. "Blood whores," they were called behind their backs, humans who gave more than was contractually required, who took pleasure in the exchange. Would she become one of them? Would she be unable to look her neighbors in the eye when she returned home?

Standing in the luxurious room that was temporarily hers, Serenity reminded herself of her purpose: to save her family and secure their future. Falling for Kane Draccus, leader of the Human Vampyr Council and a man from such a different world, had never been part of the plan.

But fate, it seemed, had a way of weaving its own pattern, heedless of anyone's careful design.

Before she could even turn on the water for her shower, her cell device beeped, the strange sound still unfamiliar to her ears. It was Evelyn, her timing either impeccable or terrible, depending on one's perspective.

The conversation was brief. First Evelyn asked whether Kane had made a feeding schedule. Once Serenity confirmed he had, Evelyn seemed satisfied, telling her she'd see her next week and to call if she needed anything in the meantime.

Serenity should have asked how to operate the unfamiliar device before Evelyn hung up, but her mind was too preoccupied. She decided she'd ask Nox instead when she saw him next. Perhaps she could bribe him with another meal before asking her questions.

She'd discovered Nox's secret love of human food by accident, finding his cookbooks tucked in one of the kitchen cabinets. Her persistent questioning had eventually worn down his resistance. Though he'd called her annoying, he'd ultimately shown her his favorite recipes once she revealed she could cook.

Gathering fresh clothes, simple cotton pajamas that felt coarse compared to the silk nightgowns Evelyn had insisted on buying her, Serenity headed for the shower at last.

As the warm water cascaded over her, reality struck anew. Tomorrow night, Kane would take her blood. The clinical language of their discussion didn't do justice to the intimacy of what would occur, his mouth on her skin, his teeth piercing her flesh, the exchange of life between them.

She touched her thigh beneath the spray, feeling for the strong beat of her femoral artery. It was so close to her most private place, where heat still lingered from earlier. Her imagination took flight again, Kane kneeling before her, his lips tracing the sensitive skin, seeking just the right spot.

This is madness, she thought, forcing herself to focus on washing rather than fantasy. Kane wasn't a potential lover; he was her patron. Their relationship was defined by contract, not passion. Whatever had happened in his office had been a momentary lapse, one that couldn't be repeated.

Reluctantly, Serenity turned off the shower and dried herself briskly. She pulled on her pajamas and climbed into the too-soft bed, her body still humming with unsatisfied desire.

As she lay in the dark, staring at the shadowed ceiling, she tried to redirect her thoughts to her family, to her mother's face when she received the first payment, to her sister's improved health once the medicine arrived. But Kane's face kept intruding, his silver-blue eyes haunting her even as exhaustion began to claim her.

In the space between waking and sleep, the boundaries blurred. She dreamed of Kane standing in her family's small home in Grove Gardens, his imposing figure somehow not out of place in the humble surroundings. In the dream, her mother smiled at him without fear, her sister laughed at something he said, and Serenity herself felt a contentment that had eluded her in waking life.

It was impossible, of course, worlds colliding in a way reality would never permit, but in dreams the impossible became tangible, if only for a moment.

With his name still echoing in her mind and the phantom sensation of his kiss still on her lips, Serenity finally surrendered to sleep, unaware that in the apartment's security room, cameras kept their silent vigil, and somewhere in the shadows of Celearius, forces moved that would soon test every connection she thought she understood.

CHAPTER TWENTY-TWO

KANE

Kane forced himself to focus on the rebellion report spread across his desk. The words blurred as his mind replayed the kiss, Serenity's soft lips, the way she'd melted against him, her fingers tangling in his hair. He ran a hand through that same hair now, the memory making his energy field crackle, sending papers fluttering.

Concentrate. Lives depended on these reports. The rebellion was escalating faster than the Council acknowledged, yet his thoughts circled back to her like a moth to flame.

What struck him wasn't just her courage in approaching him; it was how she'd looked at him. Despite everything Grove Gardens must have taught her about vampyrs, she'd shown no cowering, no pleading. Only quiet determination and something that looked remarkably like recognition, as if part of her had known he wouldn't harm her.

The memory of their first meeting at the clinic resurfaced. Her fear had been present but controlled, tempered by a resolve that ran bone-deep. So different from the terror-stricken humans who'd first volunteered as Elites after the war, their heartbeats hammering so loudly they'd filled entire rooms.

His pen scratched across the margin as he made a note about increased coordination in the attacks. The rebels were growing more strategic, more sophisticated.

This wasn't random violence anymore; it was calculated warfare designed to destabilize the fragile peace between species.

A distant memory surfaced of those early post-war days when he and Evie had drafted the Elite program. Rhyzan had been skeptical from the start. "Voluntary blood donation? You're both naïve. They'll never agree."

But they had agreed. The program had given both species a framework they could understand, willing blood donation in exchange for credits and protection. The element of choice was supposed to make the arrangement palatable.

Yet here he was, decades later, facing a rebellion that suggested their "solution" had merely created new forms of oppression. The realization sat heavily in his chest.

Kane's attention snapped back to the present as his cell device buzzed with Evelyn's distinctive tone. He stared at it a moment, weighing whether to ignore the call, but experience had taught him she would simply appear at his door if he didn't answer.

"Yes, Evie," he said, not bothering to hide his irritation.

"Let me guess," her voice came through crisp and knowing. "You're buried in reports and don't have time to talk. Make time."

"Why do I put up with you?" he asked, a reluctant trace of amusement coloring his words.

"Because I'm the only one who can take you in a fight," she retorted.

"You mean the only one I'll let take me in a fight," Kane countered, allowing himself a small smile.

"Same thing," Evelyn replied. "I'm checking in about Serenity. She mentioned you made a feeding schedule."

Kane glanced at the rebellion files, dread pooling in his stomach. "I appreciate your concern, but I can handle this."

"I know you understand the importance of keeping to the schedule," Evie said, her tone shifting to something more serious. "I won't check up on you constantly, but I need your word you'll follow through."

"You have it," he promised, touched despite his irritation by her genuine concern.

After ending the call, Kane tried to return to work. His focus lasted roughly seven minutes before Rhyzan's familiar stride echoed in the corridor. Kane didn't look up when his office door opened; only one person entered without knocking.

"I see you've entertained company," Rhy remarked, settling into the chair across from Kane's desk. He inhaled deeply, his enhanced senses cataloging the lingering scents. "The Elite was in your office. That's... unprecedented."

Kane's eyes narrowed. "Meaning?"

"Meaning I've never known you to allow an Elite into your sanctuary before." Rhy's knowing smirk was insufferable. "Didn't realize this one was special enough to warrant an exception."

The air pressure rose slightly as Kane reined in his irritation. "Why are you here, Rhy?"

Rhy's demeanor shifted to professional efficiency. "The silver from the crime scene. Sullivan found a connection."

Interest sparked through Kane's distraction. "What kind of connection?"

"The silver doesn't match any known mine in our database. Analysis turned up traces of vanadium, a rare mineral found in only a few places globally. One happens to be a processing facility in the abandoned section outside Grove Gardens."

Kane's mind raced. Grove Gardens. Serenity's district. In his experience, there were rarely true coincidences in an investigation of this magnitude. The timing felt deliberate, purposeful.

"So the silver was smuggled out of Grove Gardens?" he pressed, keeping his tone neutral despite the implications.

"Strong possibility. Sullivan's assembling a team to investigate." Rhy leaned forward. "This could be our breakthrough."

Kane rose, his decision made. "I want immediate updates on every development."

They drove through the changing districts in Kane's sedan, the transition from administrative towers to industrial complexes marking the shift in power structures. The Steel District bustled with human workers loading trucks with materials for the walls that separated Celearius from the wastelands beyond, a constant reminder of how precarious their civilization was.

Kane's enhanced senses captured everything: the metallic tang in the air, the elevated heartbeats of the night-shift workers, the grinding of machinery that never slept. The contrast between the polished administrative sector and the raw industrial energy reminded him why the alliance between their species was worth preserving, however strained.

At Sullivan's laboratory, the vampyr intelligence officer sat behind a desk groaning under evidence folders. His pale features stayed perfectly still as they entered, the unnatural immobility of their kind.

"Kane, Rhyzan," Sullivan greeted them, the silver flecks in his dark eyes catching the light. "I wasn't expecting you in person."

"The Grove Gardens connection warrants immediate attention," Kane replied, choosing to stand. His height let him survey the files spread across Sullivan's desk, his enhanced vision catching details from a distance. "What's the current status?"

"We're assembling a team to investigate the factory. Given the sensitive nature, I'm personally selecting the personnel. Preliminary findings within seventy-two hours."

Kane and Rhy exchanged a glance; the timeline was optimistic at best.

"The vanadium trace is our strongest lead," Kane observed carefully, "but I sense there's more to this than a single source."

Sullivan's pupils contracted slightly, a vampyric response to heightened attention. "Nothing concrete. We're exploring every angle, but solid evidence remains elusive."

It was the expected answer, yet it did nothing to ease Kane's certainty that crucial information was being withheld. The slight stilling of Sullivan's already minimal breathing suggested concealed knowledge.

"Contact me the moment you discover anything significant," Kane instructed, layering his voice with natural authority. "This situation is developing faster than the Council acknowledges. We need to stay ahead of it."

During the drive back, Kane methodically sorted through months of accumulated intelligence, hunting for the pattern that kept eluding him. The silver from Grove Gardens, the timing of the attacks, the choice of targets, individually explainable, but collectively pointing to a strategy he hadn't yet deciphered.

"Rhy," he said as they reached his office, "I need to review the complete file series again."

Back in his office, Kane began pulling files from his secure cabinet, spreading them across his desk. Rhy leaned against the wall, watching him pace between documents.

"When did you last feed properly?" Rhy asked after several minutes of observation.

Kane glanced up, surprised. "That's not relevant to the investigation."

"It's entirely relevant if hunger is impairing your judgment," Rhy countered. "You're no use to anyone if you collapse from neglecting basic needs."

The remark echoed Evie's concern. Having both his oldest friends voice the same worry suggested there might be truth to it.

"I'm fine," Kane said dismissively, returning to the files.

Rhy sighed, a sound carrying centuries of exasperation. "Maybe we need a different approach. We should use Sebastian."

It wasn't the first time Rhy had suggested involving Evie's Elite. For months he'd pushed for aggressive investigation into Sebastian's potential rebellion connections, though clear evidence had never materialized.

The suggestion touched on complex webs of loyalty and ethics. Using an Elite for political purposes without his full knowledge violated principles Kane had established when creating the program.

"You want me to use Evie's Elite as an unwitting asset? Absolutely not."

Rhy pushed away from the wall, his expression earnest. "Sebastian's position gives him unique access and credibility. He could infiltrate circles that would be instantly suspicious of Council connections. If he's not already involved, and I've seen no definitive evidence, he wouldn't be in real danger."

Kane's mind calculated probabilities automatically. Sebastian's background in Grove Gardens, combined with his Elite status, did place him uniquely to gather intelligence from both worlds.

But involving Sebastian would inevitably complicate things with Evie. Their friendship had weathered many storms, but this could open a rift when unity was essential.

If they were truly approaching open conflict between species, could he afford to put personal ethics over preventing war?

"Fine," Kane conceded reluctantly after a long silence. "But we proceed with extreme caution. Sebastian's safety is paramount, and Evie must be informed, though convincing her will be my responsibility."

Rhy's expression brightened with satisfaction. "I'll draft potential scenarios."

Kane nodded, already dreading the conversation with Evie. As Rhy outlined preliminary plans, Kane kept reviewing evidence files, his mind divided between the immediate investigation and the diplomatic fallout to come.

"A little bird told me you ate human food today," Rhy remarked with deceptive casualness. "The Elite cooked for you."

Kane's head snapped up, identifying the likely source. Nox. His supposedly loyal security officer had been sharing details of his private interactions.

"I'm going to terminate his employment," Kane muttered, only half joking.

Rhy laughed, a sound almost as rare as Kane's own. "Does this mean you have a particular interest in this Elite?" His smirk suggested he already knew the answer.

The question strayed into territory Kane had been compartmentalizing all evening. A flicker of real concern beneath Rhy's teasing made him answer more honestly than intended.

"She seems... different from previous Elites," he said carefully.

"Different how?"

The question invited a self-disclosure Kane rarely permitted. He shook his head, unwilling to put words to the confusing mix of attraction, protectiveness, and respect Serenity stirred in him. "Focus on developing our Sebastian strategy."

"So you admit there are personal matters to consider?" Rhy emphasized the phrase with obvious delight.

Kane felt a flare of irritation that made the lights flicker briefly. "We have more important matters than your misinterpretations."

Rhy held up his hands in mock surrender, though his smile remained. "Remember that you can't hold those walls forever, Kane. Eventually, someone will find their way through. Or perhaps already has."

The observation landed closer to the truth than Kane cared to admit. As Rhy rose to leave, Kane felt something between apprehension and reluctant hope.

"You'll need to spend time getting to know her better regardless," Rhy said, pausing at the door. "Elite-patron relationships run more smoothly with basic familiarity." He hesitated, then added gently, "Just because you've had bad experiences doesn't mean every connection is doomed. Some of the most successful pairings began with reluctance on both sides."

"Goodbye, Rhyzan," Kane replied gruffly.

"Don't forget what I said. You have only one life, eternal though it seems. Don't spend all of it in solitude because of old wounds."

With that, he closed the door, leaving Kane exactly where he'd started, surrounded by urgent work yet unable to banish thoughts of Serenity.

As night deepened, Kane wondered if Rhy might be right. Perhaps it was time to risk opening himself to connection again, despite the vulnerabilities such openness invited. Tomorrow night, he would feed from Serenity for the first time. Among his kind, feeding sometimes forged a blood bond between vampyr and donor, a rare thing, far from guaranteed. He couldn't say whether it would happen with her. Part of him suspected it might.

Perhaps that would be the beginning of something far more significant than either of them anticipated. Or perhaps it would be one more transaction in a life full of them.

The rebellion files spread before him seemed to mock his contemplation. Grove Gardens, silver weapons, coordinated attacks, all pointing to a conspiracy that threatened everything he'd worked to build. Somewhere in that web of violence and betrayal, the answers waited.

But tonight, as he finally closed the files and prepared to retire, Kane found himself thinking less about rebels and more about honey-brown eyes that looked at him without fear, and the dangerous hope that perhaps, this time, things might be different.

Time would tell. And time was the one resource Kane had in abundance, assuming the growing rebellion didn't cut his eternal existence short first.

CHAPTER TWENTY-THREE

SERENITY

The clock hands crawled toward seven as Serenity tried to keep busy, though concentration proved impossible without the comfort of home. She missed her mother and sister desperately and had been trying to reach them through Rack n' Reynolds with the cellular device, without success.

Just as she was about to give up, a strange message appeared on the screen.

We know who you are. You can help us. Meet by the fountain in the Diamond District.

Serenity's heart hammered as she sat up. The text glowed with an eerie blue light, unlike the device's normal display. She read and reread it, fingers trembling. Who were they? How did they know her? Why did they need her help? The Diamond District was where wealthy vampyrs conducted business, a place Elites rarely ventured without their patrons.

The message lingered only seconds before vanishing, leaving no trace. She frantically tapped the screen, trying to bring it back, but couldn't. In frustration she threw the device, then quickly retrieved it, relieved it hadn't broken.

Sitting on her bed, mind racing, she tried to make sense of the words. A glitch, maybe? Or sent to the wrong person. That had to be it. Yet she couldn't shake the feeling that something deliberate lay behind how the message had appeared and disappeared. She recalled whispered rumors in Grove Gardens about resistance groups working against the vampyr establishment. Was someone trying to recruit her? If so, why her? She was nobody special, just a girl from the poor district whose only notable quality was her rare blood.

The thought seemed ridiculous. What would rebels want with an Elite? She pushed the worry aside, turning to the more practical problem of learning to use the device.

Maybe she should ask Nox.

Leaving her room, she went looking for him and ran into Kane instead. He was stepping out of his office when she crashed into his imposing form. Cedar and leather, and beneath it something distinctly metallic. Blood? The scents filled her nose.

Kane moved swiftly, catching her waist and pulling her toward him. His strong hands held her firmly, keeping her from falling. The cool touch of his fingers sent shivers down her spine.

"Are you okay?" Kane asked, his voice husky and low.

Serenity nodded, unable to form coherent words. His touch lit a fire in her; she couldn't resist the pull toward him. The mysterious message was momentarily forgotten in his presence.

He seemed to notice his effect on her, his lips curving into a small smile. "What... or who were you looking for?" The slight emphasis on "who" carried a possessive undertone she hadn't noticed before.

Serenity flushed, embarrassed about her earlier panic. She hesitated. Should she tell him about the strange message? Would he believe her? Or would he think she was trying to contact someone without permission?

She tried to step away, but his arm kept her close, holding the uncomfortable nearness.

"I was looking for Nox," she managed.

Kane's grip tightened slightly. His expression turned unreadable, but his eyes darkened with something that set her heart racing.

"Why do you need Nox?" Kane asked, an undertone of displeasure in his voice.

As they stood close, his gaze dropped to her lips, and she couldn't remember what she'd meant to say. The air between them crackled.

His eyes flicked back to hers as he leaned closer. Heat radiated from his body; despite the vampyr reputation for coldness, Kane gave off a surprising warmth.

Abruptly, he pulled back, leaving her wanting. His silver eyes bored into hers, and she glimpsed uncertainty mixed with desire, a mirror of the feelings swirling inside her.

His thumb traced over her bottom lip before he drew his hand away. His silver eyes flickered with an unreadable emotion as he watched her, shoulders tensing like a predator holding itself in check.

"I need to speak with him about something important," Serenity finally whispered.

Kane's features softened. "You'll find him getting the car ready. I'm on my way out." He looked at her a moment before turning away, his footsteps making no sound, another reminder of what he was.

She watched him go, caught by the lines of his broad shoulders and muscular frame. Longing pulled at her as he moved toward the elevator, and she couldn't tell whether he felt the same draw.

"Wait!" she blurted.

Kane stopped, his shoulders tightening as he turned back. His gaze held such force it sent a tingling warmth through her.

"I wanted to contact my mom and sister, but I'm not sure how to use the cellular device." She left out any mention of the strange message, deciding to speak with Nox first.

He raised an eyebrow. "Do your mom or sister own a cellular device?"

She shook her head. "No." The word hung heavily between them, a reminder of the stark divide between their worlds.

"Then they would need to purchase one before you could call. I'll send them one and have Nox teach them how to use it." His tone was matter-of-fact, but the offer was extraordinary.

Joy lit Serenity's face. Before she realized it, she was in his arms, squeezing him tightly. His scent, cedar and leather threaded with something that was only his, wrapped around her.

"Thank you!" she murmured into his shoulder. "You have no idea how happy this makes me." She felt the brief tensing of his body at her embrace.

He looked down with a slight grin as she pulled away. "I'm glad I could help. But there's one condition." His tone shifted, taking on an edge that sent a pleasant shiver down her spine.

"What's that?" she asked softly.

"Make me something delicious tonight," he said, his grin sliding into a smirk. "Consider it payment for the cellular device."

Heat flushed her cheeks, leaving her briefly speechless. She didn't understand what was happening between them. Why was he being so considerate? Most

Elites served patrons who treated them as decorative servants. Yet Kane seemed different.

She lowered her gaze, then lifted it to meet his, nodding. "Of course. I'll make you something you'll never forget."

His smirk deepened, and warmth pooled low in her. She knew she wasn't supposed to feel this way about him, he was her patron, she should be focused on survival, but she couldn't help it.

As she turned to walk away, his hand touched her arm, stopping her.

"You know you can visit your family soon. You are not a prisoner here. You're an employee. The two weeks are an adjustment period." His words were gentle but firm.

Serenity was stunned. "I thought it was up to... my patron."

"I am your patron, and if you read the contract, you'd see it states that clearly. Most contracts include this, but it's at the Elite's discretion after the two weeks."

So all those Elites who never came back had chosen not to. She wondered how many had voluntarily decided not to see their families again, perhaps ashamed to return after accepting luxury while their families struggled.

"I wasn't aware of that part, but thank you for telling me."

He sighed. "I'll make sure you get a copy of the contract, so you know all the details."

Kane moved in a blur, and before she knew it, he was gone. The air displaced by his movement brushed her cheek like a phantom touch.

Serenity couldn't make sense of any of it. The warmth low in her body had sharpened into something more insistent, kindled by that smirk. She tried to push the feelings away, but they only grew stronger by the day.

She needed to speak with Nox, to learn the device and find out whether he might know anything about the strange message. It had felt too specific, too targeted to be random. Someone knew who she was, knew her father's legacy. The thought both terrified and intrigued her.

Drawing a breath, she decided to make breakfast while waiting for Nox to return. The familiar routine would clear her mind and maybe help her decide whether to mention the message at all.

Nearly an hour later, Nox finally appeared. He found Serenity inspecting movie discs in the theater, her fingers grazing the glossy cases as she tried to make sense of each title.

She'd never seen a movie before, having only heard about the theaters in vampyr districts. In her district, such entertainment was a frivolous luxury.

"Find anything you like?" His voice startled her, and she jumped.

She whipped around, eyes blazing. "Don't do that!"

A smirk surfaced and vanished, replaced by his usual stoic expression. "I heard you needed help with your cellular device." He pulled a random disc from the shelf and slotted it into the wall system.

Serenity sat on the plush couch, eyes glued to the massive screen as it came to life. The walls seemed to vibrate as dramatic music swelled.

"I guess there's no urgency," Nox said, but she didn't dare look away, absorbed in the images. She would ask about the message later.

When she emerged hours later, she was both horrified and awed. The movie portrayed vampyrs as horrific beasts who terrorized innocents, at least at first. It raised questions about the relationship between humans and vampyrs. The Elite system was presented as a civilized evolution, but the violence felt recent, possible.

Finding Nox on the treadmill in the gym, she stepped into his line of sight as he slowed.

"And you had me watch that because?"

He huffed for breath and shrugged. "Seemed like a good idea at the time."

"Seriously?"

"Plus, I heard it was a good movie."

She gaped at him. "I thought movies like that would be banned. Doesn't it give away vampyr secrets?"

"You already know we walk in daylight and have super strength. And that we're devilishly handsome." A smile appeared before settling back into neutrality. "Besides, humans have been making up stories about us for centuries. Most get it wrong. The truth is much more... complicated."

"I'll meet you in the kitchen in fifteen minutes. Bring your device."

She cursed under her breath, remembering she'd left it on the chair. The message. She still needed to ask him about it.

In the kitchen, Nox arrived precisely fifteen minutes later, finding her bent over the device, pressing buttons at random.

"And that is how you break it?" He chuckled, plucking the device from her fingers and demonstrating proper use.

For the next hour he patiently walked her through the basics. Each device had an assigned number; hers was 2224, Nox's was 2036. He showed her how to call by entering numbers and storing contacts. Evelyn, Rhyzan, and Kane's numbers were already saved.

He demonstrated text messaging; messages had to be short and to the point. The vampyr communication network was efficient but limited.

"U. r. an. ass." she typed to him with a mischievous grin. "Like that?"

"Exactly." He laughed, then entered three more numbers.

As he finished, the message tugged at her mind again. Should she mention it? Would he report it to Kane? But if something strange was happening with her device, he needed to know.

"Nox," she began uncertainly, "I got a strange message earlier. It said something like 'We know who you are. Meet by the fountain in the Diamond District.' But when I tried to find it again, it had vanished." She watched his face carefully.

Nox's brow furrowed, his expression turning serious. The easy rapport vanished, replaced by tense alertness. "A message? From whom?" His voice lost its warmth, going clipped and professional.

"I don't know," Serenity admitted, worrying her lower lip. "It appeared out of nowhere and disappeared seconds later. I couldn't get it back. And it looked... different. The text had this strange blue glow."

With deft taps, Nox navigated the device, his eyes scanning with laser focus. His fingers moved faster than she could follow, opening menus she hadn't seen. The kitchen suddenly felt too quiet.

After what seemed an eternity, he looked up, his brow creased with concern. "There's no record of any such message in your device history. Are you sure?"

Serenity hesitated, doubt creeping in. The message had seemed so real, so urgent. But faced with his questioning gaze and no evidence, she began to second-guess herself.

"I... I thought I saw it," she said, her voice wavering. "But maybe it was a dream. I'd fallen asleep before it happened." She didn't entirely believe that, but it was easier than insisting on something she couldn't prove.

Nox studied her closely. After a long moment, he nodded slowly, though something in his expression said he wasn't entirely convinced. "It's possible. The mind can play tricks, especially between sleep and waking."

Relief washed over her, even as part of her refused to let the message go. The Diamond District. That was a specific detail her mind wouldn't conjure without reason.

"If you receive any unusual messages in the future," Nox said seriously, "I want you to tell me immediately."

Serenity nodded, cradling the device. "I understand. I'll let you know if anything strange happens again."

"Good." Nox stood, his posture easing slightly. But she noticed how his eyes lingered on the device longer than necessary.

"So this is ICP, this is Kane's office, but what's this number?" Serenity asked, scrolling through the contacts he'd entered, curious why one had no name.

"You should call it tomorrow night and find out," Nox said.

"You'll see. I have to go now. I'll be back with him at 7 p.m. That gives you a few hours to cook something delicious."

Panic began to set in. What was she going to cook? Why had she agreed to dinner?

A number appeared on her screen. "If you need anything from the grocery store, I'm sending you the number. They can be here within twenty minutes. Just be sure to tell them you're Kane's Elite."

She nodded, flashing a grateful smile. "Thank you for this, Nox."

He grinned before turning to leave, darting around the corner with vampyr speed.

"And don't forget," he called over his shoulder, "save me some dinner!"

"Definitely," she replied with a laugh.

She played with the device a little longer, then turned her mind to what to make. The strange message still nagged at the edge of her thoughts, and more than once she caught herself glancing at the screen, half expecting that eerie blue glow to return.

Flipping through one of Nox's cookbooks, she wanted something special for Kane, something she'd never tried before. The pages were filled with dishes from regions she'd never visited, using ingredients that had been luxuries in her district. She settled on garlic butter shrimp linguine, simple enough, with most of the ingredients on hand except the shrimp.

She called the grocery store, the efficient voice on the other end asking after her preferences and suggesting an artisanal bread. These courtesies, the deference once she mentioned being "Kane's Elite," were jarring.

To pass the time until six, she watched another movie, a lighthearted story about humans with no mention of vampyrs at all. Strange, to see a world where her kind existed without the shadow of vampyr rule.

When she began cooking, the kitchen filled with garlic and seafood as she sautéed shrimp until golden, boiled the pasta to al dente, then tossed everything together with butter, salt, pepper, and fresh parsley. The colors were vibrant, pink shrimp, golden butter sauce, bright flecks of green parsley.

She set the table for three with sleek black plates and crystal glasses, filling a pitcher with water. The dark wood of the dining table reflected the soft light above. She smiled, proud of her work, hoping Kane and Nox would enjoy it.

Heat rose in her cheeks at the memory of how Kane had looked at her with those deep silver-blue eyes. There was something ancient in that gaze, something that spoke of experiences far beyond her understanding.

She set the pot on the warmer and sat in the library, watching the clock inch toward seven. The rich scent of leather-bound books surrounded her, another luxury she'd never known. The wait was agonizing until she heard the elevator ding, and her pulse leapt.

He was finally here. Despite the confusion, the fear, the lingering unease from the message, she couldn't deny the thrill at the sound of his arrival.

But beneath the excitement, the questions lingered. Someone knew who she was, knew enough to reach out to her specifically. Whether dream or reality, the message hinted at something larger, threads connecting to her father's work, to forces moving in shadows beyond Kane's elegant world. For tonight, though, she would focus on Kane and the growing connection between them that both thrilled and terrified her. The message could wait.

But as the elevator dinged, announcing his arrival, that strange blue glow flickered again at the edge of memory, refusing to be entirely dismissed.

CHAPTER TWENTY-FOUR

KANE

Kane's hunger raged through his body, barely contained by his skin. It started at his core and radiated outward until his fingertips tingled with it. He'd been fighting to hide it all day, and the craving only sharpened, threatening to burn through his restraint.

A memory surfaced unbidden: Budapest, the last time he'd felt hunger this severe. He'd been younger then, barely two centuries into existence, when a sword had opened his abdomen during a territorial dispute. The blood loss had triggered a hunger so profound he'd decimated an entire tavern before regaining his senses.

The Council had been merciful, citing his youth and the provocation. But their warning had been clear: a second incident would mean execution.

He pushed the memory away. This was different. He hadn't been injured. There was no logical explanation for this insatiable craving.

Desperate for relief, he drank six blood bags in one sitting and remained unsatisfied. Type O negative, usually his preferred sustenance, tasted flat and lifeless. The synthetic additives left a metallic aftertaste that made him grimace. Still, he'd expected it to at least dull the edge.

He drained the last bag, feeling a primal surge as he emptied it. For a brief instant the craving subsided, and he exhaled. But the respite vanished with a troubling realization: he'd never consumed so much blood at once, not since his first century after turning.

And yet it had barely dulled his hunger.

An ominous certainty settled over Kane as he stared at the empty bags. The edges of his vision shimmered with a faint red glow, the first sign his system was tipping toward bloodlust. He knew what this insatiable thirst meant. It wouldn't be satisfied until he had her.

The thought filled him with dread as his mind drifted to Serenity. He wanted her. In more ways than one. It wasn't just bloodlust; it was possession, protection, desire, emotions he'd thought himself incapable of feeling.

His resolve to avoid her had shattered the moment he kissed her. He could still taste her on his lips, feel the warmth of her body pressed to his. Every detail remained vivid in his memory. The recollection alone reignited the hunger, sending his senses into overdrive.

Kane couldn't afford to slip. He clenched his fists, fighting to suppress the relentless ache before it consumed him. His fangs had begun to lengthen on their own, a response he hadn't had outside feeding since his early years. The space behind his eyes burned, a sure sign the silver in his irises was brightening.

Evie's warning from earlier echoed in his mind. *There's something unusual about your reaction to her, Kane. If you keep resisting, the hunger will only grow worse. You must either resolve this or transfer her contract immediately.*

He'd dismissed her concern. Whatever was happening, there had to be a logical explanation.

The thought of feeding from her tonight was driving him mad. He could almost taste her blood, yet he knew he couldn't give in. He'd seen what happened when vampyrs lost control; the results could be deadly. Especially if a blood bond was forming, the first taste might trigger a frenzy he couldn't stop.

The thought of hurting Serenity was unbearable. Even here, in his office miles from his residence, he could detect traces of her, citrus and vanilla, underlaid with the unique scent of her blood. It was as if some part of his consciousness stayed perpetually aware of her, locked onto her presence like a beacon.

There was one way to sate his thirst with a willing donor, but he hated the option. It violated the Treaty that governed vampyr-human relations. The donors were willing, but only because their families were paid when they died.

Vincent. The name alone curled his lip in disgust.

The last time Kane had used Vincent's services had been before the Great War. Long before the Elite program existed, Kane had privately sought more ethical feeding methods, a leaning that had positioned him perfectly to help shape the post-war reforms.

Now, if he patronized a blood house, he'd be undermining everything he'd worked for. If the Council discovered the transgression, it would mean political ruin.

But the alternative, losing control with Serenity, was unthinkable.

He grabbed his phone and dialed a number he hadn't used in years.

"Kane? Is that really you?" the voice asked skeptically.

"It's me, Vincent." Kane's voice came out a grating rasp.

"What does the almighty Kane want with little ol' me?" Vincent's artificial Cajun accent had grown more pronounced over the years.

Kane pinched the bridge of his nose, already irritated. "I need a willing donor. Someone who knows what they're getting into."

Vincent laughed. "You do know what you're asking for, right?"

"I know exactly what I'm asking for," Kane replied through gritted teeth. The pulse in his vision had intensified to the point where he could barely tell one color from another.

"Oh, how the mighty have fallen. The great reformer, crawling back to the old ways. The Council would be fascinated to learn of this development."

Kane sighed heavily. "I'll pay double the usual price for your discretion," he said, desperation seeping into his voice.

There was a moment of silence. Kane held his breath.

"No."

His stomach dropped. "What do you mean, no?"

"It's too risky. It must be serious if you're desperate enough to reach out to me. Besides, the rebellion's activities have drawn too much attention to our operations lately. The ICP is watching blood houses more closely than ever."

Kane's hands curled into fists. "Please, Vincent. I'll pay whatever it takes."

Vincent chuckled. "You're playing with fire, and I don't want to get burned," he said before hanging up.

"*Fuck!*" Kane grabbed the silver paperweight from his desk and hurled it at the wall.

It shattered into pieces, scattering across the floor. His frustration boiled over as his anger climbed. The mention of the rebellion had struck a nerve, not because of any connection to his condition, but because it was yet another crisis demanding his attention when he could barely keep hold of himself.

His phone rang, cutting through his thoughts. He answered hastily, hoping for a solution.

"General McGraff, how may I help?" Kane asked, masking his impatience. McGraff was old-school, one of the few humans who still viewed vampyrs with open suspicion despite decades of peaceful coexistence.

"I think you should have a human help you investigate the rebellion."

Of course. Kane had been trying to get help with the rebellion for months, and now the general wanted humans involved. The rebellion had started small, whispered dissent about Elite program inequalities, isolated attacks on vampyr-owned businesses. But over the past six months it had grown more organized, more dangerous. High-ranking vampyrs had been assassinated, their bodies left with the rebellion's symbol, a skull and crossbones with "H.L." carved into their foreheads.

Kane listened skeptically as McGraff explained his reasoning. The general believed involving humans would help Kane understand the rebels' motivations. The rebellion had grown increasingly sophisticated, suggesting possible inside knowledge of vampyr security protocols.

Kane knew he needed help, but bringing a fragile human into the fold made him uneasy. Especially now, when his control was so tenuous.

"I see your point, General. And who do you propose I recruit for this task?" Kane asked, feigning cooperation while his mind raced with the implications. A human investigator could provide valuable insight into rebel motivations and methods.

"I have just the person in mind. She's experienced infiltrating extremist groups, and her family history gives her credibility with potential rebel sympathizers."

Kane considered it. Risky, but it could yield valuable intelligence if she managed to infiltrate the rebellion. Any advantage in understanding their organization and tactics would be crucial.

"Alright, General. I trust your judgment. Send her my way."

As he ended the call, apprehension settled over him. He would need to watch this person closely until he could confirm her loyalty. If the investigator learned too much or proved untrustworthy, the Council would demand her elimination, regardless of military connections.

This was the distraction he needed. He called Rhyzan about security arrangements for the human investigator, then forced himself to work, briefly pushing his hunger aside. The strategy held until he checked the clock and saw it was six-thirty.

His hunger returned in full force, accompanied by a sharp pain behind his eyes. The crimson haze had crept further across his vision, laying a red film over everything. He downed his last blood bag and two shots of vodka before heading home. The alcohol wouldn't touch his hunger, but it might dull his other senses slightly, a desperate bid to soften his awareness of Serenity.

I've survived lifetimes of temptation. I can manage this one night.

As he pulled into his building, Kane steeled himself. The place had been designed for vampyrs of his status, triple-insulated walls to dampen sound, state-of-the-art air filtration to strip away lingering scents that might trigger predatory responses. But Kane knew no technological marvel could protect him from himself.

Once he saw Serenity again, his control would be severely tested. The bloodlust heightened his senses beyond even their usual vampyr acuity. He could hear the heartbeats of the building's occupants, pick out individual scents from the apartments he passed.

When he stepped out of the elevator, she waited in the hallway, hands clasped behind her back, a warm smile on her face. Their eyes met, and an electric current jolted through him, raising the fine hairs on his arms and neck. His enhanced senses caught the subtle shift in the air temperature around them.

His pulse quickened as he took in her silky brown skin, her captivating smile, her gentle curves. The sound of her blood moving through her veins reached his ears, a melody more enticing than any music in his centuries of existence. Each beat was a siren call, drawing him closer to the edge of control.

"You're back," she murmured, her voice carrying the subtle accent of Grove Gardens.

Her presence stirred a longing for feelings he'd never thought he'd want again. He'd built walls around his emotions lifetimes ago, focusing instead on political power and intellectual pursuits. But Serenity had somehow breached those defenses without even trying.

"Yes, I'm back, and hungry," Kane admitted, his gaze locked with hers. He saw her smile falter and regretted his choice of words. "Don't worry. I promised to have dinner with you, and I always keep my promises."

Her smile returned as she led him into the kitchen. The aroma of her cooking filled the air, garlic, butter, shrimp. Under normal circumstances, the scents would have been appetizing. Now they were merely distractions from the only sustenance his body craved.

"Just have a seat. Let me serve you," she said, and tantalizing images flashed through Kane's mind. He fought to push the inappropriate thoughts away, but they persisted. The red haze in his vision deepened, and he could feel his fangs threatening to extend. He bit the inside of his cheek, using the sharp pain to pull his focus from the dangerous fantasies.

"I'm sorry. What did you say?" Kane managed, gripping the edge of the table.

"Is Nox not joining us?" she asked over her shoulder. The movement sent a wave of her scent toward him, and he had to suppress a growl. Her blood smelled different than it had this morning, richer, more potent.

"No, it will just be the two of us." Now Kane regretted sending him away. Nox's presence might have given him a buffer.

"How many slices of bread would you like?" she asked, and just then the sharp knife blade slipped across her skin, leaving a thin trail of crimson. The metallic scent of her fresh blood hit his nostrils, and his hunger flared white-hot. A single droplet welled at the cut, glistening like a ruby.

His control shattered.

The red haze swallowed his vision entirely. His fangs extended fully, pressing against his lower lip. He could feel the change in his eyes, the silver brightening to a fierce glow, pupils contracting to pinpoints. The temperature of his skin dropped sharply as his body readied itself to feed.

He closed the distance between them in an instant, hovering mere inches away. His eyes fixed on her wound, his gaze hungry and wanting. He tried desperately to back away, but the intoxicating scent was too powerful to resist. It seemed to call to him on a molecular level.

As she slowly brought her finger to her lips, his fangs lengthened further, and his nostrils flared. He could feel his self-control draining away. The primal urge pulsed through his veins as he fought it. His hands trembled with the effort of restraint.

"Don't scream, and don't take your finger from your mouth," he growled, low and menacing. He barely recognized himself; the civilized veneer he'd cultivated over centuries had peeled back, baring the predator beneath.

Serenity held her finger tightly between her lips, eyes wide with fear. Kane felt the hunger surging in him. He summoned all his strength to flee her presence, but his feet wouldn't move. It was as though some invisible force pinned him to the spot.

His eyes locked onto hers, and despite his efforts, his instincts overwhelmed him. He yearned for the taste of her blood, for the feel of it sliding down his throat and lighting up every part of him. He could hear the frantic beat of her heart, smell the warm, sweet scent of her blood. Beneath her fear he detected something else, a thread of anticipation, of curiosity. Did some part of her want this too?

"Kane, what's happening?" Serenity whispered, trembling.

He gritted his teeth and squeezed his eyes shut, trying to claw back control. "I'm sorry," he rasped. "Just don't move." If she ran, he knew the predator in him would give chase.

His mind clouded with hunger, his vision deepening to red. The scent of her blood was overwhelming. The consequences flashed through his mind, political ruin if he broke feeding protocols, possible execution if he couldn't stop himself, the devastation if he harmed her. None of it was enough to overcome the need.

The rebellion's escalation, Vincent's refusal, the mounting pressures, all of it seemed designed to test his limits. But as Serenity's pulse thundered in his ears and her blood called to him with irresistible sweetness, strategic thought dissolved into pure, primitive need.

Kane's eyes locked onto Serenity's, certain he was about to fail her.

CHAPTER TWENTY-FIVE

SERENITY

Shit.

"Just don't move," he growled.

Serenity's finger throbbed with excruciating pain as she bit down on it, trying to stem the blood oozing from the wound. Fear kept her frozen as Kane eyed her with predatory hunger. The kitchen's bright lights seemed to dim around them, as though the air itself had shifted to make room for his appetite.

She'd been careless slicing the bread, nerves making her fumble. Now the hunger blazed in his eyes, unmistakable, as his fangs lengthened, baring his primal nature. The silver of his irises had brightened to an unnatural glow that rimmed his dilated pupils.

"Don't run, and don't take your finger from your mouth," he commanded. The knife lay forgotten beside the bread, the garlic butter shrimp still on the warmer, a domestic tableau at odds with their silent standoff.

Rage and desperation collided in her chest as her mind ran the odds of escape. Her mother and sister's faces flashed before her. Would they ever know what had happened? Or would they simply receive notice of her unfortunate accident and the promised compensation?

She needed to get away before he could grab her. Her life depended on it.

Glancing around the room, her gaze settled on the garlic butter shrimp, and an idea took shape. If she could catch him off guard, maybe she could run.

"I'll catch you before you move one foot," he warned, and she knew he spoke the truth. His voice had changed, deeper, rougher, vibrating with something ancient and terrifying.

She swiftly pulled her finger from her mouth and reached for the pot. Before her fingers could graze its surface, his hands clamped around her throat like a steel vise. The crushing force cut off her air, his fingers unnaturally cold against her skin. Desperately she clawed at them, but they held with unyielding strength.

As she stared into his illuminated eyes, she silently pleaded with him to release her, but his grip only tightened. With a sharp jolt, he tilted her head to the side, baring her neck to his hungry gaze. For a moment she glimpsed the struggle in his eyes as they flickered between luminous brilliance and dark, primal hunger. Somewhere behind the monster, Kane was still fighting.

Then, without hesitation, his teeth clamped down on her flesh; pain exploded through her, an inferno of agony. Her scream echoed through the room, bouncing off the marble countertops and hardwood floors.

Her eyes rolled back as his fangs punctured her skin, drawing blood, a pain unlike anything she'd known, yet beneath it pulsed a wave of forbidden pleasure that rolled outward from the puncture site. The sensation confused and horrified her even as her body arched involuntarily toward him.

Summoning every ounce of strength, she released his wrist and reached for the heavy pot. In one swift motion she lifted it and poured the steaming contents over his head. Hot liquid splashed across his face and chest, scalding his skin and tearing an anguished cry from him. As he recoiled, his grip loosened, and he stumbled backward, his face contorted in pain.

Taking the opening, she bolted for the elevator.

Her neck, shoulder, and arm burned from the grease splatter, but adrenaline drove her muscles like rocket fuel. Every few steps the world tilted, her balance compromised by blood loss and the lingering echo of that strange, unwanted pleasure from his bite. Her fingers shook as she yanked out her keycard and slammed it against the scanner.

The instant the doors opened, she lunged inside and jabbed at the button to close them.

The doors clanged shut, and the trapped air in her lungs escaped in a stifled gasp. She trembled as Kane's howls echoed up the elevator shaft, cutting through her like jagged glass. The sound carried a rage that was barely human, a promise of retribution that ran cold through her veins.

The elevator hummed as it descended, carrying her away from the nightmare above. The distant wails gradually faded, replaced by mechanical whirring and her own ragged breathing. Her hands wouldn't stop shaking, and spots danced at the edges of her vision, symptoms she recognized from helping her father treat shock victims in Grove Gardens.

She was alive. She had survived. Yet with that realization came another, more sobering one: her family would receive nothing if she didn't return. The contract would be voided if she fled for good, leaving her mother and sister without the medical care they desperately needed.

As the elevator stopped, Serenity steeled herself. The doors opened onto the dimly lit parking garage. Harsh fluorescent lights flickered intermittently, throwing strange shadows across the concrete pillars.

Cautiously she stepped out, half expecting Kane to be waiting. The area seemed clear. She moved silently through the garage, alert for any sign of danger.

Finding the guard box empty, she carefully walked onto the deserted street. Each step sent a fresh jolt of terror through her, as if he might charge from the shadows at any moment. Above her loomed the towers of the Silver District, gleaming monuments of glass and steel that stood in stark contrast to the crumbling brick of her home district.

The further she got from the building, the more the adrenaline that had fueled her escape began to wane, leaving her cold and shivering in the frigid night air. She stumbled forward, praying she was headed toward Grove Gardens. Surveillance drones hummed overhead, their red lights scanning the streets below. She ducked into shadow whenever one passed too close, knowing an unauthorized human in this district would be reported instantly.

She crept down empty streets, her body tense and ready to flee. The shadows offered little protection, and it was only a matter of time before a vampyr caught her scent. The sweetness of her blood lingered in the air, a beacon to any predator nearby.

But she pressed on, determined to put distance between herself and Kane. As she rounded a corner into a narrow alley, a bone-chilling sense of being watched swept over her. She bolted forward, her pulse thundering in her ears. Halfway down the alley, sudden dizziness made her stumble. She caught herself against the wall, leaving a smear of blood from her neck on the rough stone. The wound had reopened.

Then, as her legs threatened to buckle, the alley opened onto a dimly lit street. Panting, she crossed it and darted into another darkened passage. An unexpected silhouette at the end made her halt, but the figure's glowing lavender eyes gave her pause. A hulking form stood bathed in faint yellow light from an overhead lamp.

He inhaled deeply, his eyes brightening as hunger flared in them. His nostrils flared as he caught her scent, his stance shifting from casual to predatory in an instant.

"Who are you?" he growled, stalking toward her, his presence filling the narrow space.

"I am no one," she stammered, pressing her hand tighter to her neck, hoping to mask the smell of her blood. "Please stay back."

Ignoring her plea, the figure kept advancing. He tapped elongated fingernails against the brick wall as he walked, a rhythmic clicking that scraped against her frayed nerves. She kept backing up until she collided with a solid form.

Too afraid to turn, Serenity froze.

"I am going to need you to do everything I say," a familiar, velvety voice whispered in her left ear.

Serenity sagged with relief as she recognized Sebastian, the Elite who had visited her in Grove Gardens just weeks before she'd been selected for Kane.

"Dex, I need you to stop right now," Sebastian called to the approaching figure.

"Bastian, she is mine. Go away," Dex retorted possessively, snapping his teeth together with an audible click.

"Unfortunately, I can't do that. She belongs to Kane Draccus."

Kane's name made Dex halt. His eyes narrowed as he scowled at Sebastian. "She is Kane's? Why should I believe you? Kane has not had an Elite in a long time. Not since the last one ended so... messily."

Serenity's stomach clenched at the implication. Kane had previous Elites? What had happened to them?

"Why would I lie? She even has her Elite ID to prove it. Also, think about what this could mean for us," Sebastian urged, positioning himself between Serenity and the looming threat. There was a calculation in his tone that hadn't been there during their brief meeting in Grove Gardens.

"I know, but her blood... it's hard to walk away." Dex inhaled again, his pupils dilating further. "It smells different. Stronger than usual."

"Stop fucking breathing and think of Haley. What does your hunger truly desire, one fleeting taste of forbidden fruit... or the rewards of patience?"

Serenity held her breath as she watched the exchange. Weariness settled into her bones while anxiety gnawed at her, but the cunning in Sebastian's eyes offered a sliver of hope. Who was Haley? And what did Sebastian mean by "rewards of patience"? The whole conversation carried undercurrents she couldn't decipher.

Dex paused, weighing Sebastian's words. He cast one last lingering look at Serenity, his predatory instinct briefly tamed by reason. With a snarl at being denied his prize, he shifted his gaze back to Sebastian. "So be it then," he growled before nodding curtly and turning away.

Sebastian turned to Serenity, his body shielding her from where Dex had vanished. "Are you alright?" His voice carried concern, but there was something else in his expression, calculation, assessment.

She nodded numbly, wincing as the movement pulled at her wounded neck. Her legs felt more unsteady by the second. He studied her before declaring, "We need to get you out of here."

Before she could move, his jaw clenched, and his blue eyes darkened with anger as he took in her injuries. "What happened?"

She touched her neck and found it wet. Looking at her fingers, she saw blood. She pulled her sleeve down to cover her hand, then pressed it to her neck.

"Here, take this." Sebastian offered a small cloth from his pocket. She placed it gently against the wound. "Come with me before we attract more unwanted attention."

But instead of leading her toward Kane's building or any direction that suggested returning her to safety, Sebastian guided her deeper into the maze of alleyways. His grip on her arm was firm, possessive even, not the gentle hand of a rescuer, but the purposeful steering of someone with a destination in mind.

"Where are we going?" she asked weakly, beginning to suspect this wasn't the coincidental rescue she'd first believed.

"Somewhere safe," Sebastian replied, a new authority in his tone that made her skin prickle. "Somewhere Kane can't reach you."

The certainty in his voice said this had been planned. How had he known exactly where to find her? How had he known she would need rescuing? The questions multiplied as her vision blurred from blood loss.

He led her through the alley until they reached an unmarked back door. He knocked three times, then banged twice, a clear code.

A woman with a bright blonde pixie cut and a sharp undercut opened the door. Her nose and lip were pierced, with more silver decorating her ears. Though her expression was unwelcoming, curiosity flickered in her eyes.

"Sebastian. You're late, and I see you brought a guest. A bleeding guest?" The woman raised her eyebrows as they entered. She closed the door, securing it with three steel bolts.

"Rose, I'm only five minutes late, and I need to see Damon so he can patch up my guest. Please open the door before you make me even later." There was an edge to Sebastian's voice that surprised Serenity; in Grove Gardens, he'd seemed so accommodating, almost subservient.

They stared each other down until Rose relented. "Fine. He's in the back, but she's already pissed."

Rose retrieved a key from between her breasts and unlocked the inner door. Piano music flooded over them as Sebastian pulled Serenity through. It was a bar like the ones she'd heard about, but modernized, with a livelier atmosphere. People laughed and talked as if they hadn't a care in the world.

The place was bathed in amber light that cast everything in a warm glow, so different from the harsh white of Kane's penthouse. The low ceiling made the room feel intimate, and the furniture was mismatched, tables and chairs salvaged from all over. On the walls hung paintings of the old world, scenes from before the Great War, when humans had been the dominant species.

Sebastian kept guiding her, greeting various patrons. They all stared at her, yet no one remarked on her presence or her injuries. Their eyes followed her across the room, some with open curiosity, others with guarded suspicion. Many of them bore scars, visible reminders of life in the human districts.

He paused to speak with a pink-haired woman with a lip ring sitting at the bar. She smiled at him until she noticed Serenity, then frowned. Sebastian leaned over and whispered something that restored the woman's smile.

"I need to take care of her first, then I'll be back for you."

He led Serenity deeper into the room until they reached a door. "Damon isn't the friendliest person, but he'll fix your neck and help you decide what to do next. Don't be intimidated by him. All bark, tiny bite." Sebastian's steady hand on her back gave her the support she needed as another wave of dizziness washed over her.

"Okay, I'll do my best," she managed weakly.

Sebastian opened the door, and she followed him through. The room was strikingly austere compared to the vibrant bar. A wooden table stood at the center, surrounded by tall shelves filled with books and equipment. A man with midnight hair sat at a desk, absorbed in a document.

Sebastian closed the door, silencing the bar noise.

"You're late. You know Starr hates it when you're late," the man remarked without looking up.

"If you look up from that damn paper, you'll see why I'm late, and you can explain it to her," Sebastian snapped.

The man glanced up, glaring at Sebastian before his gaze shifted to Serenity. Surprise crossed his face as he dropped the document and crossed to her. This must be Damon.

"Why didn't you say anything sooner? You cad." His reflective green eyes filled with concern as he gently moved her hand to examine the wound. "The bleeding has stopped. Were you burned? How did this happen?"

Serenity hesitated, uncertain whether to confide in these strangers. Her thoughts kept drifting back to Kane. What would happen to her mother and sister now? The agreement would be void if she didn't return. And beneath that practical worry lurked something else, a disturbing concern for Kane himself. Had she permanently injured him?

"Does it matter? Just help her. We ran into Dex in the alleyway. Just an FYI." Sebastian ran his hands through his hair in frustration, but Damon ignored him.

"I'll let Haley know." He focused on Serenity, scanning for other injuries. "I can see he bit you, but how did the burns happen, Serenity?"

Now it was her turn to be surprised. "How do you know my name?"

He smirked and gently replaced her hand on her neck. "Let me get supplies to clean you up, and I'll answer all your questions." He guided her to a chair, then looked pointedly at Sebastian. "She's about to collapse. Make yourself useful for once."

As soon as he left, she turned to Sebastian. "I don't think I should be here. I should go." Serenity moved toward the door, but he blocked her. "My family, they won't get anything if I don't go back. The contract..."

"You won't make it back bleeding like that, and even if you do, he might kill you. You have better odds staying here and letting Damon treat you." He stepped closer, his voice softening with practiced sympathy. "We're on the same side."

Serenity quirked an eyebrow. "The same side? Which side is that?" His eagerness made her wary. The convenient timing of his appearance was getting harder to ignore.

"He'll explain everything, I promise." Sebastian's blue eyes held hers, earnest, too earnest, she realized. This was a performance, carefully calibrated to win her trust.

"You were waiting for me, weren't you?" she said quietly, the pieces clicking together. "You knew I would run. You knew exactly where to find me."

Sebastian's expression flickered for just a moment, surprise at her perceptiveness, perhaps respect. Then the mask slid back into place. "Serenity, you're in shock. You're not thinking clearly—"

"I'm thinking perfectly clearly." Despite her weakened state, her voice carried new strength. "How long have you been watching Kane's building? How did you know I'd need rescuing?"

Before Sebastian could answer, Damon returned with a large black case. He set it on his desk and opened it, revealing medical supplies, including items she hadn't seen in years, ointment, gauze, and something else that caught her attention: small glass bottles and tins with the initials "R.W." etched into them.

Her father's personal remedies. Without thinking, she picked up a bottle of turmeric and ginger. The label bore her father's familiar cursive. "Where did you get these?"

"From your father," Damon confirmed.

Her eyes narrowed. "My father? How did you know him?" She picked up a tin of ointment in her own handwriting, the burn salve she'd prepared the week before his death.

She couldn't understand why her father would give so many supplies to someone from another district. But there had to be a reason. He was a good man who wanted to help people. Still, the discovery hinted at a side of him she'd never known, secret associations, clandestine work.

"Please let me treat your wounds first. I'll explain," Damon said. "It will be easier if I cut your shirt. I have a new one for you."

She nodded, still processing the discovery.

Damon took scissors and cut open her sleeve to the neckline. After setting them aside, he began cleaning the blood from her neck with gauze and alcohol. Her skin stung as he wiped around the deep bite mark.

"I knew your father, Richard, for quite a few years. We used his medical skills often, and we sorely miss them."

"He never told me about you." She'd never seen Damon at their home, nor had her father mentioned him.

"Likely because he didn't want you involved." He finished cleaning the bite, then opened a can of water and poured it over her burns. His movements were methodical, practiced, like her father's had been.

"Involved? In what?"

"The Human Liberation."

Serenity was speechless. She'd heard whispers of the Human Liberation but had dismissed them as distant rumor, stories about humans who fought back, who escaped, who managed to carve out freedom.

"That army is just a rumor."

"No, it's not. We're very real, and your father helped us until the day he died." There was something in his tone that suggested more to her father's death than she knew.

Serenity couldn't believe it. Her father, part of the Human Liberation. She remembered preparing cases of medicine that would vanish within days. He must have given them to this group. Was this why he'd insisted on teaching her all his remedies, making her memorize recipes even when she'd complained?

Another thought struck her. Had Kane selected her because of her father's connections? Had she been chosen specifically because of ties to the Liberation she'd never known existed?

Damon finished rinsing her burns and patted her arm dry. Blisters had formed on her skin, angry red welts that would leave scars.

"Since the blisters haven't popped, I won't bandage your arm. I can give you something for the pain if you'd like."

"No, I'm okay." She didn't want to dull her senses any further.

He retrieved a plain black T-shirt from a cabinet and handed it to her. "Let me cover the bite." He placed a small bandage on her neck. "We'll step out while you change."

Damon took Sebastian with him as they exited, giving her privacy.

Her mind reeled. Her father, part of the Human Liberation, a revelation that filled her with warring emotions. Pride at his courage clashed with hurt at his secrecy and fear for what it might mean for her family now.

Maybe running from Kane hadn't been the best decision. Had she stayed, at least her family would have received compensation for her death, money for the medicine and care they needed.

Her hands still trembled as she changed shirts. The bite on her neck throbbed with each heartbeat, and now and then a wave of that strange, disturbing pleasure would roll through her.

A knock sounded at the door. "Come in."

Damon entered confidently, Sebastian following close behind. A petite blonde woman accompanied them, her eyes fixed on Serenity. Unlike the others, who had regarded her with varying degrees of suspicion, this woman's expression was open, welcoming.

Without hesitation, she approached and embraced Serenity warmly. "Hello, Serenity," she said with a bright smile. "I've heard so much about you."

"I'm Starr," she introduced herself.

"You knew my father, too?"

"Yes, I did," Starr confirmed, a shadow of grief crossing her features. "Richard was instrumental in our early efforts." She reached out and squeezed Serenity's hand. "Have you eaten yet? I'd love to feed you."

At the mention of food, Serenity's stomach growled loudly, reminding her of the meal that had never happened.

"I'd love to learn more about how you knew my father," Serenity admitted.

Starr beamed. "Of course you would. Let's eat and talk." She glanced at Sebastian, a silent command in her eyes. "And you can tell me exactly how you happened to find Richard's daughter bleeding in the middle of the Silver District."

Sebastian's smile faltered slightly, confirming Serenity's suspicion that there was more to his timely rescue than coincidence.

As they prepared to leave the small room, the weight of decision pressed down on her. These people knew secrets about her father she'd never suspected, and they offered answers to questions she hadn't known to ask. But they also represented danger, not just to her, but to her family if she became tangled in whatever resistance her father had died supporting.

Yet what choice did she have? Kane had nearly killed her. Even if she could go back, would she survive another encounter? And if these people truly carried on her father's work, didn't she owe it to his memory to at least listen?

As Sebastian opened the door to lead her back into the main bar, Serenity understood that her old life, the quiet existence of a shopgirl in Grove Gardens, was already over. Whether she chose the rebels or returned to Kane, she would never again be the innocent young woman who had simply wanted to help her family. The only question left was which path would cost her less of her soul.

CHAPTER TWENTY-SIX

KANE

The sweet taste of her blood lingered in his mouth and flowed through his veins like liquid fire that refused to fade. It wasn't merely sustenance; it was revelation, memory, and emotion distilled into liquid form. In all his centuries of existence, Kane had never experienced anything like it. Most blood carried subtle notes of its bearer's life, fear, joy, pain, but Serenity's essence had hit him like a symphony where he'd only ever heard single notes before.

Kane lay on the kitchen floor, fingers tracing the tiles as he tried to comprehend the rush of sensation overwhelming him. The bloodlust had consumed him completely, overriding centuries of careful control in a matter of seconds. He could taste traces of sunlight on her skin, the salt of honest labor, even faint herbal notes from her father's remedies she must have handled. The complexity was staggering.

As his thirst eased, he began to regain composure, the overpowering need diminishing and leaving behind a strange euphoria laced with crushing guilt. The world around him seemed sharper, more vivid, colors deepening, sounds clarifying, as though her blood had heightened his already supernatural senses beyond their usual reach.

He had lost control, failing not only her but himself. He should have heeded his instincts and stayed away. Instead he'd let himself be drawn in by her courage, and now she wandered the city unprotected. The thought of her alone in the Silver

District after nightfall sent ice through his veins. Even for an Elite with proper identification, a woman with an open wound would draw unwanted attention from less disciplined vampyrs.

His facial wounds had healed, but a phantom sting remained. Rising to his feet, he felt the shame settle over him in full. The Elder Council would be within their rights to strip him of his position if they learned of this. Self-feeding from an Elite without consent violated every protocol he'd helped establish.

Kane made his way to the sink and turned on the faucet. Since founding the Elite program, he had been its most vocal advocate, arguing that civilized feeding arrangements benefited both species. He had testified before the Council, vouching that modern vampyrs could master their hungers. His reputation had been built on perfect discipline. Now that discipline lay in ruins around him.

The memory of sinking his teeth into her neck assailed him, an intimate, vulnerable moment he hadn't allowed himself in decades. He had craved that closeness to her life force, and for a brief instant he'd found a strange calm. The world had narrowed to just the two of them, her heartbeat synchronizing with his own dormant pulse in a rhythm that felt ancient and inevitable. But that tranquility had been shattered by scalding garlic butter, yanking him back to reality.

He exhaled, heavy with regret. The realization struck him hard: he could have killed her. The thought landed like a physical blow, a stark reminder of how close he'd come to crossing an unforgivable line. In the early days after his turning, his maker had drilled control into him through brutal lessons. *Restraint is what separates us from beasts*, Cazimir had said, standing over the drained bodies of those Kane had killed in his newborn hunger. Centuries of perfect control, undone by one woman's cut finger.

He needed to make amends, but where to begin? Perhaps he should transfer her contract to another patron, someone who wouldn't put her in danger. The thought of another vampyr claiming her clenched his jaw.

Yet Kane could feel her presence like a beacon calling to him. Her energy moved through his veins, a sensation he'd never experienced before. Blood had always been mere sustenance, but this was more powerful, more alluring. It reminded him of stories the elders told, ancient tales of blood connections so profound they transcended physical distance. He had always dismissed them as superstition. Now he wasn't so certain.

His instincts roared at him to find her, to protect her. The predator in him recognized her as precious, not prey, but something to be sheltered and guarded. He caught his reflection in the kitchen's polished steel, his eyes still carrying the luminous silver glow of feeding, though the hunger had subsided.

Kane strode from the kitchen with renewed determination. He reached the elevator and raised his arm to the scanner, but before he could touch it, the doors slid open.

Nox stood inside, eyes locked onto Kane, scrutinizing every inch of him. His nostrils flared slightly as he caught the lingering scent of Serenity's blood. Kane saw the recognition dawn, followed by disappointment and concern.

"What happened? And where's Serenity?" There was an edge to Nox's tone Kane rarely heard, not just alarm, but accusation.

The tension crackled between them as Kane searched for words. "I failed her. I'm sorry." The admission felt inadequate, a pale shadow of the remorse consuming him.

Nox's eyes widened as he stepped forward. "What do you mean you failed her?" Though he asked, the answer was already written in Kane's glowing eyes and the lingering scent of blood.

"I couldn't control myself," Kane admitted softly. "I drank from her, Nox. Savagely." The words hung between them, heavy with significance. They both knew what this meant, not just for Serenity, but for Kane's standing in vampyr society.

Horror crossed Nox's face as he stepped back. "Is she... is she okay?"

Kane nodded, relieved to offer some comfort. "She's alive... I believe. She's out there somewhere, and I need to find her." He glanced toward the window, where the city sprawled below, a labyrinth of dangers for a lone Elite after dark.

"What do you mean 'out there somewhere'? Tell me exactly what happened!" Nox stepped into the hallway, his usual deference briefly forgotten.

Kane recounted the evening. He described the brief moment of calm before the hot garlic butter pulled him back, and how close he'd come to killing her. "She defended herself," he concluded, a note of reluctant pride in his voice. "She had the presence of mind to use the food as a weapon. It gave her enough time to escape."

"Why didn't you tell us your thirst was that bad?" Nox snapped, shaking his head furiously. "Why didn't you call me?" The question carried echoes of past arguments, times when Nox had arrived to help him regain control before disaster struck.

"I thought I could handle it," Kane replied, weighed down by regret. "I know I should have stayed away. But I couldn't. There's something about her, Nox. It draws me to her, beyond just her blood." Even as he spoke, he could feel that pull, like an invisible cord connecting them across the city.

Nox's eyes narrowed. "You should have known better than to put her in danger like that. But right now, we focus on finding her before anyone else does." His expression darkened. "Especially before the Elder Council learns what happened. Isaac has been looking for any excuse to remove you."

Kane agreed. "I know. And I won't rest until she's safe." He turned to Nox, determination etched in his features. "She's out there, and she needs my help. I can feel it." It wasn't mere intuition; since drinking her blood, he had developed an awareness of her that defied rational explanation.

They moved toward the elevator together.

"We'll find her," Nox assured him, conviction in his tone. "And we'll make sure she's safe."

As they descended, Kane couldn't shake the image of Serenity's terrified expression as he bit into her neck. The moment replayed in a torturous loop. He had placed her in danger through his own actions. Now he was determined to make it right, to protect her at all costs.

The elevator doors opened on the ground floor, and they exited with Kane leading the way. The sounds of the city enveloped them, conversation, music, laughter, all amplified by his heightened senses. The Silver District was generally safe, but in certain areas, vampyrs and their appetites ruled the night.

Kane felt his senses sharpen, his body on high alert as they began their search. The darkness posed no obstacle to his vampyr sight. As he walked, he couldn't help wondering what Serenity must be feeling. Fearful and alone? Her blood in his system gave him fragmentary glimpses of her emotional state, confusion, pain, and a surprising undercurrent of determination.

A scream pierced the air, and Kane's blood iced over. Without hesitation, he bolted toward the sound, Nox close behind. His speed startled even himself; he moved faster than he ever had, the world blurring around him.

As they rounded the corner, they found a vampyr and his Elite pressed against a wall, feeding consensually. The Elite's expression was one of bliss rather than terror, the regulated feeding process releasing endorphins. Kane's feeding from Serenity had been anything but proper.

He gritted his teeth in frustration. This wasn't what he sought. He was about to turn away when he heard a faint whisper that sounded like Serenity's voice. It wasn't physical; her actual voice couldn't possibly carry this far. It was an impression, a sensation that bypassed his ears and spoke directly to his consciousness.

He signaled for Nox to wait, then cautiously followed the direction of the sound. Moving deeper into the alley, he found it empty. Closing his eyes, he focused on the tenuous link between them. She was alive, but frightened. Not here, but somewhere to the east.

Nox motioned to him. "Come, Kane. We need to call Rhy so we can cover more ground. We must alert the ICP, especially if she's bleeding." His expression grew grave. "But we need to be careful how we phrase it. If they realize you've broken feeding protocols..."

Reluctantly, Kane acknowledged the wisdom of it. Involving the Inner City Police was risky; they would question how Serenity came to be injured. But they had resources and manpower he lacked.

Pulling out his phone, he dialed Rhy's number, thoughts racing as he waited. As Chief of Security in Celearius, Rhyzan oversaw the vampyr police of both the Inner and Outer City, commanding extensive resources while remaining one of Kane's most trusted allies.

"What's going on?" Rhy asked, concern evident in his voice.

"It's Serenity," Kane managed. "I... I drank from her. And now I can't find her. We need your help." The admission came hard, each word leaden with shame.

A long pause followed, tension building in Kane. Finally Rhy responded.

"I'll be there," he declared firmly. "Don't move. We'll find her." His tone was neutral, professional. "And Kane... the HV Council doesn't need to know about this. Not yet."

Kane ended the call and turned to Nox, worry in his eyes. "He's on his way, but we need to find her."

Nox nodded. "You really care for her, don't you?" he asked quietly as they navigated the shadowed streets. "Not just as an Elite, but as..."

Kane didn't answer right away. When he'd selected Serenity from the Elite candidates, he'd been drawn to her spirit, her resilience. He hadn't anticipated the connection that formed between them, one that now reached beyond the normal patron-Elite bond.

"She deserves better than what I've given her," he finally replied. "I owe her that much at least."

As Kane moved through the labyrinthine streets, he pushed aside the gnawing fear and focused on his sense of her. He could still feel her, anxious and on edge, yet with that underlying determination that impressed him. Though he couldn't pinpoint her location, he knew she was alive. The link between them held steady, her life force stronger in his awareness than before.

His heightened senses caught the faint sound of footsteps echoing through the dark. He halted, listening intently, silver eyes scanning his surroundings. Then a sharp scent reached him, Serenity's distinctive citrus and vanilla, mixed with a metallic tang he recognized.

Blood.

Her blood. But not fresh; the scent was hours old, a lingering trace where she had passed. Kane inhaled deeply, focusing on the subtle notes that made her scent unique. She had been here, moving eastward as he'd sensed. Toward the Waterside Cross district, where human establishments operated under tenuous permits.

Where she might find help, or far greater danger.

As they followed the faint trail, Kane's mind raced with possibilities. The rebellion had been escalating, targeting Elite gathering places, using increasingly sophisticated tactics. If Serenity had stumbled into their network while fleeing him, she could be walking into a trap far worse than his momentary loss of control.

The irony wasn't lost on him: in trying to protect her from his own darkness, he might have delivered her straight into the hands of those who saw her as nothing more than a weapon to use against him.

CHAPTER
TWENTY-SEVEN

SERENITY

They took Serenity to a small diner tucked between two apartment buildings. Its mirrored windows hid it from the street, one of their safe havens after dark. Unlike the gleaming chrome and glass of Kane's residence, this place had a worn authenticity, chipped paint on the door frames, uneven floorboards that creaked underfoot, the lingering scent of decades of cooking.

"If you ever need to find us again, look for places like this. Specifically, search for this mark." Sebastian pointed to a small skull and crossbones near the bottom of the door, so tiny and well-blended among the graffiti that she'd have missed it unless she was looking.

She racked her brain, trying to recall where she'd seen the symbol before. It danced at the edge of memory, just out of reach. Her thoughts scattered as throbbing pain shot through her arm. She winced and pressed her hand to the burned area, feeling the heat radiating from the wound.

Inside, the lights were low, and the walls were painted a warm, inviting yellow, a stark contrast to the cool blues and silvers of vampyr design. Booths lined the perimeter, several people enjoying late-night meals. Most of the diners bore subtle markers of human hardship, patched clothing carefully mended rather than replaced, the slight thinness of those who never quite had enough, calloused hands from manual labor. Yet there was laughter here, genuine and unrestrained.

They settled into an empty booth, and a waitress with a kind face approached. A thin scar marked her left cheek, disappearing beneath her collar, the distinctive trace of vampyr claws. She'd survived an encounter, yet here she was, continuing her life with quiet dignity.

"Can I start you off with some drinks?" she asked.

"Cokes all around," Damon responded. "Cheeseburgers for everyone and fries for the table." His movements were precise, economical, a man who wasted neither words nor gestures. His green eyes constantly scanned the room.

Starr waited until the waitress was out of earshot before speaking quietly. "I know you have questions, Serenity. Your father didn't get the chance to tell you much." As she spoke, she twisted a thin silver bracelet around her wrist, a nervous habit that belied her otherwise composed demeanor. "Your father and mine were friends before the war. They went to medical school together, and during the conflict, they formed a group called the Resistance."

Serenity knew about the caves where she'd been born; her mother had shared stories about their life there during the final days of the thirty-year war. Her father had played a significant role in the peace treaty, though the specifics had always stayed murky. She remembered asking about the caves as a child, how her father's expression would cloud over, his hands gripping whatever he held too tightly.

"When the vampyrs approached them with the treaty, my father and yours disagreed. My father wanted to keep resisting, but with your mother pregnant, your father was ready for peace. In the end, my father conceded and signed alongside him."

"Wait, why would our fathers be the ones to sign the treaty?" A memory surfaced, her father being greeted with unusual deference when they visited other districts, the way older residents would straighten when he entered a room.

Starr and Damon exchanged glances. Starr continued, "Our fathers led the Resistance. Do you remember seeing this?" She pulled a piece of paper from her pocket bearing a skull and crossbones with the letters H.L. above it.

Why did it seem so familiar? Then realization dawned. She'd glimpsed this symbol on medicine boxes and in his medical journals. Once, when she was twelve, she'd found it scratched into his old wooden desk. When she'd asked about it, he'd quickly covered it, saying it was just an old doodle from his student days.

"It looks familiar?" Starr asked, studying her expression.

She nodded, biting her lip. "Good, because this next part may surprise you. For the past decade, we've been rebuilding the human resistance as the Human Liberation, with your father's help. We supplied the medical ingredients he needed, and he helped us create weapons against the vampyrs."

"Weapons?" Serenity's eyes widened. She recalled her father's insistence on teaching her about certain herbs and compounds, plants with no apparent medicinal use that he'd claimed were "important to understand."

"Silver weapons are part of it, but your father's real contribution was different," Starr explained, lowering her voice. "He found ways to... level the playing field. To make vampyrs more vulnerable when we needed to defend ourselves."

"What do you mean?" Serenity asked, though part of her wasn't sure she wanted to know.

Damon's expression grew serious. "Your father was brilliant. He understood things about vampyr physiology that most humans never learn, and he used that knowledge to help protect our people." He paused, choosing his words carefully. "Let's just say his medical background proved invaluable in ways beyond traditional healing."

"My father helped create weapons? He was a healer. This doesn't make sense." She thought of his shed with its double-locked door and complex ventilation system. Those mysterious stains on his hands, the ones she'd assumed came from medicinal herbs, took on an ominous new significance.

The waitress arrived with their food, interrupting her thoughts.

Damon watched her leave before speaking. "Your father wanted to keep you away from all this because of your blood. I'm honestly surprised you survived tonight after Kane tasted you."

Starr continued, "After my father died, I took command and worked with yours until his passing. Tonight was fate. Sebastian was meant to find you. We tried sending a message to your cellular device but weren't sure if you received it."

Serenity took a sip of soda, her first in nearly ten years. She sighed, focusing on the present. "That strange blue text? I saw it briefly before it disappeared. I thought I was imagining things."

"What we really want to know is why you became an Elite," Starr asked casually, though her eyes stayed fixed, weighing every reaction.

Serenity poked at a fry, frowning. "I had no other option. I'll do whatever it takes to save my mother and sister. They're sick and need medication to survive."

Her voice broke as she remembered how close they'd come to losing Beth last winter during an asthma attack.

"I'm sorry. We should have reached out sooner," Starr said, squeezing her hand. "We can provide all the medicine they need."

Grateful as she was for Starr's compassion, Serenity wanted to know one thing. "Does this mean I don't have to go back? I'm not sure I even can return." The memory of Kane's silver-blue eyes shifting to predatory hunger made her shiver. Yet beneath the fear lay something more confusing, the brief moment before he bit her when she'd glimpsed his inner struggle.

"Technically no, but we'd prefer you did," Damon said. "We know it's dangerous, but you could be crucial. We need intelligence to gain an advantage in this war."

Sebastian leaned forward, his blue eyes filling with what seemed like heartfelt concern. "Serenity, I know this is overwhelming after what you've endured. But think about it. You've seen firsthand what they're capable of. What Kane did to you tonight, that's who they really are beneath the civilized facade."

His voice carried pain, as if he spoke from personal experience. "I've seen how they treat Elites when they think no one's watching. The contract you signed, it doesn't protect you the way they claim. You've essentially handed him complete control over your actions. You're bound to his will, effectively his property."

Serenity felt tears threaten as the memory of the attack flooded back, Kane's cold hands around her throat, the terror of being completely helpless.

"But here's the thing," Sebastian continued softly, reaching across to touch her shoulder. "You don't have to be powerless anymore. Your father found a way to fight back, and now you can too. Not just for yourself, but for your family. For every human who's been forced into this system."

Starr gently touched Damon's arm, then turned back to Serenity with empathetic eyes. "What Sebastian means is that this goes beyond you or your family. It's about humanity's future. We've been oppressed too long, and we finally have a chance to fight back. But we need you."

Through the window, she caught a glimpse of Inner City Police officers moving through the streets, their search intensifying.

"Unfortunately, you have to decide tonight, because they're already looking for you," Damon said. "But don't worry. They won't find you here. This place has safeguards against vampyr detection."

Serenity wouldn't call herself brave, but she was determined. If her father believed they could defeat the vampyrs, who was she to question it? Memories of his quiet wisdom surfaced, how he'd insisted their worth as humans wasn't measured by vampyr standards, but by how they cared for one another.

"What exactly would I need to do?" she asked.

Starr beamed. "You know who your assigned vampyr is?"

"Yes, he's the Head of the HVC," she replied with a heavy sigh.

"Good. Information is our greatest need. Right now, we need to locate where he holds human prisoners. We know he uses caverns outside the walls, but we can't pinpoint where."

"How would I find that information?"

"Likely in his office," Damon replied, "but more importantly, listen carefully. He may speak freely in your presence, assuming you won't understand or care."

Serenity recalled Rhyzan mentioning a murder to Kane. "I think... I might already have something. Earlier today, I overheard Rhyzan mention a murder to Kane."

"A murder?" Starr looked at her sharply. "Do you remember details?"

"Not exactly. It was mentioned briefly, no names or locations. But Kane seemed troubled by it. He asked if there were any witnesses, and mentioned something about a 'pattern' they needed to investigate."

Starr and Damon exchanged glances. "We know about this. It was a victory, but details like that matter. Understanding their reactions could give us a crucial advantage."

Serenity nodded, apprehension building in her. Spying on Kane mixed fear with an unexpected hesitation. Memories of his silver-blue eyes and commanding presence filled her thoughts. The intelligent gleam when they discussed books, the surprising gentleness before the hunger took over, the way he'd promised to help her contact her family, these moments warred with the terrifying predator who had attacked her.

Sebastian noticed her hesitation. "I know it's scary to think about going back to him. After what he did..." His voice softened with understanding. "But you're stronger than you know. And you won't be alone. I'll be there to help you navigate this. We'll find ways to communicate safely."

He paused, letting his words sink in. "Think about your sister, Serenity. Beth is only twelve, right? In a few years, she'll be old enough to be selected as an Elite.

Do you want her to feel Kane's hands around her throat, his fangs piercing her skin?"

The image of Beth, frail and vulnerable, standing in Kane's penthouse as he looked at her with hunger, sent ice through Serenity's veins. No. Her sister already suffered enough with her illness.

Sebastian held her gaze, his eyes urgent. "Your father spent years fighting to prevent that future for her, for all human children. This is your chance to finish what he started. To make sure no other girl has to go through what you did tonight."

She drew a breath, steeling herself. "About his office..."

"We can arrange access," Starr said.

"He has cameras everywhere. How will I relay information back?"

"You'll give it to me," Sebastian said. "Communication will be easier since we're both Elites. You're permitted to interact with each other."

"Especially now that he'll be considered a 'savior' for returning you," Damon added.

"And the cameras?"

"We'll create opportunities for you to access his office. Otherwise, be mindful of your movements and your timing. If you're caught snooping, act naive, like you don't understand what you're looking at, then leave immediately," Starr continued.

"If you're caught, deny everything. Claim you were lost, confused after the attack. They'll expect you to be traumatized. Use that," Damon added.

Sebastian smiled reassuringly. "Don't be frightened. I've been spying for years without detection. Let her finish her meal and consider it. I'll bring her back when she's ready."

Starr and Damon nodded, then stood to leave. Before walking toward the door, Starr turned to Sebastian. "Don't take too long. Soon every vampyr in the city will be searching."

Serenity caught sight of her reflection in the mirrored window, pale face, exhausted eyes, the edge of a bandage visible above her collar. Could she really do this?

After they departed, Sebastian's tone softened. "I know that was a lot. I'll get a milkshake while you think and enjoy your burger."

Sebastian moved to the counter, leaving her alone with her thoughts.

Serenity forced herself to eat, the simple act lending a brief normalcy. She turned their request over, weighing the risks. Could she make such a monumental decision so quickly? Yet this was her chance to truly make a difference. She couldn't help thinking of her father, and resenting that he'd never told her. Perhaps he'd tried but didn't think she was ready, or, more likely, he'd wanted to protect her.

Through the window, she watched sleek black vehicles with tinted windows cruise slowly down the street, vampyr security forces. The search was escalating.

Sebastian returned as she sipped her Coke. "So... how was the burger?"

"Delicious. I can't remember the last time I had one like that."

"That's because it's real meat. Only the best in the Silver District." Sebastian slid into the seat across from her. "Have you decided?"

She grimaced. "I'm uncertain. I don't want to endanger my family."

"Listen, I understand this is frightening. But I promise you, if you're worried about your family, don't be. We'll keep them safe." He paused, studying her face. "Think about your little sister. Do you want her to become an Elite?"

The image of Beth in Kane's world, vulnerable to the same violence Serenity had suffered, hardened her resolve. She would rather die than let Beth endure that terror.

She drew a breath, her body tensing with determination.

"Yes. I'll do it," she declared firmly. "For my family. I hate that so many people are dying, and if there's any way to stop it, I'll help."

Sebastian smiled encouragingly. "You'll make a difference. If you're finished, we can head back."

They returned to the bar and found Damon and Starr in his office.

"I'll help," Serenity announced.

"I knew you would." Starr embraced her. "Thank you. Your father would be proud."

"I'll help, but I need your assurance that if something happens to me, you'll take my family to safety."

Damon approached, meeting her gaze directly. "I promise on my life that I'll see your family not only reaches safety but receives the medical care they both need."

The sincerity in his eyes reassured her.

"How do I explain who treated my injuries?"

"Leave that to me," Sebastian assured her. "We'll say I found you wandering disoriented and took you to the Silver District clinic."

Starr touched her arm. "Listen carefully. We're searching for the places they hold human prisoners. Specifically, we need to find a prisoner named Jon Sinclair. They're keeping them in caverns, but we need precise locations. They use coordinates, so if you find any, memorize them. Don't write anything down."

Damon retrieved a photograph from his desk and handed it to Starr. She showed it to Serenity, an image of her father with another man who shared Starr's blonde hair and blue eyes. Both wore jackets bearing the skull and crossbones.

Serenity's chest ached at seeing her father so young and vibrant. There was that familiar determined set to his jaw, but something else too, a fire in his eyes she'd only glimpsed on occasion. This was a side of him she'd never fully known, the fighter, the leader, the revolutionary.

"Just in case you needed more proof."

"I won't let you down," she promised.

"Alright. Sebastian, get her back. We'll contact you in two days on your cellular device. Watch for a text at noon. If you sense danger, leave immediately." Starr gave her a final hug before departing.

Sebastian turned to Serenity. "Now, let's get our story straight. Remember, from now on, you're always being watched. Every expression, every word, it all matters."

Serenity nodded, steeling herself for what was to come. She would return to face the creature who had nearly killed her, and somehow find the strength not only to hide her fear but to carry out her mission. For her family. For her father's legacy. For all of humanity.

But she couldn't help wondering: when she looked into Kane's silver-blue eyes again, would she see the monster who had attacked her, or would the confusing pull she felt toward him make her mission impossible to complete?

CHAPTER TWENTY-EIGHT

RHYZAN

Rhyzan's sharp gaze followed Sebastian as he escorted Serenity out of the twenty-four-hour urgent care clinic. His heightened vision cataloged every detail: the slight tremor in her hands, the careful way she held her injured arm, the barely perceptible tilt of her head to keep pressure off the bite wound. Twenty minutes earlier, Glen had called to tell him that Sebastian had come in with an injured Elite bearing second-degree burns and a vampyr bite. Before Glen even recited her donor ID number, Rhyzan had known it was Kane's Elite.

The scent of antiseptic and burnt flesh reached him through the closed windows, a reminder of the sensory curse that came with enhanced abilities. Beneath those medical odors, he detected Kane's signature on the bite wound. A marking. Unintentional, perhaps, but unmistakable to one who had known Kane for centuries.

Sebastian's appearance was no surprise; Rhyzan had been monitoring him for months, aware of his recruitment efforts. He strongly suspected Sebastian was behind the corruption of several Elites, most notably Ava, Kane's former Elite, whose betrayal nearly a year ago had confirmed Rhyzan's worst fears about Sebastian's infiltration methods.

Ava had been different from the other cases. Her hatred ran deeper, her desire for revenge more personal. Where Sebastian typically recruited Elites who had been mistreated by their patrons, Ava had been well cared for by Kane, even intimate with him. Yet somehow Sebastian had still managed to turn her, convincing her to attempt murder during what should have been their most vulnerable moment together.

The memory of that night still haunted Kane: Ava raising a silver blade above him as he lay defenseless, her eyes filled with a rage that seemed to come from nowhere. Only Kane's reflexes had saved him, stopping her hand inches from his heart. Even now, months after her capture and detention, Ava refused to explain her actions or reveal who had recruited her. Her silence spoke volumes about the Liberation's ability to corrupt even seemingly loyal Elites.

A flash of movement made Rhyzan sink lower in his seat. An Inner City Police patrol cruised by, the officers unaware their Chief of Security was conducting personal surveillance. Officially, he should have assigned this task to subordinates, but some matters required his direct attention, especially when they involved both a Council member's Elite and possible rebel recruitment.

Unfortunately, he lacked concrete evidence to support his suspicions. Neither the Council nor Evie were convinced Sebastian had ties to the Human Liberation. For years, Rhyzan had tracked his movements, ever since discovering encrypted communications linking him to unsanctioned activities. His name appeared only through coded references, part of a meticulous effort to cover his tracks that made formal accusations impossible.

The pattern was becoming clear. Every few months, another wave of Elite disappearances occurred, followed by increased attacks against vampyrs. Though the investigations consistently reached dead ends, Rhyzan recognized the methodology. Sebastian's approach was sophisticated; he targeted vulnerable Elites in moments of crisis, positioning himself as savior and protector before gradually introducing them to Liberation ideology.

The recent supply depot attack exemplified their evolving tactics. The facility had been hit with military precision, guards eliminated with silver weapons, medical supplies redistributed to unregistered humans in the forbidden zones beyond the walls. Two days later, Sebastian had been spotted in that sector, ostensibly visiting a patron's residence, but his route had taken suspicious detours.

Serenity Wright might be the key to finally proving Sebastian's involvement. The trouble was, it could come at the cost of his friend's heart. Rhyzan and Kane had stood together through centuries, from the blood-soaked battlefields of the Great War to the delicate Treaty negotiations. Kane's rare capacity for compassion had often balanced Rhyzan's pragmatism, making them effective partners in Celearius's formation.

Guilt weighed on him. Serenity radiated an innocent warmth, her silky black curls framing her face elegantly even in her current state. She didn't deserve to be tangled in this dangerous game, just a pawn on a board controlled by more powerful players.

Rhyzan had seen too many innocents caught in ideological crossfire. The early post-Treaty days had been especially brutal, with extremists on both sides resisting peaceful coexistence. He had lost Alex to human radicals who opposed the Treaty, his lover, a vampyr who had believed in a world where their two kinds could live side by side, murdered for that belief. Perhaps that explained his particular hatred for those who claimed violence was the only path to justice.

The question now was whether Sebastian would recruit Serenity, and if so, whether she would accept. From Rhyzan's brief surveillance since her selection as Kane's Elite, she possessed a quiet determination and intelligence that made her valuable to either side.

More intriguing was how Sebastian might respond when eventually pressed to become a spy for the vampyrs. Rhyzan anticipated resistance but could be persuasive. Sebastian's known weakness for protecting other Elites might provide the necessary leverage. The Liberation wouldn't sacrifice their most valuable asset lightly, but faced with exposure, they might have little choice.

A flash of headlights from an approaching vehicle sent Rhyzan sliding further down. He couldn't risk recognition; unauthorized surveillance of an Elite could raise questions he preferred not to answer, even to the Council.

He kept watching as they waited roadside until Nox's car appeared. Sebastian opened the door, and both climbed in. A smart move, returning Serenity himself positioned him as rescuer rather than potential kidnapper. It might even earn him additional access to Kane's residence for "wellness checks" on the traumatized Elite.

Now Rhyzan would need to watch the Elite in the coming days to determine whether recruitment had occurred. If so, it presented an opportunity to track her movements and potentially uncover rebel headquarters or detailed plans. She could become his unwitting spy within the organization.

The stakes were escalating. Intelligence reports suggested the Human Liberation was planning something significant. Whispers from Rhyzan's informants spoke of a new weapon, chemical agents engineered specifically to target vampyr physiology. If those rumors proved true, thousands of lives hung in the balance, Kane's among them.

Ava's actions suggested the Liberation was moving beyond isolated attacks toward systematic warfare. The psychological component was especially concerning, using turned Elites to strike at the heart of vampyr society, exploiting the trust inherent in patron-Elite relationships.

The time for action had arrived. He needed evidence to convince the Council and Evie of Sebastian's involvement, but he also needed to understand the Liberation's broader strategy. Were they planning coordinated strikes? Had they developed the rumored chemical weapons? How many other Elites had been compromised?

His tactical mind whirred with possibilities. The first step would be additional surveillance on Sebastian, perhaps tracking devices on personal items. At the same time, he needed passive monitoring inside Kane's residence, focused on the areas where Serenity and Sebastian might interact. Resource allocation would be tricky; with the recent surge in rebel activity, his department was already stretched thin.

Then there was Kane to consider. His friend would resist any suggestion that his Elite might be compromised. Kane's judgment was often clouded by his persistent belief in human goodness, admirable but dangerous in these unstable times. Rhyzan would need to proceed carefully, gathering irrefutable evidence before approaching him.

Ava provided a template for what might happen with Serenity. If Sebastian successfully recruited her, would she become another intelligence asset like most of his converts? Or would her trauma at Kane's hands, combined with whatever familial pressure the Liberation exploited, turn her into another weapon like Ava, beautiful, deadly, and ultimately uncontrollable?

For a moment, doubt flickered through Rhyzan's mind. Was he letting personal history color his judgment? His failure to protect those he loved had left wounds that never fully healed. He pushed the thought aside. The attacks were real, the threat substantial. His personal history merely lent additional motivation to necessary work.

With that resolution firmly in mind, Rhyzan started his engine, its low purr vibrating beneath him. He watched Nox's car disappear around a bend, then turned his own vehicle in the opposite direction. There were preparations to make, resources to gather, surveillance to establish, his next move to plan.

The game was entering a new phase. Sebastian had shown his hand by personally rescuing Kane's Elite, casting himself as her savior and protector. Now Rhyzan would show his, turning Sebastian's own tactics against him, using the recruitment of Serenity Wright to finally expose the network that threatened everything they had built.

"Celearius will not fall while I draw breath," he whispered, an oath renewed with each new threat. He would protect this fragile peace, this imperfect city where humans and vampyrs lived side by side, however uneasily. Even if it meant using Serenity. Even if it meant betraying Kane's trust for a time. Even if it meant becoming the thing he had once despised, a manipulator of innocent lives for the sake of a greater cause.

The weight of long years pressed on him as he drove toward the Cavern 47. Behind its gleaming walls, he would set in motion the machinery that might finally end the rebellion, or at least cut off its most effective recruiter. The Liberation had used Sebastian's access to Elite society for too long. Now it was time to turn that access into a liability.

As he pulled into his private garage, Rhyzan's phone buzzed with an encrypted message from one of his deep-cover operatives. *Package delivered to target location. Subject appeared receptive to contact. Awaiting further instructions.*

A cold smile crossed his features. The breadcrumbs had been laid. Soon Sebastian would make his move, and when he did, Rhyzan would be ready to spring the trap months in the making. The rebellion thought they were hunting Kane's Elite. They had no idea they were walking into a snare designed by someone who had been hunting them far longer than they had been hunting vampyrs.

CHAPTER TWENTY-NINE

KANE

The elevator's chime announced their arrival with mechanical precision. Kane stayed concealed in the shadows, his vampyr senses cataloging every detail as Sebastian escorted her into the apartment. The antiseptic scent barely masked the metallic tang of her blood, while her elevated body temperature and the subtle favoring of her unburned side registered as clearly as if she'd spoken her pain aloud.

Sebastian recounted finding her near the Waterside Cross gate, another piece in the puzzle that had troubled Kane for months. The area had become a focal point for suspicious activity, yet Sebastian always seemed to have a legitimate reason for being there. Tonight's excuse was chocolates from Birmingham's Artillery for Evelyn's supposed birthday. Kane filed the detail away; Evie's actual birthday was months off.

The faint tether in his consciousness, a connection he'd felt since tasting her blood, pulsed with her fear. The sensation disturbed him more than the hunger itself. In all his centuries, he had never experienced such awareness of another being. The ancient texts spoke of blood bonds, dismissed by modern vampyrs as superstition, but Kane had lived long enough to know that old knowledge often held truth.

She hadn't moved from the elevator threshold. While Sebastian and Nox failed to notice, Kane caught the tremor in her stance, the acceleration of her heartbeat, a rhythm now intimately familiar. His gaze shifted to the blisters on her arms, physical evidence of his transgression, and the bandage concealing his bite mark.

The memory of Budapest surfaced unbidden, the last time he'd lost control. Cazimir's words echoed across the centuries: *Control isn't about never feeling hunger. It's about mastering it, moment by moment, for eternity.* That lesson had shaped Kane's existence until tonight, when his discipline crumbled beneath an inexplicable compulsion.

But it was more than hunger that stirred in him. Her blood had carried notes of an essence that lingered like the finest vintage, yes, but something deeper had awakened, a protectiveness that went beyond mere predatory instinct. The realization troubled him. In his position as Head of the Human Vampyr Council, such vulnerability could be catastrophic.

His movement caught her attention. Their eyes met across the space, and he witnessed something remarkable: fear transforming into determination. She stepped toward him, then again, until she reached the boundary of shadow that hid him. Most humans cowered in his presence; she walked straight into the darkness to face him.

"You must have a death wish," he said, curiosity warring with wariness.

"Possibly," she replied with steady composure. "But I think if you were going to kill me, I wouldn't have made it this far."

"True." Kane found himself genuinely intrigued. In centuries of dealing with humans as Council Head, few had shown such courage. "I could kill you now. Right where you stand."

She trembled slightly, he caught the spike of adrenaline in her scent, before steadying herself. "Then you'd have to find another Elite. You and I both know Evelyn would force you to get one."

Astute. As one of the Elite program's architects, his failure would be seen as evidence that even controlled vampyrs couldn't be trusted. The political fallout would destabilize the delicate balance he'd spent decades building. Hardliners would gain support for more restrictive human policies.

"So we have reached an impasse," he said gravely.

Her response cut through the layers of political maneuvering with startling directness. "I can't go home because I need the credits, and you can't kill me because you'd have to find a new Elite."

If only she understood the full truth. The blood bond made releasing her impossible even if he wished it. He could sense her presence in the building like a second pulse, feel the echoes of her emotional state through the connection. Ancient vampyr courts had considered such bonds sacred, granting the human partner special protection. Those customs had faded, replaced by the clinical efficiency of modern systems.

Kane stepped closer, the tension building between them. Her pulse quickened, but beneath the fear lay something else, a shift in her scent that made his restraint waver. His strategic mind warred with emotional impulses he hadn't felt since Becca's death.

"Perhaps there is another way," he said, his voice carrying a dangerous undertone. "I could make a deal with you."

"A deal?" Wariness colored her tone.

"If you allow us to begin again, I will ensure your family receives all necessary care at no cost, for as long as you remain with me." The offer surprised even him; using his Council authority for personal matters violated his own principles. Yet the thought of her leaving, of anyone else approaching her, ignited a protective fire that burned fiercer than bloodlust.

She considered the proposal, conflict evident in her silence. When she finally looked up, her beauty struck him like a physical blow, not merely aesthetic appeal, but what the ancient Greeks called *kalon*: beauty that reflected inner worth. Her courage, determination, and resilience combined into something that transcended attraction.

Memories of his mother's stories surfaced, tales of brave maidens and honorable knights that had shaped his understanding of courage before his turning. He'd been the youngest son of a minor noble, more interested in books than battles, when the endless night had claimed him.

"Yes," she said at last.

Relief flooded through him. "Thank you. Perhaps we should start tomorrow. You need rest after tonight's ordeal."

"Goodnight... Kane."

His name on her lips sent a shudder through him, an intimate act by ancient standards. The sound resonated beyond mere hearing, triggering responses that momentarily stunned him. In all his centuries of deals and negotiations, none had affected him so profoundly.

Once she disappeared upstairs, Kane moved behind Sebastian with vampyr speed, startling him. "You found her where?"

"Near the Waterside Cross entrance," Sebastian stammered.

"Lucky timing." Kane's tone stayed neutral despite his suspicions. Waterside Cross had been flagged repeatedly for rebel activity, meetings, contraband exchanges, unexplained disappearances. "What brought you to that area?"

Sebastian lifted a distinctive red and gold bag. "Chocolates for Evelyn's birthday from Birmingham's Artillery."

Kane knew Evie's actual birthday. The inconsistency, like the others Nox had noted, added to a growing pattern of discrepancies. Sebastian's nervousness seemed excessive even for the natural human fear around vampyrs.

"You will tell no one what happened tonight," Kane commanded, placing a hand on Sebastian's shoulder. "Especially Evelyn. If I discover otherwise, the academy is always seeking donors."

Sebastian swallowed hard and nodded before retreating to the elevator.

Could Sebastian's love for Evie drive him to rebellion? Kane understood love's power to push people to extremes. Galandrea, his human lover before turning, had inspired him to risk everything before fever claimed her. Becca, his vampyr wife for nearly a century, had died in flames trying to save human children from a burning schoolhouse. Love made people dangerous, unpredictable, and vulnerable.

That was why Kane had delayed acting on Nox's suspicions. He couldn't shatter Evie's happiness without concrete proof. After centuries of solitude, she'd finally found contentment with Sebastian.

"You need to heal her," Nox said, appearing behind him.

"It's forbidden." Kane moved toward his office, the ancient law clear in his mind; direct healing of humans by vampyrs was prohibited even in extreme circumstances.

"We do plenty of 'forbidden' things. Technically, nearly killing an Elite is attempted murder."

Kane's growl reflected his frustration. He pressed his hand to the door until the lock clicked, then entered with Nox following.

"She'll be fine," Kane said hollowly.

"She'll be in pain all night."

Kane paused while shuffling papers. "The clinic provided nothing?"

"Glen said she refused."

Another puzzle. Why decline medication after such trauma? Pride? Fear? Or distrust of strangers after his attack, a thought that sent guilt lancing through him.

"Could we get something to her?"

"Not unless Sebastian escorts her again. If you or I take her, it goes on record." Nox's reminder stung. Kane's own regulations, designed to protect humans from vampyr exploitation, now kept him from helping the one human he'd harmed.

Kane grabbed Nox by the throat, pushing him against the wall. "Be quiet. I need to think."

"No, you need to heal her," Nox said through clenched teeth. "How will you explain her injuries to Evelyn?"

The truth deflated Kane's anger. Evie was one of his closest friends, but friendship wouldn't stop her from confronting him about harming an Elite. Her disappointment would be harder to bear than any political consequence.

"Damn it! I hate when you're right."

After Nox left, Kane slumped into his chair, the weight of what he'd done crushing him. He poured amber liquid into a crystal glass and downed it in one motion. The burn sliding down his throat was a harsh reminder of his brutality.

The prospect of healing her through a blood exchange made him uneasy. Such intimacy went far beyond feeding; it was sacred, forbidden for good reason. The connection he already felt from tasting her blood throbbed in his consciousness like a second heartbeat. Would giving her his blood strengthen that bond beyond his ability to control it?

Yet the older laws demanded he make amends. In the ancient courts, a vampyr who injured a human under his protection was bound by blood oath to heal that injury or face disgrace. Those traditions resonated in him despite centuries of modern governance.

It had been ages since he'd healed a human with his blood. The process required precise control, too little would be insufficient, too much could overwhelm her system. In his current state, with her blood still singing in his veins and the memory of her fear fresh, could he hold the necessary restraint?

Kane rose from his chair, his decision settling into place. He would heal her injuries and accept whatever followed. The risk was enormous, for his political position, for the bond's potential strengthening, for his own carefully maintained control. But the alternative, letting her suffer from wounds he'd inflicted, was unacceptable.

As he moved toward the door, the ancient part of him that remembered honor and responsibility overrode the modern politician who calculated risks.

Sometimes the right choice was also the dangerous one. Tonight, for her sake and perhaps his own salvation, he would choose right over safe.

CHAPTER THIRTY

SERENITY

Serenity collapsed against her closed door as Nox's relentless questioning finally ended. The vampyr had circled back to the same details again and again, her escape from Kane, Sebastian's timely rescue near Waterside Cross, every moment between the attack and their return. His penetrating silver gaze had hunted for inconsistencies with surgical precision, forcing her to hold to the story she and Sebastian had carefully constructed.

Strangely, she'd dreaded Nox's interrogation more than facing Kane directly. While Kane's presence intimidated her, she realized her fear centered on his capacity for violence, not on him as a person. The predator beneath his civilized exterior terrified her, but the man who'd shown unexpected remorse... that complicated everything.

A sharp throb lanced through her wounded arm, followed by a pulsing pain in her neck that kept time with her heartbeat. The mirror reflected angry red blisters and the bandage over Kane's bite, visible evidence of how quickly their arrangement had unraveled.

She regretted refusing pain medication at the clinic. Her father had always said pride had no place in healing, but she'd needed clarity, couldn't risk anything dulling her wits while she navigated this dangerous new role. Though calling herself a spy felt surreal; yesterday she'd been stocking shelves, and now she was gathering intelligence for the Human Liberation.

The night's revelations churned in her mind. Her father, the gentle healer who'd dried her tears and taught her medicinal herbs, had been a revolutionary. A member of the Liberation. Perhaps even someone who'd killed vampyrs.

It explained the abundant medical supplies, the secretive behavior, those monthly "supply runs" to the Inner City. The pattern was obvious now, and she felt foolish for never questioning it. Had Papa intended this for her all along? The careful lessons in observation, in memorizing details, even in lying convincingly to district officials, had it all been preparation for this moment?

Knowing about the Liberation earlier might have changed everything. She wouldn't have needed to become an Elite, would never have met Kane. Her family would have been safe, receiving medications through Liberation networks. Instead, by agreeing to spy, she'd placed them in greater danger than ever.

What have I done?

A sharp electronic beep interrupted her spiraling thoughts. She followed the sound to the cellular device Kane had provided, finding a message: *This is my number. Save it. Sebastian.*

She stored the contact as Nox had shown her. Just as she prepared to step into the bathroom, a soft knock echoed at her door.

Please not Nox again. She couldn't endure another interrogation. But if not him... Kane. The possibility sent an involuntary shiver through her, part fear, part something she didn't want to examine.

The knock came again, gentler this time.

Squaring her shoulders, she opened the door.

Kane filled the doorway, but his stance lacked the predatory edge from earlier. Instead he seemed almost hesitant, uncharacteristically uncertain.

"You refused pain medicine at the clinic?" His brows furrowed with concern.

The question took a moment to register through her mental fog. "I'm fine," she asserted, her voice stronger than intended. "No need to worry."

His gaze dropped to the angry blisters on her arms, wounds from her desperate defense, not his feeding. Instinctively she shifted to hide them, suddenly conscious of her vulnerability.

Pain flickered across Kane's expression as he caught the protective movement. Not physical discomfort, but something closer to shame. "You agreed we could start over tomorrow?"

"Yes," she admitted hesitantly, recalling their earlier exchange.

"Before we begin fresh, I need to fix what I did to you."

"Fix?" She frowned, uncertain of his meaning. After what had happened, any suggestion of him doing something else to her body made her tense.

He noticed her reaction, his expression softening. "I won't hurt you again, Serenity. I want to heal your wounds."

"How?" Curiosity cut through the apprehension. She hadn't known vampyrs possessed any healing ability beyond their own regeneration. If it were true, it could revolutionize treatment for countless human ailments.

Then another thought struck. If vampyrs could heal humans, why allow such suffering in the districts? The question added another layer to her growing suspicions about vampyr rule.

Kane averted his gaze, inhaling sharply. "By giving you my blood."

"I don't understand. How will that heal me?" Blood wasn't medicine, at least not for humans.

He shifted uncomfortably, glancing down the empty hallway. "I shouldn't be telling you this. It's expressly forbidden by Council law. As Nox pointed out, we can't let Evelyn discover what happened tonight."

Understanding dawned. "So you want to heal me to hide my injuries from Evelyn?"

He ran a hand through his raven hair, looking away before meeting her gaze. "Essentially, yes."

Serenity tried to suppress the laughter bubbling up in her, and failed. After everything, the attack, her escape, learning about her father and her recruitment as a spy, the mighty Head of the HVC stood at her door, wanting to hide his transgression from his friend.

It was the most human trait she'd witnessed in him, suggesting that perhaps vampyrs weren't so different after all. Even the most powerful feared disappointing those they cared about.

When she regained her composure, she noticed a slight smile on his face. The expression transformed his features, softening the sharp edges and lighting his eyes. She imagined how devastating a full smile might be, if this hint could alter him so completely.

"How exactly will your blood heal me?"

"My age has given my blood properties that let me heal humans," he explained, his voice lowering. "The ability manifests in vampyrs over three centuries old, but even then it's rare. Perhaps one in fifty develops it. And it's strictly forbidden."

"Why?" If his blood could heal, it was a precious gift. Yet he spoke of it with shame.

"The Healing Statutes were established after the Compassion Riots of 1658," Kane said, surprising her with the historical detail. "Humans discovered that certain elder vampyrs could heal wounds and cure diseases. They began hunting these vampyrs, capturing them, draining their blood for medicinal use. Many died, both vampyrs and humans."

"That's terrible," Serenity said, genuinely disturbed.

"After order was restored, the Council forbade healing and purged all mention of it from public records. Few humans remember now; it's become myth, a fairytale about vampyr magic. If humans knew the truth, it would destabilize the peace we've maintained."

His explanation made sense. If humans discovered vampyrs could heal, chaos would follow. Yet part of her wondered how many human lives might have been saved if the ability had been shared carefully rather than hoarded. How many children in Grove Gardens had died of treatable wounds while vampyrs attended galas?

Focus on the mission, her father's voice whispered in memory. *One step at a time.*

"Why risk it for me?" she asked, her voice trembling slightly. The question mattered; his answer might reveal where she truly stood with him, how she might use their relationship to gather information.

Kane hesitated, the tension crackling between them. His silver eyes softened as they searched hers, vulnerable, stripped of his usual facade, revealing something ancient and weary beneath.

"Because I owe you," he murmured, his voice heavy with emotion. His hand moved instinctively, brushing the hair from her face, his fingers lingering too long. "For the pain I've caused."

His gaze dropped briefly before meeting hers again, something raw flickering within. "You didn't deserve any of it. And yet you're still here, looking at me as if I'm not the monster I've spent centuries becoming."

His fingers brushed her cheek tentatively, as if asking permission. For a charged moment, the world narrowed to just the two of them, suspended in a fragile connection that transcended their roles.

"You're not a monster," Serenity heard herself say, surprising herself with her candor. "You've made mistakes, yes. But that doesn't make you a monster."

His sharp intake of breath revealed his surprise. "You have an uncanny way of seeing through me, Serenity. Few have dared over the centuries. Fewer still have survived the attempt."

The confession stirred something in her. A genuine compassion rose, and she regarded him with renewed curiosity. Perhaps there was more to Kane than the heartless overlord the Liberation portrayed.

That complexity could make her job harder. It was easier to spy on someone you despised, easier to justify deception when your target embodied everything you opposed. If Kane was capable of remorse, kindness, connection... where did that leave her?

She pushed the uncomfortable thought aside. Her family's safety came first. Kane's offer to cover their medical expenses, something the Liberation couldn't guarantee, made betraying him feel increasingly wrong. But she'd given her word, and too many people depended on her.

"You're willing to break your own laws to heal me?"

Kane nodded, his silver eyes meeting hers. "Yes. For you."

She weighed his words and their implications. If he'd risk censure for her now, what else might he share? What Council secrets might he reveal if she nurtured this unexpected connection?

Taking a deep breath, she decided. "Okay."

"You can't tell anyone," he warned. "It would breach your Elite contract, punishable by immediate termination."

She really needed to read that document. "You mentioned providing a copy?"

"I'll have it delivered tomorrow. Now, will you let me heal you?"

Serenity searched his frame for deception, but saw only the same vulnerability from moments ago, cloaked beneath his composure yet still visible.

"Are there side effects I should know about?"

His voice was reassuring, almost gentle. "No lasting harm. The few I've helped over the centuries had no negative consequences. The most noticeable immediate effect is enhanced senses for a few hours, sounds louder, colors more vivid, touch more sensitive. It can be disorienting, but it passes."

That didn't sound alarming, and her arm throbbed. Without proper care, the blisters could become infected. The clinic's treatment had been deliberately basic, negligence, she suspected, since the doctor had recognized her as an Elite her patron had injured.

She opened her door wider. "Come in."

He stepped inside cautiously, his frame seeming too large for the modest room. She noticed how he slowed his movements, perhaps aware of how his vampyr speed might unnerve her.

Keeping the door open for propriety and her own reassurance, she moved to the bed, unable to stand any longer as exhaustion overtook her.

Kane remained near the door, keeping a respectful distance. "I know you're tired. This shouldn't take long, and you may feel more energetic afterward."

She nodded, her face contorting as a sharp pain lanced through her arm.

"This would be easier if I sat beside you. Would that be alright?" He indicated the space next to her, careful not to assume agreement.

She nodded again, her gaze drifting to the ceiling as another wave of pain radiated outward.

The mattress dipped as he sat carefully, keeping inches between them. "Your arm must hurt badly," he said gently, real concern in his voice.

She could only nod.

"I'll bite my wrist and place a few drops in your mouth," he explained. "My blood is potent. You'll only need a small amount."

Serenity's pulse quickened, but she recognized this as her best chance for relief. Still, a lifetime of warnings about blood contamination made her hesitate.

Sensing her reluctance, Kane added, "Vampyr blood carries no human diseases. It's highly antiseptic, part of why it heals. The process is safe."

His reassurances, paired with another wave of pain, decided it for her. She nodded her consent.

His fangs extended gracefully, gleaming as he brought his wrist to his mouth and punctured the pale skin precisely. Dark crimson welled up, almost black in the soft light.

"Lean back," he instructed, his voice low. "Open your mouth slightly."

Serenity regarded him warily, a final uncertainty flickering. But with pain coursing through her and the mission requiring his trust, she had little choice. Taking a deep breath, she tilted her head back and parted her lips.

Kane held his wrist above her mouth, letting three drops fall onto her tongue.

The sensation was immediate and overwhelming. Rather than a metallic tang, his blood carried an astonishing sweetness, honey laced with exotic spice, the rarest wine aged for centuries, nothing earthly she'd ever tasted. Before she could stop herself, her hand closed around his wrist, instinctively drawing it nearer for more.

He allowed one additional drop before gently pulling away, his expression caught between amusement and concern. "That's enough. More could be a problem."

The taste lingered, haunting in its complexity. She found herself unconsciously licking her lips, trying to capture any remaining trace.

Kane brought his wrist to his mouth, sealing the wound with a practiced motion. It closed instantly, leaving no mark.

A sudden warmth bloomed in Serenity's chest, spreading outward like the spiced heat from moments before. When it reached her burns, the sensation shifted into a peculiar tingling, effervescent, like thousands of tiny bubbles beneath her skin.

She watched in astonishment as the angry blisters began to fade, the swelling visibly receding with each beat of her heart. Within moments her skin had returned to its normal color and texture, the pain completely erased.

Kane leaned forward, his face inches from hers as he carefully removed the neck bandage. His scent enveloped her, not cold stone but a rich complexity: aged leather, cedar, a hint of cloves, and beneath it all a warm musk that seemed strangely human.

"The bite mark is healing," he observed with satisfaction. "How do you feel?"

Before she could answer, the world transformed. Colors sharpened to a painful brilliance, her muted blue bedspread suddenly vivid as a summer sky, the wooden furniture revealing intricate patterns she'd never noticed. Sounds became distinct and overwhelming: the climate system humming, distant guard conversations two floors below, and most distinctly, a powerful rhythmic thumping that filled the room.

Thump. Thump. Thump.

She searched frantically for the source, her gaze locking onto Kane's chest. She watched, mesmerized, as his shirt rose and fell with each beat.

His heart. The heart she'd been told vampyrs no longer possessed in any meaningful way. Without conscious decision, she pressed her palm to his chest, feeling the steady, powerful rhythm beneath her fingertips. Slower than a human heartbeat, more deliberate, but undeniably alive.

As she touched him, his eyes darkened, pupils dilating until only a thin ring of silver remained. The connection between them shifted, and an electric current passed between her fingertips and his chest. His gaze locked with hers, and something inside her answered instinctively, a primal recognition that had nothing to do with fear and everything to do with desire.

Her heightened senses registered every detail with overwhelming clarity: the imperceptible movement of air as he breathed, the subtle warmth that belied the myths of vampyr coldness, the muscle shifting beneath his clothing as he leaned closer.

She imagined, with startling vividness, how his lips might feel against hers, how that silky black hair might wrap around her fingers. The thoughts came unbidden, inappropriate, and dangerous for both Elite and spy, yet she couldn't banish them.

"I'm sorry," she said, withdrawing her hand though it pained her to. "I got distracted by your heartbeat. It beats differently."

"Yes," he agreed, his voice lower than before, vibrating through her enhanced hearing in a way that sent shivers down her spine. "What you're experiencing is blood-sense, your perception temporarily heightened to something closer to vampyr awareness."

He traced a finger over her hand, seemingly idle, but the sensation was electric, each nerve ending registering the touch with exquisite clarity. She watched, trans-fixed, as he painted invisible patterns across her skin, every movement sending constellations of pleasure up her arm.

Her breathing grew shallow as he turned her hand over and brushed his lips against her palm, so gently it might have been the touch of butterfly wings. The contact shocked her entire system, every nerve firing at once in cascades of sensation that made her gasp.

Just as the feeling threatened to overwhelm her, Kane pulled away, his usual stoic expression returning, though something unreadable flickered in his eyes. Emotions surged within Serenity, disappointment at the lost contact, curiosity about his restraint, fascination with her body's response, and beneath it all a raw, pulsing desire that made her heart stumble.

"Are you alright?" Kane asked, his voice carefully controlled, though she caught the concern beneath it.

"I'm... fine," she stammered, heat rising to her cheeks as the swell of feeling threatened to spill over. The pain had vanished completely, replaced by an ex-quisite sensitivity that made even cloth against skin feel like a caress.

She didn't understand what was happening. The heightened senses Kane had mentioned made sense, but this burning need for him, this magnetic pull, was that normal? Was it because he was her patron, because he'd fed from her, or something unique to the two of them?

Despite the questions racing through her mind, she couldn't deny the pull toward him, beyond conscious control, as though her body recognized something her mind hadn't yet grasped.

Without thinking, she reached for him again. Her hands found his chest, the cool fabric, the solid strength beneath. She wanted to undo a button, to touch the hidden skin, but some vestige of self-preservation held her back.

Her eyes met his, finding an inscrutable heat there. She swallowed hard, her throat parched from the unyielding tension. A soft sound emerged from deep in his chest, part growl, part sigh, a primal response that could have been warning or invitation.

"Kane," she whispered, barely audible above her pounding heart. Though his name felt foreign on her lips, it seemed right, as though she'd been meant to speak it all along.

He didn't respond at once. Instead he watched her with the stillness of an ancient predator, restraint in every line of him. She braced for rejection, for him to retreat behind the propriety that governed vampyr-Elite relations.

Instead, he moved closer.

"Yes, Serenity," he answered, his gaze never leaving hers. Something in the way he said her name transformed it, no longer just a word but a sacred invocation. The air between them seemed charged as he reached out, fingers gently tucking a loose curl behind her ear. The simple gesture felt more intimate than anything she'd experienced.

His touch was cool against her feverish skin, a soothing counterpoint to the fire spreading through her veins. She leaned into his hand, her eyes fluttering closed as she savored the contact. A soft sigh escaped her, embarrassingly wanton to her own ears.

"Is this normal? The way I feel... is it just the blood?"

The question hung heavy with vulnerability. Kane stayed silent, his eyes scanning her face as though memorizing every detail.

"No," he finally replied, honestly. "I've healed humans before. This connection is something else entirely."

It should have frightened her, confirmation that this went beyond the expected effects of his blood. Instead she felt a strange relief. At least she wasn't imagining the pull between them, the invisible thread drawing them together despite every reason they should stay apart.

His hand slipped from her face, leaving a coolness behind like a ghostly reminder. The loss of contact was almost painful, her enhanced senses craving the stimulation he'd provided.

The recognition of her longing settled over her, undeniable. Acting on pure instinct, she leaned forward and pressed her lips to his.

The kiss began hesitantly, a question rather than a statement, a line crossed that could never be redrawn. For one eternal second, Kane remained perfectly still, and Serenity feared she'd misread everything, made a catastrophic error that endangered not only her mission but her life.

Then his arms encircled her, pulling her against his chest as he returned the kiss with matching hunger. The restrained power in his embrace made her feel at once vulnerable and utterly safe, a paradox that somehow made perfect sense.

Every point of contact sent electric currents cascading through her, her enhanced senses amplifying each one to a nearly unbearable degree. The heat between them built fast, a bonfire from what should have been a spark, as they moved together with a synchronicity impossible for two beings who'd known each other so briefly.

"Serenity," he murmured against her lips, pulling back to meet her eyes. Her name carried both warning and supplication. "We shouldn't," he whispered, though his eyes, now almost black with desire, conveyed a different message.

"I know," she replied breathlessly, even as she drew him back.

What am I doing? The thought flickered through her mind. *I'm supposed to be spying on him, not...*

But the blood-enhanced desire pulsing through her demanded satisfaction, and some traitorous part of her heart whispered that this felt more real than any mission ever could. Kane's offer to cover her family's medical expenses echoed in her mind, generous beyond anything the Liberation could promise. How could she betray someone willing to risk so much for her family?

Because people are counting on you, her father's voice seemed to whisper. *Because the Liberation needs this.*

The war between duty and desire made her pull back slightly, breathless and conflicted. Kane's eyes searched hers, and she wondered if he could see the battle raging within her, spy against woman, mission against heart.

"We should stop," he said finally, his voice rough with suppressed longing.

"Yes," she agreed automatically, though every cell screamed in protest.

They lay still, his forehead pressed to her shoulder, his breath warming her skin in rhythmic waves. She could still hear his heartbeat, slightly faster now, and his scent enveloped her completely.

As her own heartbeat gradually slowed, reality began to intrude. The magnitude of what had nearly happened settled over her like a physical weight. They'd entered dangerous territory, crossing boundaries that existed for good reason.

She couldn't afford to forget who Kane was, Head of the Human Vampyr Council, architect of the policies keeping humans subordinate, nor what she'd promised the Liberation. She'd agreed to spy on him, to betray whatever trust developed between them. The thought sent guilt lancing through her, guilt that had nothing to do with the mission and everything to do with the man still holding her as though she were precious.

With a heavy sigh, Serenity disentangled herself and slipped off the bed, immediately missing his warmth. The enhanced sensations still coursed through her, making even the air against her skin almost painfully sharp.

"I'm sorry," Kane said, sitting up, self-reproach evident in his rigid posture. "I took advantage of your vulnerable state. The blood effects can be overwhelming the first time."

"It's okay," she assured him softly, though nothing was okay. Everything had changed between them in ways neither could articulate. "We can blame it on side effects. Another thing erased when we start over."

He nodded, his jaw tightening as he rose from the bed. His movements were measured as he straightened his clothing, an act designed to rebuild the walls between them.

"Then I'll bid you goodnight. The effects should subside within the hour and be gone by morning."

"Thank you for healing me," she said, offering a strained but genuine smile.

"Don't thank me," he replied bitterly, gripping the doorknob hard enough to leave indentations. "I don't deserve your gratitude."

After he left, Serenity shivered, her body still vibrating from his touch. Every nerve ending remained painfully aware, processing sensation with a force that left her dizzy.

The Liberation was counting on her. Her family's safety depended on keeping her focus, on using Kane's obvious attraction to extract valuable information. Sebastian had warned her about this very scenario during their drive back.

He'll be vulnerable after what happened, Sebastian had said quietly. *Guilt makes even vampyrs susceptible to manipulation. Use it if you can, but don't get caught in your own game.*

Had she already failed by responding so genuinely to Kane's touch? The line between performance and truth had blurred dangerously, the boundaries between duty and desire bleeding together like watercolors.

Touching her lips, still tingling from his kisses, she berated herself for yielding so quickly. For centuries, vampyrs had used seduction as a weapon against humans. Was she experiencing something real, or falling victim to techniques Kane had perfected over lifetimes?

What have I gotten myself into?

She examined her newly healed arms. No trace of injury remained, not even the faintest discoloration. The burns had been erased completely, as though they'd never happened.

Her fingers moved to her neck, probing gently for the puncture wounds. They too had vanished, leaving only smooth skin beneath her touch, and the ghost-memory of his lips trailing fire along the same path.

The healing properties of Kane's blood were remarkable. She wondered if he understood the potential it held for human medicine. Diseases that claimed countless lives in the human districts might be curable through carefully administered vampyr blood. Or perhaps he did understand, and that was exactly why it was forbidden; such knowledge would upend the carefully maintained imbalance of power. Her father would have given anything for access to it. How many patients had he lost who might have been saved with a few drops of elder vampyr blood?

The immediate question was how to handle Sebastian. Should she tell him about the healing? About the unexpected intimacy? She couldn't explain the sudden absence of her injuries without raising suspicion, yet sharing the truth would mean revealing Kane's forbidden ability, information the Liberation would undoubtedly exploit, possibly putting Kane at risk.

Why am I worried about his safety? The thought disturbed her. *He's not my friend. He's my... enemy.*

Yet the vulnerability he'd shown tonight, the glimpse of the man beneath the vampyr, made simple hatred impossible, the kind of hatred that would have made her task so much easier. Her father had died fighting vampyr rule. Her mother and sister depended on her securing their safety. She couldn't falter because of misplaced feelings for someone who, despite his moments of kindness, remained part of the system oppressing her people.

Banishing the troubling thoughts, she turned on the shower, adjusted the temperature to a comfortable lukewarm, and stepped in, hoping to wash away the confusion along with the day's residue.

The moment the water touched her skin, paradise turned to purgatory.

What should have been a gentle cascade became an assault on her enhanced senses. Each droplet struck like a tiny missile, sending shockwaves through nerve endings still amplified by Kane's blood. A prickling sensation crawled up her limbs, spreading until every inch of her registered the water's touch with excruciating clarity.

She tried to adjust the temperature, but the dial slipped from her trembling fingers. The pounding of the water grew louder by the second, magnifying in her sensitive ears until it sounded like a roaring waterfall rather than a simple shower.

Her heart hammered in response to the sensory overload, each beat echoing through her skull. She tried to cover her ears, but her own pulse was louder still, a thunderous drumming that shook her bones.

The bathroom brightened by degrees, the normal light becoming blinding as her enhanced vision struggled to cope. Colors shifted and warped, the white tiles taking on iridescent qualities, shimmering with rainbows that shouldn't exist. The effect was disorienting, forcing her to close her eyes against the visual chaos.

With her sight shut off, her other senses compensated, growing even more painfully acute. The rhythm of water against skin went from uncomfortable to agonizing. Every nerve felt exposed, raw and defenseless against the relentless pelting.

She reached for the faucet, desperate to stop the water, but her limbs felt disconnected, responding sluggishly. Panic rose in her chest, constricting her breathing as the overwhelming input continued without mercy.

The pleasure that had coursed through her earlier had completely inverted, becoming a pain so severe it transcended ordinary experience. White-hot agony clouded her mind, rendering coherent thought impossible as she writhed beneath the water's assault.

A memory surfaced through the haze, Kane's warning about side effects, his careful administration of just a few drops. Had she taken too much when she'd grasped his wrist? Was this the consequence of human greed for vampyr power?

Unable to bear it any longer, Serenity released a bloodcurdling scream that echoed off the shower walls and spilled into the bedroom beyond.

CHAPTER THIRTY-ONE

RHYZAN

Rhyzan stood at the threshold of a hidden tunnel, its entrance cleverly disguised within the walls of Levees. The makeshift bar, strategically placed just outside Grove Gardens' fortified walls, provided perfect cover for the rebels' underground activities. The mingled scents of sweat, alcohol, and damp earth permeated the air, each distinct to his vampyr senses. He could separate the sharp tang of human perspiration from the sweeter notes of various liquors, and beneath them, the mineral richness of soil that hadn't seen daylight in decades.

This discovery could be the breakthrough he'd been hunting since the rebellion's first stirrings. Six high-ranking vampyrs had been executed in the past six months alone, a coordinated campaign that bore the hallmarks of organized resistance rather than random violence. As Chief of Security, each death weighed on him personally. He had sworn an oath to protect Celearius, and these tunnels might finally lead him to those threatening its stability.

He fixed the Outer City Police member with a sharp, inquisitive glare. "And you did not know about these tunnels?" he challenged, his heightened hearing easily catching the officer's accelerated heartbeat, the unmistakable rhythm of deception.

The official averted his gaze, unable to meet Rhyzan's eyes as the weight of the truth bore down on him. For the past five minutes, Rhyzan had pressed relentlessly for answers, receiving only stammered half-truths and evasions. The scent of fear poured off the man, a sour note that grew stronger with each question.

Tension hung in the air, the mystery of the hidden tunnels creating an unsettling atmosphere. Rhyzan could taste the apprehension like copper on his tongue, a sensation unique to vampyrs of his age and sensitivity.

Kurt, the doorman, had already revealed the sinister arrangement between the owner and the OCP: scheduled raids to capture unsuspecting humans for blood donations. The tunnels below provided escape routes for those fortunate enough to evade capture. The practice was technically legal under Outer City regulations, though frowned upon by the Inner City Council that Kane headed. Another example of the gap between official policy and ground-level reality that the rebels exploited so effectively.

Three pathways existed within the tunnel system. Two led back into the Outer City, while the third posed the greatest threat. It wound deeper into the abandoned ruins, where only rubble remained. That wasteland beyond the outer walls had once been Boston's northwestern suburbs before the Great War. Now it served as a buffer zone between Celearius and the wilderness, the Abandoned City, a perfect hiding place for those who wished to operate beyond the reach of vampyr authority.

Rhyzan's mind whirled with possibilities, calculating probabilities with the precision that had made him indispensable to Kane for centuries. The recent attack pattern suggested the rebels had established at least three operational bases; one had been discovered and neutralized last month in the Eastern District. If his theory was correct, their main headquarters would sit equidistant from all the attack sites for optimal coordination. This tunnel could lead directly to that central command.

Either way, they were now closer to uncovering the rebels' plans and ending their uprising against the OCP. His informant's intelligence about the bar and the tunnels had proven accurate. That same informant had mentioned a major operation in the works, something involving a weapon of considerable danger. The thought sent a chill through Rhyzan's centuries-old blood. He needed to find their headquarters before such a weapon could be deployed.

The OCP official kept shifting nervously beside him, visibly uncomfortable with the direction of the conversation. The Outer City Police, technically under Rhyzan's authority but practically autonomous in their daily operations, had grown increasingly unreliable as the rebellion gained momentum. Some officers were merely incompetent, but others... their loyalties were suspect.

Rhyzan turned to him, his voice low and menacing, the subtle harmonics that only vampyrs could produce making his words reverberate in the human's chest. "You knew about these tunnels, didn't you? And you didn't report them?" He let a hint of his true age and power seep into his gaze, a technique that made even brave humans quail.

The official hesitated, eyes darting. Rhyzan could hear the man's joints creak as his muscles tensed, smell the adrenaline flooding his system. "I... I had heard rumors about rebels possibly using them, but I wasn't certain," he stammered. "We were just here for the blood donors." That last statement carried the unmistakable cadence of truth amidst the nervous falsehoods.

Rhyzan studied him, his enhanced senses confirming the honesty of that final claim. The officer was corrupt, certainly, a participant in the unsanctioned blood-harvesting operation, but likely not directly tied to the rebellion. With a disgusted shake of his head, he dismissed the man, knowing no further useful information would come. He made a mental note to have the officer's activities investigated more thoroughly later. Corruption was a cancer that often metastasized into treason.

He signaled two other officers to follow as he squeezed through the crevice leading to the three-way division. Taking the leftmost tunnel, which carried a faint acidic odor reminiscent of the Abandoned City, he continued until he reached a ladder. The scent profile changed as they progressed, traces of gunpowder, chemical compounds, and beneath them, the medicinal herbs that reminded him of the remedies Richard Wright, Serenity's father, had been known for. Another potential connection that couldn't be dismissed as coincidence.

Cautiously ascending, he listened for activity above. His vampyr hearing reached well beyond the human range, catching the faint scurry of rodents in the walls and the gentle shifting of dust disturbed by distant movement. Hearing nothing significant at first, he was about to lift the covering when voices filtered through.

"Stop being an ass, Jax. She did it for her family."

"Yeah, that's bullshit, Tori. She could have come to me."

Rhyzan listened intently, his mind automatically cataloging vocal patterns and inflections. The male voice, Jax, carried the distinctive accent of Grove Gardens' eastern section, while the female, Tori, spoke with the more refined cadence of someone who had spent time in the Inner City. Two people, arguing about a third, a woman who had apparently made a difficult choice for her family's sake. His thoughts went immediately to Serenity Wright, whose Elite contract had been driven by her family's need for medical care.

Carefully, he raised the cover and peered out, his eyes adjusting instantly to the change in light, another vampyr advantage that let him see clearly in near-total darkness.

The area appeared deserted, though the voices sounded clearer now. Instructing the officers to hold their positions, he hoisted himself up and emerged into an open space cluttered with abandoned machinery. The smell of rust and oil hung in the air, mixing with the unmistakable scent of humans, at least three distinct individuals by their pheromone signatures. He crept silently behind the equipment for a better view, moving with the preternatural grace that made vampyrs such effective predators.

A woman and a man stood several yards away, deep in heated discussion. The third person remained partly hidden in the corner, but Rhyzan could hear his breathing, male, older than the other two, with a slight rasp that spoke of respiratory issues common among those raised in the more polluted human districts.

"Jax, you already know you can't afford their medicine no matter how hard you work. She did what she thought best to save her family." The woman placed her hands on the man's shoulders, pressing her forehead to his. "She'll be fine. You just need to support her when the time comes."

"Yeah, Jax. Don't be mad at her. She means too much to us... to you," the other male voice added from the corner, confirming Rhyzan's count.

The conversation hardened Rhyzan's suspicions into near certainty. They had to be discussing Serenity Wright; the timing was too perfect, the circumstances too aligned. This Jax seemed to have a personal connection to her, perhaps romantic, judging by the emotion in his voice. More importantly, the phrase "when the time comes" suggested future plans involving her. If she had indeed been recruited, she could become an invaluable asset, a direct line into Kane's inner sanctum.

Three people present. Rhyzan would need to proceed cautiously, uncertain how many more might be nearby. His senses detected no other humans in the immediate vicinity, but rebel groups were known to use techniques that masked their presence from vampyr detection; certain herbs and chemical compounds could temporarily dampen a scent signature.

He retreated slightly toward the opening and gestured for the officers to ascend quietly. They climbed up to join him. He signaled three individuals, possibly more, and advised caution. Both officers were among his most trusted, humans who had served under him for years and proved their loyalty repeatedly. Still, they lacked his abilities and would be vulnerable if the confrontation turned violent.

Stepping out from behind the machinery, Rhyzan startled the group. They tensed at once; the man in the corner reached toward his pocket while the other two stepped apart. Rhyzan raised his hands in a non-threatening manner. His preternatural vision caught the glint of metal in the corner man's pocket, a weapon, though probably not silver, judging by the duller reflection.

"Just relax," he said softly, modulating his tone with the subtle harmonics vampyrs used to calm agitated humans, not mind control as folklore suggested, but a physiological response hardwired into the human nervous system. "I mean you no harm." The half-truth came easily after centuries of intelligence work.

The man eased slightly, withdrawing his hand from his pocket but keeping it nearby. "Who are you?" he demanded, his posture betraying his readiness to fight despite the apparent compliance.

Rhyzan introduced himself as a commander in the vampyr military, explaining that he'd followed a lead to the tunnels. He emphasized that he wasn't there to harm them but to learn why they were using these passages. The partial truth would be more effective than outright deception; his centuries of interrogation had taught him that people were more likely to reveal information when they believed some facts were already known.

The woman spoke, her voice quavering. "We're not hurting anyone. We just wanted a safe place to gather." Her dilated pupils and microexpressions read as fear, but also determination, the characteristic blend he'd seen in many rebel sympathizers.

Studying them with his heightened senses, Rhyzan registered more to the story. The subtle shift in their pheromones as they spoke, the almost imperceptible changes in their muscle tension, all of it marked partial truths offered in place of whole ones. They weren't professional operatives, but they were definitely hiding something significant.

He approached, scanning their faces for signs of deception, moving with deliberate slowness to avoid triggering a violent response. "What do you mean by a safe place to gather?" His hearing caught the slight rise in Jax's respiration, the woman's swallow, the corner man's fingers tightening around whatever was in his pocket.

"Exactly what it sounds like," Jax snapped, eyes flashing with defiance. The sharp spike in his adrenaline told Rhyzan he'd struck a nerve.

Rhyzan's eyes narrowed, the silver in his irises brightening, a subtle vampyr response to a potential threat that humans often found unsettling. "It's illegal for you to be outside Celearius's walls. You'll be arrested and detained for the night." He kept the consequences moderate on purpose, a night's detention rather than the harsher penalties technically available. The approach often yielded better results than immediate threats.

"We aren't going anywhere with you!" Jax shouted, grabbing a burning log from the fire and hurling it at Rhyzan, who dodged easily, the projectile passing through the space he'd occupied a heartbeat earlier. Human attacks always seemed to unfold in slow motion to his perception.

"Jax, don't!" the man in the corner warned, too late. His reaction was telling; clearly the older man held some authority in the group, perhaps even leadership.

Rhyzan frowned at the sudden aggression. Something deeper was at work here, more than humans simply seeking a meeting place. The ferocity of Jax's response suggested personal stakes beyond an illegal gathering. Combined with their earlier conversation about a woman who had sacrificed for her family, the picture was taking clearer shape.

He stepped closer, his voice calm but firm. "That was unnecessary. Officers, arrest them." He could have subdued all three himself within seconds, but letting the human officers make the arrests maintained the pretense that he was merely a military commander rather than the Chief of Security investigating rebel connections.

The officers moved forward cautiously. One quickly secured the woman while the other apprehended the man in the corner. Rhyzan swiftly arrested Jax, who was reaching for another piece of wood. His vampyr strength made restraining the struggling human effortless, like guiding a child's movements.

Jax fought as the cuffs were applied, forcing Rhyzan to tighten them considerably. The human's wrists would bruise, but nothing worse. Rhyzan had centuries of practice in applying exactly the right amount of force to subdue without causing permanent damage.

Ignoring Jax's protests, Rhyzan marched him toward the exit with the others in tow. He needed to determine why they were using the tunnels and who else might be involved. More critically, he needed to establish whether Serenity Wright was indeed the woman they'd been discussing, and if so, what her role might be in whatever they were planning.

As they emerged back into Levees, Rhyzan couldn't shake the feeling that there was more to uncover. The hidden meeting space they'd found through the tunnel was too small to be a main headquarters, likely just an outpost or meeting point. The real center of operations remained hidden, perhaps elsewhere in the Abandoned City, or maybe even within Celearius itself.

He loaded the suspects into the police vehicle and transported them to the nearest OCP headquarters. The Outer City Police compound stood as a stark reminder of the division between Inner and Outer Celearius, functional rather than aesthetic, built to project authority rather than blend with the surrounding architecture. Unlike the gleaming structures of the Silver District where Kane resided, these buildings carried the utilitarian stamp of military efficiency.

He needed to inform Kane of his discoveries and request permission to explore the Abandoned City further. This development, coming on the heels of the incident with Serenity, warranted immediate attention. If the rebels were indeed recruiting from within Kane's household, the threat level had escalated significantly.

Pulling out his cellular device, he dialed Kane's number. The connection established almost immediately, one advantage of the vampyr-maintained communication network that operated independently of the unreliable human infrastructure.

"Speak," Kane answered, clearly irritated, unsurprising given the night's events with his missing Elite. Rhyzan caught a tension in his friend's voice that went beyond mere annoyance. Something had happened since they'd last spoken.

"I found something intriguing today." Rhyzan kept his tone measured, professional, despite the potential significance of his discovery.

Kane responded with a resigned sigh that carried through the connection with perfect clarity. "Define intriguing." The background sounds suggested Kane was in his private quarters rather than his office, unusual at this hour.

"We apprehended suspected rebels in the Abandoned City. They claim they're simply 'gathering,' but I suspect a connection to the recent executions," Rhyzan reported, watching the police car's flashing lights disappear into the distance. He deliberately withheld his suspicions about Serenity until he had more concrete evidence. Kane's emotional state seemed precarious, and accusations without proof would do more harm than good.

"Humans? In the Abandoned City?" Kane paused, and Rhyzan heard his friend's breathing shift, a sign of heightened attention only another vampyr would catch.

"Yes," Rhyzan confirmed, "and we found a hidden tunnel from Levees, the old bar outside Grove Gardens, leading into the Abandoned City." The strategic implications were significant. If rebels could move undetected between districts through these passages, the security protocols they'd built were fundamentally compromised.

"We know about the tunnels." The plural caught Rhyzan's attention; Kane wasn't alone, perhaps Nox was with him, or more concerning, Serenity herself.

"But not the third. It's unmarked on our current maps." The revelation should have drawn immediate concern from Kane, whose security instincts had been honed over centuries of threat and conflict.

"The third..." Kane trailed off as a faint scream pierced through the phone line from his end. The sound was distinctive, female, pained but not terrified, with a quality that suggested it hadn't been induced by violence but something else. Rhyzan had heard similar sounds during healing sessions, when vampyr blood was administered to humans. "*Fuck.*"

Then the line went dead.

Rhyzan stared at the device, his mind racing through possibilities. The timing was too perfect, the connections too numerous to dismiss. More troubling was the possibility that Serenity Wright now stood positioned between two worlds, Kane's inner circle and the rebel organization, a perfect conduit for intelligence in either direction.

He pocketed the device and turned toward the police headquarters, his expression grim. The interrogations would need to be thorough, methodical, and above all, discreet. If Serenity Wright was indeed connected to these rebels, Kane needed to know, but not before Rhyzan had gathered irrefutable evidence. Their centuries of friendship demanded nothing less than absolute certainty before he delivered news that might shatter Kane's trust in his Elite.

The Abandoned City waited, its secrets secure in the darkness for now. But not for long. Rhyzan would return with more resources, more men, and he would find whatever the rebels were hiding in those ruins. The security of Celearius, and perhaps the safety of his oldest friend, depended on it.

CHAPTER THIRTY-TWO

SERENITY

Her hands searched frantically for the shower door, fingertips screaming as they grazed the glass. The water had gone from a gentle cascade to countless needles piercing her skin. Each droplet sent lightning through her nerve endings, as if her skin had been flayed open and every receptor laid bare. The water's rhythm against the tile crescendoed into a deafening roar that threatened to split her skull.

The scent of her soap, vanilla and citrus that had seemed mild before, now assaulted her nose like chemical warfare. Even the steam felt wrong, each inhaled molecule coating her lungs with fire. Her thoughts fragmented as her consciousness splintered under the assault.

She screamed again as panic welled in her, the sound reverberating inside her head like thunder.

The bathroom door burst open, wood crashing against the wall with a force she felt through the shower glass. Hurried footsteps pounded against the tile, each step an earthquake.

The shower door was thrown open, and Serenity stumbled out, crying and shaking. Water droplets clung to her skin like acid, her body trembling violently as the air itself scraped against her.

Strong arms caught her as she lurched forward. Her bare skin registered the texture of his shirt, each fiber distinct and abrasive, yet beneath that pain, his embrace offered a security she'd lacked for so long. She pressed against him, anchoring herself in his presence.

For just a moment, fear flashed through her mind, *remember what he did to you*, but the thought dissolved beneath the tidal wave of sensation.

"Serenity, what's wrong?" Kane's voice was low, edged with an unfamiliar vulnerability, as though her distress tore at something in him. The vibration of his words traveled from his chest to her cheek, gentler than the other sensations bombarding her.

Nox's footsteps echoed in the small space. "Here, put this around her," he instructed, his voice a harsh whisper that felt like sandpaper on her eardrums.

When Kane tried to wrap what she assumed was a towel around her, the sensation became unbearable, rough and scratchy, like fire igniting her hypersensitive skin. Every thread felt like a wire brush against raw nerves. She cried out in agony, and Kane immediately discarded the fabric, his movement creating a breeze that swept across her wet skin like winter wind.

Her breaths came in sharp, shallow gasps, her body convulsing. The taste of copper filled her mouth; she'd bitten her tongue without realizing it. The metallic flavor blended with something else, something sweet and ancient that lingered from when Kane had given her his blood.

"Shit. Serenity, what's wrong?" Concern filled Kane's voice as he studied her trembling form. His silver-blue eyes had darkened with worry, the color shifting like mercury.

She cupped her hands over her ears, pressing hard, trying to block out the amplified world, her thundering heartbeat like war drums, the steady drip from the showerhead crashing like boulders, Kane's voice cutting through the chaos. Even her eyelashes brushing together when she blinked was excruciating.

"Please," she whimpered, her voice breaking. "Make it stop." The words tore from her throat, ragged with desperation.

Kane's hold tightened. While his shirt rasped against her hypersensitive skin, the stability of his embrace paradoxically grounded her, pulling her back from the sensory chaos. His body ran cooler than human, blessed relief against her feverish skin. The contrast between the pain of contact and the security of it created a disorienting duality.

"Serenity," he said softly, barely audible, his lips near her ear. "I need you to breathe me in. Do you understand? Breathe me in." The command carried an undercurrent of power that bypassed her conscious mind, reaching something primal in her, a new awareness awakened when his blood entered her system.

His words anchored her, drawing her back from the overwhelming sensation. She inhaled deeply, shakily, and his scent, warm leather, cedar, and something inherently him, ancient and predatory yet strangely comforting, filled her lungs. It soothed her frayed nerves like a balm, his essence somehow neutralizing the hypersensitivity. She exhaled slowly, then inhaled again, her body beginning to relax. The tightness in her chest eased as her frantic heartbeat steadied, falling into rhythm with his slower, steadier pulse.

"Good girl," he murmured, his tone steady and reassuring. "You're doing so well. Just keep breathing." His hand moved along her spine in soothing circles, careful not to press too hard.

Nox hovered at the edge of her vision, his usual sardonic expression replaced by genuine concern. "I've never seen this reaction before," he said quietly to Kane. "Not even with—" He stopped abruptly when Kane shot him a warning glance.

As her senses quieted, the world dimmed. The bright lights blinked out, leaving them in soft darkness. She barely registered Nox's retreating footsteps as Kane shifted, holding her close while gently guiding her to stand. The absence of light brought immediate relief, as if someone had turned down the volume on all her senses at once.

"I'm going to stand you up now," Kane said, his voice a low vibration through her. "But I need you to stay still. Don't move, all right?" His words carried that same subtle power, not forcing compliance but making it the path of least resistance.

Her nod was almost imperceptible, but enough. He eased her to her feet, his hands never leaving her bare skin, making sure she wouldn't collapse. The cool tiles beneath her offered slight relief, though water droplets still clung to her body, stinging faintly as they slid down her hypersensitive skin.

In the darkness, the silver of his eyes gleamed with an otherworldly light that should have frightened her after what had happened in the kitchen. Instead she found it mesmerizing, a point of focus in the chaos of sensation.

"Serenity, may I touch you now?" he asked, his voice threaded with tenderness and concern. She nodded again, unable to speak but trusting him in a way that surprised even her. A small part of her mind whispered warnings, the memory of his fangs at her throat, the kitchen attack, her own vulnerability, but those thoughts seemed distant, unimportant against her immediate need for relief.

His hand moved to her back, impossibly gentle. Instead of pain, she felt a soothing warmth spread through her, dulling the raw sensation that had consumed her moments before. It radiated from his touch like ripples on water, his vampyr ability to heal working through the link his blood had already established. The burning subsided wherever the warmth traveled, replaced by a tingling pleasure that made her sigh.

Kane pulled her closer, pressing her against his bare chest. The steady presence of his body enveloped her like a protective cocoon. She realized he'd stripped off his shirt and pants while Nox cut the lights, leaving only his briefs to avoid aggravating her raw skin further. The fine dusting of hair on his chest tickled her cheek, but pleasantly now, her hypersensitivity transformed from torture to heightened awareness under his influence. Despite the intimacy, she didn't feel exposed. She felt protected.

"Does this feel better?" His voice was soft, his breath brushing her temple.

She nodded, her body sagging against him as she released a shaky sigh. "Yes." The word came as barely more than an exhale, but in the silence of the bathroom, it was enough.

"Good," he murmured. "Now, I need you to open your eyes." His thumb traced the curve of her cheekbone, feather-light.

With effort, Serenity blinked them open. She met his silver-blue gaze, filled with concern. Worry etched his features, his normally stoic mask shattered by her suffering. She'd seen him as patron, as predator, but never like this, never vulnerable. The fierce protectiveness in his expression made something flutter in her chest, a warmth separate from the healing spreading through her limbs.

"Hi," she whispered, her voice trembling but steadying with each breath.

"Hi," he replied, his lips curling into the faintest smile. The way his gaze held hers, determined and filled with a depth she couldn't name, made her feel like the only person in the world who mattered. Despite standing naked before him, she felt a surprising comfort, as though his presence alone could shield her from everything.

An unfamiliar sensation bloomed in her, warm and strange and impossible to identify. There was a peculiar awareness, like catching movement at the edge of her vision, but when she tried to focus on it, the feeling slipped away. Her body hummed with an energy that hadn't been there before, a subtle vibration beneath her skin that was both foreign and oddly comforting.

The realization should have terrified her, this strange new awareness coursing through her veins along with his blood. She felt different, changed in ways she couldn't articulate. There was an odd sense of completeness, as though some missing piece of herself had quietly clicked into place.

What is happening to me? The thought flickered through her mind. *Why do I feel so... settled?*

"Can you tell me what happened?" he asked softly, their faces mere inches apart. His pupils dilated slightly as he studied her, cataloging every detail of her condition.

Her lips parted as she struggled to explain. "In the shower... the water felt fine at first. But then... it started to hurt. My skin—" She paused, swallowing hard as the memory made her shudder. "It felt like it was burning. And the sound... became too loud. I couldn't even touch the door. Everything was... too much." Words seemed inadequate to capture the overwhelming assault, how even the air had felt like it was flaying her alive.

"Shhh... calm down," he reassured her, his voice steady as his hands rubbed gentle circles over her back. "Keep taking deep breaths. Breathe me in." His scent filled her lungs again, calming her racing heart, building a bubble of peace around them both.

She obeyed, taking another breath of him, and the tension in her body eased further. The pain receded to memory, replaced by a languid warmth wherever his skin touched hers. Her awareness of him sharpened, the steady rhythm of his heart, the subtle shift of muscle beneath his skin, centuries of power contained in his seemingly human form.

"It's my blood," he explained, guilt weighing his words. "I've never seen it cause such a strong reaction in a human before." His brow furrowed, centuries of experience suddenly inadequate to the situation. He looked younger somehow, uncertainty breaking through his usual confidence.

"I've never heard of this either," Nox's voice cut in from the doorway. Serenity instinctively shrank closer to Kane, who shifted to shield her from Nox's gaze. The movement was protective, possessive in a way that should have alarmed her but instead made her feel secure.

Something in Kane's posture changed as Nox spoke, a subtle tension that rippled through the muscle beneath her cheek. His arms tightened around her almost imperceptibly, and she found herself drawn closer to his chest, as though he were shielding her from view.

"Serenity, look at me," he said, gently tipping her chin so her eyes met his again. His silver-blue gaze was steady, searching hers for something she didn't fully understand. In the darkness, the silver in his irises seemed to glow with an inner light, beautiful and inhuman.

She gazed back as he examined her, feeling strangely calm despite everything. There was a quality to his presence that quieted the chaos in her mind, as though his nearness alone had a soothing effect she couldn't explain. She found herself watching the play of silver light in his irises, mesmerized by the depth of concern she saw there.

The intimacy of the moment overwhelmed her, standing naked in his arms, vulnerable yet feeling safer than she had in months. Whatever was happening between them felt significant, though she couldn't say why.

"SLEEP," he commanded, firm yet soothing, laced with the undeniable power of his compulsion. The word resonated through her entire being, bypassing her conscious mind to touch something deeper. The compulsion washed over her like a wave, irresistible not because it forced her will, but because it offered the perfect relief her overwhelmed mind craved.

Her body relaxed instantly, the trembling subsiding as her eyes fluttered closed. Kane's voice echoed in her mind, lingering long after the word had been spoken. Serenity whimpered as a shiver ran down her spine, not from fear but from the pleasure of surrender. Her body draped against his, defenseless and at his mercy. The steady rhythm of his heart beneath her ear seemed to draw hers into time with it, two beats gradually falling into harmony.

"I've got you," he murmured into her hair, fingers tracing gently up and down her back. She melted into his touch, letting the rhythmic strokes soothe the last traces of pain.

As consciousness faded, a distant part of her mind wondered if she should fear this connection, whether she was losing herself in something beyond her understanding. But those thoughts dissipated like morning mist, inconsequential against the profound relief and security of Kane's embrace.

Her last coherent thought before sleep claimed her was how well she fit against him, as though she'd been made to rest in the circle of his arms. His heartbeat beneath her cheek had become the most soothing sound in the world, steady and strong, a promise of safety through the dark hours ahead. Even his scent seemed to wrap around her like a lullaby, drawing her deeper into peaceful surrender.

Slowly, she drifted into the most restful sleep she'd known in years, cradled against his chest like something precious he would guard through the night.

CHAPTER THIRTY-THREE

KANE

Kane's arms enveloped Serenity as he wrapped the plush towel around her sleeping form. He carried her effortlessly into the bedroom, where her scent filled the air, jasmine and rose, stronger now to his heightened senses, beneath it the faint citrus-vanilla of her soap, and beneath that still, the subtle trace of his own blood under her skin. Nox had already pulled back the crisp sheets, and Kane gently laid her on the mattress before tucking the bedding around her.

He sat on the edge of the bed and ran a hand through his tousled hair, the centuries-old habit doing nothing to calm the unfamiliar storm brewing in him. The connection he felt to her pulsed like a second heartbeat, something he'd never experienced in all his long existence.

"This Elite sure knows how to give us trouble," Nox joked, trying to lighten the tension.

Kane's head snapped up, silver eyes flashing dangerously. "Nox. Shut up." His fingers curled into fists, knuckles white with the effort to hold control. "I need to think." The bond to Serenity throbbed in him, a bridge he hadn't expected and couldn't explain.

"That should not have happened to her," he muttered, his brow furrowed. "Enhanced senses, yes, but not to the point of excruciating pain." The echo of her scream still resonated in his bones; it had reached him before the sound itself did, a phenomenon that troubled him more than he cared to admit.

Nox hesitated before speaking cautiously. "It could be her blood type. Have you ever healed anyone with AB negative before?"

"No," Kane replied, shaking his head. "The list of humans I've healed is painfully short." Limited by both law and his own reluctance ever since the Blood Plague had decimated both species.

"Then how did you know skin-to-skin contact would work?"

"I don't know. It seemed right." The compulsion had come over him as naturally as breathing once had. If the towel had been abrasive, clothing would have been too. He'd needed to touch her, to give comfort through direct contact.

His eyes moved around the room, searching for answers in the shadows. The last time he'd felt this protective was centuries ago, with Becca, before the Great War, before he'd hardened himself into the leader this world required.

"Evie—" Nox began, but was swiftly cut off.

"No," Kane snapped. "I won't involve her. She'll be furious about why I had to heal Serenity in the first place." Evie would demand answers, wielding her authority as head of the Elite Program to investigate the incident thoroughly. The last thing he needed was her scrutiny when he didn't understand what was happening himself.

A beep sounded from his discarded pants. Nox handed them over, and Kane retrieved his device. "Rhy," he muttered.

"Is everything alright? What was that scream?"

Kane sighed, rubbing his tense neck. "It was the Elite, but she's fine now."

"Why did she—"

"No reason," he cut Rhyzan off, avoiding the explanation. "She's fine. Tell me about this third tunnel. Did you find evidence of rebels?"

After a brief silence, Rhyzan answered, "Even better. I found three humans in an old factory. One tried to attack me; his hatred for our kind was obvious."

Kane's brows drew together. "Part of the rebellion?" A familiar dance they'd performed for decades, hunting those who refused to accept the world as it was.

"Possibly. I've taken them into custody, but I'd like to explore the area further with Council permission."

"Send me your location. I'm on my way." He ended the call, then turned to Nox, who handed him his shirt.

"Call me when she wakes," Kane said, glancing at sleeping Serenity as he tucked in his shirt. "The side effects should wear off before then." He could still taste the sweetness of her blood, a memory that lingered like fine wine.

Nox nodded, his gaze following Kane toward the door. "But what if they haven't worn off?"

Kane paused with his hand on the doorknob, looking back at Serenity. He shouldn't leave her like this. She ought to sleep through the night, but his blood shouldn't have affected her so severely either. What if she woke and the effects persisted?

Guilt weighed on him as his gaze lingered on her peaceful form. He would rather stay and make certain her condition didn't worsen. But Rhyzan's matter couldn't be ignored. The dutiful Councilor in him warred with the protective guardian she'd awakened.

"Then do what you can to make her comfortable. And call me immediately."

Nox nodded firmly, assuring him he'd care for her.

Kane took one last look at Serenity before leaving. Her black curls spilled across the white pillow, a contrast that burned itself into his memory.

Her presence lingered in his thoughts like a haunting melody as he walked to his car. Every fiber of him yearned to turn back, a connection unlike anything he'd known, even with Becca. What truly unsettled him was feeling her pain before her scream reached his ears, a bond that transcended the physical senses.

They were connected on a deeper level, intertwined in a way he couldn't explain. He'd just poured himself a drink when the bottle slipped from his hand and shattered on the floor. Without hesitation, he'd rushed toward her room, drawn by an invisible thread pulling taut between them.

He was grateful she'd been susceptible to his compulsion. The power to make her sleep might have failed with his blood in her system, as vampyr blood often granted humans a temporary resistance. Kane shuddered, thinking what might have happened if he couldn't have made her sleep. The Elder Council had strictly forbidden relationships between vampyrs and humans for good reason; though blood bonds were only myths whispered among humans, the emotional attachments created vulnerabilities neither species could afford in positions of power.

But this couldn't be that. Blood bonds were legend, fairy tales told to explain the rare cases of vampyr-human devotion in ancient times. What he felt was simply... protective instinct. Heightened by her unique blood type, perhaps, but nothing more.

This, whatever it was, would have to wait. Her well-being was in Nox's capable hands. He needed to focus on ending the rebellion, not on his Elite.

Kane gripped the steering wheel of his black Maserati, his knuckles white from the pressure. He forced himself to start the engine and pull out of the garage, her scent still clinging to his skin like a promise.

He concentrated on navigating the quiet Silver District streets until he reached the CityCentre gate, which lowered to let him pass. Instead of heading to the Council garage, he turned left toward what appeared to be a storage building, its facade meticulously designed to look mundane to human eyes.

A button on his rearview mirror opened the storage door, and he drove inside. Once it closed, he acknowledged the lone guard, whose eyes reflected the same silver glow as his own. The guard entered a code that revealed an entrance to the underground tunnels.

The quickest route to the districts and beyond the city walls. A handful of high-ranking vampyrs knew about these passages, remnants of infrastructure built during the darkest days of the Transition. He navigated the maze of tunnels expertly until he emerged into a cave outside Easton's walls.

Another button opened a camouflaged rock door, and he sped toward the destination marked on his phone.

Upon arrival, an officer informed him Rhyzan was inside, standing by the cavern wall speaking with an OCP officer.

"Where are these tunnels?" Kane asked, interrupting their conversation, his senses cataloging the subtle scent of human fear in the air.

Rhyzan looked up, his expression grim. "Right through here."

Kane followed him through an unexpected crevice in the rough stone wall, their footsteps echoing off damp surfaces as they descended into the dark cave system. The air was cool and musty, with a metallic hint lingering at the edge of perception, blood, old but unmistakable. The tunnel forked, and Rhyzan pointed out a small skull and bones marked above the entrance to the leftmost path.

"Interesting choice of decoration," Kane muttered, running a finger over the symbol. The rebellion had grown more sophisticated over the years, evolving from simple riots to organized resistance with codes and systems. The Human Liberation's signature mark; he'd seen it carved into the foreheads of six dead vampyrs in the past six months.

They continued through twisting passages until the cave gave way to an old sewer system. They walked until they reached a ladder leading up to faint light. As they climbed out, Rhyzan indicated another skull and bones drawn near the exit.

The space had clearly once been a bottling factory, now repurposed as some-one's hideout. Piles of old furniture and empty bottles littered the area, casting long shadows in the dim light filtering through narrow windows. Kane's eyes adjusted instantly, revealing details invisible to human sight.

"I found them here. They were discussing someone making a decision that the hostile one disliked," Rhyzan told him.

Kane's eyes scanned the area, searching for clues to determine whether this was a rebellion hideout or merely a gathering place for humans. He'd seen both during his centuries of governance and had learned to tell the patterns apart.

"You took them into custody?"

"Yes, they're being transported to the cavern now."

"Good." Kane's lips thinned as he surveyed the surroundings, his nostrils flaring as he worked through the complex tapestry of scents.

He searched thoroughly but found nothing that conclusively marked this as merely an escape spot. Then a familiar trace lingered in the air, jasmine and rose, unmistakably Serenity's natural scent beneath everything else. His pulse quickened against his will. She'd been here.

The realization hit him like a physical blow. His Elite, the woman currently sleeping in his bed recovering from his blood's effects, had been in this rebel hideout. When? How recently? The scent was faint but present, meaning she'd been here within the last few days.

Questions cascaded through his mind. Had she been captured and brought here? Rescued from here? Or... had she come willingly? The possibility ran cold through him. Could Serenity be connected to the Human Liberation? Could her presence in his life be more than coincidence?

He forced his expression to stay neutral, not wanting to alert Rhyzan until he understood more. But inside, everything had shifted. The woman he'd healed, comforted, felt inexplicably drawn to, was she his salvation or his destruction?

"Either the humans we caught are extremely foolish for gathering here, or they're rebellion members stupid enough to use this as a shelter," Rhyzan mused, kicking a bottle across the floor.

"I suspect the former, but hope for the latter," Kane replied automatically, his mind racing. Catching another familiar scent in the air, sex, and something distinctly human, his thoughts drifted to Serenity for a moment before he refocused. He decided to check the upper level, where older scents might reveal more about who had used this space.

As he turned the rusty handle and pushed open the door, his nostrils caught lingering traces of intimate activity and the faint acrid smell of burnt metal and gunpowder, distinctive and unmistakable.

"Rhy, come here."

Rhyzan appeared instantly at his side. "Interesting."

"I authorize you to interrogate them for information, but proceed cautiously in case they truly are just trespassers," Kane instructed, though his tone had gone colder. The discovery of Serenity's scent here changed everything.

Rhyzan nodded, already crouching to retrieve a piece of paper with faded writing.

Kane moved deeper into the room, boots crunching on debris scattered across the floor. The place was in disarray, but there was a pattern to the chaos that his experienced eye could detect.

A makeshift pallet lay in one corner, the source of the intimate scent. Among the debris were worn handwritten notes and maps, plans of some kind. It looked like trash to the untrained eye, but Kane knew better. He carefully picked up one note, squinting at the faded ink to make out its content.

His blood iced over as he deciphered partial words: "Council meeting," "security rotation," "Elite access." This wasn't just a rebel hideout; it was an intelligence-gathering operation. And Serenity's scent was woven through all of it.

"Rhy," he called without looking away. "Can you make out what this says?"

Rhyzan peered over his shoulder at the paper. "Hard to tell... looks hastily written."

Kane folded the paper and slipped it into his pocket. "We need to seal this area for further investigation. Inform the OCP and send a collection team."

"On it," Rhyzan replied, stepping away with his device.

Kane examined the room carefully, his mind piecing together the implications. If Serenity was connected to this operation, everything about their relationship took on new meaning. Her application to become an Elite, her presence in his life, even tonight's healing, could it all be part of an elaborate infiltration?

The thought should have filled him with rage. Should have triggered the cold, calculating response he'd perfected over centuries of leadership. Instead he felt something far more dangerous: uncertainty. Because despite the evidence suggesting betrayal, he couldn't forget the terror in her eyes during the sensory overload, the way she'd trusted him to help her, the way she'd fit so perfectly in his arms.

Was she an exceptional actress, or was she as caught off guard by their connection as he was?

He kept moving through the room, examining faded papers with new urgency. Old maps depicted neither Celearius nor the Abandoned City, but when he noticed an out-of-place picture of a subway station, he spotted a faint arrow marked on the wall, then another.

Following the trail of rusted marks, his gaze led to an old vent. Using his pocket knife, he pried it open, the metal protesting with a screech. Through the dust and cobwebs, a glimmer caught his attention. Reaching into the opening, his hand emerged clutching a small metal box.

Despite its size, it felt heavy. He examined its edges, looking for clues or an opening mechanism. His fingers traced along the sides until he found a combination lock.

"Sir, are we ready to seal the area?" an OCP officer asked, entering the room.

Kane slipped the box into his pocket and replaced the vent cover. "Yes, I'm finished. My team is en route to collect everything. Fine the bar owner and close the establishment for twenty-four hours. Allow business to resume afterward." No need to alert the rebellion unnecessarily; let them think they'd only found a decoy hideout.

The officer nodded. They made their way out of the dimly lit cave system, footsteps fading with each step.

After giving final instructions, Kane hurried to his car and drove home, his mind filled with conflicting thoughts. The relief he'd expected to feel at seeing Serenity safe warred with the new knowledge that she might be anything but innocent. The box weighed heavy in his pocket, but the pull toward his Elite weighed heavier still.

As he drove through the empty streets, Kane found himself caught between duty and desire, between the evidence of betrayal and the inexplicable connection that drew him to her like gravity. Whatever the truth about Serenity Wright, he would uncover it. The question was, when he did, would he have the strength to do what duty demanded?

The thought of her sleeping peacefully in his bed, trusting him to protect her, made his chest tighten with an emotion he didn't want to name. Tomorrow he would have answers. Tonight, he would simply have to live with the uncertainty, and the growing fear that the woman who'd begun to heal something broken in him might be the very person destined to destroy everything he'd built.

CHAPTER
THIRTY-FOUR

SERENITY

Serenity's head throbbed gently as she opened her eyes to morning light filtering through unfamiliar curtains. For a moment she lay still, wrapped in an unexpected contentment at odds with her last memories of excruciating pain. The pillow beneath her cheek carried a cool, masculine scent, cedar and leather and something distinctly Kane, that hadn't been there before. The sheets beside her held a subtle indentation, as though someone had lain there watching over her through the night.

She inhaled deeply, confirming her suspicion. Kane had been here, not just to bring her to bed but to stay beside her. The realization sent conflicting waves of comfort and alarm through her. Taking inventory of herself, she noticed yesterday's pain was conspicuously absent, no aching muscles, no burning skin, no raw nerves screaming at the slightest touch.

That was when everything else came rushing back.

The attack. Her escape. The Human Liberation. The truth about her father. And most shocking of all, she had willingly consumed Kane's blood.

What was I thinking?

She should have refused and endured the pain. But when the agony drowned her, his offer had seemed like her only lifeline. She remembered his wrist at her lips, the intoxicating sweetness spreading across her tongue, the inexplicable hunger for more. The memory sent an involuntary shiver through her that had nothing to do with fear.

She rolled over, pressing her face into the pillow where his scent was strongest. Had he sat watching over her all night? The thought should have disturbed her, a vampyr guardian observing her in vulnerable sleep, but instead it wrapped around her like a protective cocoon. Her fingers traced the slight depression in the mattress, and she imagined his weight there, his silver eyes keeping vigil.

Even with her senses back to baseline, she couldn't shake the lingering awareness of Kane that hummed beneath her skin. It was as if some invisible thread connected them now, letting her sense his presence in the building, or rather, confirming his absence. The sensation was both unsettling and oddly comforting.

Was this normal after consuming vampyr blood? The possibility troubled her almost as much as her mission to spy on the very being who had saved her from that pain, the same being who had apparently kept watch over her through the vulnerable hours of the night.

A loud grumble interrupted her troubling thoughts. Her stomach protested its emptiness, reminding her she hadn't eaten since breakfast yesterday. She sat up, pulling back the covers, and realized with a jolt that she was completely naked beneath them.

Heat flooded her cheeks. Kane had carried her, wet and unclothed, from the shower to the bed. The same Kane who had kissed her so fiercely. And now, it seemed, the same Kane who had remained by her side through the night, a silent guardian whose scent still clung to her sheets and skin.

"This is ridiculous," she muttered, pushing herself out of bed with more force than necessary. Her family needed her. She couldn't afford to be distracted by whatever strange effect Kane's blood had on her system.

She hurried to the closet and selected a simple lavender dress that covered her from neck to knee, the most modest option in her Elite wardrobe. As she pulled it on, her fingers traced the places where burns and bite marks should have been. Nothing remained, not even the faintest scar to evidence what had happened. Kane's blood had erased it all, as though rewriting history itself.

Sighing, Serenity made her way to the bathroom, brushing her teeth and coaxing her curls into some semblance of order. She studied her reflection critically. Same honey eyes. Same full lips. Same dark skin. Nothing outwardly changed, yet she felt fundamentally different, as though Kane's blood had rewritten something in her on a cellular level.

With new determination, Serenity descended to the kitchen. As she approached, she could hear two male voices in hushed conversation. They fell silent as she entered, both Nox and Rhyzan turning to look at her with an uncanny synchronicity that underscored their inhuman nature.

"Feeling better?" Nox asked, genuine concern etched on his features. Rhyzan's gaze was more clinical, his eyes moving systematically from her face to her neck to her arm, checking for evidence of last night's injuries, no doubt.

"Yes," she replied, taking a seat beside Nox, deliberately placing him between herself and Rhyzan's scrutinizing stare. "Just a slight headache."

"Hungry?" Nox asked.

She nodded, feeling oddly shy under their combined attention.

"I'll make you breakfast," Nox offered, pushing his chair back. He cast a warning glance at Rhyzan. "Behave."

The familiarity between them suggested a relationship that went well beyond professional courtesy. How long had they worked together? Decades? Centuries? The thought of such extended lifespans still boggled her mind.

She raised an eyebrow at Rhyzan, whose hard stare hadn't wavered despite Nox's warning.

"Would you like eggs and..." Nox paused, extracting a clear plastic bag of meat from the refrigerator. He sniffed it suspiciously, nose wrinkling. "I think this is sliced ham?"

She smiled, amused by his uncertainty with human food. "I would love some."

Trying to appear relaxed, Serenity attempted to meet Rhyzan's gaze, but the weight of his stare made her look quickly away. What did he know? What did he suspect? Her heart rate ticked up at the thought that he might have discovered her connection to the Liberation. *Calm down*, she told herself. *Vampyrs can detect an increased pulse, and anxiety will only make you look suspicious.*

"I heard you had quite the adventure last night," Rhyzan commented, setting his cellular device down slowly.

Last night had indeed been an adventure, one that had fundamentally altered her understanding of the world. The knowledge that her father had been a key figure in the Human Liberation brought both pride and pressure. She carried his legacy now, continuing work he'd deemed important enough to risk his life for.

If she succeeded in her mission, locating where the vampyrs held human prisoners, particularly this Jon Sinclair person Starr had mentioned, she could potentially help free dozens of humans. Her family could escape to safety with the Liberation's help. Freedom from vampyr control seemed tantalizingly possible.

Yet as she sat in the kitchen, watching Nox crack eggs with preternatural precision, her thoughts kept circling back to Kane. The way his eyes had burned when he looked at her. The gentleness of his touch despite his immense strength. The taste of his blood, sweeter than anything she'd ever known.

"I don't know if I'd call being afraid and thinking you're going to die an adventure," Serenity replied, deliberately turning her attention to Nox's work. The rich aroma of cooking meat filled the kitchen, momentarily distracting her from her churning thoughts.

"So, Sebastian found you? Where exactly?" Rhyzan's tone carried a predatory edge that set her on guard.

She tensed, recalling Sebastian's strict instructions about their cover story. Any inconsistency now could endanger everything, the mission, the Liberation, her family.

"Leave her alone," Nox interjected before she could respond. "I already questioned her thoroughly last night." He tossed ham into the sizzling pan with more force than necessary, spattering oil. "Don't you have somewhere to be?"

The protection surprised her. Why would Nox shield her from Rhyzan's questioning? Another mystery in a household already overflowing with them.

She studied Rhyzan covertly as he glared at Nox. Though dressed in the same elegant style as Kane, something about him seemed fundamentally different, colder, more calculating, as though he viewed humans as pieces on a strategic board rather than as individuals.

"So, you work for him. For Kane? Like Nox?" she asked, steering the conversation away from Sebastian and her escape.

"Yes and no." The cryptic response was typical of vampyr communication, giving nothing away.

"May I ask what you do for him?" She layered her voice with innocent curiosity, though in truth, any information about Kane's inner circle could prove valuable to the Liberation. Her stomach rumbled again as the aroma of cooked ham intensified.

"I oversee security and help train vampyrs at the academy," Rhyzan replied, his tone suggesting this was common knowledge hardly worth discussing. "And I assist Kane with human and vampyr relations when needed."

Human and vampyr relations. Such a sanitized term for what likely involved hunting down humans like herself who dared challenge vampyr authority. Did he know about the Human Liberation? Was he working to undermine them even now?

Before she could probe further, Nox placed a plate before her, eggs cooked to perfection, ham seared golden brown, a glass of fresh orange juice.

"Eat," he instructed with unexpected gentleness before taking the seat beside her.

"So, you're like his second in command?" she asked Rhyzan between bites, building a profile of Kane's power structure in her mind.

"Yes." The single syllable carried unmistakable pride.

She took another bite, chewing slowly while she gathered courage for her next question. "Where is he?" The question came out more softly than intended, betraying an interest beyond casual curiosity.

Rhyzan's expression held suspicion while Nox's showed a mix of concern and subtle amusement. Neither answered right away.

She took a bite of ham and waited, feigning nonchalance while her heart thumped traitorously faster.

Finally Nox broke the silence. "He's attending a Council meeting. He'll return within the next hour or two."

The thought of seeing Kane again sent an involuntary flutter through her stomach that had nothing to do with hunger. *Focus*, she chided herself. *Remember why you're here. Remember your family.*

Her mother's tired eyes and gaunt features flashed in her mind, the toll of her illness written in every line of her face. Then Beth's image followed, her brilliant sister, whose potential would be wasted if her condition kept deteriorating. They depended on her. The medical care Kane had arranged would help for now, but only the Liberation could offer true freedom.

"Was it the smell of my blood that made him bite me?" she asked abruptly, redirecting the conversation. "Like the doctor at the clinic?" She fixed her gaze on Rhyzan, noting how his eyes narrowed at the mention of the clinic.

Nox turned sharply toward Rhyzan. "What doctor? What happened at the clinic?" His confusion seemed genuine. "No one informed me about an incident with a doctor."

"Because there was nothing to report," Rhyzan replied, his dismissive tone belied by the tension in his shoulders. "The doctor is under control now. She broke protocol and clearly wasn't field-ready."

Serenity suppressed a shudder, imagining what "under control" might mean in Rhyzan's terminology. Yet Kane had committed the same transgression. "But Kane also lost control," she pointed out, concern in her voice. "Will he face punishment?"

The question surprised even her. Why should she care about Kane's welfare? He was the enemy, the very embodiment of the system she was working to undermine. Yet the thought of him suffering consequences for actions that had ultimately led to her healing troubled her in ways she couldn't fully articulate.

Rhyzan studied her with renewed interest, as though the question had revealed something significant. "No, he won't be punished," he said finally. "Even if last night's incident warranted consequences, he's not easily harmed." The implication was clear; Kane's position and power shielded him from accountability that would destroy lesser vampyrs.

She took a casual sip of juice, trying to ease the sudden tension. "So he can't be punished?" she asked, more pointed than she intended.

"Why?" Rhyzan countered, leaning forward slightly. "Would you like to see him punished?"

The question caught her off guard. Just days ago, her answer would have been an unequivocal yes. Any vampyr who harmed a human deserved whatever justice the universe delivered. But now, knowing it was her neck he had bitten, her pain he had ended with his forbidden blood...

"No," she admitted quietly, surprising herself with the truth of it. "I don't want to see him punished. He did heal me, which he wasn't obligated to do."

"Speaking of healing," Nox interjected, throwing Rhyzan a warning glance, "you understand the importance of discretion. Especially regarding Evelyn."

"Yes, of course," Serenity assured him. "We discussed it last night."

A particular memory surfaced with startling clarity, the moment Kane's blood had touched her tongue. It had been an explosion of sensation, like nothing she'd ever experienced. Rich and sweet, carrying notes of honey and something indefinable that sang along her nerve endings, kindling a primal desire for more. Even now, the memory made her mouth water with shameful longing.

"Does everyone react that way when given vampyr blood?" she asked, unable to contain her curiosity.

"No," Nox replied curtly. "We're unsure why you responded so dramatically to his blood. Our theory involves your unique blood type."

"Reacted? How did you react to his blood?" Rhyzan asked, sudden interest sharpening his features.

"As you said earlier, nothing to report," Nox cut in with unusual sharpness. "She had a reaction. It's over now." Rhyzan glared at him, clearly irritated by the deflection.

The tension between them fascinated Serenity. Clearly these vampyrs didn't communicate as seamlessly as she'd assumed. Their relationship seemed complex, professional respect undercut by personal friction. Such divisions could be exploited by the Liberation, if properly understood.

She finished her meal in thoughtful silence, her mind cataloging every interaction for later. As she rose to clear her dishes, a sudden chill raced across her skin, raising goosebumps along her arms. Her pulse quickened, responding to something beyond conscious perception.

He was here. She knew it with inexplicable certainty.

The elevator dinged as she placed her dishes in the sink. She kept her back turned, steeling herself for his arrival. *Remember your mission. Remember who you are.*

"You're back early," Rhyzan observed. "The meeting must have gone poorly."

"McGraff is an idiot," Kane declared, his rich voice sending an involuntary shiver down her spine despite her resolve. "He still refuses to acknowledge the security breach as a systemic threat."

"Three more weeks until his retirement," Nox offered consolingly. "Have they selected his replacement yet?"

Serenity could feel Kane's gaze on her back like a physical weight, but she kept washing her dishes, needing these few moments to compose herself before facing him. The strange connection she'd felt earlier sharpened with his physical presence, as though an invisible cord pulled taut between them.

It was just the blood, she told herself. A temporary side effect that would fade. Nothing more.

"They have two candidates under consideration," Kane replied, his voice softer now. "The final vote takes place next week."

Silence fell, broken only by the gentle sound of running water. Serenity focused on the simple task of washing her plate, trying to ignore the weight of Kane's attention. Then a warm hand pressed gently against the small of her back, and she startled. She hadn't heard him approach, another reminder of the preternatural abilities that made vampyrs so dangerous.

Her hands stilled beneath the flowing water as electricity seemed to arc from his touch through her entire body. She swallowed hard, desperately trying to compose herself before turning to face him.

"Good morning," he greeted, his voice smooth as aged whiskey. "How are you feeling?"

She turned off the water and reached for a towel, using the mundane action to buy precious seconds. "I'm fine," she replied, aiming for nonchalance and missing by a mile. "And you?"

A hint of a smile played at the corner of his mouth. "Better, now that I've confirmed your recovery."

Glancing around, she realized that Rhyzan and Nox had disappeared, leaving her alone with Kane in a silent kitchen that suddenly seemed too small. Her heart accelerated despite her best efforts to stay calm.

He stood close, not touching her, but near enough that his scent enveloped her. Leather and cedar and something uniquely him that made her want to lean in and breathe deeply, as she had during last night's crisis. His eyes flickered, the silver-blue irises momentarily illuminating before he closed them briefly, visibly exerting control.

When he reopened them, his eyes had returned to normal. "I'm pleased you're feeling better," he said, his tone more formal now. "I have the contract you requested."

He retrieved a stack of stapled papers from his briefcase on the table. She moved closer, acutely aware of his presence with every nerve ending. His scent intensified, and she closed her eyes for a moment, savoring it with a reaction that felt instinctive rather than chosen.

When she looked again, his eyes had illuminated once more. His gaze dropped to her lips, lingering there with a heat that made her gasp softly. He looked away immediately, extending the contract toward her. As she reached for it, their fingers brushed, the briefest contact that nonetheless sent a jolt of awareness through her entire body. He stepped back quickly, putting distance between them.

"Please review this at your convenience," he said, his voice carefully controlled. "Let me know if you have questions."

He collected his briefcase and moved toward the door, pausing at the threshold. His eyes remained illuminated, betraying emotions his composed expression concealed.

"A cellular device was delivered to your family yesterday," he said quietly. "Nox programmed their number into your device. You may call them whenever you wish."

The unexpected gift hit her like a physical blow. Communication with her family, the ability to hear their voices, to know they were well, to ease their worries about her, was more precious than any luxury his wealth could provide. In that moment the carefully constructed narrative of "evil vampyr overlord" cracked, revealing something more complex beneath.

Without conscious thought, she crossed the kitchen and threw her arms around him, embracing him with genuine gratitude. "Thank you," she whispered, her voice thick with emotion. "Thank you so much."

His briefcase thudded to the floor as he gently disengaged her arms from his waist. But instead of stepping away, he remained close, his illuminated gaze traveling slowly to her lips. They trembled slightly in response, anticipation warring with the voice of duty in her mind.

He leaned closer, his breath warm against her skin. Her heart hammered, torn between contradictory impulses. He wanted to kiss her. More alarming, she wanted him to.

The rational part of her mind screamed warnings. This was dangerous territory. She was here to gather intelligence for the Liberation, to find information about the human prisoners, to honor her father's legacy. Getting emotionally involved with Kane would compromise everything. Yet looking into his silver eyes, seeing the vulnerability there alongside the desire, she felt her resolve waver. This wasn't the monster the Liberation had described. This was a man who had healed her at great personal risk, who had watched over her through the night, who'd been thoughtful enough to arrange communication with her family.

What if they're wrong about him? the traitorous thought whispered. *What if there's more to this than the Liberation understands?*

"Serenity," he murmured, her name a question on his lips.

For a moment she almost surrendered to the pull between them, almost let herself forget everything except the way he was looking at her, the way his nearness made her heart race, the way every instinct told her to lean into his strength.

But then her mother's face flashed in her memory, gaunt, tired, depending on her daughter to secure their survival. Beth's labored breathing echoed in her mind, a reminder of what was at stake. The Liberation was counting on her. Her father had died for this cause.

No. The voice of reason finally broke through the haze of desire. *This isn't real. Remember your mission. Remember who you are.*

"I'm sorry," she said, pulling away with an effort that felt like tearing part of herself free. "Thank you again for the gift." She retreated to retrieve the contract, needing physical distance to clear her head. When she turned back, the doorway stood empty.

Serenity pressed the contract against her chest and took a deep breath. She just needed to find the information about the human prisoners, and then she could go home. She would make her father proud by continuing his work. She would secure her family's safety. She would fulfill her mission.

But as she returned to her room, contract in hand and Kane's scent still lingering in her nose, doubt gnawed at the edges of her certainty. The man who had just given her the gift of her family's voices didn't match the evil overlord the Liberation had painted.

She needed to call her mother and sister. That tangible link to her real life, her real purpose, would surely ground her again. It had to. Because if it didn't, if this strange connection with Kane kept growing despite her best efforts, she would be forced to choose between her father's legacy and her own heart. And that was a choice she wasn't sure she was strong enough to make.

CHAPTER THIRTY-FIVE

KANE

"And what was that?" Rhyzan inquired as Kane entered his office, his tone deceptively calm. His sharp, assessing gaze, framed by dark hair against pale skin, held an edge that demanded answers. The bookcases that usually lined the walls had been pushed aside, revealing security monitors that displayed feeds from throughout the building. On the larger screen, Kane's foyer showed Serenity ascending the stairs.

Kane felt Rhyzan's nostrils flare subtly, a vampyr tell that he was sampling the air, likely detecting traces of Serenity's blood mingled with Kane's own scent. Rhyzan's pupils dilated slightly before he controlled the reaction, a change imperceptible to humans but obvious to Kane.

"No, you may not," Kane replied curtly, setting his briefcase on his desk. He straightened to his full height, shoulders squared, a centuries-old posture of dominance. Rhyzan, however, met his gaze unflinchingly, a silent reminder that while he respected Kane's position, he was no subordinate to be intimidated. Kane discreetly pressed a button under the desk. The bookcases began sliding shut, concealing the security cameras.

"Can I at least know why you chose to heal her last night?" Rhyzan pressed, keeping his physical distance, a calculated move that showed deference while asserting his right to question. "I heard she had a bad reaction."

Kane's jaw tightened, fangs instinctively lengthening before he forced them back. "She was hurt, and I healed her to stop her pain," he explained, his voice deepening with authority. "She had a bad reaction, but I think it was just from healing too fast." He added sharply, "Satisfied?"

Rhyzan crossed his arms, his stance mirroring Kane's authority. "No, but we have more important matters to discuss." His expression conveyed the gravity of their situation while making it clear he was letting the subject drop by choice, not by command.

Kane knew Rhyzan wouldn't let this go easily. A Council member sharing blood with an Elite, even for healing, crossed lines established after the Blood Riots. If Rhyzan knew, Evie would soon storm through his doors demanding explanations.

"We do. Have any of the humans begun to talk?" Kane moved toward the window, keeping his back to Rhyzan to hide the tremor in his hands, an aftereffect of Serenity's blood coursing through his system. Her essence amplified his senses; he could hear conversations three floors below with painful clarity.

"Yes. Two are innocent, but the third one, his hatred for our kind runs deep. His pulse doesn't elevate when he lies about Liberation involvement. He's been trained."

Kane turned, interest piqued. The Liberation had evolved from scattered protests to organized resistance, their tactics growing more sophisticated with each attack. "Let the other two go. Do you have more on him?"

"We're gathering it now. Should have it by this afternoon." Rhyzan's eyes flicked to Kane's wrist, the same wrist Serenity had grasped last night. Kane subtly adjusted his sleeve.

"Good. The doctor's killer isn't talking, and there's only so much we can do without killing him. Until then, send in Chloe for the softer approach."

Rhyzan raised an eyebrow but said nothing. Chloe's empathic abilities made her invaluable for interrogations; she could sense emotional truths beyond physical reactions.

"Have we deciphered any of the messages found with him?"

"Unfortunately, no. But we sent them to Kregan, south of us. They have a codebreaker who might help." Rhyzan stood, moving toward the door. He paused deliberately, his eyes meeting Kane's with meaning. "Your Elite... her presence lingers on you, even now." His voice stayed neutral, but Kane caught the underlying warning.

"Good. We need to solve this soon. I have a feeling things are going to escalate."

After Rhyzan left, Kane examined the interrogation files. They couldn't even find the killer's name, no trace of him anywhere. It made him wonder if humans still lived in the cave systems beyond the Abandoned City, operating entirely off their radar.

The rebels could be working in shadow networks, just as Serenity had before becoming his Elite. The thought sent unease through him, particularly after discovering her scent at the Liberation hideout.

Kane closed the files and moved to the window. Outside, Celearius stretched before him, the gleaming Silver District giving way through Quartz to the weathered buildings of Easton beyond. Somewhere out there, the Liberation plotted their next move, potentially with information Serenity had gathered during her time among them.

The discovery of her scent in that rebel hideout had shattered his fragile sense of security. Everything about their relationship took on new meaning, her application to become an Elite, her presence in his life, even last night's healing. Could it all be part of an elaborate infiltration?

He closed his eyes, and unbidden, an image of Becca surfaced, his vampyr wife from centuries past. Her golden hair illuminated by candlelight, her musical laugh, the way her amber eyes gleamed when she smiled across the formal Council chambers. They had been equals, partners in building the early foundations of Celearius.

Serenity was nothing like Becca. Where Becca had been sunshine and gentle curves, Serenity was midnight and sharp edges. Where Becca had accommodated his ambitions, Serenity challenged his authority at every turn. Yet somehow, both women had found their way past his defenses.

But unlike Becca, Serenity might be his enemy.

He couldn't pinpoint when it had happened, but Serenity was no longer just a means to satisfy his hunger. She had become something more, a connection he hadn't sought yet couldn't deny. After centuries of treating humans as mere sustenance or political tools, Serenity stood before him as an enigma. This unexpected attachment threatened the walls he'd meticulously built since Becca's loss.

Kane's fingertips brushed his desk, registering each grain of the wood with startling clarity. Her blood in his system had transformed all his senses, making even familiar textures feel newly discovered. He remembered the silk of her skin as he'd carried her to bed, the flutter of her pulse against his fingertips, the weight of her body against his chest. His fangs descended fully at the memory, a visceral reaction he hadn't felt in decades.

These feelings weren't transient, despite his resistance. The blood bond had created something deeper than simple attraction. Even now, he could sense her presence in the building like a steady pulse at the edge of his awareness, a distraction that pulled him from matters of state security.

The cruel irony didn't escape him. If Serenity was indeed connected to the Liberation, then he had fallen for his own enemy. The woman whose blood sang through his veins, whose presence had begun healing something broken in him, might be the very person assigned to destroy everything he'd built.

And yet, despite the evidence, the scent in the rebel hideout, the convenient timing of her Elite application, the way she'd survived an attack that should have killed her, Kane found himself reluctant to accept her guilt. The terror in her eyes during the sensory overload had seemed genuine. The way she'd trusted him to help her, the way she'd fit so naturally against him, her gratitude for the family communication device, could all of it be an act?

Kane sat in silence, contemplating what pursuing this connection would mean. For centuries he had held his convictions steadfastly, never deviating from duty and discipline. But now he was being drawn into an unpredictable current that could destroy them both. As Head of the Human Vampyr Council, taking an interest in any human brought complications. If that human was also a spy for the Liberation, it could unravel the fragile peace he'd spent decades building. The Council chambers would echo with accusations of bias, of compromised judgment, and those who opposed his moderate policies would seize on the perceived weakness.

The thought of her betrayal cut deeper than it should have. Deeper than was wise for someone in his position. But the alternative, that she was innocent, that this connection between them was real, carried its own dangers. How could he maintain objectivity in human affairs when one particular human had claimed such a significant piece of his heart?

His rational side insisted such a relationship would be disastrous, for her, for him, for everything he strived to maintain in Celearius. The city balanced precariously on the edge of another war. He couldn't allow distractions, even as he longed to throw caution aside and claim her.

And yet the safest place for her was at his side, where he could ensure no harm came to her, from his kind or from her own. The universe seemed to mock him with the cruelty of it: the safest haven for Serenity was beside the very creature who craved her blood most.

Kane recognized the truth he'd been avoiding. In all his centuries, no threat to Celearius had ever felt as dangerous as what he felt for this human, or as impossible to resist. Whether she was innocent or guilty, whether she loved him or was using him, the bond between them had already changed everything.

Lifetimes of discipline, potentially shattered by a single drop of her blood. And despite the evidence of betrayal, despite the rational voice warning him of danger, he still wanted more.

The question now was whether he would let wisdom or desire guide his next move. Whether he would protect Celearius from the threat she might represent, or protect her from the consequences of whatever role she played in the Liberation's plans.

As he stood at the window, watching the city he'd helped build spread out below him, Kane realized that for the first time in centuries, he wasn't sure which choice he would make.

CHAPTER THIRTY-SIX

SERENITY

Serenity pressed the button on her device and held it to her ear. Her pulse quickened at the soft click of connection, followed by her mother's voice, familiar yet distant through the speaker.

"Hello?"

"Mom." Warmth streaked down her cheeks, tears falling silently. "Mom." The word held everything she couldn't say: her fear, her longing, the weight of her secrets. Though only days had passed, the distance between Grove Gardens and the Silver District seemed to span worlds.

Her sister's voice cut through her mother's quiet sobs. "Serenity? Is that really you?"

"Beth." The tightness in her chest eased slightly. "It's so good to hear you. Is Mom okay?"

"I'm fine," her mother said, her voice steadying. "That man who delivered this yesterday... he didn't even speak. Just handed over the device and said to wait for your call."

Nox. Had to be. She could picture his stoic expression as he carried out Kane's errand.

"I've missed you both so much," Serenity said, running her fingertips along the unfamiliar luxury of her bedspread, soft cotton that bore no resemblance to the rough fabric of home. "Tell me everything."

Beth cleared her throat. "Jax has been stopping by these last few days."

Not surprising. His anger at her choices didn't extend to abandoning her family. Whatever his feelings toward her, his sense of duty remained intact.

"Did you give him my letter?" Serenity leaned back against the headboard, bracing herself.

A pause stretched through the connection, Beth's hesitation audible. "Yes. He... he didn't take it well."

The expected answer still landed like a physical blow. Jax had been more than a neighbor: confidant, protector, the shape of a future she might have had. She'd thrown that away the moment she signed the Elite contract.

"In what way?" she asked, needing to measure the damage.

"He read it and then crumpled it up." Beth's voice dropped. "He said nothing, but his eyes, Serenity... he looked broken."

Broken. The word lodged beneath her ribs like a splinter. She'd done that to him, to the boy who'd taught her to hunt small game when food was scarce, who'd stood between her family and danger more times than she could count.

Serenity swallowed hard. "Are you eating well? Has Mom been taking her medicine?"

"They delivered groceries and both our medicines yesterday," Beth replied, smoothly accepting the change of subject. "A nurse came to administer Mom's treatment properly, and a doctor is scheduled to visit at the end of the week for checkups on both of us."

"I'm fine," her mother interjected. Her tone shifted, becoming the one Serenity recognized from serious conversations. "Tell me the truth. Are you okay there? Really okay?"

Serenity glanced toward her bedroom door, aware that somewhere in this apartment, vampyrs might be listening. The walls in the Silver District might be thicker, but secrets still found ways to travel.

"I'm adjusting," she said carefully. "Everything here is... different."

"How has he been treating you?" The question carried unspoken fears.

Serenity's mind flashed to Kane's eyes watching her across the morning kitchen, to his hands steadying her in the bathroom, to his lips almost touching hers before she'd pulled away.

"He's been... considerate." The word felt inadequate. "I don't see him often."

Her mother's relief whispered through the connection. "Stay vigilant, baby. Remember what I taught you."

About watching for signs of vampyr aggression, about protecting herself, about the small gun with silver bullets now hidden in her closet. "I remember."

"I have good news," Serenity continued, curling her legs beneath her. "He's going to cover yours and Beth's medicine. Separate from my monthly payment."

"What?" Suspicion edged her mother's voice. "Why would he do that?"

Serenity thought quickly. "He asked why I became an Elite. I told him about the medicine costs, and he offered. Said it comes with being his Elite."

"And what does he want in return?"

The question hung between them, loaded with implication. What would her mother think if she knew about the blood exchange? Their almost-kiss in the kitchen after he'd given her the communication device? The way her body responded to his nearness like a compass finding north?

"Nothing specific." Serenity kept her voice neutral. "He hasn't... demanded anything inappropriate." The half-truth tasted bitter.

"Just be careful," her mother warned. "Vampyr or human, men usually want the same thing."

And what if I want it too? The thought surfaced unbidden. The memory of Kane's touch sent electricity dancing across her skin, the gentle pressure of his hand at her back, the cool brush of his breath, the strange hunger in his silver eyes.

"Serenity?" Beth's voice broke through her dangerous thoughts. "Can you come visit soon?"

The simple question pierced straight through her. "I'll try, Beth." She pictured her sister's face, the same dark curls, the same stubborn set to her chin, but softer, more vulnerable.

"Mom, has my first payment gone through?" Serenity asked, focusing on practical matters.

"Not yet, but they said the fifteenth. That's today, isn't it?"

Serenity made a mental note to ask about the payment schedule. "Yes. You should receive it soon."

"Tell us about it there," Beth urged, curiosity breaking through the melancholy. "What's it really like?"

Serenity described her surroundings, the market's array of fresh produce she'd never seen in Grove Gardens, shops with clothes that weren't patched and faded, buildings with functioning climate control. With each detail, the disparity between their worlds grew sharper, guilt threading through her wonder. She alone enjoyed these luxuries while her family continued to struggle.

The device beeped, its display dimming as the battery weakened.

"I need to go," Serenity said, watching the lights fade. "The device needs charging. I'll call again tomorrow."

"Please stay safe," her mother urged. "We love you."

Serenity hesitated, one question burning in her mind. "Mom, before I go, did Dad ever mention helping other districts with medical supplies?"

The silence stretched long enough that Serenity wondered if the connection had failed. Then she heard muffled movement, her mother covering the receiver, perhaps speaking to Beth.

"He mentioned it occasionally," her mother finally answered, her voice careful. "Why do you ask?"

"I met someone who had his remedies. Someone from outside our district."

Her mother's breathing changed, becoming measured. "Your father had many secrets, Serenity. Some I wasn't privy to. But I believe he did what he thought was right."

"Was it right?" Serenity pressed, her heart pounding.

"This isn't a conversation for now," her mother said softly. "But your father gave his medicine to help build a better future, especially for you girls."

Relief loosened the knot in Serenity's chest. Her father's involvement with the rebellion hadn't been a lie. She wasn't betraying his memory by continuing his work.

"This person you met," her mother continued, her voice dropping further, "be careful who you trust. Remember that everything you're doing helps us too."

The device beeped again, more insistently.

"I love you both," Serenity whispered. "Tell Jax to keep checking on you."

"We will."

The screen went dark, leaving Serenity alone with the weight of confirmation. Her father had been a rebel. Her mother knew. The path she'd chosen carried their blessing, but that knowledge did little to quiet the turmoil within her.

She set the device down, her gaze drifting across the room, the plush carpet beneath her feet, the delicate curtains filtering the sunlight, the fresh flowers on the nightstand. Each luxury underscored how far she'd traveled from her former life. The Liberation was counting on her to find information about the human prisoners, particularly Jon Sinclair, that could help free dozens of people and finally strike a real blow against vampyr control.

But thinking of the Liberation inevitably led to thinking of Kane, and the growing connection that threatened to compromise everything.

The contract on her bedside table caught her attention, its official seal gleaming in the afternoon light. Maybe understanding its terms would give her clarity, remind her of her purpose here, and the stakes involved.

She picked up the document, settling back against the pillows. Many provisions were familiar from her briefing at the clinic, but details caught her attention that hadn't been emphasized before.

One pint of blood per weekly feeding, or two in "emergency circumstances." What constituted an emergency? Kane's hunger? Medical necessity? War?

Her eyes lingered on section 12.4: "Sexual Conduct Between Patron and Elite." The clinical language detailed that while physical relations weren't prohibited, they required "explicit verbal consent" that couldn't be compelled through vampyr influence. Further, any Elite who engaged in such relations could request reassignment without penalty if the relationship became "untenable."

Heat crept up her neck. Had Kane read this section? Was he expecting her to share more than her blood eventually? The thought of his hands on her skin, of surrendering to the pull she felt toward him, sent dangerous warmth spiraling through her.

Focus on the mission, she reminded herself, reaching for the pen in her nightstand drawer to note questions in the margin.

When she reached the compensation section, her breath caught. The standard Elite stipend ranged from $2,500 to $5,000 credits monthly. Her own figure: $10,000 credits.

Serenity sat up straighter. Double the maximum standard rate. With Kane covering her family's medical expenses separately, this could transform their lives. Repair the house. Move to Easton. Maybe even better schooling for Beth.

But why was he paying her so much? Was it her rare blood type, or something more personal?

Payment distribution: the fifteenth of each month. Today. Had her family already received it? The thought of her mother and Beth finally having financial security after years of struggle brought fresh tears to her eyes.

She set the contract aside, restlessness driving her to her feet. The room suddenly felt confining, its luxury a gilded cage. Despite the soft bed and beautiful furnishings, she longed for the worn comfort of home, the creaky floorboard outside her bedroom door, the faded quilt her mother had made, the familiar sound of Beth's humming.

And Jax. His absence left a hollow space she hadn't anticipated. Would he ever forgive her? The image of his face, strong jaw tight with disapproval, dark eyes wounded beneath their anger, rose in her mind. Their relationship had teetered on the edge between friendship and something more. Now it might be beyond repair.

Serenity paced, her mind racing. So many questions needed answers. How to charge the communication device. Whether her family had received the payment. What "emergency circumstances" might force a second blood drawing. What Kane expected of her beyond feeding.

What she expected of herself.

She stopped at the window, looking out over the manicured gardens of the Silver District. Somewhere beyond those pristine hedges lay Grove Gardens, with its struggling crops and crumbling infrastructure. Somewhere out there, the Liberation plotted their next move, waiting for the intelligence she'd promised about prisoner locations and vampyr weaknesses. And somewhere here, Kane moved through his day, perhaps thinking of her as she thought of him.

The contradiction tore at her. The Liberation painted vampyrs as uniformly evil oppressors, yet Kane had shown her unexpected kindness, healing her at great personal risk, arranging medical care for her family, giving her a way to reach them. These weren't the actions of a heartless monster. And still, Starr and Damon had shown her evidence of vampyr cruelty, of humans held in caverns, of a system built to keep her people subjugated. Her father had died fighting vampyr rule. The Liberation needed her intelligence to free prisoners and save lives. Both things seemed true at once, and she didn't know how to hold them together.

She needed answers. Nox could explain the device charging, perhaps confirm the payment transfer. But for the contract questions, she needed Kane himself.

Seeing him would be dangerous. Not because she feared harm from him, but because each encounter weakened her resolve, blurring the lines between ally and enemy, between duty and desire. Still, she couldn't complete her mission by hiding in her room. The Liberation was counting on her to find information about Cavern 47, about security protocols, about anything that could help their cause.

Serenity gathered the contract and device, her decision made. Finding Kane might deepen her confusion and strengthen the pull she felt toward him, but it was the only way forward, for her mission and for understanding whatever was happening between them.

Her hand hovered over the doorknob, hesitation warring with determination. This was necessary. Dangerous, but necessary.

She took a steadying breath and stepped into the hallway, the contract clutched to her chest like armor, in search of the vampyr who had saved her, fed from her, and somehow begun to unravel everything she thought she understood about herself and her world.

She had a rebellion to serve and a family to protect. But as she moved through the elegant hallways of Kane's residence, she couldn't escape the growing fear that her heart might already belong to the enemy.

CHAPTER THIRTY-SEVEN

KANE

No matter how Kane tried to concentrate on the interrogation video, his thoughts drifted back to Serenity. Her blood pulsed through his system, transforming his awareness of her into something supernatural. He found himself tracking her movements through the apartment without conscious effort, her presence impossible to ignore even through walls and floors. For the third time in an hour, his finger hovered over the security feed button.

He tapped it, bringing up the hallway outside her room. The door remained closed, just as before. The camera couldn't penetrate her private quarters, one of the few protections Elites retained, but he knew she was behind that door. His senses told him so, the blood bond creating an awareness that transcended physical barriers.

He closed the feed with a frustrated hiss, fangs instinctively descending before he forced them to retract. The hunger was worse after tasting her, sharper, more specific. His body now recognized her blood as unique nourishment, craving it with an urgency that disturbed him. Centuries of carefully cultivated control, eroded by a single taste.

Kane returned to the interrogation footage, the silver flecks in his eyes brightening with focus. A young man, perhaps twenty-four or twenty-five, with the lean build of someone raised on restricted rations, sat bound to a metal chair. Across from him stood Sullivan, Kane's most trusted agent. They had worked together to suppress this rebellion for five years, ever since humans had kidnapped, tortured, and dismembered Sullivan's little sister, Elena. The trauma had transformed Sullivan from a moderate into one of Kane's most ruthless agents. Finding her severed limbs arranged in the Liberation's signature pattern still turned his blood cold.

Sullivan moved closer to the captive, his shadow elongating across the concrete. The cell's harsh lighting cast hollows beneath the young man's eyes, but there was no fear in them, only defiance.

"Where is your headquarters in the Abandoned City?" Sullivan's voice was deceptively quiet.

The Council suspected the rebellion kept a headquarters beyond Celearius but had no concrete evidence of its location. The rebels also maintained safe havens within the city itself, yet whenever Kane thought he'd found one, it would already be cleared. Someone was feeding them information, a thought that now carried new weight given Serenity's scent at the rebel hideout.

What they truly needed to learn was how many humans, and possibly vampyrs, were involved, and who led them. The Liberation's increasingly sophisticated attacks suggested inside knowledge of vampyr security protocols.

Sullivan had interrogated the young man for hours, yet he'd offered nothing but profanity.

"You are going to tell me what I want, even if this takes weeks," Sullivan growled, dragging his military-grade knife down the captive's leg. The fabric parted with a soft hiss, revealing skin unmarked by the blade's passage; Sullivan's control was precise.

Kane leaned closer to the screen. The young man's pulse stayed steady even as Sullivan's imposing frame cast a shadow over him. Unusual. Most humans couldn't control their fear response so completely. Professional training, perhaps, the kind the Liberation gave their operatives.

Kane was about to turn off the video when Sullivan struck the captive, snapping his head to the side and exposing a tattoo on his neck. Kane paused, enhancing the image and zooming in on the marking. He couldn't make it out clearly, only that it resembled a serpent or dragon curling around itself, similar to the one found on the doctor's killer, but with subtle differences. He made a note to request a higher-resolution image. Perhaps it denoted rank within the rebellion.

A subtle shift in the air drew his attention before his ears registered the soft footsteps approaching his office. The scent of her reached him first, jasmine and rose with a hint of honeysuckle, ambrosia that made his throat constrict with hunger. His senses heightened, focusing with predatory keenness on the hallway beyond his door.

It was her. He didn't need to open the door to know. Her blood called to him, a siren song that resonated in his marrow. The awareness their exchange had created told him exactly where she stood, the rhythm of her heartbeat, even the slight acceleration that suggested nervousness.

Instead of pressing the door button, he rose to open it himself, each movement measured to conceal the hunger roiling beneath his composed exterior. His hand paused on the handle as he took a steadying breath, willing the silver in his eyes to recede to normal.

The door swung open just as her knuckles met air.

"Hi," she smiled tentatively, color rising in her cheeks. "I'm sorry to bother you. I tried to find Nox, but he seemed busy. If I'm interrupting, you can just turn me away."

She launched into an explanation about charging her communication device and questions about the contract. Kane found himself entranced by the movement of her lips, the way her teeth occasionally caught the soft flesh when she hesitated. It would be so easy to capture them with his own, to taste the warmth there, to follow the pulse beating visibly at the hollow of her throat.

The predator in him noted details beyond her words: the slight tension in her shoulders, the way her gaze flickered past him toward his office, the careful placement of each step as she unconsciously assessed her surroundings. These weren't the movements of an innocent Elite seeking help with her contract. These were the practiced observations of someone gathering intelligence.

"So, would you be able to help me?" she asked, her expression hopeful.

Kane blinked, forcing himself back to the present. "Of course." He opened the door wider, gesturing her inside with a fluid movement that kept a careful distance between them.

He stepped aside as she entered, her scent washing over him in a wave that tightened every muscle in his body. Her familiar fragrance now carried subtle notes of his own essence, the biochemical signature of their exchange lingering beneath her natural perfume. Their scents had intertwined, marking her in ways imperceptible to humans but unmistakable to his kind.

Yet as she moved into his office, he noticed how her eyes swept the room with practiced efficiency, cataloging the screens, the documents on his desk, the security monitors he'd hastily closed. Was she memorizing the layout? Searching for something specific? The possibility that she might be here for reasons beyond contract questions ran cold through him.

"I hope I'm not intruding," she said, breaking into his thoughts. Her eyes met his briefly, curiosity flickering across her face before she glanced away.

"Your presence is never an intrusion," he replied, his voice smooth as molten silver. It was true, despite the growing suspicion that her presence might be more dangerous than he'd realized. He had never desired any human's company before her; she remained an enigma that woke his centuries-old curiosity even as she potentially threatened everything he'd built.

He returned to his desk, closing the security feed and surveillance screens with subtle gestures. The interrogation footage vanished as he removed several sensitive documents from view, acutely conscious of what she might observe. Council members who brought Elites into their confidence rarely stayed Council members for long, especially if those Elites had ties to the rebellion.

"You mentioned your communication device needed charging." He pressed a hidden button beneath his desk, activating the mechanism that raised a chair from the floor. "Please, sit."

"Thank you." She settled into the seat, the fabric of her dress rustling softly against the leather. The sound reached his ears with crystal clarity. "Yes, I was talking with my family when it died."

"May I see it?"

She nodded, extending her hand to offer the device. As he reached for it, their fingers brushed, a momentary contact that sent electricity racing up his arm. The heat of her skin against his cooler touch triggered an instantaneous response: a tightening in his chest, a sharpening of his senses, a keen awareness of the mere inches separating them.

When he opened the device, it powered on; its battery only depleted, not dead. Her heartbeat quickened, the rhythm changing from nervousness to something more complex. He studied her face, trying to understand the source of her anxiety. Was she hiding something about the call? Had she spoken to someone beyond her family?

"The device doesn't require a charger. It's self-sustaining and will recharge itself." He closed it, placing it on his desk with care. "It should be fully functional within the hour if you let it rest."

"Oh, I didn't know."

"I apologize. I should have explained when I gave it to you." The words were formal, but beneath them lay an awareness of all the things he hadn't explained, about being his Elite, about the blood exchange, about the dangers that might come with both. About the possibility that she might be tied to the very rebellion he was fighting.

She glanced uncertainly at the device before looking down at the contract in her hand. The thick packet represented a binding not just of legal obligation but of something deeper, a connection neither had anticipated, one that could prove catastrophic if she was indeed working for the Liberation.

"I'd be happy to answer any questions about the agreement."

She looked away, appearing embarrassed. The scent of her discomfort reached him, a subtle shift in her natural fragrance. His office suddenly seemed too confining, too formal with its stark lines and leather furnishings. The austere space reflected his public persona rather than the private self that responded to her.

"How about we continue this somewhere more welcoming? The library, perhaps," he suggested, an impulse that surprised even him. If she was gathering intelligence, the library would be safer, no sensitive documents or security feeds for her to observe.

She brightened immediately, the tension easing visibly from her shoulders. "I would love that."

He waited for her to rise before pressing the button to lower the chair into its recessed position. His hand hovered near the small of her back as he guided her to the door, not quite touching but close enough to feel the heat radiating from her body.

Closing the office door, he led the way down the corridor, acutely aware of her footsteps behind him. The rhythm of her heart followed him like music, slightly elevated, but steadier now. Was her nervousness about the contract questions, or about successfully completing whatever intelligence mission had brought her here?

"Have you visited it yet?" he asked, glancing back at her. In profile, her features took on a different quality, softer, more vulnerable than when she faced him directly with that stubborn defiance he found so intriguing.

"No," she replied. "There's only one library in our district, more of a closet with a few books. I look forward to exploring your collection."

The casual mention of Grove Gardens' deprivation stirred something uncomfortable in him. The inequities between human districts and vampyr ones were necessary, he'd always believed, a natural reflection of species hierarchy. Yet hearing it from her perspective cast it in a different light. Or was this calculated manipulation, designed to evoke sympathy?

"I can recommend titles you might enjoy, if you tell me what subjects interest you," he offered as they reached the library door.

"Thank you," she said, stepping through. "I would appreciate that."

The library spread before them, walls lined with volumes collected over centuries, tall windows letting natural light spill across reading nooks and comfortable seating. Unlike his office with its sleek surfaces and stark functionality, this room embraced a traditional warmth: rich mahogany shelves, deep velvet chairs, wool carpets over hardwood floors.

He settled automatically into his favorite spot, the corner window seat overlooking the city, with a view of the ocean in the far distance. She lingered by the shelves, trailing her fingers over the book spines with a reverence that pleased him despite his suspicions. He took a moment to appreciate her presence in this private space, even as he wondered what information she might be seeking.

She wore a simple lavender dress that hugged her curves before flaring at the waist. His gaze traveled from her bare feet along the delicate bones of her ankles and the gentle curve of her calves. It would be so easy to—

His thoughts scattered as she cleared her throat. Looking up, he realized she'd caught him staring. Instead of fear or disgust, her eyes reflected a hunger that mirrored his own. For a moment he was overwhelmed by the urge to press her against the bookshelves and kiss her breathless, to taste the pulse at her throat, to claim her in ways that went beyond mere feeding.

The silver in his eyes flared before he forced his features back to neutral, though his fangs stayed painfully extended behind closed lips.

"What questions do you have?" His voice emerged lower than intended, rough with restraint.

Her heartbeat accelerated, the sound filling his ears. She sat by the window on the opposite side of the room, a wise distance to keep between them. Wise, but unsatisfying.

"Come." The word escaped unbidden, carrying a command he hadn't meant to voice. He cleared his throat. "Come, sit beside me... so we can review the contract together."

With a nod, she gathered the document and cautiously approached. He shifted to make space for her on the cushioned seat, the air between them charged with unspoken tension. As she settled beside him, her fragrance surrounded him, jasmine and rose and honeysuckle layered over lemon and vanilla, with that indefinable element that was uniquely hers.

Outside, clouds passed over the sun, casting momentary shadows across the library floor. Beyond the window, the Silver District continued its carefully regulated existence, unaware of the precipice on which its Councilor stood. A relationship with an Elite would be frowned upon but tolerated. A true bond with a potential spy, however, that could destroy everything he'd built.

"What questions can I answer for you?" He turned to face her, careful to keep that crucial distance, aware they balanced on a knife's edge of propriety and desire, duty and hunger, trust and potential betrayal.

And there it was, the thing he couldn't reason his way around: even knowing what she might be, even with the evidence stacking against her, he wanted her closer, not farther. That was the danger no security protocol could address. Not what she might do to Celearius, but what she had already done to him.

CHAPTER THIRTY-EIGHT

SERENITY

The lavender dress had been a mistake. Serenity hadn't considered the consequences when she'd chosen it that morning, the whisper of fabric against her bare legs, the way it would leave her skin exposed as she sat beside him. Now, with each subtle shift of her body, her thigh brushed the rough texture of his tailored pants, sending shockwaves of awareness through her nerves.

Focus, Serenity.

She glanced down at the contract, afternoon sunlight streaming through the library windows to illuminate her hurried notes in the margins. The familiar scent of leather-bound books and paper surrounded them, but it couldn't ground her against the magnetic pull of Kane's presence.

"It mentions you can take two pints of blood in case of an emergency," she said, tapping the relevant paragraph with her fingertip. "What exactly constitutes an emergency?"

A hint of appreciation flickered across his features. "Situations where I might sustain injuries requiring accelerated healing. The additional blood would help me recover more quickly."

"Wouldn't taking that much blood be fatal?" Her pulse quickened at the thought.

"Not necessarily," he said, his tone softening. "You would require immediate medical attention to prevent shock, but many humans have survived such donations." The corner of his mouth lifted slightly. "Rest assured, I have no intention of becoming injured anytime soon."

"Good to know," she replied, unable to suppress a nervous laugh.

Kane leaned slightly closer, his voice lowering to a more intimate register. "More importantly, I would always seek your consent first, circumstances permitting."

The sincerity in his words sent an unexpected warmth through her chest. Despite everything, he recognized her autonomy, her right to choose. This wasn't the behavior of the monster the Liberation had described.

She straightened the pages on her lap, gathering courage for her next question. "Does the Elite Taskforce actually function as described? If an Elite needed protection..."

Something hardened in Kane's expression, not anger, but a sober recognition of reality. "If a vampyr files a complaint, action is immediate. For Elites..." He sighed, the sound unexpectedly human. "The taskforce operates in two divisions, vampyr and human. Rhyzan has attempted repeated collaboration with the human division regarding Elite mistreatment. Too often, Elite complaints about vampyrs disappear before reaching his desk." Frustration colored his tone. "Enforcement has proven challenging without human cooperation."

The revelation settled uncomfortably in Serenity's stomach. The protections outlined in her contract might be merely words on paper. Yet it wasn't as simple as vampyr cruelty; humans seemed equally responsible for the broken system, refusing cooperation that might benefit their own kind.

Another crack in the Liberation's narrative. How much of what Starr and Damon had told her was accurate? How much was propaganda designed to recruit desperate people like herself?

"Any other questions?" Kane asked, his gaze lingering on her face in a way that made her skin tingle.

She had one final question, one she knew she shouldn't ask yet couldn't suppress. Her fingers traced over section 12.4, drawing his attention back to the document.

"The contract specifies that any sexual conduct between us requires documented agreement from both parties. Is this standard for all Elite contracts?"

She raised her eyes to his, finding his gaze transformed, molten silver shot through with pinpoints of darker blue, fixed on her with a heat that stole her breath.

"Yes," he responded, his voice dropping to a register that seemed to vibrate through her bones. "The arrangement was never designed to include physical intimacy, though it often evolves that way to enhance the feeding experience."

The implication sent warmth cascading through her body. "So the bite, it doesn't always hurt like that first time?"

Kane's expression shifted as he closed his eyes a moment, then rose from the window seat in a single fluid motion. The sudden absence of his warmth left her unexpectedly bereft.

He moved to stand before the window, sunlight filtering through the specially treated glass to silhouette his powerful frame. For several heartbeats, he remained silent.

"No," he finally said, his back still to her. "What you experienced wasn't... typical. That night—" His voice roughened with what sounded remarkably like regret. "I never intended to cause you pain. I waited too long to feed, allowed my hunger to become unmanageable."

The confession surprised her, both its content and the vulnerability it revealed. "And if you were to feed again? Would it be different?"

Kane turned slowly to face her, his expression carefully composed though the silver in his eyes stayed bright. "It could be," he said quietly. "With proper preparation and... mutual anticipation, the experience can be quite different."

The space between them seemed to contract despite the physical distance. Serenity became hyperaware of every sensation, the soft cushion beneath her, the weight of the contract in her hands, the quickening of her pulse that she knew he could hear perfectly.

"When will you feed from me next?" The boldness of her question surprised even her. "Will you set a regular schedule?"

Kane remained motionless, a statue carved of marble and shadow. When he finally spoke, his voice carried a strain she'd never heard before, control stretched to its limits. "Regular feeding would prevent what happened before. It would spare you that pain." He paused, his shoulders tensing visibly. "But it's not... uncomplicated."

Curiosity propelled her forward, one cautious step closer. "Why not? Isn't it simply part of our arrangement?"

The laugh that escaped him held no humor, only bitter acknowledgment. He turned to face her fully, and the raw emotion in his eyes nearly stopped her heart.

"That's what it's supposed to be," he said, the words precise yet weighted. "Clinical. Practical. A transaction." He raked his fingers through his dark hair. "But feeding isn't merely taking blood, Serenity. It transcends the physical. It becomes..." He searched for the word. "Intimate."

"Intimate," she repeated, barely above a whisper.

"A connection forms that neither participant can fully control. Thoughts, emotions, sensations... they bleed across boundaries that should stay fixed."

Her heart hammered against her ribs as understanding dawned. This was information the Liberation could use, the intimate vulnerability vampyrs experienced during feeding, the potential for a human to influence them in those moments. Intelligence that could prove invaluable to the rebellion.

Yet the thought of exploiting Kane's vulnerability felt like a betrayal.

"I don't want to experience that pain again," she admitted, hating the vulnerability in her voice.

"You won't," he assured her, certainty hardening his features. "I give you my word."

"How can you be certain?"

Kane studied her for a long moment, something shifting in his expression, the mask of authority slipping to reveal something older, more contemplative.

"The feeding ritual is fundamentally an exchange of vulnerability," he began, each word carefully chosen. "The vampyr reveals his primal nature, allowing the human to witness raw need, dependency. And the human offers trust in their moment of greatest exposure. I denied us both that exchange. I promise you, Serenity, that will never happen again."

His words wrapped around her like silken cords, at once binding and freeing. Trust. Vulnerability. Exchange. The framework he described transformed what she'd viewed as predatory into something almost sacred. And it revealed exactly the kind of weakness the Liberation sought to exploit.

"Alright," she breathed, nodding slowly. "I... trust you."

The tension in his frame visibly eased, though something darker remained in his eyes, a hunger of a different sort. "That means more than you can know."

The air between them changed, charged with an electricity that raised goosebumps along her arms. She needed to leave. This was becoming too dangerous, not to her body, but to her mission. To her heart.

She rose from the window seat, the rustle of her dress against her skin unnaturally loud. "That's all the questions I had. Thank you for your answers."

"Of course," Kane replied, his voice a low rumble she felt rather than heard.

She turned toward the door, her legs unsteady beneath her. Three steps. That was all she managed before the whisper of movement behind her was her only warning.

Kane moved with impossible speed, his body suddenly before her, backing her against the nearest bookshelf. His hands planted on either side of her head, caging her without touching her. His presence surrounded her completely, the rich aroma of cedar mingled with cologne and that unmistakable essence that was uniquely his.

A gasp escaped her, more surprise than fear. Her heart thundered, blood rushing in her ears, yet beneath the instinctive panic bloomed something darker and more insistent: desire.

"I won't hurt you." His words emerged as a solemn vow, his eyes searching hers.

Strangely, she believed him. Despite everything, against all logic, she trusted his word.

"I'm sorry," he murmured, his voice rough with restraint. "I can be... overwhelming."

Yet in his gaze burned something beyond hunger, a question, a need for connection that mirrored her own confusion.

His gaze dropped to her lips, desire evident in the tightening of his features. He moved with excruciating slowness, giving her every opportunity to refuse. She should. Every rational thought demanded it.

But rationality had abandoned her the moment he touched her.

His lips met hers with unexpected tenderness, a contrast to the powerful body now caging her. The taste of him was intoxicating, something ancient and complex that defied description. Her hands moved of their own accord, one gripping his shoulder while the other tangled in the soft hair at the nape of his neck.

She had never felt so consumed, so desired, so terrifyingly alive. Her pulse roared in her ears as he explored her mouth with practiced skill, drawing responses from her body she hadn't known were possible.

This is wrong, her mind whispered. You're supposed to be gathering intelligence, not falling for him.

But as his mouth descended to her neck, trailing feather-light kisses along her throat, all coherent thought fled. When his hand lifted her leg, hooking it around his hip, the new position pressed his hardness against her most sensitive point, drawing a gasp from deep in her chest.

Their bodies found a rhythm together, a slow, deliberate grinding that built tension in her lower abdomen, coiling tighter with each movement. Books trembled on the shelves behind her, witnesses to their transgression.

When his fangs grazed the sensitive skin of her throat, fear and arousal mingled into a potent cocktail that stole her breath. Instead of pulling away, she tilted her head, offering better access.

What am I doing? The Liberation. My family. My father's legacy.

But Kane's need, his restraint, the careful way he held her as though she were precious, it all felt more real than any ideology.

"Serenity," he growled against her skin, her name a prayer and a curse. "I need—"

"Yes," she whispered, then with greater certainty, "Yes."

His fangs penetrated her flesh, and the initial sharp pain transformed almost instantly into something transcendent. Heat bloomed from the bite, spreading through her bloodstream like liquid gold, setting every nerve ending alight. Each pull of his mouth answered with a pulse of ecstasy that radiated outward.

The connection he'd described became real, thoughts, sensations, emotions bleeding between them until she couldn't tell where she ended and he began. His pleasure at her taste, her surrender to his touch, all merged into a single experience that built toward an inevitable peak.

When the climax finally broke, the force of it stole her voice, waves of pleasure crashing through her. Her entire body shuddered against him, her soul laid bare in this most intimate act.

As the sensation gradually subsided, reality crashed back with crushing force. Despite the passion they'd shared, the fundamental truth remained unchanged: she was a spy, a rebel, bound by loyalty to her family and their cause.

But she could no longer deny her attraction to Kane. It transcended physical desire, reaching toward something she dared not name.

Conflicting emotions warred in her. She had chosen her path, aligned herself with the rebellion against vampyr rule, and her family's safety hung in the balance. If Kane discovered her involvement... The thought sent ice through veins still warm from his touch. Would his feelings for her, whatever they might be, outweigh his duty to his kind?

She had to trust her father's judgment, his belief that fighting for human liberation was worth the risk. Yet a traitorous part of her longed for Kane's touch, for the sanctuary of his arms, for the connection that had momentarily united them.

No. She couldn't allow herself to be swayed. Her curiosity was satisfied, and her role now was clear: gather information for the rebellion, then sever every tie. No more stolen kisses. No more transcendent pleasure. No more pretending this could be anything more than what it was, a dangerous liaison with an inevitable end.

Kane cleared his throat, drawing her attention back to his composed features. Only the lingering darkness in his eyes betrayed what had passed between them. "Would you like me to amend our contract?"

The question sent her heart racing anew. Did she want to formalize this aspect of their relationship? Make official what had been spontaneous, emotional, possibly unrepeatable?

She knew the logical answer. There could be no future where this ended well. The Liberation was counting on her. Her family needed her. Her father's sacrifice demanded justice.

"Kane," she said firmly, pushing aside the whispers of desire still echoing through her body. "No."

The word hung between them like a blade, cutting through the intimacy they'd shared with surgical precision. Something shuttered in his expression, the warmth in his eyes cooling to polite distance.

"I understand," he replied, his voice returning to its formal register. "Perhaps that's for the best."

But as he stepped back, creating a physical distance that felt like an ocean between them, Serenity couldn't escape the growing certainty that she'd just made the biggest mistake of her life. She watched him retreat behind his walls of authority and control, and wondered if the price of loyalty might be higher than she could bear to pay.

CHAPTER THIRTY-NINE

RHYZAN

"Why didn't you tell me about the blood reaction?" Rhyzan demanded, pressing Nox against the elevator wall with controlled force. His palm registered the familiar tension in Nox's shoulder, a body he'd mapped intimately across centuries.

"Because I didn't want you running back to Evelyn with information she doesn't need," Nox countered, straightening his jacket with that precise movement Rhyzan had once found endearing. Now it only emphasized the careful distance between them.

"They're both my friends. I decide what's relevant." The silver flecks in Rhyzan's eyes brightened as his frustration sharpened. Kane's situation was growing more volatile by the day, and Serenity represented both salvation and catastrophe in equal measure.

Four centuries as Kane's Second had taught him to read the subtle signs, the way Kane's jaw tightened when discussing territorial disputes, the careful modulation of his voice during Council sessions. But this Elite had introduced variables Rhyzan couldn't predict or control.

The blood reaction confirmed his worst fears. Not only was she valuable enough to start wars, her AB negative blood type made her a strategic asset any opposing faction would kill for, but Kane's loss of control proved even his legendary discipline had limits. If she was indeed working with the Liberation, they'd identified Kane's greatest weakness and positioned themselves to exploit it.

"She's dangerous, Nox. Her blood type alone makes her a target every rebel faction will pursue." Rhyzan's tactical mind catalogued the implications as they exited the elevator. "And if Sebastian recruited her..."

"You think leaving them alone is wise?" Nox asked as they reached the garage, the question carrying layers of meaning beyond the obvious.

Rhyzan caught the keys with fluid precision, his fingers brushing Nox's palm a moment longer than necessary, a touch that triggered unwanted memories of an intimacy now reduced to professional cooperation.

"He needs this connection," Nox continued, sliding into the passenger seat. "She might be exactly what he requires to move beyond his grief."

"If she doesn't betray us first." Rhyzan backed out of the garage, his grip tight on the wheel. "I know Sebastian got to her."

The certainty in his voice was backed by months of surveillance data, communication patterns, suspicious absences, the carefully orchestrated timing of his appearance at Serenity's location. Sebastian had played his role perfectly, casting himself as rescuer rather than recruiter.

"She could provide the evidence I need to expose Sebastian to Evelyn," Rhyzan said, navigating through the gate as the guard saluted. His files on Sebastian were comprehensive but circumstantial. Direct proof of recruitment would give him leverage to act.

"Or we could give her reason to trust us," Nox suggested, his gaze fixed on the manicured landscape of the Quartz District. "Turn her to our side willingly."

"And have her betray her own kind?" Rhyzan's scoff held bitter experience. "Humans remain loyal to their own, a truth I've watched destroy more than one bond."

The memory of Alex surfaced unbidden, the lover he'd lost lifetimes ago, a vampyr who had believed humans and their kind could live as one and had died for that belief, murdered by anti-Treaty radicals who saw her conviction as treason. The wound had never fully closed, and the scars of it shaped how he weighed every alliance since.

"She might choose differently, if her feelings for Kane deepen," Nox persisted. "What I witnessed in Kane's office suggested real attraction."

"Attraction can be weaponized." Rhyzan had observed enough Liberation tactics to recognize sophisticated manipulation. "They're recruiting smarter assets now, ones capable of holding deep cover while extracting critical information."

As they approached the Galeway District, Rhyzan's mind turned to operational priorities. The security protocols he'd implemented after the recent attacks required constant vigilance. Three vampyr deaths in coordinated strikes had proven the Liberation possessed both organization and resources.

The gate guards performed their inspection with practiced efficiency, checking for hidden passengers, scanning for unauthorized materials, verifying their identities through multiple security layers. Rhyzan had designed these protocols himself, modeling them on both ancient defensive strategies and modern surveillance techniques.

"Let's stop by Unit 28 on the way back," Nox said as they passed through the checkpoint. "I want to get sweet potatoes for Serenity."

The unexpected request drew Rhyzan's attention, a genuine enthusiasm in Nox's voice he hadn't heard in decades. Perhaps Kane wasn't the only one being affected by their new Elite. The thought of Nox cooking again brought an unexpected comfort, a glimpse of the domesticity they'd once shared.

Driving past the utilitarian storage buildings toward Cavern 47, Rhyzan marveled at Kane's foresight in preserving the surrounding forest. The natural barrier provided perfect camouflage for their most sensitive security installation while deterring casual exploration.

The hidden entrance responded to his coded signals, the rock wall sliding open to reveal the illuminated tunnel. Their footsteps echoed softly as they made their way through multiple checkpoints to the detention area.

"Where's Chloe?" Rhyzan asked, scanning the monitors displaying each cell.

"In there with him now," the guard replied, indicating monitor six.

On screen, their most effective interrogator was working her particular magic. Chloe's delicate features and recent Turning allowed her to pass for human, a deception that had yielded crucial victories during the Border Conflicts with rogue factions from Kregan.

The young man they'd captured near the bar sat across from her, his athletic build and defiant posture suggesting military training. But already his resistance was crumbling under Chloe's expert manipulation.

"I hate them too," Chloe said, crossing her legs with calculated casualness. The prisoner's dilated pupils and quickened breathing revealed his growing attraction, exactly as she'd intended.

"But you work for them," he replied, suspicion warring with desire.

"Not by choice. They have my daughter." The desperation in Chloe's voice sounded completely real, a performance honed through dozens of similar extractions.

"She's still using that story," Nox commented, leaning close enough for his scent to stir buried memories.

"It works every time." Rhyzan shifted away while keeping his professional detachment. "Humans are predictably emotional about family bonds."

The prisoner's hatred blazed across his features as he denounced vampyrs with vehement passion. Such indoctrination in someone so young suggested the Liberation's recruitment had evolved beyond simple grievance into systematic ideological conditioning.

Chloe rose gracefully, approaching with the confident, predatory grace that belied her lethal capabilities. Her whispered words drew him closer until their faces nearly touched.

"The only way we can talk is if I show interest in you," she murmured, glancing toward the camera. "They'll shut off monitoring if they think romance might produce offspring. More food sources for them."

The lie was brilliantly constructed, playing to Liberation propaganda while positioning intimate contact as rebellion rather than seduction. When he kissed her deeply, Rhyzan knew they had him completely.

"Turn off the camera light," Nox instructed the guard. "Did our seductress extract anything useful yet?"

The guard consulted his notes. "Yes, sir. He gave us a name. Jax Thornton."

"Excellent." Nox's satisfied smile carried an anticipation Rhyzan recognized from more intimate settings. "Cross-reference that name with our Sinclair files."

The name triggered recognition in Rhyzan's strategic memory. If this Jax connected to Jon Sinclair, they might finally have the thread to unravel the entire Liberation network, and potentially confirm Sebastian's involvement.

He watched Chloe expertly build rapport with their prisoner while he considered the larger implications. Every piece of intel brought them closer to dismantling the rebellion, but also closer to the truth about Serenity.

If she was indeed their spy, Kane's growing attachment would become another vulnerability to exploit. But if she could be turned to their side, a turned asset with access to Liberation secrets could prove invaluable, especially one whose blood type made her indispensable to Kane.

The possibility intrigued him despite his natural suspicion. Either way, the coming days would decide whether Serenity meant deliverance or ruin for Celearius. And Rhyzan would be watching every moment, ready to act when the truth finally emerged.

His duty to Kane and their people demanded nothing less.

CHAPTER FORTY

KANE

No.

The word echoed through his mind with the finality of a blade severing steel. After everything that had happened in the library, her gasps against his mouth, her body yielding to his touch, the exquisite surrender as his fangs pierced her throat, she had refused him. The rejection burned like silver against his skin, more painful than any wound he'd taken across all his centuries.

Kane stood motionless beneath the punishing spray of cold water, each droplet a futile attempt to extinguish the fire coursing through his veins. The icy torrent did nothing for the hunger clawing at his control; if anything, it sharpened his awareness of her lingering scent on his skin, the phantom taste of her blood on his tongue.

With a sound that was half-sigh, half-growl, he twisted the fixture, silencing the water. Steam hadn't fogged the mirrors; the temperature had been far too cold for that luxury. His reflection stared back: silver eyes still dilated with want, jaw clenched against memories that threatened his carefully maintained discipline.

He should have kept his distance. Should have let her leave instead of caging her against those books like some medieval lord claiming his prize. Yet when she'd turned away, something primal had shattered his control, centuries of civilization reduced to nothing by the sight of her retreating form.

"Control," he muttered, reaching for the familiar mantras. *"Distance. Focus."*

The words felt hollow now, insufficient armor against what she'd awakened in him.

Kane dressed with mechanical precision: dark trousers, crisp white shirt, leather shoes polished to a military shine. Each movement was deliberate, designed to center him through routine. Yet beneath the practical motions pulsed the relentless desire to seek her out, to continue what they'd begun.

The obligations of his position scrolled through his mind: interrogation footage to review, security protocols to update, Council meetings regarding territorial expansion. Yet all of it felt secondary to the need thrumming in his veins, the need for her.

Pathetic. Dangerous.

As he rounded the corridor toward his office, a familiar figure came into view. Serenity stood before his door, shifting nervously from foot to foot in a distinctly human display of uncertainty.

The sight sent electricity through his system. He forced his features into neutrality, though his fangs pressed insistently against his gums.

"I—I forgot my communication device," she explained, honey-brown eyes meeting his briefly before darting away.

"Of course. I'll retrieve it for you." His voice emerged rougher than intended, betraying the control he'd fought to rebuild.

She stepped aside as he unlocked the door, keeping a careful distance. He noted the movement with irritation and grudging approval; at least one of them showed sense. As he entered, he deliberately avoided drawing breath, knowing her scent would only sharpen the hunger threatening his composure.

The device vibrated against his palm as he retrieved it from his desk. Instinctively, he glanced at the illuminated screen, noting how her heartbeat immediately picked up.

I wanted to check up on you. Let's grab a coffee. Meet me downstairs. S.
Sebastian. Of course.

"Seems you've made a friend," he remarked, extending the device toward her. The slight curve of her lips as she read the message didn't escape him, despite her attempt to suppress it. An image flashed unbidden through his mind: Sebastian's elegant features contorted in agony, blood streaming from wounds designed for maximum suffering.

The violent fantasy brought a moment of satisfaction before he banished it with practiced discipline.

"Yes, I think I did. Thank you." Her fingers brushed his as she took the device, the brief contact sending fire up his arm. She hesitated, shifting her weight. "Is it... acceptable for me to see him?"

Everything in him, every predatory instinct, every possessive impulse honed over centuries, screamed to refuse. To forbid it. To carry her to his chambers and claim her so thoroughly that no other would dare approach what was his.

Instead, he forced the words through clenched teeth. "You're free to move throughout the Silver District. However, inform either Nox or myself before leaving, and continue masking your scent."

Relief softened her shoulders as her device buzzed again, her pulse jumping in response. The sound of her quickened heartbeat filled his ears.

He watched her type her reply, slender fingers dancing across the screen. For the hundredth time since her arrival, he battled the urge to close the space between them, to reclaim what they'd shared. Instead he stayed rooted, hands clenched until his knuckles whitened.

"Thank you," she murmured, turning to leave. His gaze followed the gentle sway of her hips beneath the simple dress. Desire and frustration surged through him as he wrenched his attention away.

Once alone, Kane tried to focus on the interrogation footage. Three times he tried. Three times her lingering scent, jasmine and rose and the distinctive undercurrent of her blood, pulled his mind back to her. Even the ticking of his antique clock seemed to echo her sighs.

After the third failed attempt, he closed his eyes, immediately assaulted by an image of her sprawled across his desk, papers scattered, eyes wide with desire. The fantasy was so vivid he could almost taste her skin.

Intolerable. He would relocate to his city office until he regained proper control.

As he gathered his jacket, something metallic clattered from its pocket, the tin box he'd discovered at the human gathering place near Grove Gardens. Its surface had been worn smooth by handling, a faint skull and crossbones etched into the tarnished lid.

He pried the container open, revealing a small key and a folded note. The key was unmistakably old-fashioned brass, with the number fifty-nine engraved into its surface. Train-station design.

The note's message was brief but telling: *The future is ours. Protect it with your life.*

No train stations existed within Celearius, a deliberate security measure. The nearest functioning station stood in Kregan, sixty miles to the southwest. But buried beneath the rubble outside the walls lay the remnants of the old transit system, abandoned since the final bombing campaign.

This tangible lead demanded immediate investigation.

Pocketing the items, he left his quarters for the city offices. Despite his resolve to focus on the development, he found himself glancing at the corner café as his vehicle passed. Through the windows, he spotted her instantly, seated at a small table, fingers wrapped around a steaming cup, smiling at Sebastian's unseen face.

Jealousy crashed through him with violent force, briefly darkening his vision. His grip tightened around the steering wheel, vampyric strength leaving deep impressions in the handcrafted leather.

He would need to have it replaced. Again.

Accelerating away, he forced his attention back to strategy. The rebellion had grown increasingly bold, clinic bombings, assassinations, sabotage of blood transport vehicles. Sebastian's carefully cultivated charm had always struck Kane as performative.

At the CityCentre checkpoint, the guard extended a scanner. Kane pressed his finger against the device, feeling the familiar prick as it sampled his blood. The machine pulsed green, and the reinforced gate slid open.

The underground garage welcomed him with harsh fluorescent lighting and the scent of damp stone. Stepping from his vehicle, anger still coursing through him, he slammed the car door with excessive force, then delivered a precise kick that left a significant dent.

The childish display did little to ease his frustration, and he knew Nox would look at him with that particular mixture of disappointment and amusement he'd perfected over centuries.

Yet he couldn't banish the image of Serenity's smile as she talked with Sebastian. She was his Elite, not his mate. Sustenance, not a partner. Nothing more.

Yet the connection he felt defied rational explanation, a primal claim that seemed written into his very cells. Even Becca, his beloved wife, had never evoked this consuming territorial response.

The executive elevator awaited him, accessible only to Council leadership. Kane placed his palm against the scanner, felt the sharp prick as the system drew blood, watched the panel pulse green before the doors opened.

As he ascended, he composed himself behind the impassive mask that had served him for centuries in Council chambers.

The security guard at the elevator bank straightened as Kane emerged. A subtle nod was exchanged, and the reinforced door buzzed open to admit him to the executive wing.

He passed Kaelen's workstation, noting the meticulous organization that characterized everything his assistant touched. Kaelen himself embodied the same precision: crisp shirt, tailored trousers, hair arranged with mathematical exactitude.

"Sir, I didn't expect you for another hour," Kaelen greeted him, rising swiftly.

"I finished earlier than anticipated. I need David in my office immediately with the pre-war infrastructure maps," Kane replied, his tone clipped.

"Of course, sir. Would you like me to bring Syn?" Kaelen offered, referring to the synthetic blood substitute.

Kane fixed his assistant with a glacial stare and continued toward his office without responding. The shutters activated automatically, revealing the sprawling city below, twenty years of vision transformed into this functioning metropolis.

Becca had once told him he needed to identify and cultivate a human leader who shared his vision of coexistence. Thus far, every human authority figure had proven disappointingly shortsighted, corrupted by their brief lifespans into prioritizing immediate gains over sustainable progress.

"Sir. David will arrive within five minutes," Kaelen's voice broke into his contemplation as the assistant placed a bottle of Syn on his desk before retreating.

David entered shortly after, his arms laden with rolled maps and documents. The archivist's appearance spoke of countless hours in the climate-controlled record repositories: glasses perched precariously, dark hair disheveled, clothing rumpled.

"Have you been sleeping in the archives again?" Kane inquired.

David's expression confirmed his guilt. "I've been conducting critical research. If we intend to expand beyond the current boundaries, we must develop methods to neutralize residual radiation for human populations."

"We have sufficient time."

"Humans do not," David countered with unusual assertiveness. "The earlier we implement reversal protocols, the better the outcomes." He spread his materials across the conference table. "You didn't specify which maps you required, so I brought the comprehensive set."

"I need to locate the nearest train station outside the walls. I believe one might be buried beneath the rubble outside Grove Gardens."

David rifled through his materials, extracting a large-format map. "This depicts Celearius before Outer City development. Red for rail networks, green for sewage infrastructure."

Kane focused on the section near Grove Gardens' outskirts, where multiple green lines converged toward the former city center.

"Show me the pre-war configuration."

David overlaid another map. "Orange designates the original rail system."

An orange line intersected precisely with the green tunnels near where Kane had found the box, confirmation that the rebellion had repurposed the old transit infrastructure. He traced the pathway to the nearest station, roughly two miles from the discovery site.

"Kaelen," he called, not bothering to raise his voice.

"Yes, sir." His assistant appeared instantly.

"Where is Sullivan?"

"Resting in the Solarium, I believe."

"Wake him."

Kane returned his attention to the maps, calculating the most efficient approach to the buried station. The subterranean infrastructure would have deteriorated significantly. Exploration would require specialized equipment and personnel trained in navigating unstable environments.

"You summoned me?" Sullivan's voice preceded him into the office, still rough with interrupted sleep. He wiped blood from the corner of his mouth while tugging his shirt into place.

"Thank you, David. Leave the maps for now." The dismissal was polite but firm.

Sullivan approached with casual predatory confidence, his auburn hair tousled from sleep, a calculating alertness in his dark, silver-flecked eyes. "I take it my recreational period has concluded."

"How perceptive." Kane retrieved the tin from his pocket and tossed it toward his security chief.

Sullivan caught it effortlessly, examining first the note, then the key. "Locker fifty-nine," he noted, glancing between the key and the maps. "This promises to be an extended operation."

"Indeed. You'll likely find your objective here." Kane indicated the probable location. "Select a small team, experienced individuals capable of absolute discretion."

"I have several candidates in mind. We'll be prepared within the hour." Sullivan captured the relevant map section on his communication device.

"Keep me informed once you're on site."

After Sullivan departed, Kane remained at the table, studying the maps with renewed focus. Whatever waited in locker fifty-nine would provide actionable intelligence about the rebellion's structure and objectives.

Minutes later, he returned to his desk and activated his private surveillance system. The wall panel slid aside, revealing high-definition screens displaying real-time footage throughout Celearius. His attention immediately fixed on the Silver District.

He manipulated the controls until he located the café where he'd last seen Serenity. The table she'd occupied was now empty. A faint disappointment registered before he dismissed it as irrelevant.

Yet his hand seemed to operate independently, navigating the surveillance system to access the internal cameras within his residence. The image shifted until movement caught his eye.

Serenity emerged from the elevator, a flaky pastry held delicately between her fingers. The high-resolution camera captured every detail: the slight flush coloring her cheeks, the contemplative expression, the graceful economy of movement that distinguished her.

He switched viewing angles, following her progress with a focus that disturbed even him. She opened the refrigerator, selected milk, her slender fingers wrapping around the glass with a gentleness that evoked inappropriate thoughts.

She settled at the kitchen table, taking a small bite of pastry. Her eyes closed for a moment in appreciation as flakes scattered against her lips. The simple pleasure in her expression triggered a complex response, hunger, certainly, but also a peculiar satisfaction in witnessing her enjoyment.

Without conscious intent, he traced a finger down the screen, following the contours of her face. The action shocked him back to awareness.

This was unacceptable. She had explicitly rejected his advances, and he had given his word to respect her boundaries, a promise he intended to honor regardless of the hunger gnawing at him. His code, developed through eras when such behavior was common among his kind, remained inflexible: consent was inviolable.

As she savored the final morsel, her communication device emitted an alert. She froze mid-motion, eyes widening as she read the message. Unmistakable panic flickered across her features before she steadied herself with a deliberate breath. Composure settled over her like a mask.

Kane leaned forward, curiosity piqued. Who would send her a message capable of evoking such a reaction? Sebastian again? Or someone else entirely?

After disposing of her food packaging and washing her hands, she departed for her private quarters. Kane tracked her progress until she disappeared into her room, where no cameras had been installed.

Perhaps a strategic approach would yield answers. A shared meal would provide the perfect setting to disarm her defenses, allowing conversation to develop naturally while establishing a more balanced dynamic.

He still owed her a proper dinner, after all. Their first attempt had ended in his attack, and today he'd taken her blood without the courtesy of the nourishment he'd promised.

"Kaelen," he called.

"Yes, sir?"

"Make a reservation for this evening at Les Reines. Inform them that my Elite will accompany me."

Kaelen's eyebrows rose fractionally in surprise. "Yes, sir. At what time?"

"Six-thirty," Kane decided. Early enough to avoid ostentatious social displays, yet late enough for proper preparation.

"I'll see to it immediately."

Kane hadn't missed his assistant's momentary lapse in composure. He understood the source; it had been years since Kane had voluntarily taken part in Celearius's social rituals. Perhaps this outing would benefit not only his relationship with Serenity but his own neglected need for experiences beyond strategy sessions and security briefings.

He was about to deactivate the surveillance system when something unusual caught his attention. The central monitor flickered subtly, a digital anomaly that most observers would attribute to routine fluctuation. But Kane, intimately familiar with his custom-designed network, recognized it for what it was: external interference.

His suspicion sharpened when he noticed the timestamp in the corner: two days prior, not the current date and time.

Someone had penetrated his security system, replacing live footage with a pre-recorded loop.

Cold fury replaced all other concerns as he reached for his communication device, already calculating the system vulnerabilities that would require immediate attention.

Security had been compromised. Everything else was secondary.

But as the connection established, one thought blazed through his tactical assessment with uncomfortable clarity: if someone could breach his private surveillance, what else might they have accessed? What other secrets lay exposed?

And more troubling still, had they been watching when he'd fed from Serenity in the library? Had they witnessed his moment of complete vulnerability, when centuries of control had crumbled at her touch?

If the rebellion possessed footage of that encounter, they would understand exactly how to weaponize his greatest weakness against him.

"Nox," he said the moment the line connected. "My surveillance has been breached. Come to the city office. Now."

CHAPTER
FORTY-ONE

RHYZAN

"It's just a minor glitch, nothing to be alarmed about. Isolated to your end. The team is already working on a fix," Nox explained to Kane, his voice carefully measured. The lie was necessary, for now.

Rhyzan's fingers flew across three separate keyboards, each connected to a different security subsystem. The blue glow of the monitors cast sharp shadows across his face, highlighting the tension in his jaw. Emergency protocols had activated the instant they detected the intrusion, but whoever had breached Kane's personal security was sophisticated, dangerously so.

Wall-mounted screens displayed fragmented views of Kane's residence: empty foyer, kitchen with its abandoned milk glass, corridors leading to the private quarters. Rhyzan had designed this system with multiple encrypted backups and parallel monitoring networks, impossible to hack completely, yet evidently vulnerable enough for a historical feed injection.

"Twelve minutes," he murmured, studying the timestamp data scrolling across his auxiliary screen. "They maintained access for twelve minutes before detection."

The self-criticism was harsh but justified. In security operations, twelve minutes was an eternity.

When Nox received Kane's urgent call, followed by the encrypted alert codes, Rhyzan had abandoned their interrogation mid-session, leaving Chloe to keep extracting information from their captive. He'd anticipated countless potential threats across the centuries, but direct penetration of Kane's private security hadn't ranked high on his probability matrix.

A miscalculation he wouldn't repeat.

With practiced efficiency, he'd traced the digital signature, then executed a specialized countermeasure developed for precisely this contingency, a passive tracking protocol that let him observe the observers without alerting them to his presence. Now he could see exactly what the rebels were seeing: carefully selected views of Kane's supposedly empty apartment.

Three security specialists worked at adjacent stations, one tracing the signal origin, another reinforcing secondary systems, the third documenting anomalies for forensic analysis.

"Perhaps they've realized Kane isn't there," Nox suggested after ending his call. The usually unflappable vampyr couldn't quite conceal his concern, his typical sardonic expression replaced by genuine worry. "They may abandon the attempt."

Rhyzan shook his head, silver-flecked eyes narrowing as he studied the infiltration patterns. "This breach is too sophisticated, too targeted." He pulled up secondary displays showing the encryption characteristics. "These patterns align perfectly with incidents we've traced to Sebastian's network. The algorithmic fingerprint matches exactly, the same signature we documented during last month's clinic attack."

Centuries of suspicion hardened into certainty. "Sebastian recruited her. Kane inadvertently created the perfect opportunity, isolated, vulnerable, already primed to distrust vampyr authority."

The surveillance feed suddenly shifted, focusing with uncomfortable precision on Serenity's bedroom door. The movement wasn't random; whoever controlled the system was waiting for something specific.

"They're monitoring her specifically," Rhyzan observed, a cold certainty settling in his chest. "Positioned the surveillance to track her movements."

"Do you think she'll act?" Nox asked, his voice uncharacteristically tight.

The question hung between them, laden with implications neither wished to voice directly. If she betrayed Kane, the consequences would reach far beyond her execution. The fragile political balance Rhyzan had spent centuries crafting would fracture along factional lines. Hardliners would seize on Kane's lapse in judgment as proof that his human sympathies clouded his reasoning. Kane's position on the Human Vampyr Council hinged on his reputation for absolute control, and that carefully cultivated image would crumble if his own Elite proved to be a Liberation agent.

The timing couldn't be worse, with Bosa's militants testing the borders and human unrest growing in the outer districts.

On the central monitor, the bedroom door opened. Serenity emerged, glancing furtively down the corridor before stepping into view. Her movements carried none of the casual confidence she'd shown earlier; each step was careful, measured, the behavior of someone crossing a line.

"She received a message the day after arriving at Kane's," Nox said quietly. "While I was teaching her the communication device."

Rhyzan's head snapped toward him, his composure abandoned. "When did this happen?" The words escaped as a harsh demand, his normally measured tone replaced by an edge that centuries of diplomacy had kept in check.

"She seemed confused about whether it had actually happened," Nox replied, holding an outward calm that didn't match the unease in his eyes. "The message was vague. Could have been misdirected, or harassment."

Rhyzan's jaw tightened, the muscles visibly clenching beneath pale skin. "Or she was lying. Feigning confusion to avoid suspicion, a common enough tactic."

Before Nox could respond, the security system registered an alarming development. All localized alarm protocols within Kane's apartment deactivated at once, a master override that should have required direct physical access to the central hub.

"They've compromised the secondary failsafes," one technician reported. "Attempting to reinitiate remote protection protocols."

"Don't," Rhyzan commanded sharply. "Let them believe they have complete control. We learn more by observing their operations."

His gaze returned to the monitor displaying Serenity's cautious progress. Each step carried her closer to Kane's private chambers, areas even Elite donors rarely accessed.

"If she's working with them, what would they want her to find?" Nox asked pragmatically.

Rhyzan considered with the thoroughness that had kept Kane's regime secure through three decades of attempted insurrections. "Access codes. Security protocols. Kane's movement patterns. Perhaps something more specific, the identities of Council informants within the rebellion. Kane keeps physical records of sensitive intelligence in his private safe."

History taught that trust was the most exploitable vulnerability in any security system. He'd witnessed other betrayals, Elites poisoning their patron's blood supply, coordinated attempts to trap vampyrs on rooftops at sunrise.

On screen, Serenity paused where the corridor branched, left toward the library, right toward Kane's office. Her hesitation was brief but noticeable, a moment of decision captured in high definition.

"Her choice reveals everything," Rhyzan murmured, leaning forward. "Kane's office means treachery."

The seconds stretched as they watched her internal struggle play out. Finally, she turned right, toward Kane's office.

"Implement observer protocol seven," Rhyzan instructed without taking his eyes from the monitor. "Full passive surveillance. No intervention unless she attempts to remove physical evidence or breach the main security hub."

"What if she accesses Kane's private files?" a newer specialist asked.

"We let her," Rhyzan replied coldly. "We need irrefutable evidence of her collusion with Sebastian. Kane won't accept anything less."

Presenting Kane with suspicion or circumstantial evidence was futile. Only undeniable proof would overcome Kane's remarkable capacity for self-deception where those he favored were concerned, a rare weakness in an otherwise formidable leader.

"If she betrays Kane after forming such an obvious connection..." Nox left the thought unfinished.

Rhyzan's expression hardened. He'd witnessed Kane's devastation after Becca's death; that Kane had shown interest in anyone after such loss was miraculous. That he might be betrayed by the first woman to breach his defenses was potentially catastrophic.

"Kane survived losing Becca," he stated flatly. "He'll survive this."

Yet even as he spoke the reassurance, doubt crept in. Kane had been different with this Elite from the start, more affected, less controlled, vulnerable in ways Rhyzan hadn't witnessed before. If this ended badly, the consequences wouldn't be limited to broken trust. Kane's fury would be both personal and political, a dangerous combination in someone with his power.

On the monitor, Serenity reached Kane's door, hesitating with her hand poised above the access panel. Her expression reflected clear internal conflict, fear warring with determination.

But there was something else in her face that gave Rhyzan pause. Not the cold calculation of a trained operative, but real anguish. The pain of someone betraying everything she'd begun to care about.

Perhaps that was what made her so dangerous. Unlike previous infiltrators who'd kept their emotional distance, Serenity's feelings for Kane appeared unfeigned, which made her betrayal all the more devastating, and her potential value to the Liberation exponentially greater.

"Her attachment to Kane makes her either our greatest asset or our most dangerous threat," Rhyzan observed, adjusting the monitor resolution to capture every detail of her expression. "If we can turn her back to our side, she becomes invaluable intelligence about Liberation operations. If not..."

He left the alternative unspoken. They both understood what happened to confirmed spies.

As Serenity's hand finally descended toward the scanner, Rhyzan made a strategic decision. This moment would determine not just her fate, but potentially the future of human-vampyr relations in Celearius.

The choice now was whether to stop her before she completed the act, or let her proceed and gather the intelligence they needed to destroy the rebellion entirely.

CHAPTER
FORTY-TWO

SERENITY

Serenity stood frozen outside Kane's office, her hand hovering inches from the access panel. The hallway shadows seemed to close around her as her heart hammered against her ribs. Every instinct screamed at her to run back to her room, yet she couldn't move, trapped at the threshold of a decision that would change everything.

The memory of Kane's kiss burned through her mind, the careful strength in his hands as he'd held her against the library shelf, the surprising gentleness when his fangs had pierced her throat. She touched her neck where the marks had already faded, her body responding with a shiver that had nothing to do with fear.

This is wrong.

After reluctantly telling Sebastian about Kane's healing abilities, carefully omitting their intimate encounter, she'd been surprised to learn the rebels already had this intelligence. They'd been watching Kane for years. She was simply confirmation.

Sebastian had promised contact today with new instructions, but she hadn't expected this sudden opportunity. The rebels had somehow disabled Kane's security system, giving her precious minutes to search for the information they desperately needed.

Freedom waited beyond this betrayal. Her family. Her district. Her father's legacy, all of it would benefit if the rebellion succeeded in securing equal rights from vampyr control. Yet guilt stayed with her like a physical weight. Kane had protected her, fed her, respected her boundaries when she'd refused to formalize their physical relationship. He'd arranged payment for her family's medicine.

Was he truly the enemy my father fought against?

The security light above the panel shifted from steady red to black, confirmation that the rebels had successfully breached the system. Her opportunity had arrived. Time was running out.

She could walk away. Tell Sebastian she couldn't do it. Kane wasn't the monster they believed him to be.

Yet her father's face appeared in her mind, his kind eyes, his firm belief that humans deserved more than mere survival under vampyr rule. She owed him this. She owed her people this.

With trembling fingers, she pressed her palm to the scanner. It resisted briefly before the door slid open with a soft hiss.

The office beyond was dimly lit by the setting sun streaming through the large windows. Every surface gleamed with flawless order, not a paper misplaced, not a speck of dust marring the polished wood. The space embodied Kane's personality: controlled, organized, impenetrable.

Her communication device buzzed against her palm.

"Serenity." Starr's voice crackled through the speaker, tight with urgency. "Find his computer."

She slipped inside, closing the door carefully behind her. Each footstep seemed thunderous against the hardwood despite her efforts at silence. The air carried Kane's scent, cedar and leather, unmistakably his.

The computer sat flush against the desktop near the window, its screen dark. Growing up in Grove Gardens, she'd barely seen a working computer, let alone used such advanced technology.

"I've never used anything this sophisticated," she admitted, fear creeping into her voice.

"It's alright," Starr reassured, her tone softening for a moment. "I'll guide you through each step. Look for a power button, likely along the screen's edge."

Serenity traced the sleek display until her fingers found a small, nearly invisible depression. She pressed gently.

The screen illuminated, casting blue light across her face. Instead of the technical interface she'd expected, the display showed a breathtaking landscape, an ancient forest bathed in golden light, impossibly tall trees reaching toward a crimson sunset. The image seemed incongruous with Kane's austere office, a glimpse of unexpected beauty in his strictly controlled environment.

"Access the system portal," Starr instructed. "Touch the icon in the lower left, then select the search function. It looks like a magnifying glass."

Serenity followed the directions, her fingertip leaving a tiny smudge on the pristine surface. The forest disappeared, replaced by symbols she didn't recognize.

"Type 'Command Box' and press Enter."

"There's no keyboard."

"Touch the surface directly in front of the monitor."

When Serenity placed her fingers against the cool desktop, a keyboard materialized beneath her hands, keys glowing with soft blue light. The technology was so far beyond anything she'd encountered that it momentarily stole her breath. This was Kane's world, a realm of possibilities humans in districts like hers could barely imagine.

She carefully typed the command. A black rectangle appeared, followed by a blinking green cursor.

"Enter   this   access   code   exactly: export.function.activat e {1ZC70-AZJ21-56GLH} ACCESS."

Serenity's fingers shook as she typed each character. What would happen if the system detected unauthorized access? Would alarms sound? Would Kane be automatically notified? She glanced nervously at the closed door, half-expecting it to burst open.

When she pressed the final key, the screen filled with racing code, green symbols moving faster than her eyes could follow. Her mouth went dry as she watched the system being methodically compromised, each line carrying her another step deeper into Kane's private world.

This is wrong.

The thought came with startling clarity, but too late. Three pulsing dots appeared, showing the remote infiltration continuing. She had crossed a line from which there was no return.

"Nothing's happening," she whispered after tense seconds stretched into a minute.

"Just a moment more," Starr replied, concentration evident in her voice as rapid keystrokes punctuated her words. "Their security is... impressive."

The screen suddenly flashed green: ACCESS GRANTED.

"We're in," Starr announced triumphantly.

Relief briefly washed through Serenity before guilt crashed over her. She watched folders open automatically, the rebels now controlling the system remotely through her access point. Documents flashed by, reports on district resource allocation, security protocols for the Inner and Outer Cities, population statistics organized by blood type and occupation.

"We need to hurry," she urged, her voice barely above a whisper.

"Don't worry," Damon's deeper voice replaced Starr's, meant to be calming. "Kane remains at his CityCentre office. Our watchers confirm it. We wouldn't risk your safety."

"What about Nox and Rhyzan?" she pressed, remembering the vampyrs' ability to move silently.

"They left the city an hour ago," Damon replied with precise detail. "Sebastian is with Evelyn, keeping her occupied. Your position is secure."

As folders continued cycling through the display, a particular label caught her attention: 'Becca.' The name was unfamiliar, yet the folder held a prominent place among Kane's files.

Curiosity overcame caution. Who was Becca, and why did Kane keep a special file about her? Serenity's fingers moved almost on their own, selecting the folder.

A password prompt immediately appeared.

"What happened?" Starr's voice returned, edged with concern.

Serenity's gaze swept the office, searching for clues. Unlike Kane's carefully austere space, one personal item hung on the wall near the window, a small, exquisitely detailed painting in an antique frame. The image showed a woman seated beside a lake, her expression peaceful yet somehow melancholy. From her position, Serenity could just make out words at the bottom: 'lac d'amour.'

"One moment," she murmured, standing to examine the painting closely.

The woman possessed a haunting beauty, golden hair framing delicate features, amber eyes gazing out with an emotion Serenity couldn't name. The canvas had been painted with extraordinary skill, capturing not just appearance but essence. This wasn't merely art; it was memory preserved. The placement, directly in Kane's line of sight from his desk, spoke volumes about its significance.

Something constricted in Serenity's chest as understanding dawned. The woman in the painting must be Becca. The way Kane had positioned it, where he would see it each time he looked up, suggested a meaning far beyond casual decoration.

"Serenity?" Starr called insistently. "What are you doing?"

She returned to the computer, her fingers hovering over the keyboard. "Just a second," she replied, typing 'lac d'amour' into the password field.

The screen paused briefly before the folder unlocked, revealing dozens of sub-folders and files. Images flooded the display, the same woman captured in count-less moments: laughing in a garden, reading beside a window, sleeping peacefully. In some sketches Kane appeared beside her, his expression transformed by some-thing Serenity had never witnessed in him, an unguarded joy.

This was someone he loved. His wife.

The realization struck with unexpected force. She had known, in theory, that Kane had once been married, but seeing proof of that relationship, the tenderness preserved in these images, made him human in a way she hadn't anticipated. The man who had held her against the library shelves with such controlled passion had once loved this woman with his entire being.

"Serenity!" Starr's increasingly worried voice pulled her from her contempla-tion. "What are you accessing?"

"Nothing relevant," she replied, closing the gallery with surprising reluctance. She kept searching until another folder caught her attention: 'Cavern 47.'

The rebels had mentioned this location before. Sebastian had identified it as potential weapons storage, though he'd been frustratingly vague about its exact importance. Finding concrete information had been one of their primary objectives.

"I think I've found it," she told Starr, selecting the folder.

As its contents began to load, Serenity couldn't shake the feeling that she had crossed more than one line today. She had come seeking information for the rebellion, but had instead stumbled onto something unexpectedly personal, a glimpse of Kane not as the powerful Council leader, but as a man who had loved and lost.

Kane wasn't the cold, calculating tyrant the Liberation had described. He was a man carrying grief across centuries, someone who had once known joy and had it torn away. Someone who deserved better than her deception.

What am I doing to him?

As the Cavern 47 files opened, revealing detailed schematics and security protocols, Serenity realized with crystalline clarity that this moment would haunt her forever, regardless of which side ultimately claimed victory in the war between humans and vampyrs. She was betraying someone who had shown her nothing but protection and care. Someone who still loved a woman three centuries dead. Someone who might, impossibly, be learning to care for her.

The thought nearly made her flee the office entirely, but the weight of her father's memory, her family's needs, and the rebellion's cause kept her rooted in place as she fed Kane's secrets to his enemies.

Even as her heart broke a little more with each stolen file.

CHAPTER
FORTY-THREE

RHYZAN

"This is going to break him," Nox whispered, the blue glow from the monitors casting harsh shadows across his face as they watched Serenity access Kane's private files. His normally confident voice betrayed an unusual vulnerability.

Rhyzan remained motionless, only his eyes tracking every micro-movement on the high-definition display. The rebels' infiltration had penetrated all seven security layers he'd designed over decades. What they didn't realize was his deliberate strategy: he'd left one firewall intentionally vulnerable, a calculated risk that let him monitor their every action while they remained oblivious to his surveillance.

"He has survived far worse betrayals," Rhyzan replied, his tone carrying the certainty of centuries spent witnessing Kane's resilience. Yet even as he spoke the reassurance, something darker stirred in his chest as he watched Serenity navigate Kane's most private spaces.

Around them, technicians worked in focused silence, interrupted only by the soft beeps of the monitoring systems. Rhyzan adjusted the controls, lowering the temperature further; cold optimized vampyr cognitive performance and enhanced their tracking.

His fingers moved with practiced precision across the custom interface, selectively curating the digital landscape the rebels explored. He methodically deleted truly sensitive intelligence: complete informant networks, the plans for the containment facility beneath Easton, psychological profiles of captured rebel leaders.

What remained served his purpose, records of the assassination attempt on Dr. Mercer, the Elite doctor whose car the rebels had rigged, and, most crucially, the early intelligence on Jax Thornton.

"Their retrieval pattern indicates they're mapping strategic vulnerabilities rather than seeking personal information about Kane," Rhyzan observed, analyzing the rebels' digital footprints. "They're identifying access points, defensive weaknesses. This isn't reconnaissance; they're planning a specific operation."

He positioned the Thornton file with care, embedding subtle tracking code that would let him follow its movement through rebel networks once acquired. The bait was calibrated precisely, neither obvious enough to trigger suspicion nor hidden enough to escape discovery.

"Which priority will reveal their leadership structure?" Nox asked, leaning closer to the display. "Personal connections or tactical objectives?"

"They're copying both files at once, but accessing Thornton first," Rhyzan noted with interest. "Emotional decision-making superseding tactical analysis. Their commanders aren't pure strategists; they're driven by personal stakes."

His eyes narrowed as he traced the thin scar along his jawline, an unconscious habit that emerged only during complex calculations. "They'll begin searching for Cavern 47 soon. We must prepare a trail leading exactly where we want them."

"Sebastian remains the obvious conduit," Nox suggested, his long-standing suspicion of Evelyn's patron evident in his tone.

"No," Rhyzan countered, his gaze fixed on Serenity's image. Her movements revealed a nervous energy layered over an underlying determination, qualities that had grown more apparent since her arrival. "She'll relay intelligence to Sebastian. Her position provides us something uniquely valuable: credible deniability."

The philosophical difference in their approaches reflected decades of collaboration. Where Nox favored direct confrontation, Rhyzan had learned through centuries of political maneuvering that indirect methods often proved more effective. Kane required both perspectives, the hammer and the scalpel.

On screen, Serenity's fingers hesitated over Kane's computer as she accessed a folder labeled 'Becca.' Rhyzan's expression tightened imperceptibly. Of all Kane's files, this was the most personal, the carefully preserved memories of his greatest love and loss.

"She's accessing his wife's files," Nox observed quietly.

Rhyzan watched as Serenity opened image after image, Kane's private gallery of a marriage that had spanned a human lifetime and more. The paintings, the sketches, the intimate moments captured with an artist's devotion. His friend had poured his grief into those images, preserving every detail of their life together.

A muscle twitched in Rhyzan's jaw. This went beyond mere espionage; it was a violation of Kane's most sacred memories. Yet strategically, her discovery served his purposes. Witnessing Kane's capacity for profound love would complicate her mission, introduce an emotional conflict he could exploit.

"She's seeing who he truly is," Rhyzan murmured, his analytical mind cataloguing the implications. "Not the Council leader or the vampyr authority, but the man who loved Becca with his entire being. This changes her perception fundamentally."

"Is that advantageous or problematic?" Nox asked.

"Both." Rhyzan's fingers stilled on the controls as he watched Serenity's expression shift from curiosity to something approaching anguish. "She's realizing the depth of what she's betraying. This internal conflict makes her either more valuable as an asset or more dangerous as an adversary."

The rebels completed their data extraction and instructed Serenity to exit the system. Before the connection terminated, Rhyzan erased all traces of their passive surveillance and restored Kane's security protocols. The most effective traps were those the target never suspected existed.

Serenity slipped from Kane's office, the door closing silently behind her. The camera feeds tracked her progress through the residence until she reached her quarters, communication device still in hand as she severed contact with her handlers.

"I'll retrieve her device later," Rhyzan noted. "Standard rebel protocol suggests quantum encryption and signal scattering, but future contact attempts will allow triangulation of their operational area."

He shifted the main monitor to display Celearius's northern section, the region where signal analysis indicated concentrated rebel activity. Their tactics had evolved significantly in recent months, suggesting either new leadership or outside assistance. Both possibilities concerned him.

"What's our next move?" Nox asked, straightening from his position over the console. Unlike Rhyzan, who could remain motionless for hours during surveillance, Nox retained more human mannerisms, subtle movements, shifts in position, expressions of restlessness.

"We wait," Rhyzan replied, his voice carrying the weight of centuries spent observing enemies. "And prepare Cavern 47 for the inevitable breach attempts."

He gestured to the senior technician, who immediately began implementing enhanced protocols.

Nox ran a hand through his dark hair, an uncharacteristic frustration from someone who typically held rigid self-control. "I truly believed she would be different. The way Kane responded to her... I haven't seen him that engaged since Becca."

The mention of Kane's wife sent a shared memory rippling between them; both had witnessed the devastating aftermath of her loss firsthand. Three centuries of Kane's careful reconstruction, the deliberate rebuilding of his capacity to function beyond mere existence.

Rhyzan's expression softened marginally, the only sign of his internal conflict. He had advocated for Kane to accept another Elite specifically to draw him from the emotional abyss he'd inhabited since Becca's death. That Serenity had succeeded where others failed made her betrayal particularly regrettable.

"She is different," he acknowledged, examining the facility schematics on the tactical display. "Her effect on him has been... significant. More than anticipated." He marked several access points requiring additional security. "But containing this rebellion must take priority. If Kane's attachment compromises our ability to prevent further bloodshed, the calculation is clear."

"Nothing about this is clear," Nox countered quietly.

Rhyzan met his oldest friend's gaze directly. "Our duty remains unambiguous. When this concludes, if circumstances permit, we'll find him another companion. Someone equally compelling, but without ties to Grove Gardens' rebel sympathizers."

The admission carried weight. Rhyzan had genuinely hoped Serenity might become the stabilizing influence Kane had lacked since Becca. Her fearlessness in their presence had been refreshing; most humans crumbled under his scrutiny alone. Under different circumstances, she might have been exactly what Kane needed.

He disliked the necessity of manipulating her, recognizing that the rebels were likely exploiting her family's vulnerable position. Unlike contemporaries who viewed humans as inherently expendable, Rhyzan held a more nuanced view, developed across centuries. Humans demonstrated remarkable adaptability; some had shown loyalty and courage to match any vampyr he'd known.

"When this concludes," he added quietly, "I'll ensure her punishment reflects the coercion she's likely under. She needn't suffer excessively for being exploited."

Nox's expression revealed surprise at the unexpected mercy. "You've developed greater sympathy for humans."

"I've developed a better understanding of power dynamics," Rhyzan corrected, returning his attention to the surveillance feeds. "She's a pawn manipulated by more experienced players. Our true target remains whoever coordinates these increasingly sophisticated operations."

Yet watching her access Kane's memories of Becca had stirred something unexpected in his calculations. Serenity's genuine distress at violating Kane's privacy suggested a conscience beneath the rebellion's facade. Perhaps there was more to work with than simple family loyalty.

The irony wasn't lost on him: Kane's greatest vulnerability might become their greatest asset. If Serenity's feelings for Kane deepened sufficiently, her emotional conflict could be leveraged to turn her against her handlers entirely.

"Increase surveillance on all Cavern 47 entry points," he instructed the security team. "Triple the patrol frequency while maintaining the existing routes; we don't want to signal awareness of a potential breach. Prepare the containment cells in the lower levels. I anticipate guests soon."

For now, he would keep using Serenity as an unwitting double agent, feeding carefully selected intelligence through her to the rebellion while gathering data on their structure and objectives. Kane didn't require these details yet; the knowledge would only compromise his judgment and potentially alert Sebastian to their suspicions.

The pieces were finally converging toward an endgame. After five years of patient maneuvering, the rebellion's leadership was about to emerge from the shadows, drawn by information too valuable to resist investigating in person.

When they did, Rhyzan would be waiting.

But first, he needed to determine whether Kane's growing attachment to his Elite would be the saving of him or the ruin of them all. The answer would depend on which proved stronger: Serenity's loyalty to her mission, or her feelings for the man whose heart she'd just witnessed through three centuries of preserved memory.

Either way, Rhyzan would ensure Kane survived the revelation. Even if it meant destroying the first happiness his friend had found since Becca's death.

CHAPTER FORTY-FOUR

KANE

The excavation feed flickered across Kane's monitor, casting cold blue light through his office. After two grueling hours navigating crumbling infrastructure, Sullivan had finally reached the abandoned transit system beneath the city's foundations. His team moved like shadows through the ruins, their progress measured in cautious steps across unstable ground.

On screen, Sullivan's operatives uncovered a half-collapsed passageway concealed behind debris. Ancient stairs, worn smooth by countless forgotten commuters, descended into darkness toward the pre-war rail tracks. Each movement was deliberate, each placement calculated on the treacherous footing.

"I believe we're approaching the target coordinates," Sullivan's voice crackled through the static-laden speakers. "Structural damage exceeds initial assessment. Additional personnel required for safe clearance of obstacles."

Kane studied the tactical display showing their position relative to the coordinates he'd extrapolated from David's maps. They were within a hundred meters of where locker fifty-nine should be, assuming decades of decay hadn't collapsed the entire station.

"Nox and Rhyzan are en route to your position," Kane replied, his fingers steepled beneath his chin. The rebellion had gained momentum across recent months, disappearing Elites, assassinated officials, sabotaged integration programs he'd spent decades developing. Whatever the rebels had deemed worthy of such elaborate concealment might finally provide the key to dismantling their organization entirely.

The camera angle widened as two familiar figures navigated the debris with predatory grace. Even dust-covered and disheveled, Rhyzan moved with the calculating precision that had made him Kane's security chief for centuries. Beside him, Nox's more fluid movements revealed his younger Turning, though he was no less lethal.

"Reinforcements have arrived," Sullivan confirmed, straightening to acknowledge their presence with the subtle nod vampyr operatives used for formal greeting.

Nox immediately assessed the blockage, his expression shifting to wry amusement. "This promises to be entertaining," he muttered, already calculating structural integrity and removal sequences.

"Excellent," Kane responded through the crackling speakers. "Push through with necessary force. I require immediate intelligence on that locker's contents." He didn't need to emphasize the mission's importance; all three understood that whatever the humans had hidden might provide the leverage to end this rebellion for good.

"Understood," Sullivan replied with the absolute reliability that had made him Kane's preferred field commander.

Kane disconnected the feed, the screen darkening to leave him alone with the weight of leadership accumulated across his long existence. He leaned back in the ancient leather that creaked softly, closing his eyes with a slow exhale. His office's usual sanctuary of order now felt stifling rather than peaceful.

Instead of strategic considerations, Serenity's face materialized unbidden in his mind's eye. Not flushed with desire as she'd been in the library, but serene and contemplative as she'd appeared that morning, sunlight catching her dark curls while she sipped tea by the window, unaware of his observation.

His surveillance system waited a single keystroke away; he could monitor her movements throughout his residence with one command.

Kane's fingers hovered over the controls before he pulled back with a frustrated exhale. This preoccupation was becoming dangerous. With the rebellion threatening everything he'd built, he couldn't afford the distraction she represented, regardless of how uniquely her blood called to him.

Perhaps requesting the dinner reservation had been impulsive. Though Kaelen had confirmed the arrangements an hour earlier, doubts crept in about the wisdom of his decision. She represented a beautiful, defiant distraction he could ill afford during these dangerous times.

He should contact Kaelen immediately and cancel.

Kane reached for his communication device, Kaelen's direct line displayed, when something stopped him.

No. He wouldn't cancel.

There was something about her that transcended mere physical attraction, the resilience that had let her survive his initial attack, the courage that allowed her to meet his gaze without flinching, the adaptability that helped her navigate a world utterly foreign to her former existence. These qualities had reached past his carefully constructed barriers to touch something he'd thought permanently dormant.

She was nothing like Becca. Where his wife had been gentle wisdom personified, Serenity was determination forged in hardship. Becca had known him only as statesman, diplomat, architect of integration. She had never witnessed the predator lurking beneath his civilized veneer. Had he shown Becca even a fraction of the aggression Serenity had endured, she would have fled, rightfully so.

Yet Serenity had not run. Even after experiencing his hunger at its most primal, she had stayed. That fact continued to puzzle him.

The antique Parisian clock showed 5:15 p.m. with quiet precision.

He needed to leave immediately. Dinner preparation required minimal effort, but he wanted time to change properly. Despite the pressing matters awaiting resolution, an unexplainable anticipation quickened his movements as he gathered his personal effects.

As the private elevator ascended toward his residence, Kane felt an unfamiliar sensation uncoiling within him, something between nervousness and eagerness he hadn't experienced in decades. This strange emotional mixture should have troubled him more than it did. He had negotiated peace between warring factions, had guided civilization's rebuilding from humanity's ashes, yet dinner with one woman unsettled him like nothing else.

The moment the elevator doors parted to reveal his penthouse, regret twisted through him with powerful force.

This dinner will be exquisite torture.

Serenity stood near the windows, the dying sunlight catching her form in a golden embrace that transformed her from merely beautiful to breathtaking. The dress she wore, elegant simplicity in burnished gold, complemented the warm undertones of her skin. Her normally loose curls had been swept up, revealing the graceful lines of her neck and her delicate collarbones. Small golden earrings caught the light when she turned toward him, emphasizing the natural luminescence of her skin.

Kane remained frozen in the doorway, captivated. His carefully maintained vigilance faltered as the rebellion's concerns receded, this woman commanding his complete attention. Through their connection, he felt her initial nervousness at noticing him, followed by a warm appreciation as their eyes met.

"Hi," she said, breaking the spell. "Someone named Kaelen called and explained you were planning dinner. He said I should be ready when you returned."

Her words washed over him, requiring several heartbeats before he could respond. He had witnessed the rise and fall of countless civilizations, yet this moment rendered him as awkward as a newly Turned vampyr.

"Yes," he finally managed. "I find myself... in debt for two meals, given our interrupted first attempt. I require only a moment to change into appropriate attire."

She nodded gracefully, stepping aside. Yet his feet felt weighted, refusing to move past her. An overwhelming urge to touch her seized him, to confirm she was real, to feel the warmth that haunted his thoughts. His hand lifted involuntarily before he caught himself, lowering it with effort. Through their connection, he sensed her mixture of caution and intrigue mirroring his own internal conflict.

The air between them seemed charged with unspoken possibilities, a tangible current that made his skin prickle with awareness. Her heartbeat filled his enhanced hearing, slightly elevated but steady, both soothing and maddening.

"I shall only be a moment," he said finally, breaking the charged silence before it consumed them both.

In his private chambers, Kane changed methodically into dinner attire, selecting a charcoal jacket that complemented rather than matched her golden dress. As he adjusted his cuffs, he silently berated himself for agreeing to this dinner. One meal wouldn't erase the complications of the library. One evening couldn't undo the intricacies of their situation.

Yet even as the logical arguments mounted, he found himself opening the concealed safe. Inside, nestled in aged velvet, lay his mother's necklace, one of the few possessions he'd preserved through countless relocations across the centuries. The simple golden pendant, an unbroken circle suspended from a delicate chain, had adorned his mother's neck in the only drawing he possessed. She had died when he was seven, long before his transformation, her face now a faded memory, but her legacy preserved in this tangible link to his human origins.

He had shown it to no one since Becca's death. Yet now, without understanding his own motivations, he carefully removed it and closed the safe. Before rational thought could intervene, he returned to where Serenity waited.

"I believe the only element missing is suitable accompaniment," he said, holding up the golden circle. "This should complete your ensemble."

Serenity's eyes widened as she examined the jewelry, genuine appreciation mixing with hesitation. Through their bond, he felt her surprise and a deeper emotion, a feeling she tried to conceal.

"It's absolutely beautiful," she said softly. "But I couldn't possibly wear something so valuable. Even these earrings feel excessive."

"As Evelyn often reminds me," Kane found himself saying, "there is no such thing as excess when beauty is properly adorned." The words surprised him, almost playful, a tone he rarely employed. "Please, allow me to place it on you. Occasional indulgence is permitted, and tonight seems particularly fitting."

She studied him with piercing eyes that seemed to perceive more than he intended to reveal. A silent assessment passed between them before she turned, presenting her back in a gesture of trust that affected him more deeply than it should. Their connection vibrated with the significance of the small act, her willingness to make herself vulnerable despite everything between them.

As she gathered her curls from her neck, Kane stepped closer, allowing himself one unguarded moment. He inhaled deeply, capturing her distinctive scent, the artificial vanilla and lemon unable to fully mask the natural ambrosia beneath. The proximity made his fangs ache with remembered pleasure, her taste still vivid in his memory.

With care, he draped the necklace around her throat, the gold warming instantly against her skin. His fingers brushed her nape as he secured the clasp, and he felt her subtle shiver in response. Their blood bond intensified with the nearness, creating a feedback loop that threatened to overwhelm his carefully maintained control.

His hands felt unexpectedly empty as he regarded her, the golden circle resting against her skin as though it had been designed for her rather than crafted centuries before her birth.

"Are you prepared to depart?" he asked, surprised by the slight roughness in his voice.

She nodded, a small smile playing at her lips. "I'm ready whenever you are."

Through their connection, he sensed her genuine pleasure and excitement about the evening, emotions uncomplicated by the strategic considerations clouding his own anticipation.

"Then let us proceed," he said, extending his arm in a gesture belonging to earlier, more formal eras.

Yet beneath the surface of her excitement, he detected an undercurrent of guilt flowing through their bond, a subtle shadow darkening otherwise bright emotions. The sensation mirrored his own misgivings so precisely that he momentarily confused their origins.

The pendant at her throat looked as though it belonged there, as though it had found its rightful home after centuries of waiting. He focused on that simple truth rather than examining the dangerous complexities of their emotional entanglement.

It is merely dinner, he reminded himself as they walked toward the elevator. A simple meal between two individuals with a complex arrangement.

Even as he thought it, he knew the lie for what it was. Tonight was a dangerous step into uncharted territory, and Kane, master strategist though he was, had no contingency plan for what might follow.

Their connection hummed between them like a live current, promising something neither could yet name, while somewhere beneath the city his most trusted operatives worked to uncover secrets that might change everything.

CHAPTER FORTY-FIVE

SERENITY

Serenity stepped into the elevator beside Kane, the brass walls reflecting her worried expression back at her. Her heart hammered so loudly she feared he might detect it, might somehow sense the betrayal still fresh on her fingertips. Guilt wrapped around her ribs like a vise, tightening with each floor they descended.

The confined space intensified his presence. The cedar-and-leather scent uniquely his, threaded with a faint spice, the controlled power evident in every measured movement, all of it pressed against her senses, demanding attention. Her mind filled with images from the library: his lips on hers, his body pressed against her, the transcendent sensation when his fangs had pierced her throat.

Heat bloomed low in her belly at the memory. Touching the marks on her neck afterward, she'd found they'd already healed, leaving only slightly raised skin as proof. Even that gentle self-exploration had sent electric sensations racing through her, nearly driving her to seek more.

It's wrong to want him, she reminded herself. He represents everything I should oppose.

Yet her body responded to his nearness as though governed by its own rebellious agenda.

The soft chime jolted her back to awareness. Cheeks burning, she stepped onto polished concrete, her heels echoing in the vast garage. She tried to create distance between them, as if physical space might order her chaotic emotions.

Somewhere across the city, Starr and Damon would be analyzing the stolen files, scanning for the information they'd convinced her was crucial. Once they confirmed they had what they needed, they would extract her from this luxurious prison. Instructions would come tonight. She just needed patience and composure for a few more hours.

First, though, she had to survive dinner while pretending normalcy as her conscience screamed betrayal and her body hummed with awareness.

Lost in the internal struggle, she didn't hear him call her name. His gentle touch on her arm sent electricity straight to her core, nearly making her gasp.

He stood close behind her, heat radiating against her back. The air between them crackled with unspoken tension. His gaze felt like a physical touch, the whisper of expensive fabric as he shifted his weight making her skin prickle with awareness. A terrible certainty settled in her bones: no matter how far she ran, she'd never escape his effect on her.

His hand found the small of her back, guiding her toward a sleek white vehicle. The simple touch burned through the thin fabric, leaving a warmth that lingered even after he moved to open her door with centuries-practiced courtesy.

She settled into the soft leather, the sophisticated interior showing a quiet luxury. The door closed with a satisfying finality, sealing her in a space that carried his scent. The dashboard's array of buttons and displays tempted exploration, technologies she'd only glimpsed from afar in Grove Gardens.

When he joined her, his presence seemed to shrink the interior. A single button brought the engine to purring life. An unfamiliar symbol flashed on the screen before changing to a detailed map of Celearius shown in ways she'd never seen.

He moved the lever with practiced ease, R for reverse, then D as they glided forward. She studied his movements with scientific precision, memorizing details: the foot pressure controlling speed, the measured turns of the wheel, the easy confidence with which he navigated the underground structure. In Grove Gardens, driving was reserved for wealthy humans or vampyr officials.

The dashboard screen zoomed to display the Silver District, a blue dot tracking their movement along streets she was beginning to recognize.

"Is this a tracking device?" she asked, curiosity overriding caution.

Kane glanced at the screen, amusement warming his typically expressionless features. "In a manner of speaking, though its primary function is navigation. I consider it one of humanity's most brilliant inventions. I wish it had existed centuries earlier."

His soft laugh captivated her. This glimpse of lightness in his guarded manner made her want to uncover more.

"You think a direction-giving machine ranks as mankind's greatest achievement? That seems underwhelming, considering our inventions."

"Do you have a superior candidate?" he asked, navigating streets gradually filling with evening pedestrians.

"The car itself? Perhaps communication devices?" She gestured around them.

His rich laughter filled the space, transforming his severe features and creating fine lines around his eyes that spoke of a rare amusement.

"Useful tools, certainly, but not necessarily the most profound," he countered thoughtfully. "Without direction, without knowing where one stands relative to a desired destination, even the fastest car or the clearest message lacks purpose."

"Fair point," she agreed, smiling. "A map only benefits those willing to admit they're lost. Someone certain of their destination needs no guidance."

A real smile appeared as they slowed at the checkpoint separating Silver from the exclusive Quartz district. The guards recognized him immediately, requiring neither identification nor inspection.

They entered Quartz, instantly recognizable by the crystal-like structures catching and reflecting the fading sunlight into dazzling patterns. Clean streets hosted people in clothing costing more than her family's monthly expenses, some focused on devices, others enjoying the evening air carrying tantalizing hints of distant ocean.

This district housed the influential Human-Vampyr Council members, the political elite who shaped policy from comfortable offices before returning to luxurious Waterside Park homes. There, private docks extended into the vast ocean that had once terrified humanity but now represented one of their few remaining connections to the pre-vampyr world.

Serenity had dreamed of seeing that endless blue expanse since childhood, imagining standing at the edge of something so immense and untamable. In secret fantasies, she'd pictured finding boats and sailing away with her family beyond vampyr territories, to rumored places where humans lived freely.

A sigh escaped before she could stop it.

"Is everything well?" Kane asked, concern evident.

"Yes, sorry," she replied, forcing lightness. "I sometimes get lost in my thoughts." She redirected with an effortful smile. "Will you reveal our destination, or maintain the mystery until we arrive?"

His increasingly familiar laugh resonated again. "Les Reines."

"The Queens?" she translated, confused. "You're taking me to see royalty? I thought we were having dinner."

Another delighted laugh. "It's a restaurant. Perhaps the finest French establishment in Celearius. Your knowledge of the language is unexpected."

Heat crept up her neck at the misinterpretation. "My father taught me what little French he knew. I picked up Italian and Spanish phrases too, languages preserved in the medical texts he salvaged."

"Your father was a physician, correct?"

"Yes," she confirmed, a familiar ache blooming. "He tried to teach me everything before he died. I hoped to become a nurse, continue his work in our district, but..." She trailed off, current reality making the conclusion obvious.

Kane nodded, something unreadable flickering across his expression. "Life seldom follows planned paths."

The observation carried an experiential weight that reminded her of the vast gap between them. How many human lifetimes had he witnessed, diverted by circumstances beyond their control?

She turned to the window rather than pursue the unsettling thought. Their reflections merged on the glass, her golden dress catching the sunset's last rays, his darker silhouette stark beside her.

The car eventually slowed before a distinctive building surrounded by ornate iron railings designed like climbing roses. As Kane opened his door, a young attendant emerged.

"Good evening, Mr. Draccus," the valet greeted respectfully, accepting the electronic key. Kane circled to her side with unhurried grace, extending his hand in a gesture echoing customs older than the gleaming city around them.

As her door opened, the bracing scent of saltwater filled her senses. She inhaled deeply, the oceanic air filling her lungs with something dangerously like hope. This scent represented everything beyond vampyr control, the vast, untamed nature that had existed before their rise and would continue long after.

Kane cleared his throat softly. His expression as he offered his hand held something almost tender, as if he recognized and respected this moment of private yearning.

She placed her fingers in his, the contact sending immediate warmth up her arm despite the coolness of his skin. They entered a marble-floored foyer with private elevators, approaching the one marked "Les Reines" in elegant gold script.

The elevator ascended in tense silence, his hand resting lightly at her back. The simple touch sent heat through her body, stirring memories of the library, how quickly that controlled touch had transformed into passionate urgency.

She risked a glance at his profile, immediately regretting it when she found his eyes already fixed on her. The hunger in his silver-blue gaze matched her forbidden thoughts, creating a loop of desire that threatened to consume rational thought. Since he'd drunk from her, she swore she felt echoes of his hunger amplifying her own.

The soft arrival chime broke the moment. His expression remained intent, questioning, a silent communication that needed no words.

Despite her body's demands and the pull of their blood bond, she broke eye contact, lowering her lashes in silent refusal. She couldn't give him what he wanted, not after betraying his trust hours ago, not when her loyalty lay elsewhere.

He accepted her unspoken answer with a barely noticeable tightening of his jaw, then guided her toward the restaurant entrance.

"Good evening, Mr. Draccus," the host greeted respectfully. "Your table will be ready momentarily."

Serenity stood quietly, surveying her surroundings with academic interest. The restaurant showed a refined luxury, deep burgundy walls, intimate lighting creating pools around each table, crystal chandeliers spreading mesmerizing patterns of light.

The clientele was carefully curated, couples in quiet intimacy, business discussions, romantic meetings. She studied them anthropologically, trying to determine which might be vampyr couples, which Elites with patrons, which human officials granted rare privilege.

As her eyes swept the room, they locked unexpectedly with familiar emerald ones.

Damon.

Shock rippled through her. Through their connection, she felt Kane's brief concern at her fear spike before she could mask it. Damon sat near the far wall across from a woman with vibrant red hair. The woman's attention absorbed in her device allowed Damon to acknowledge Serenity with the slightest nod before returning his focus to his companion.

Questions exploded like fireworks. Damon was an Elite? How was this possible? Why hadn't he shared this critical information? Was his position strategic, or had he been hiding it from the rebellion itself?

Before she could process the implications, Kane's breath warmed her ear. "Our table is ready."

They crossed the main dining area, ascending steps to a raised section with eight tables positioned for maximum privacy while offering spectacular views. Six overlooked the glittering cityscape, while two faced the distant ocean, now turning molten gold as the sun began its final descent.

Her breath caught as the host led them to one of these premium tables. Despite her efforts at composure, genuine delight spread across her face at the unexpected gift. Through their connection, she felt Kane's pleasure at her reaction.

"Will you be dining this evening, sir?" the waiter asked, addressing only Kane while presenting a single menu.

"Tonight, I will dine with my Elite," Kane responded, making the statement more significant than the simple words suggested.

After presenting Serenity with her own menu, the waiter suggested wines with practiced precision.

"The Pichon would be excellent," Kane decided with casual confidence.

Serenity turned to the panoramic ocean view. The sunset transformed the surface into shimmering amber and crimson, stirring an ancient human connection to the vast wilderness that had existed before vampyr dominance.

"The view has captured you," Kane observed, a small smile playing at his mouth.

"It's breathtaking," she admitted. "I wish I could smell the ocean again. Feel it against my skin..." The wistful comment escaped before she could stop it.

"The view is indeed spectacular," he agreed, though his tone suggested he wasn't referring to the ocean.

Their gazes locked in silent communication as the waiter returned with the wine and service.

"I gather Elites have limited freedom here," she observed when they were alone.

"Some vampyrs impose strict regulations on their Elites," Kane explained, lifting his glass. "Particularly regarding interactions with others. Vampyrs can be territorial about what they consider theirs." His gaze flickered briefly to her neck, where the feeding marks had faded. "Staff won't address you directly without my explicit permission. It's respect, and protection."

She raised an eyebrow, studying the respectful staff positioned strategically around the dining room. His explanation illuminated another facet of vampyr society, the elaborate layers of protocol governing seemingly straightforward interactions.

She lifted her glass, inhaling the complex scent before a careful sip. Though she'd seen wine occasionally in Grove Gardens, she'd never tasted anything of this quality. A rich complexity flooded her senses, dark fruits and subtle spices yielding to something earthy and sophisticated.

"You don't object to my speaking with others?" she asked, curious about his personal boundaries compared to societal norms.

"No," Kane replied with surprising directness. "You're my Elite. I trust your judgment."

The simple statement landed with unexpected weight. He trusted her. The irony sent fresh guilt surging through her. She took another, larger sip of wine, hoping the alcohol might dull the edge of her self-recrimination.

"Could I place the order myself?" The question was partly experimental, testing the boundaries he'd explained.

"If you wish." A subtle smile played across his features. "I'll inform them they have permission to interact with you directly."

When the waiter appeared, Kane granted permission for direct address. After a momentary adjustment, the server turned toward Serenity.

"I'll have the Potatoes Dauphinoise and the Bouillabaisse," she decided. Then, feeling unexpectedly bold, she added, "And he'll have the Boeuf Bourguignon and the Salmon en Papillote."

The waiter's eyes widened before he turned uncertainly toward Kane. She'd just ordered for one of Celearius's most powerful vampyrs as though he were a human companion.

Kane studied her with an unreadable expression before nodding. "As she said."

Relief flooded her as she felt his amusement rather than anger at her boldness through their connection.

"I thought we might sample each other's selections," she explained.

His lips curved into that rare, transformative smile. "You could never appear improper, and I find your solution elegant."

She observed him across the table, struck by the careful control evident in every movement. Each gesture was precise, measured, the product of centuries of self-discipline. His silver-blue eyes gleamed with intelligence and something more complex.

"Why did you select me as your Elite?" she asked, breaking the companionable silence. "You could have chosen someone less... complicated."

He set his glass down with deliberate calm, his gaze sharpening. "You assume my criteria excluded complications. Perhaps you underestimate your value, Serenity."

"My blood type. I understand its rarity—"

"No," he interrupted quietly but firmly. "Not exclusively your blood."

He leaned back, shadows playing across his angular features as he studied her with unnerving focus. "Yes, your blood is exceptional," he acknowledged, something primal flickering behind his composure. "But there are other consi derations... more than you realize."

His cryptic response intrigued her more than a straightforward answer might have.

His expression shifted suddenly to concern. "When did you last eat properly?"

"This morning... no, apples and peanut butter around midday."

"Perhaps slow down on the wine," he suggested gently rather than condescendingly. "Have you had wine before?"

"No." She'd forgotten its alcoholic properties in the enjoyment of a new experience. Accepting the wisdom with reluctance, she set down her glass.

The waiter arrived with the first courses as Kane directed that water be brought immediately.

"Eat," Kane encouraged, his gaze attentive on her face.

Though tempted to resist on principle, the rising scent proved irresistible. Saffron, seafood, and herbs combined in a symphony that made her mouth water and her stomach respond embarrassingly. He was right; she needed food after drinking on an empty stomach.

His steady gaze prompted her to sample the fragrant broth. The explosion of flavor drew an involuntary sound of pleasure from her throat, a moan she hadn't meant to voice. Lost in the discovery, she didn't immediately notice Kane's reaction.

What she saw took her breath away more effectively than any physical touch.

Desire burned in his silver-blue eyes with a heat that made her skin flush hot then cold. Heat seemed to radiate from him in palpable waves, his usually controlled expression transformed by a naked hunger that had nothing to do with food. Through their connection, his desire hit her like a physical force, making her gasp. Her body responded instantly, liquid warmth pooling low, her thighs tightening against a sudden ache.

The waiter returned with water. "How is everything?"

"Go. Away," Kane growled without breaking eye contact with Serenity.

The waiter vanished.

With deliberate, predatory movements, Kane dipped his spoon into his stew, extending it across the table to her lips in silent offering. Though some distant rational part of her suggested refusing the intimate gesture, the rich smell compelled her to part her lips. He placed the spoon in her mouth with careful precision, withdrawing it slowly and leaving another explosion of flavor, tender beef, red wine, aromatic herbs in perfect harmony.

"Eat," he instructed again, his voice dropping to a register that seemed to vibrate directly against her skin.

As she continued, she couldn't deny the evidence of her body's response, the dampness gathering between her thighs, her nipples tightening against the silk, a flush spreading across her chest and throat. Their connection amplified each sensation.

"The soup is exquisite," she managed, barely audible.

"Yes," he confirmed, satisfaction rumbling beneath the syllable.

She couldn't escape his magnetic gaze, at once thrilling and terrifying. In the intimate lighting, the silver in his irises seemed to glow with an inner light, creating an otherworldly aura that reminded her of his fundamental difference from humanity.

His hand moved suddenly across the table, not taking hers, but brushing a stray curl from her face with unexpected tenderness. She shuddered involuntarily, her pulse jumping visibly at her throat.

"Serenity," he murmured, her name barely audible above the ambient restaurant sounds.

Her heart stumbled at how he spoke it, as though the syllables themselves were precious. She glanced up through her lashes to find him studying her with an expression she'd never witnessed, the silver gleam softened to something almost human in its vulnerability.

"Kane," she responded, matching him, his name unfamiliar yet right on her tongue.

She wanted to refuse him, to explain she couldn't be what he needed, that their worlds were too different. Instead, she found her hand moving across the table toward his, pulled by a force that seemed to work independently of her conscious will.

Just as their fingertips approached contact, his expression changed dramatically, the warmth vanishing beneath an expressionless mask as though a curtain had closed. He withdrew his hand with fluid grace, leaving hers suspended awkwardly. Confusion and disappointment tangled in her chest.

"Kane Draccus! Is that truly you?" a feminine voice sang from behind Serenity, a false sweetness carrying a predatory undertone she instantly recognized as vampyr.

"Remain silent and avoid eye contact, particularly with her Elite," Kane whispered urgently, his manner completely transformed.

"Elise," he acknowledged with polite recognition but no warmth.

Serenity kept her eyes fixed on her soup as instructed, though instinct urged her to turn. Her side vision caught nothing, but she realized she could see their visitor's reflection in the window beside them.

The vampyr woman appeared deceptively delicate, petite with dark hair flowing around a heart-shaped face. Golden eyes sparkled with calculated liveliness, hiding a predatory assessment. Behind her stood a tall, broad-shouldered male radiating controlled power.

Damon.

His eyes found hers in the reflective surface, holding her gaze briefly before deliberately looking away. The confirmation hit like a physical blow. Damon wasn't just with the rebellion. He was an Elite, bound to a vampyr patron, living the existence he and Starr had convinced her to risk everything escaping.

"It's been forever since I've seen you dining out," Elise continued melodiously. "I had no idea you'd acquired a new Elite, especially after what happened to your last one. We could have joined you for a more... stimulating evening."

"She's still quite new," Kane replied smoothly. "I'm still breaking her in properly."

Serenity bit the inside of her cheek to keep from reacting to the demeaning description. She kept watching the window reflection, capturing their figures despite their standing behind her. The casual intimacy with which Elise touched Damon, owning, possessive, spoke volumes. When Elise's hand squeezed his rear with bold ownership, Damon's responding smile carried a warmth that couldn't be faked.

Confusion and betrayal churned in her stomach. How long had this deception been maintained? Did Starr know about Damon's true position? Such an important detail couldn't be hidden within the rebellion's inner circle. Which meant they'd deliberately kept Serenity in the dark, manipulating her while hiding crucial information.

"Enjoy your evening," Elise purred before walking away, her hand still possessive on Damon.

Serenity maintained the submissive posture until they were safely gone. Then she raised her eyes to Kane, unable to completely hide a flash of anger.

"Break me in?" she repeated, her voice low but sharp.

Kane's expression remained impassive until Elise and Damon had completely gone. Only then did regret flicker across his features.

"Elise wields considerable Council influence," he explained. "To maintain my ability to affect policy, I occasionally need to present certain... appearances."

Serenity reached for the wine before reconsidering and taking water instead. Her fingers trembled slightly against the cool glass as her mind raced with the implications, both about Kane's political maneuvering and Damon's unexpected status.

"I apologize," Kane said, a surprising sincerity in his voice. "I'll make amends... again."

She took a long drink, trying to calm the emotional storm. The cold water helped clear her head, bringing a reluctant understanding of the political necessity. "I understand the need for strategic posturing, though I don't have to like it."

His expression softened at her pragmatism. "Most wouldn't understand so readily."

She almost smiled at the irony; her connection to the rebellion had taught her plenty about the necessity of deception and political theater. She returned her attention to her meal, though the past minutes' revelations had considerably diminished her appetite.

When she was halfway through her dish, she felt a gentle tap against her plate. She looked up to find Kane offering his selection, suggesting an exchange. The gesture was unexpectedly intimate, sharing food in an almost human way. The simple act seemed to strengthen their inexplicable connection.

The salmon melted against her tongue, but this time she couldn't prevent the soft sound of appreciation that escaped. The moment the involuntary moan left her lips, she felt the weight of his gaze like a physical touch.

Cautiously, she looked up to meet his hungry gaze, and knew that whatever happened next would change everything between them.

CHAPTER FORTY-SIX

KANE

If she made that sound once more, he would break.

Kane gripped the table's edge, the fine linen crumpling under fingers that had once torn stone with far less provocation. Centuries of disciplined control unraveled with each small sound of pleasure escaping her lips. He had made the grave error of allowing himself to breathe deeply in her presence, a decision he now recognized as both self-indulgence and tactical mistake.

She turned away, her attention caught by the ocean stretching toward the horizon beyond the glass. The dying sunlight transformed her dark curls into hints of amber and mahogany his enhanced vision caught even in the restaurant's subdued lighting. The simple joy illuminating her features at that endless blue view stirred something long dormant, a reminder of his own first glimpse of the sea lifetimes ago, when the world still held wonders unexplored.

Centuries of existence had taught him to distrust such impulses, yet here he sat, a being who had witnessed empires rise and fall, anxiously awaiting attention from a human woman who had entered his life mere days ago.

The absurdity should have triggered contempt. Instead, it inspired something dangerously close to wonder.

"Earlier today, you received a message that seemed to... disturb you," he observed casually, though his enhanced hearing had caught every nuance of her elevated heartbeat as she read it.

"It was from my sister," she replied with remarkable steadiness. "She mentioned my mother was unwell again. Nothing serious, but enough to concern me. I feel helpless, unable to care for them directly."

Kane studied her carefully. He sensed real family concern, that much rang true, yet something else lurked beneath it, a dissonance he couldn't identify. Centuries of reading human expressions told him concealment lay behind her explanation.

"Perhaps we could arrange a visit," he suggested, watching surprise flicker across her features. Through their connection, he felt emotion surge: hope, longing, gratitude, washing away the earlier undertone of deception. "Not immediately, but soon. It might ease your concerns to confirm their wellbeing in person."

The authentic feeling flowing between them nearly overwhelmed him, raw, unfiltered emotion that couldn't be feigned. Whatever secrets she harbored, her attachment to her family was unquestionably real.

"I would... that would mean more than I can express," she managed, her voice thick.

Kane felt himself softening despite centuries of practiced detachment. Her gratitude reached him with unmistakable clarity, tugging at parts of himself he'd believed dormant. "Family bonds shouldn't be severed unnecessarily. Your transition is difficult enough without complete isolation from those you cherish."

He sensed a sudden emotional twist through their bond, something resembling guilt, though he couldn't determine its source. It vanished quickly, as though deliberately suppressed.

"Thank you," she said simply, restraining herself, carefully controlling what she allowed to surface.

The waiter appeared with their second courses, disrupting the charged moment. As they shared dishes, exchanging plates with unexpected intimacy, Kane observed conflict playing across her features, subtle changes that might have been imperceptible without his enhanced senses.

"Is something troubling you?" he asked, keeping his tone neutral despite his growing concern. "You seem... preoccupied."

She shook her head, forcing a smile that didn't reach her eyes. "Just overwhelmed by the day. Everything is still so new."

The explanation seemed plausible, yet what flowed between them conveyed a deeper distress than simple adjustment would warrant. Still, he chose not to press, signaling subtly for dessert instead.

As they shared the Tarte Tatin, Kane observed a shift in her demeanor. He sensed her perception of him changing, barriers lowering, preconceptions dissolving. The experience was unexpectedly intimate, feeling someone's view of him transform in real time.

"In my centuries of existence," he admitted when she asked about the weight of immortality, "there are moments when accumulated memory becomes... challenging to bear. Human lives burn brightly before extinguishing. Vampyr existence resembles twilight, neither darkness nor light, extended beyond its natural boundaries."

Something fundamental was shifting between them in that simple exchange.

In the private elevator descending toward the garage, the silence amplified the tension. The confined space sharpened his awareness, her accelerated heartbeat, the subtle change in her breathing, the faint flush rising along her throat. Desire flowed in both directions, creating a feedback loop that tested his practiced restraint.

"Serenity," he said, her name emerging as a question.

She turned toward him, pupils dilating as she found him closer than expected.

"Yes?" she breathed, barely audible even to his enhanced hearing.

"Tonight has been... unexpected."

A smile curved her lips. "Yes, it has."

"I find myself reluctant for it to end," he admitted, the confession revealing more vulnerability than intended.

When her hand moved across the car's center console to rest on his, all pretense of concentration vanished. He risked a glance her way, but she gazed out at the passing city, as if the touch were casual rather than the serious breach of protocol it represented.

Her uncertainty mixed with desire mirrored his own conflicted feelings. The blood bond hummed between them, transmitting emotions too complex for words.

Once in his penthouse, he sensed her growing tension, a slight stiffening of her posture, a hesitation in her movement that hadn't existed earlier. Her emotional struggle intensified, though he couldn't identify the exact cause.

"Are you feeling unwell?" he asked, his concern evident.

She shook her head wordlessly, her remarkable eyes meeting his with an intensity that seemed to reach past his carefully constructed walls.

Unable to resist the pull between them, he approached slowly, giving her the opportunity to withdraw. When she remained, he gently took her hands, the contact letting him feel her inner conflict more clearly.

"I apologize if something has caused you distress," he said softly, searching her face for clues. "Tonight was meant to remedy my earlier transgression, not create additional discomfort."

What he sensed through their bond made his breath catch, unmistakable desire matching his own, a loop of mutual wanting vibrating in the space between them. Yet beneath it lurked what felt distinctly like regret.

Acting on instinct rather than calculation, he reached up to tuck a stray curl behind her ear, his fingers tracing the graceful line of her jaw before continuing down the column of her throat. As his touch drifted over her pulse point, she closed her eyes, a soft sound of pleasure escaping her parted lips.

The sound tested the outer limits of his control. Every aspect of his being wanted to claim that mouth that had haunted his thoughts since their first encounter.

Before his restraint completely shattered, she surprised him with a sudden movement, throwing her arms around him in a startling embrace. The simple human gesture, so common in mortal interactions, so rare in his extended existence, momentarily froze him.

How long since anyone had embraced him without wanting something in return? The realization of his loneliness struck with unexpected force as her warmth penetrated his carefully constructed armor.

"I wanted this evening to transcend the ordinary," he confessed, his voice resonating through both their bodies. "I hoped to demonstrate through action rather than words that I am not the monster your people's stories might suggest."

"I know," she murmured against him. "And I appreciate the gesture... more than I can properly express."

Slowly, she pulled back to lift her gaze to his. The vulnerability in her expression created an answering recognition within him, a shared uncertainty that transcended the difference in their power.

"Kane," she began, his name reverent and tentative on her lips. Her hand rose to his face, fingers trembling as they traced features unchanged for centuries. "I never considered you a monster."

He sensed the truth in her words. After centuries hiding his nature behind authority and control, being seen, truly seen, as more than a predator was both terrifying and liberating.

"And I... I am not afraid of you."

Something primal and permanent broke free at her declaration. All careful restraint, centuries of practiced control, dissolved against the simple truth of her acceptance. Their senses flared with shared emotion, a loop of desire and connection that transcended the physical.

His lips found hers with exquisite gentleness despite the storm raging within, a butterfly touch testing her response, seeking confirmation that her words meant physical consent. When she leaned into the contact rather than pulling away, he deepened the kiss gradually, hands threading through the silk of her curls to angle her exactly where he wanted.

Without breaking the kiss, Kane lifted her easily, guiding her legs around his waist before carrying her to his chambers. Her weight felt like nothing to his strength, yet the trust in her surrender touched him more deeply than any burden he'd ever carried.

They moved together like celestial bodies finding their orbit, pulled by a force stronger than choice. The invisible tether between them resonated with shared feeling, making it difficult to tell where his desire ended and hers began.

"I need your words, Serenity," he said when they reached his bed, his voice rough with the effort of control. "Tell me clearly that you want this... that you want me."

"I..." Her answer faded into a heavy silence as doubt flickered across her face, her desire warring against something darker, guilt, perhaps, or fear of consequences.

"We need not continue," he said gently, ignoring his body's protests. "Your comfort supersedes all else."

She looked back at him, something settling in her expression as she made her decision. He could sense her inner conflict resolve into determination.

"Yes, Kane," she finally whispered, her answer carrying the weight of a sacred promise rather than casual permission. "I want this connection. I want you."

All remaining doubt disappeared. He claimed her mouth with new purpose, slower now, deeper, savoring rather than consuming.

He began exploring her body with unhurried care, discovering through touch and taste the places that drew her strongest responses. His lips traced the smooth column of her throat, instinct guiding him to the pulse point where he applied gentle pressure with blunt teeth rather than sharp fangs.

As their intimacy deepened, Kane felt his fangs descending involuntarily, a physiological response impossible to suppress when heightened emotion combined with physical connection. The hunger for her blood grew increasingly insistent, merging with sexual desire until the two became indistinguishable aspects of the same primal need.

"Serenity," he managed through gritted teeth, his voice strained with the effort of restraint. "I need—"

Before he could complete the request, she turned her head in wordless offering, exposing the elegant line of her throat in a gesture of trust that affected him more profoundly than the physical pleasure surrounding him.

With careful precision, he allowed his fangs to pierce the delicate skin at the exact angle to maximize pleasure while minimizing discomfort. The first taste of her extraordinary blood triggered a cascade of sensation unlike anything in his long experience. Their bond flared with blinding force, thoughts and emotions merging as legend had spoken of but few modern vampyrs ever experienced.

As they approached the peak together, their shared pleasure created a union transcending the physical, approaching something almost spiritual. When release claimed them both, it surged beyond anything either had anticipated.

Drawing her closer afterward, he marveled at the simple perfection of the moment. A profound contentment unlike anything he'd known in decades, perhaps centuries, settled within him as he watched her relax toward sleep.

Looking down at her peaceful expression, he pressed a gentle kiss to her forehead. Every molecule of his being vibrated with awareness of her, his ancient body recognizing something his logical mind hesitated to name. He could feel her dreams beginning, hazy images of ocean waves and golden light.

Nothing outside this room held significance compared to her presence in his arms. He vowed silently to fulfill her every desire, to protect her against any threat, to bind their existences beyond the limitations of her human lifespan.

The peaceful silence shattered with the sudden, insistent vibration of his communication device. Reality intruded with jarring abruptness, dragging him from their shared intimacy back to the responsibilities that defined his existence.

We found it.

Three words capable of altering the future of Celearius, potentially ending the rebellion that threatened everything he'd built. The locker's contents might finally provide the leverage to dismantle the insurgency's leadership rather than merely addressing symptoms.

He should have felt triumph. Instead, looking at Serenity's peaceful form amid the tangled sheets, he experienced a disquieting premonition, as though two separate aspects of his existence were accelerating toward an inevitable collision.

With a reluctance bordering on physical pain, he extracted himself with preternatural grace, moving without disturbing her rest. Even at a distance, he could feel her peaceful slumber, a secondary awareness running parallel to his own consciousness.

Yet beneath that peace, he sensed something troubling through their bond, a tension, a secret perhaps, that disquieted him more than he cared to admit.

With centuries of practice compartmentalizing emotion, he composed his response: *I will meet you at the office.* Whatever awaited him at the locker, whatever strategy emerged from its contents, he would return to her before dawn if he could.

The silent promise offered cold comfort against the growing certainty that forces beyond his control had been set in motion, that the peace he'd found in her arms might prove as fragile as the human holding him there.

CHAPTER FORTY-SEVEN

KANE

The cold white light of Cavern 47's meeting room cast harsh shadows across the faces of his three most trusted partners. Nox, Rhyzan, and Sullivan waited with controlled tension, their freshly showered appearance unable to mask the underground dust Kane's sharp senses detected, evidence of their hard journey beneath the city.

Nox stood at attention, his dark suit matching his precise nature. Two hundred years of friendship allowed Kane to read the subtle signs others missed, the slight tightness around his eyes that signaled an important discovery. Beside him, Rhyzan's pale face remained carefully blank, though a muscle twitched repeatedly in his jaw. Sullivan leaned against the desk with forced casualness, the network of scars across his face more visible under the harsh lighting.

Kane's enhanced senses automatically catalogued the room's contents, cleaning products, individual scents, and something else... old paper, faded ink, the musty smell of long-sealed metal. His body tensed with anticipation.

"Where is it?" he demanded, silver eyes scanning the room. Her scent still clung to his skin despite his shower, jasmine and rose mixed with more intimate notes that momentarily distracted him.

"On the table," Nox replied, nodding toward the window.

Kane crossed to the table in measured strides, his fingers touching worn blueprints, paper yellowed with age, corners softened from repeated folding. Something deeply wrong radiated from the document as he lifted it under the light.

His eyes widened as they tracked across the detailed diagrams. A precise circle, elegant yet engineered to exacting tolerance. Within its boundaries, a vial connected to an automatic release mechanism with a ten-second delay trigger. Scientific notations filled the margins in practiced handwriting.

"What the hell am I looking at?" Kane asked, his voice dangerously soft.

The silence stretched taut. Three vampyr hearts marked time in the stillness.

"They've created a weapon to release an airborne disease," Rhyzan confirmed, stepping beside him.

Kane's fingers tightened on the paper as he calculated the threat to Celearius's population. "A biological weapon engineered for vampyrs."

"More insidious than that," Rhyzan corrected, shaking his head. "The disease targets humans exclusively."

Kane's brow furrowed. "Explain."

"The formula doesn't kill humans directly," Rhyzan continued, his finger tracing a molecular diagram. "It changes human blood chemistry into a substance deadly to vampyrs. The compound would remain dormant in human carriers while making their blood toxic to our kind. One drop would cause paralysis; three would be fatal."

The implications took shape with terrifying clarity. Thousands of humans in Celearius, the Elite Program, the blood banks, all of them potential weapons.

"They mean to starve us," Sullivan added, draining his glass. "Introduction into the water supply or spray dispersal would suffice. The formula affects all mammals with compatible blood chemistry, humans and livestock alike."

"Maximum effectiveness through multiple deployment methods," Rhyzan elaborated, turning the blueprint over to reveal additional plans. "Large-caliber projectiles for spray dispersal across populated areas. Wind patterns, population density, maximum coverage, all of it calculated."

Kane absorbed every detail with flawless clarity, trajectory angles, dispersal rates, chemical stabilizers. "This suggests they have artillery, or plan to steal ours."

"Already checking inventory," Rhyzan confirmed. "Teams are conducting physical verification."

Kane nodded, a ghost of approval flickering across his features. "Bring Evie to authenticate this formula. Her expertise is essential."

Before his instruction could be acted on, Nox stepped forward, his expression grave in a way Kane had witnessed only a handful of times across their shared centuries.

"There's something else you need to see first," Nox said, his voice carefully neutral.

He dismissed Sullivan with a look, waiting until the heavy door sealed behind him. Then Nox carefully took the blueprints from Kane's hands, placing them on the polished surface and positioning a magnifying device over the document's lower corner.

"Here," he said simply.

In the magnified view, tiny letters became visible: Dr. R. J. Wright.

Wright. The name teased Kane's memory, familiar yet elusive. His perfect recall sorted through centuries of information with lightning speed.

Rhyzan approached with unusual hesitation, placing a manila folder atop the blueprints. The simple beige cover bore a name that caused Kane's heart to stutter, a physiological impossibility that nonetheless occurred.

Serenity Renee Wright.

His hands trembled almost invisibly as he opened the folder. Richard James Wright, father to Serenity Renee Wright.

Her father. The creator of a weapon designed to wipe out vampyrs.

"Verify this," Kane whispered.

"Confirmed through multiple sources," Rhyzan replied. "We cross-checked the handwriting with medical documentation. There were additional notes in a second cache. The connection is undeniable."

Kane's fingers pressed against the paper hard enough to dent the surface. Serenity's scent, the memory of her skin against his chest as she'd slept in his arms hours ago, seemed to mock him now.

"There's more," Nox stated, moving to Kane's private terminal.

The screen displayed security footage from Kane's residence, timestamped earlier that day. Serenity stood before his office door, uncertainty evident in her posture. Kane watched in perfect stillness as she entered, moved to his computer, and began accessing files with unexpected skill.

Something cold and ancient stirred within him, a predator's recognition of betrayal. The woman who had awakened something beyond mere hunger in all his centuries had used that very connection against him.

"When?" he asked, his voice unnaturally calm.

"During our questioning of the clinic prisoner," Rhyzan replied carefully.

"She triggered the security alert," Kane realized. The pieces aligned with mathematical precision. While he'd been consumed with thoughts of her, she'd been stealing his information. While he'd taken her to Les Reines, she'd reported to her handlers. While he'd made love to her with unprecedented abandon, she'd carried secrets that could destroy everything.

Fury surged through him with such force that the lights flickered. Ancient instinct demanded immediate action, to confront, to punish, to eliminate the threat.

His jaw clenched audibly, fangs descending despite his efforts at control. "How could I have been so blind?"

"Sebastian recruited her, as predicted," Rhyzan stated carefully. "The night of her first feeding incident. The pattern aligns with his methods."

"You have proof now," Kane said, gesturing toward the screen. "She met with him at the café, an extensive, unsupervised conversation. Arrest him immediately."

"No."

A contradiction from anyone else would have carried severe consequences.

"Explain," Kane demanded.

"This presents an unprecedented strategic opportunity," Rhyzan elaborated. "She provides a direct connection to the rebellion's inner circle, our first substantial lead in five years. They believe they've successfully planted an operative within Celearius leadership. And it creates a pathway for Chloe's deeper infiltration."

Kane's brow furrowed slightly. "Continue."

"Chloe has established rapport with the prisoner, Jax. While not formally affiliated with leadership, he maintains contacts who can make introductions. She's convinced him she needs help recovering her fictional daughter from vampyr custody."

Rhyzan's precision momentarily overrode Kane's emotional storm. "The rebellion believes they have an Elite with classified access. They'll task her with gathering more. The strategic leak of modified plans through Chloe can reach the rebellion's leadership by way of Thornton."

"Then they'll instruct their Elite to acquire weapon components by any means necessary," Kane concluded, his tactical thinking extending the implications. The image of Serenity using their connection to extract information sharpened his sense of violation.

"We create convincing fakes and destroy the originals," Kane decided. "I will not risk authentic documentation."

"I'll commission the replacements immediately," Rhyzan agreed. "Evie can modify the formula to appear viable while ensuring any implementation fails."

"Proceed," Kane instructed. "Leak the modified plans through Chloe. I'll speak with Evie personally about Sebastian."

After Rhyzan departed, Kane turned toward the floor-to-ceiling windows overlooking his city. Celearius glittered in the darkness, unaware of the invisible war within its boundaries. The lights of the human districts burned alongside vampyr territories, a visual integration representing the coexistence he'd fought to establish.

Betrayal and rage coursed through his system like liquid nitrogen, freezing rational thought beneath primal response. His flawless memory recalled every moment with Serenity, her laughter, her wonder at the ocean, the way her body had yielded to his in perfect harmony. Those treasured memories now burned like acid.

A growl emerged from deep in his chest, a sound belonging to ancient forests rather than modern cities. His reflection revealed eyes shifted from silver to obsidian, the pupils expanding in response to extreme emotion. Centuries of civilization receded beneath the personal betrayal.

He had believed her different, had allowed himself to believe in her sincerity despite ages of evidence that trust was a luxury his kind couldn't afford. The realization that his emotional response had been weaponized struck deeper than any physical wound.

His fist clenched involuntarily, fine cracks appearing in the reinforced glass beneath his palm before he registered the lapse. With considerable effort, he pulled back from the edge of rage.

Yet beneath the fury churned something else, grief, sharp and unexpected. He had trusted her, had opened pathways long sealed against harm. The admission that he'd begun to care, that he'd envisioned possibilities beyond their arrangement, wounded more deeply than any strategic implication.

"For what it's worth," Nox observed quietly, "she's acting for her family's welfare. She believes this is their only path to security."

"I reached that conclusion," Kane replied, his voice carefully controlled. "I require complete intelligence on her father, every detail. And arrange a supervised family visit this week."

Nox hesitated briefly. "That might change her perception of you. If she sees genuine care—"

"This is not about changing her perception," Kane interrupted, his voice hardening. "It's about preventing her from suspecting I know of her activities."

He caught Nox's disappointment in the glass's reflection, the subtle expression before it was masked. His oldest friend held more optimistic views of human nature than Kane's experience justified.

Emotion couldn't interfere with his primary directive. Celearius represented centuries of work, a coexistence model essential for both species' survival. The rebellion threatened not merely his authority but the delicate balance established at tremendous cost.

Kane settled at the console, activating Serenity's infiltration footage once more. With clinical detachment, he analyzed her movements, her methods, her approach. The tactical portion of his mind catalogued her techniques for future reference.

Yet beneath the analysis, his consciousness remained haunted by sensory echoes, the phantom pressure of her fingers across his chest, the delicate rhythm of her pulse as she'd slept against him. She had gazed at him with such apparent openness, a warmth in those honey-brown eyes that now stared back with devastating duplicity.

His jaw tightened as he observed her methodical exploration of his files. Natural grace concealed calculated purpose, each movement serving a specific end rather than the spontaneous expression he'd believed it to be. The contrast between the woman who'd come apart in his arms and the operative on his screen created an almost physical pain.

Two opposing forces warred within him, the part that yearned for her presence despite all rational knowledge of her deception, and the cold fury demanding retribution. The conflict manifested in throbbing tension and unnatural stillness as his muscles locked against the opposing impulses.

Regret and determination intertwined as he acknowledged the necessity of hardening himself against her. The emotional walls he'd lowered in her presence would have to be rebuilt stronger. Yet he feared the foundation had been compromised beyond repair, that her brief presence had created irreparable cracks in his defenses.

He studied her image one final time, committing to memory the exact curve of her cheek, the precise shade of her skin, the determined set of her shoulders. Then, with deliberate finality, he deactivated the display.

Drawing a measured breath, Kane compartmentalized his emotions with centuries of discipline. He retrieved his communication device and initiated contact with his most trusted advisor.

"Evie," he began as the connection established, his voice betraying nothing of the storm raging beneath his reconstructed composure. "We need to discuss Sebastian. I have evidence you need to see immediately."

The game had entered its final phase. The woman who had briefly claimed his heart would now serve as the unwitting instrument of her own cause's destruction.

Behind his composed exterior, something essential continued to break, a loss he could acknowledge to no one, least of all himself.

CHAPTER FORTY-EIGHT

SERENITY

Serenity buried her face in the soft pillow, inhaling Kane's scent, cedar and leather that had somehow become comforting rather than alien. The silk sheets whispered against her bare skin, a luxury that would have seemed impossible weeks ago in Grove Gardens.

Her stomach clenched with hunger, but a more pressing realization crashed over her like ice water: she wasn't in her room. She was in his.

Panic surged through her as the unfamiliar shadows took shape, the massive armoire, the clean architectural lines, the space designed for someone who had stripped away all unnecessary sentiment. She pushed back the heavy duvet and sat upright, the climate-controlled air raising goosebumps across her naked skin.

Memory returned in vivid flashes, his body against hers, the exquisite sensation of his fangs at her throat, the whispered endearments in languages she didn't recognize but somehow understood. Her fingers drifted to the puncture marks, already healing thanks to his blood. The phantom echo of pleasure made her press her thighs together against the renewed ache.

Through their connection, which still hummed beneath her skin like electricity, she could sense his absence from the building. The awareness should have been impossible, yet it felt as natural as breathing.

Why did he have to show such tenderness? Why couldn't he have stayed cold, cruel, dismissive, anything that would have made her mission easier? Behind his controlled exterior, she'd discovered an unexpected gentleness that made her betrayal feel like acid in her veins.

The automatic curtains parted, revealing Celearius at night. The city sprawled before her in divided light, the human sectors already darkening, the vampyr territories coming alive. But her attention fixed on the distant shimmer where moonlight caught the ocean's surface.

Her father had described it countless times, its vastness, its constant motion, the salt and mystery in its scent. Though geographically close to Grove Gardens, the shoreline remained forbidden territory. Military checkpoints ensured that coastal access stayed a privilege of the inner districts.

How many nights had she imagined standing at that infinite blue expanse? The fantasy that appeared unbidden now included Kane beside her, showing her shores he'd known for centuries. The domesticity of the image shocked her, its casual assumption of a future that couldn't exist.

She forced herself away from the window and located her dress, slipping it over her head. Her undergarments had vanished, casualties of his eagerness the night before. The memory sent heat through her before reality quenched it.

With a final glance at the rumpled sheets and the hypnotic ocean view, she slipped from his bedroom, closing the door silently.

The hallway stretched before her, softly illuminated by recessed lighting that activated at her movement. Each step felt weighted with competing impulses, her heart pulling her back toward the warmth she'd abandoned, her mind pushing her forward toward duty.

A faint glow leaked from beneath his office door. She paused, hand half-raised to knock, the desire to see him again nearly overwhelming her resolve.

No. Her father's voice echoed in her mind. She couldn't risk further entanglement. One more moment in his presence and she might confess everything, consequences be damned.

With a shaky exhale, she moved past his door toward the kitchen. Her purse rested where she'd left it, but her attention caught on the packaged leftovers from Les Reines, tangible evidence of a connection she couldn't afford. She quickly stowed them in the refrigerator.

Heart racing, she climbed the stairs to her room with careful steps. As her door closed with a soft click, she heard another door opening downstairs. Frozen against the wood, she held her breath, straining for approaching footsteps. The possibility of confronting Kane now, when her defenses were shattered and her emotions raw, terrified her more than any physical threat.

After several tense moments of silence, she moved toward her bed, searching beneath the pillows for her communication device. She'd left it behind deliberately, afraid a message might arrive while she was with Kane.

The screen revealed nothing. She sank onto the mattress, exhaustion settling into her bones, not merely physical fatigue, but the bone-deep weariness of carrying contradictory truths.

Guilt carved hollow spaces beneath her ribs. She had stolen from Kane, violated the trust of a man who had shown her a consideration she'd never expected. Yet hours later, she'd welcomed him into her body, shared a connection that felt real despite every rational argument against its possibility.

She should never have agreed to Starr and Damon's proposal so hastily. The clinic attack had left her reeling, and the revelation of her father's rebellion involvement had created an obligation she hadn't properly examined. Grief and confusion had made her vulnerable to manipulation.

Now a different path beckoned, one that might allow for the changes her father had sought without the bloodshed the rebellion seemed determined to provoke.

Her gaze drifted to the framed photograph on her nightstand, her family before her father's death, his arm around her mother's shoulders, Beth balanced on his knee. His smile radiated the warmth and conviction that had defined him. Would that man, the healer who had treated vampyrs and humans alike, approve of what she'd become?

Tears welled as she reached for the frame, her fingers tracing the glass. Part of her desperately wished he could guide her through this impossible situation. But the dead remained silent, and the living had to make their own choices.

She wiped the moisture from her cheeks, drawing a deep breath. Sebastian should have contacted her by now. His silence amplified her anxiety.

Where was Cavern 47? What made their prisoner so important that innocent lives had been endangered? The questions multiplied, each one deepening her doubts about the cause she'd committed herself to.

A cold weight settled in her stomach as she prayed the rebellion hadn't deceived her, hadn't placed her family at risk for goals they had no intention of sharing. With growing desperation, she typed a message to Sebastian.

Hey.

The word seemed absurdly inadequate, but anything more specific might create evidence she couldn't afford if Kane accessed her communications.

Minutes stretched as she waited, each second amplifying her doubts. What if Sebastian had abandoned her? What if the information she'd risked everything for was worthless? The fear that she'd compromised herself for nothing threatened to overwhelm her.

The device's vibration made her jolt.

Are you alone?

Unknown number. Her heartbeat thundered as she typed: *Yes.*

Go into the bathroom and turn on the shower.

This wasn't Sebastian; he would have responded directly. This level of secrecy suggested higher-level operatives, increasing both her anxiety and her wariness. With growing unease, she moved to follow the instructions.

Water hissed to life as she adjusted the temperature, steam fogging the mirror. She sent another message: *I'm in, and the shower is running.*

Is the door closed and locked?

After securing the door: *Yes.*

The device vibrated with an incoming call. Her finger hovered a moment before she accepted.

"Hello?" Her voice emerged barely above a whisper.

"Serenity." Damon's familiar voice echoed in the tiled space, tension evident in his clipped tone. "Sorry for the late contact. We needed to verify certain information you provided. Is your situation secure?"

The question carried multiple meanings. Was she safe? Would he pretend she hadn't seen him at the restaurant with Councilmember Elise? The memory of his submissive posture contrasted sharply with his authoritative manner now.

"Yes, everything seems normal. I don't think he suspects anything." Her free arm wrapped around her waist. "Why? Has something happened?"

The pause stretched her nerves tighter.

"We've encountered problems, Serenity." Tension filled each word. "The information you obtained was important but incomplete. Cavern 47 contains more than we initially thought. Your position has become... essential. We need you to maintain your placement longer than planned."

The weight of his request pressed against her chest, making it difficult to breathe. The rushing water suddenly seemed too loud, the bathroom too small, the walls closing in.

"Why can't you get this information?" The words escaped before she could consider their implications. "You're an Elite as well. To a Council member, no less."

The silence confirmed she'd crossed an unspoken boundary. When Damon finally responded, his voice had hardened.

"Yes, I am." The admission carried no pleasure. "But Elise doesn't have the necessary clearance regarding Cavern 47. Her position grants different access than Kane's. This is our only viable option."

The revelation should have comforted her; Damon understood her complexity because he lived the same double life. Instead, it deepened her suspicion. If he'd maintained this deception, what else might the rebellion conceal?

"What if I refuse, Damon?"

"Then we lose our advantage in this phase," he answered with brutal candor. "But we won't force compliance."

The statement carried an unspoken finality. The thought of betraying Kane further, of delving deeper into deception while sharing his home and possibly his bed, created a physical ache beneath her breastbone.

"There must be another approach," she murmured, her voice smaller than intended. "Another person with access..."

"I understand what we're asking." A genuine sympathy softened his tone for a moment. "But the reality is clear. Kane rarely selects Elites; sometimes decades pass between choices. Your blood type makes you uniquely valuable to him, providing protection even if suspicions arise. He might hesitate to eliminate you when others wouldn't receive the same consideration."

The clinical assessment of her value contrasted painfully with Kane's tenderness hours earlier. Was Damon right? Did her rare blood make her disposable to the rebellion but indispensable to Kane?

Yet another truth lurked beneath her discomfort: the thought of Kane selecting a different Elite provoked a jealousy so fierce it bordered on rage. The emotion shocked her with its possessive nature, its assumption of a relationship that couldn't survive the revelations to come.

"I need your promise on one matter," she stated, surprising herself with sudden resolve.

"Anything within our capacity," Damon replied immediately.

"If things go bad, if I'm discovered, you'll ensure my family stays safe." Not a question but a non-negotiable condition.

The pause stretched longer, background noises suggesting Damon might be consulting someone off the line. "Yes. We can guarantee that protection."

Relief washed through her, loosening the tightness in her chest a fraction. "Then I'll continue."

"We appreciate your commitment." The formal phrasing suggested others might be listening. "Sebastian will contact you tomorrow morning. Delete these messages before exiting. This call record will erase automatically when we disconnect."

"Understood."

"I'll contact you in three days. Be extremely careful until then." The line went dead with abrupt finality.

She spent several minutes permanently deleting the text exchange, checking twice to confirm the call had vanished. With no further reason to maintain the pretense, she stepped into the shower, hoping the water might cleanse more than her skin.

Heat penetrated her tense muscles yet brought none of the relief she desperately sought. Behind closed eyelids, images of Kane kept materializing, his silver eyes darkening with desire, the rare smile transforming his austere features, the careful tenderness of his hands. Each memory twisted the guilt deeper.

When she finally emerged wrapped in a plush robe, a bone-deep chill had settled despite the steam. Her fingers trembled securing the belt, the fine material feeling like undeserved luxury.

She sank onto the edge of her bed, a soft sound of despair escaping before she could contain it. Her existence had always been defined by external struggles, her father's death, securing food, maintaining hope in a district designed to crush it. But this new enemy lived within her own heart, and she had no strategy to combat it.

Torn between competing loyalties, to her father's legacy and to the man whose trust she'd violated, between her obligation to the rebellion and the uncomfortable questions their methods raised, she moved through a minefield where every step threatened destruction.

The pressure built within her chest until she wanted to scream, to release the fury and terror coiled beneath her breastbone. Instead, she swallowed the sound, forcing it down along with the tears that threatened to overwhelm her composure.

She had made her choice, committed to a path that permitted no deviation. All that remained was seeing it through to whatever end awaited: redemption or destruction, freedom or imprisonment, life or death.

The certainty brought no comfort as she stared into the darkness beyond her window, where the same ocean Kane had shown her stretched invisible in the distance, close enough to sense but impossibly out of reach, like every dream she had ever dared to harbor.

CHAPTER
FORTY-NINE

EVELYN

"You found these outside Celearius?" Evelyn asked, her gaze sharpening as she examined the weapon plans spread across her metal desk. Her auburn hair caught the evening light filtering through the tinted windows as she leaned forward, emerald eyes shifting like the sea, keen and sharp with focus.

"Only hours ago," Kane replied, his voice weighted with an exhaustion she recognized from their darkest centuries together.

"Ingenious design." Her fingers traced the detailed drawings, pausing at the chemical formulas in the margins. Her scientific mind automatically catalogued the implications. "This wouldn't just make humans deadly to us. It would transform their blood into a weapon."

"Elaborate." Kane stepped closer, bringing the familiar scent of cedar and something metallic, stress, perhaps, or the lingering aftermath of feeding.

"A single drop of human blood containing this compound would prove fatal on contact." She rotated the plans, studying the chemical structures for weaknesses. "The molecular bonds here create flawless vampyr toxicity. We couldn't eliminate them without destroying ourselves, a perfect stalemate."

"You find genocide clever," Kane observed, an eyebrow raised in that expression she'd known for centuries.

"Being analytical ensures survival, Kane. You taught me that in Vienna." She touched the old silver microscope on her desk, a keepsake from bloodier times. "Emotion clouds judgment when facing extinction."

Her voice stopped as she noticed the signature: R. J. Wright.

The Elite's father.

Evelyn's eyes lifted to meet Kane's intense gaze. He'd already seen the connection, understood its implications before bringing these plans to her.

"This doesn't prove her involvement," she reasoned. "These plans appear roughly seven years old, judging by the paper's deterioration. Even if she assisted, she likely couldn't have comprehended what she was helping create."

Kane's face darkened, silver eyes flashing with a fury she'd witnessed only during their worst defeats. "You're wrong. She is involved."

His rage revealed how much this Elite affected him, something Evelyn hadn't fully grasped until now.

"Kane," she whispered, understanding flooding through her. "I should have been more thorough during intake, conducted additional screenings, but her rare blood type made me careless. I was too eager—"

"The blood type wasn't the issue, Evie," Kane interrupted, his hands clenched white-knuckled. "She passed every test you administered. This runs deeper." He began pacing with uncharacteristic agitation.

"How much deeper?" Evelyn asked, concern replacing curiosity.

Kane stopped beside the tall windows overlooking Waterside Cross, where elegant glass buildings appeared peaceful in the evening light, concealing the turmoil beneath. "The weapon represents only a fragment of a larger threat. The Liberation has been systematically recruiting active Elites."

Evelyn's breath caught. Did he know about Sebastian? Probabilities and risks cascaded through her consciousness.

"How?" she asked, her voice rougher than usual.

Kane remained silent, his reflection in the glass showing the minute facial changes she'd learned to interpret centuries ago during their first uneasy partnership. He appeared to be gathering strength for a difficult revelation. Finally, he turned toward her, his eyes displaying a guilt she recognized from Prague.

"Sebastian."

Ice flooded Evelyn's system, a physiological reaction she couldn't suppress despite centuries of emotional control. The truth settled within her, confirming her worst fears. No escape remained.

"I suspected as much," Evelyn admitted, her typically fluid speech becoming clipped.

"Suspected?" Kane's voice dropped to a growl, his eyes darkening like storm clouds. "Why didn't you report your concerns?"

"I lacked concrete evidence. Only behavioral patterns and anomalies. I..." Her words trailed off as she met his gaze, guilt creasing her features. She looked away, her fingers gripping the edge of the desk. "I wanted to be mistaken."

Regret, an emotion she typically dismissed as inefficient, gnawed at her as she watched him silhouetted against the city lights. She bore partial responsibility for the chaos threatening their civilization.

"You believe he recruited Serenity," she stated, dreading what his confirmation would mean.

"Yes. He's the sole Elite she encountered during the critical period—"

"That our surveillance detected," she interjected, her mind racing through the possibilities.

"Precisely. That documented observation recorded," Kane agreed with their old conversational precision.

"Alternative contact methods exist beyond our monitoring," she added urgently, moving toward her computer terminal. "Allow me to question him. I can leverage our research collaboration to extract information without arousing suspicion."

Kane crossed the room swiftly, pinning her against the wall with controlled force, his arm across her throat, restraining but not harmful. Their faces inches apart, his eyes bored into hers with an intensity that had once leveled cities.

"Under no circumstances can he suspect we know of his recruitment activities," he stated, each syllable precisely measured. "He would detect your interrogation immediately."

"Understood," she replied calmly, meeting his gaze with centuries-old mutual respect. "But action is necessary, Kane. This isn't merely another Elite. This is Serenity Wright. Her father's blood flows through her veins, and if the Liberation gains access..."

"What makes her lineage significant?" Kane's grip loosened slightly.

"It's essential for the weapon to function." She pushed him away with measured force, returning to examine the blueprints. Her fingers traced the chemical diagrams, eyes absorbing every detail. "The compound requires a natural stabilizer to hold its reaction together, and that stabilizer is her blood type. AB negative.

Serenity is the only known source in Celearius, perhaps anywhere. I've tracked the trait through generations of the Wright line. Without it, the reaction destabilizes and the weapon is inert."

Meeting his gaze again, she observed the turmoil in his silver eyes, an emotional complexity she'd witnessed only during Vienna's crisis. He continued studying her expression, searching for the deception her centuries-old mask might conceal.

"Serenity is the crucial component," she said softly, her scientific objectivity briefly yielding to deeper concern. "It was never only that her blood was rare. It's that her blood is the key."

Kane moved to the table, seizing the plans. Fury marked his features as he nearly destroyed the documents before restraining himself. He cursed in a language he hadn't used in lifetimes, breathing deeply to regain control.

"You care for her," Evelyn observed, a rare analytical slip.

Instantly, Kane's mask returned like reinforced barriers. "Personal considerations are irrelevant to operational requirements," he replied coldly. "Arrange her family visitation request. I'll accompany her personally, which will enable a property search without suspicion."

His tone brooked no argument, though Evelyn's enhanced senses detected the subtle aromatic changes that betrayed his emotional investment.

"I'll contact Rhyzan regarding the preparation logistics. Meanwhile, your disposal instructions for these plans?"

"Work with Rhyzan to create convincing duplicates, ones capable of deceiving human scientists under rigorous examination. We intend to place them for rebel discovery. Chloe may have already established contact."

Evelyn studied the plans again, her mind working through the replication challenges. "Feasible, but we must address any embedded codes and recreate the signatures flawlessly."

"I trust your capabilities. Rhyzan will handle the authentication details. I want functional plans in rebel hands by tomorrow evening."

"Certainly. I'll calibrate the equipment for optimal results," she assured him.

As Kane prepared to depart, Evelyn felt an unusual concern rising, an inefficient emotion she typically suppressed. "For what it's worth, I believe the Elite benefits you, and she likely doesn't fully comprehend her position."

Kane sighed heavily, a human habit retained through centuries. "She will facilitate this rebellion's termination. That constitutes my sole requirement."

He departed without observing the brief melancholy that crossed Evelyn's features before her expression resumed its clinical neutrality. She reached for the secure communications to contact Rhyzan.

She found herself contemplating, with uncharacteristic emotion, how circumstances might have differed without their accumulated centuries of secrets and deceptions. Yet duty and species loyalty superseded personal desires and hopes.

Her fingers touched the silver microscope as she whispered to the empty laboratory, "Sebastian, what have you done?"

CHAPTER FIFTY

RHYZAN

Rhyzan and Nox stood in tense silence, their eyes fixed on the screen in Kane's office. The room was cast in the faint blue glow of the monitor, harsh against their heightened senses, highlighting the hardened lines of their faces as they watched the scene unfold in Kane's apartment. Kane and Serenity were locked in a heated embrace, their bodies melding together as if no force could tear them apart.

Rhyzan's verdant eyes narrowed, the silver flecks catching the light as his gaze roamed over the intimate display. The blue glow illuminated his sharp, aristocratic features, the high cheekbones and sculpted jaw that had remained unchanged for centuries. The shadows accentuated the unreadable expression on his face, but beneath his composed exterior, the faintest flicker betrayed something else: concern, perhaps even fear. The scent of old books and leather that permeated Kane's office suddenly felt suffocating.

Beside him, Nox shifted, his stance betraying his unease, the muscles visibly contracting beneath the pale skin of his jaw. Though his face remained impassive, Rhyzan caught the way his fingers curled into fists at his sides, the veins beneath his marble skin pulsing with ancient blood. They didn't need to speak to know what the other was thinking; centuries of shared hunts, battles, and secrets had created an unspoken language between them. But this was something neither of them had anticipated in their long existence.

Kane's hands slid down Serenity's waist, pulling her closer with that preternatural strength now carefully restrained. His movements were reverent, possessing the predatory grace that marked their kind, yet tempered with a tenderness

Rhyzan had not witnessed in his oldest friend for centuries. The look in Kane's silver eyes was enough to make Rhyzan's chest tighten. It wasn't merely the hunger that defined their kind; it was far more dangerous. It was filled with longing, devotion, and the one thing that had no place in the precarious world they had built: love.

Rhyzan clenched his jaw, feeling his own fangs press against his lower lip, a visceral response to the tension flooding the room. Kane had always been a master of control, a leader who placed duty above all else since the Transition. And yet here he was, letting his guard down for a human who, against all odds, had pierced the armor he had worn for centuries. It was a sight that filled Rhyzan with a complicated blend of admiration and dread, churning in his stomach like ice.

"She's more to him than an Elite," Nox muttered, his voice low enough that only another of their kind could hear it, as if speaking the words aloud would make them more real. His eyes remained fixed on the screen, where Kane pressed his forehead to Serenity's, his expression tender in a way neither of them had ever seen. "This isn't just a distraction or a feeding ritual."

Rhyzan's lips pressed into a thin line, his brow furrowing. "No," he murmured, his voice heavy with implications that spanned centuries of their shared history. "It's not."

The room held only the faint hum of the monitors and the distant heartbeats of humans in the building below, sounds imperceptible to mortal ears. The weight of what they were witnessing hung heavily between them. This wasn't a fleeting moment of passion but a fundamental shift, a crack in the foundation of the world they had worked so hard to preserve.

"You realize what this means," Rhyzan finally said, his voice steady despite the turmoil brewing within him. His eyes flicked to Nox, who still stared at the screen as if trying to will the scene away. "If word of this relationship gets out..."

"It could destroy everything," Nox finished, his voice sharper now, tinged with frustration. He dragged a hand through his raven hair, the tension in his shoulders evident beneath his tailored jacket. "The Elders and the HV Council won't stand for it. The humans will see it as a weapon against us. And the other vampyrs—" He stopped himself, his jaw tightening again. "They'll see it as weakness. A violation."

Rhyzan turned back to the screen, his gaze hardening. Kane and Serenity were speaking now, their words lost to the silence of the feed, but the way they looked at each other spoke volumes. There was no hesitation in Kane's movements, none of the calculated precision that had kept him alive through the Great War. There was no fear in Serenity's gaze, none of the instinctual terror humans typically masked in close proximity to their kind. They were two people who had found something worth risking everything for.

The sight stirred a memory in Rhyzan, one he had buried long ago beneath the weight of responsibility. He glanced sideways at Nox, his expression softening just enough for a moment of vulnerability to emerge. "Do you think he knows what he's doing? The risk he's taking?"

Nox's gaze flicked to him, his usually impassive face betraying a flicker of emotion in eyes that had witnessed civilizations rise and fall. "Do any of us?" he replied, his voice quiet, tender. "But if anyone can walk that line between our world and theirs, it's him."

Rhyzan let out a low sigh, his fingers brushing the ancient wood of the desk as he leaned forward. The burden of centuries pressed down on his shoulders, the weight of countless decisions made for the survival of their kind. But something about Nox's calm, steady, familiar presence eased some of his tension. Their proximity, their unspoken bond forged in blood and battle, felt like a lifeline in the storm.

"We have to protect him," Rhyzan said firmly, his voice carrying the authority that had made lesser vampyrs tremble. "And her."

Nox's lips quirked into the faintest semblance of a smile, though it didn't reach his eyes, eyes that had witnessed too much suffering to be easily lightened. "You think he'd let us? He's been fighting his own battles since before you and I ever stood beside him."

"No," Rhyzan admitted, a ghost of a smile playing at his lips, revealing the slightest hint of fang. "But that doesn't mean we won't."

They stood side by side, the glow of the screen casting them in sharp relief against the darkness of the room. The air between them crackled with unspoken tension, not only about Kane and Serenity, but something deeper, something they had ignored for far too long across the centuries they'd walked together. Rhyzan's gaze lingered on Nox longer than necessary, his eyes searching that ageless face for something he couldn't name but had felt stirring since the night they'd first shared blood.

"We've faced worse," Nox said softly, breaking the silence. His voice was steady, but there was a warmth to it that Rhyzan couldn't ignore, the same warmth that had sustained them through countless winters and wars. "And we'll face this, too." He turned slightly, meeting Rhyzan's gaze directly. "Together."

Rhyzan nodded, his resolve settling into place, quiet and immovable as stone. "Together."

In the dim light of the monitor, their eyes held a conversation their lips dared not speak, while on the screen, Kane and Serenity continued their own forbidden dance, immortal hearts beating against the rhythm of a world that would tear them apart if given the chance.

DON'T FORGET!

If you were captivated by Kane and Serenity's forbidden love story, mesmerized by the dark world of Celearius, or found yourself rooting for love to triumph over impossible odds, please consider leaving a review! Your thoughts help other readers discover BOUND and mean the world to indie authors like me.

Don't forget their story continues in MARKED and it's going to be a wild ride.

Also by Charley Black

The Elite Series
Bound
Marked
Destined – August 2026

Within the Darkness Trilogy
Entwined Within the Darkness
A Dance Within the Darkness
Forever Within the Darkness

Blackwater Chronicles – Standalones
A Symphony of Shadows
A Requiem of Flames – TBA

About the Author

THIS STORY LIVES IN the space where loyalty is tested, secrets cut deep, and nothing is ever as simple as it seems.

I've been writing since I was twelve, always drawn to stories that blur the line between danger and desire, fantasy and reality. The characters I create rarely behave, and I've learned to follow where they lead—even when it gets messy.

I'm Charley Black, and I write dark paranormal and fantasy romance filled with morally gray characters, emotional intensity, and worlds where love is never safe, but always unforgettable. I live in Rhode Island with my family, where I balance writing, work, and motherhood—though the worlds I build are far more chaotic than my everyday life. For me, storytelling is about connection—pulling readers into immersive, emotional journeys and leaving a mark long after the final page. Thank you for stepping into this world with me... and for staying until the end.

You can connect with me on:
Instagram: @authorcharleyblack
TikTok: @authorcharleyblack
Facebook: @authorcharleyblack
Subscribe to my newsletter:
Website: www.charleyblack.com